Slovo Ne

Vorobey

A word is not a sparrow

By Philip Scholz

ISBN: 9798776002489

4

Table of Contents

6

Chapter 1

Katherine lay still, listening. She heard faint noises, but she couldn't be sure where they were coming from nor what was happening to cause them.

She was lying on her bed, her wrists tied to the headboard with a dishtowel from their kitchen. Her reddish-blonde ponytail had been undone, her long strands either cascading over her shoulders or pinned under her back, and she was naked.

Ben was nearby, bound to a chair with wire from his workbench and gagged with another dishtowel from their kitchen. Katherine wasn't gagged, but she understood the consequences of raising her voice. Her neck was still sore from the hands-on demonstrations.

Katherine and Ben were sure the man was still in the house. The bright red numerals on their clock radio told them it was 3:13 in the morning. That was more than six hours since he'd ambushed them when they returned home from dinner with Ben's parents up in Hunt Valley. Though they were exhausted, neither dared to nod off with him still in the house.

The man had laid out everything he needed prior to their arrival, having raided their drawers and dressers for binding and gagging supplies. He'd subdued them with ease when they entered through the front door. His gun was a helpful incentive for inspiring cooperation. He only needed to point it at Katherine in order for her to obey his command to undress.

"Very nice," he'd complimented when surveying her body before he made her lie on the bed.

He'd already raped her twice tonight, insisting Ben watch from his seat. During each assault, he taunted the couple by reminding them about the power he had over them.

"I'm in charge," he said. "You couldn't stop me if you tried. I always get who I want."

He also exaggerated his climaxes with loud grunts, after which he hurled a derision at Ben.

"She's quite a ride," he said. "She ever make it that good for you?"

Returning to the bedroom at random times to scare or further taunt them, he searched through the house during the interims. They could hear him opening and closing doors and drawers, rifling through their belongings, and helping himself to food in their kitchen. He even stopped to catch David Letterman in their den.

Straining to listen for any sign of his return, Katherine couldn't hear anything. Her arms had long ago gone numb due to the makeshift restraints. Having cried through most of the ordeal, her makeup was well-smeared, her Picasso-like visage not hindering the second rape. She looked at Ben, seeing the bruises on his arms from fighting his own restraints without success. He looked back at her, his eyes wild with the desperation she felt. Her mind went back to when the man forced her to bind him to the chair.

"Is he gone?" Katherine asked, her voice low and hoarse due to his physical warnings about no loud noises.

Ben sat stock-still, seeming to listen as well. Neither of them heard anything, but they couldn't be sure he was gone. The silence might be another mind game.

Katherine looked at the clock on the nightstand. 3:14. They usually woke up at 6:30 and were at work by 8:00. They wouldn't be missed until then and no one would immediately start looking for them.

She saw no way to loosen her bonds and Ben's predicament seemed to be the equivalent despite her efforts not to tie him too tight. If someone called to inquire about their whereabouts, they'd only be able to listen to any new voice messages. They'd likewise be unable to answer any knocks at their front door. Katherine shuddered at the thought of being found naked and tied to her bed, assuming someone thought to force their way in to investigate. These outcomes were all assuming they'd survive this ordeal.

Katherine froze. She thought she heard something. A creak? Was the man coming back? It'd been about ninety minutes since he'd raped her the second time. Was he ready again? Could he be ready again? Katherine feared the telling sound of a zipper being pulled down.

She saw a flash of movement by the open bedroom door. Then, he was in the room, keeping the lights off this time. Dark as it was, she could tell he was tall and slim, maybe an athlete. He wore dark jeans, a gray shirt, and a green army jacket. She'd managed to see his face earlier when he hovered over her. He looked young, maybe around hers and Ben's ages. He was clean-shaven, had a small nose, and large hazel eyes. His hair was short and probably blond. Katherine recited these features in her head, hoping to be able to repeat them later.

The man moved closer, pulling out his gun. He paused for a second to take aim. He shot Ben in the side of his head … just one bang echoed throughout the house. There was no hesitation.

Katherine gasped and coughed as her husband's body jerked sideways. Blood dripped onto his shoulder as he then swung forward, his head and shoulders slumped over as far as his bindings would allow.

As Katherine's mind registered what she'd just witnessed, the man turned to her, his gun still raised. He was aiming at her face as he stepped closer. It was perfectly steady.

"No!" Katherine cried just before she heard the shot.

* * *

He slipped into the alley and climbed up the fire escape to the second floor. Finding the window he wanted, he pulled his KA-BAR out of his backpack. Admiring the blade for a moment, he wedged it into the window. It took about a minute, but he was able to pry the stubborn window open. It didn't help that the building was probably erected back in the fifties. The frame felt old and stubborn as he pushed it up, but it did move far enough.

He crawled inside and found himself crouching on a small counter in a small kitchenette, perched like a parrot right next to the sink. He hopped down and studied his surroundings. There was the usual stove, fridge, sink, and a second, even smaller counter. A tiny table with three mismatched chairs were stuffed into the only open corner. Someone had left a plastic cup on the table. Stepping closer and sniffing, he figured it was some kind of alcoholic beverage … something college kids liked to drink to look sophisticated.

There was no door. Instead, the kitchenette opened into a main room of the small apartment. Hearing a television running, he moved forward, hitching his backpack higher on his shoulders.

The room was dark except for the television. A talk show was playing, but his Auburn Lovely was fast asleep. She had been kind enough to lie on the couch in such a way that the light from the TV screen illuminated her upper half. Her long, red hair framed a peaceful face, complete with a relaxed smile, and her white t-shirt hinted at a fit figure with a chest other people would notice. The shirt had a logo. He couldn't see enough of that in this dim light, but he didn't care. The shirt would soon be gone.

Leaving his Auburn Lovely to sleep for now, he turned to see a short hallway with three doors, two on the left and one on the right. The one on the right was open. Beyond it was a small bedroom and it was easy to determine it was empty.

He moved forward, passing between the couch and the television. His shadow didn't disturb his Auburn Lovely as it disrupted the TV's light. Right then, the audience happened to laugh at the talk show host's remark, but he wasn't listening to what said host had uttered.

The first door on the left was a small bathroom. He studied it quickly and shut the door again. Moving down the hall, he tried the next door.

This was another bedroom, if one could call it that. The space was as small as the one across the way, though it seemed to be proportional to the rest of the meager apartment. There was just a thin bed, a dresser, closet door, and a small desk, all of it crammed in there. He could hardly identify the carpet.

He could see a figure beneath the blanket on the bed and took a couple steps forward.

Illuminated by light slipping through slivers in the blinds over the window, this girl was blonde. She too looked peaceful in sleep. He could hear her breathing. Her t-shirt was gray. Most of her body was under the blanket and she had her back to him, so he couldn't determine much more. The shallow lump beneath the blanket suggested she too was in good shape.

His thoughts returned to his Auburn Lovely in the main room. He then remembered Susanne and the anger rose again. Knowing he needed to focus, he took a few deep breaths to calm himself. It would only be a few more minutes. He could have what he came for, but he needed to focus.

He set his backpack down and unzipped it. He pulled out his KA-BAR again, along with a roll of duct tape. Peeling off a long strip, he cut it with his knife. His heart raced as he braced himself. He had to be quick.

Pocketing his KA-BAR, he grabbed the blonde's shoulder and pulled. She was light and rolled over easily. As he anticipated, she also woke up just as easily.

Ready for this, he slapped the tape over her mouth with his other hand before she could scream. She'd only gotten out a squeak and was now reduced to muffled pleading as she registered his dark, strange shape in her room.

Before she could rise from the bed, he pulled his KA-BAR back out and stabbed her just below her left breast. As her shirt tightened around her chest due to the force of the knife, he noticed her breasts were smaller than those of his Auburn Lovely. Good thing he'd already made his choice. It was never a contest.

He pulled the knife out and stabbed her again, this time in her stomach. the blonde was fighting against him now, her arms and legs flaying as she tried to land a blow anywhere.

But she was Losing blood quickly. Unimpeded, he stabbed her two more times. Her hand slapped his shoulder, which he hardly noticed as he plunged the knife in a fifth time. His arm was getting tired, but the adrenaline was making up for that. He kept thrusting the blade in and out of her. She moaned and gurgled, but this would be inaudible to anyone more than five feet from the bed.

After the ninth or tenth time, she was still. The bed was now soaked with her blood. So was he, but that didn't matter. He listened as the air escaped through the multiple holes in the blonde's chest. It was like hearing a balloon deflate. There was also still a faint, gurgling sound, but he wasn't concerned. He'd done his research and knew there was no hope for her.

Satisfied, he took his KA-BAR and tape back into the main room. His Auburn Lovely hadn't moved. She couldn't have heard the blonde's 's muffled screams and the struggle had been brief. If she'd heard anything, she would have thought it was the television.

He stood over her, readying himself. He'd planned this out since he saw her the previous week. Now, he'd have her.

He cut off another piece of tape. His Auburn Lovely was already facing him, so it was easy to tape her mouth shut. All he needed to do first was set his KA-BAR down by his feet.

She woke up as he was doing this. Like the blonde, she tried to fight him. She also tried to scream, only to realize she was gagged.

He grabbed her wrists and yanked her off the couch. He outweighed her by at least thirty pounds, so it was an easy maneuver.

He forced her to her knees, pressing her face down into the couch cushion while holding her wrists with his other hand. Grabbing the roll of tape, he wrapped several layers around the struggling girl's wrists. She was kicking the floor in some lame attempt to free herself, but the rug nicely muffled her bare feet's thuds. Like her friend, he could hear her muffled pleas.

When her wrists were secure, he pulled her off the couch. He laid her on the floor so she could look up at him. He grabbed his KA-BAR from the couch and held it up for her to see its shining blade by the light from the television.

"Be good," he growled as he slid the blade beneath her shirt. "Be very, very good for me."

He was slowing down now, enjoying her anguished pleas mixed with the sound of his knife cutting through fabric. He knew that, thanks to the television's light, his Auburn Lovely couldn't miss her friend's blood on his clothes. The sight terrified her. This was what he was here for and he intended to saver it, moving the blade like a paintbrush over an artist's canvas. It ran along the seams of her jeans and between the cups of her bra, rendering each garment useless in turn.

Removing one article of clothing after another, he remembered when he first saw her. It was fate. He was just working with no expectations. He didn't know why she was out, but that didn't matter. His Auburn Lovely was gorgeous and he wanted her. He'd long perfected the plan and she was the final piece.

He studied her. He followed her. That was how he learned where his Auburn Lovely lived. With some casual surveillance of the building, he learned about her friend/roommate. A simple query about a fictitious plumbing problem with an oblivious neighbor got him the exact location of their apartment within the dwelling he hadn't been able to access. Seeing the fire escape in the alley, he knew he was meant to visit her.

His Auburn Lovely was soon naked and crying, her tears glistening as they ran down her face. Setting his KA-BAR and her shredded clothes aside, he unzipped his pants, smiling at her agonized shriek. Even gagged, she sounded so good.

Time seemed to stop. All sound around them ceased, or maybe he didn't care to hear it as he took her. He did listen to her muffled sobs and gasps, feeling even more excited.

It was soon over. He'd have liked to go longer, but biology wasn't allowing it. Still, she had been almost as good as he'd imagined. At least she cooperated more than Susanne.

As he got off her, his Auburn Lovely closed her legs and rolled onto her side. Despite all her crying and muffled blubbering, she hadn't resisted. She'd understood his warning about being good.

He picked up his KA-BAR again and pushed her face-down on the rug. As she tried to swivel her head to see what he was doing, he plunged the knife into her back, just missing her spine. Blood spurted out around the blade and over the handle. His Auburn Lovely screamed, struggled, and kicked the floor again. There was still hardly any noise. He kept stabbing, finding her easier to kill than the blonde. It felt so good to feel her slowly going limp beneath him and he kept piercing her again and again.

When she was still and stopped breathing, he rose to his feet and headed to the bathroom. He had some work left to do, but he first wanted to take a shower. He had blood all over him and he couldn't leave the apartment looking like that.

* * *

Working on his paper in the kitchen, Christian Becker paused when Lydon rose and walked across the main room. It seemed he hadn't shut the bedroom door completely as the dog pushed it open without encountering resistance and continued on his apparent mission.

Christian then heard Sasha moving through the bedroom while addressing the dog, who was always eager to be the first to greet anyone when they woke up in the morning.

"No," Sasha was saying to the insistent animal. "Me only."

She closed the door to their bathroom and Christian soon heard the shower running. He resumed working as a defeated Lydon returned to his spot on the round rug beneath the kitchen table. While he loved his guide dog work, helping Christian negotiate the busy streets of Washington, D.C., he loved having more than his handler living in the same dwelling. When out of harness, he sought attention from each of them in turn as often as the day would allow.

Sasha came into the kitchen a few minutes later, smelling of shampoo and body wash. Her long blonde hair was still damp, clinging to the oversized t-shirt she wore over her petit frame.

Christian was engrossed in his paper again, his earphone in his right ear so his screen reading software didn't disturb Sasha or anyone living on the other side of the apartment's paper-thin walls.

"What's got you pecking away so eagerly?" Sasha queried, finding coffee in the coffeemaker and retrieving a mug from a cabinet. "Working on the novel?"

Christian was planning his first publication, a legal thriller broken down into a five-part series. It was originally supposed to be one book, but the draft was proving to be too long for that to work.

"A paper I'm behind on," Christian explained, still concentrating on the computer as Lydon circled them both in a Figure 8 pattern. "I haven't gotten as far on it as I need to."

That would have been Sasha's second guess. She had left Christian working at this table the previous evening. He'd climbed into bed about two or three hours later. They'd both been exhausted and barely said "good night" before falling asleep.

Christian supposed the adrenaline of the looming deadline got him going now. With the curtains to their windows still closed, he sat at their table in a Capitals t-shirt and boxer shorts, his bare feet appreciative of being set on the rug.

"Mind if I turn on the radio?" Sasha asked, taking a sip of coffee.

"Konechno," Christian said.

He'd been practicing his Russian. Sasha had no idea what he'd said or if his pronunciation was correct, but she supposed this was an affirmation. She moved along the counter towards the radio scanner she kept by their phone. She switched it on and continued drinking as the kitchen filled with static-laced chatter.

"This is 2036 requesting a license check," a DC Metro Police Officer was saying. "My computer's down."

He proceeded to recite the license plate number.

"You know they have apps that do that?" Christian asked, wondering what the neighbors thought if they heard this. No one had complained yet.

"I use that too," Sasha replied, still listening to the scanner. "It drains my phone battery though."

"Chto by ni," Christian muttered, surrendering.

As the newest addition to the Washington Post's Local Crime and Public Safety section, she was always keen to hear about the police's activities. Earlier that year, she'd managed to be the first reporter to arrive at the scene of an armed robbery, earning a rare smile from her editors when the story was posted within an hour of the incident.

"No wants or warrants," a police dispatcher replied over the scanner.

"Copy that," the officer acknowledged.

"You have plans this weekend?" Sasha asked.

"My father wants to take us to lunch," Christian replied, lifting his fingers from his laptop's keyboard and running one hand through his dark-blond hair.

Sasha nodded. It was Wednesday, so she supposed this wasn't short notice. Plus, she wanted to be supportive.

Christian and his father weren't close. In fact, the latter had been absent for most of Christian's life after impregnating his mother. The two only started talking when Christian was in college and their chats and meetings were still infrequent, despite Christian's father seeming to be trying. At least he was supportive of the engagement and promised to attend the wedding. He also seemed to understand there was no place for him in the actual ceremony.

"Attention all units in District 2," the dispatcher was saying and Sasha turned to listen. "Be advised of a possible Homicide at the Summerset Building on Idaho Avenue Northwest. Any available units, please respond."

Sasha's mind was racing. She knew the Summerset building. It was near the University of the District of Columbia, where Christian was currently attending night classes. The building was just a few blocks away. It'd be a ten-minute walk … faster if Sasha took her bike.

"I'll make you a sandwich!" Christian called as she raced across the main room.

As she hurried back to the bedroom, a curious Lydon behind her, Sasha heard a beeping in her right ear and cursed. This would only slow her down.

Chapter 2

In his eighteen years with the Metropolitan Police Department, Detective Joseph Conway had seen several brutal crime scenes. This was one of them.

A technician from the medical examiner's office had finally zipped up the bag containing Rachael Holden's nude body. The girl's features, both natural and induced by her killer, had been photographed and documented for the past hour with the veteran investigator supervising the process. In all that time, she lay on the floor, her hands on her spread thighs, remnants of tape still on her wrists.

Joseph studied the rest of the room. It seemed largely undisturbed, the struggle having been confined to the area right in front of the couch. The thick, dark-blue rug was covered with blood and the green couch had dark stains across its front.

"How many times did he stab her?" Joseph asked the technician from the Medical Examiner's Office, who was packing up her equipment.

"I counted eighteen wounds, all on her back," the medical examiner replied with a sigh. "We'll confirm it during the autopsy. I'd guess any one or two of them would have killed her."

"Overkill."

Joseph said this more to himself than anyone else as he glanced at the closed body bag. It took serious rage to do that. Rachael Holden was just over five feet tall, so her killer probably overpowered her with ease, but to do this was something different. Then, there was the position he'd left her in. Naked and lying face up with her hands on her spread thighs and her feet pointed towards the front door, as though inviting anyone entering the apartment who was interested. Her long, red hair had been brushed and arranged to frame her face and her lips had been pushed up into a smile. The girl was sexualized in death.

"How'd he do that with her lips?" Joseph asked.

"He probably pushed her lips up as rigor mortis set in," the technician replied. "This one knows what he's doing."

Wanting to focus on something else, Joseph moved into the kitchenette, where a crime scene technician was still dusting for and lifting prints.

"Anything?" he asked.

"These prints look small," the technician replied. "Probably the residents', but we won't be sure until the medical examiner gives us their prints for elimination. Til then, I'm collecting everything. I've got as many unidentifiable smudges as actual prints to work with here."

Joseph looked through the kitchenette's only window, which was still open. Given the front door had been left undisturbed, this was the killer's likely entry and exit point. A technician was outside on the fire escape, having already found pry marks to support this theory. He seemed to have found nothing else significant, or Joseph just hadn't heard about anything else which was significant. Joseph knew a couple officers were sent to search the alley down below. He hadn't heard anything from them either.

"How's it going?" someone said.

Joseph turned to see his partner, Detective Hadrian Hasselle. Hadrian had been in one of the apartment's bedrooms, where the other victim, Ellie Stets, was found.

"Nothing useful," Joseph said. "You?"

"Same," Hadrian replied. He had a slow, methodical way of speaking. It was as though nothing could ever rush him. This characteristic developed its own legacy after Hadrian allegedly talked down a murder suspect who was about to shoot him after having killed four people in a grocery store holdup.

"You wanna give me that gun?" was the only thing the detective was purported to have said, never drawing his own weapon.

The suspect, facing multiple life sentences without parole, complied. Ever since then, many cops referred to Hadrian as "Yoda", a term he seemed to find endearing.

"As bad as Rachael?" Joseph asked, focusing on where they were again. Though he was half a foot taler than his partner, there was a reason they split up to each focus on one victim.

"Suppose that's a judgement call," Hadrian remarked. "The wounds look just as bad, though he stabbed Ellie in the chest instead of the back. The posing's about as provocative."

Joseph nodded, having seen it during a brief visit to that bedroom. Ellie Stetz had been posed face-down on her bed, her face in her pillow and her knees under her so her backside stuck up. Her pants and underwear were around her knees and her t-shirt was up by her shoulders. Probably because of the bed's position in the room, the killer had taken the mirror off the adjacent bathroom's wall and mounted it in her room so anyone coming in would immediately face the reflection of his work. It was as sickening as the real thing.

"He took his time with that," Hadrian remarked. "That mirror wasn't ripped off the wall. He worked to get that thing down and rehang it."

"Meaning he hung around after the girls were dead," Joseph said. No victim would lie there and allow their assailant to do this without trying to escape.

Two crime scene technicians were still in the bathroom, collecting any samples they could find. The empty towel rack and damp plastic curtain suggested someone had showered in there recently and took the towels afterwards to further hide potential evidence.

"Ellie die about the same time as Rachael?" Joseph asked.

Hadrian nodded.

"Medical examiner estimates 1:00 this morning," he said. "The building superintendent found them around 7:30 after the downstairs neighbor complained about a leak in the ceiling."

"You think that was the killer's doing?"

"I doubt it. Why rush to get someone in here? The girls weren't going anywhere. Plus, the more time before someone walked into this horror show, the more time he'd have to get away. After all, he took his time to clean up and set the stage to his liking. God knows how long it took him to set all this up."

Joseph nodded. He supposed their best chance at a lead was to talk to the neighbors and the victims' friends. Both girls were undergraduates at the University of the District of Columbia, according to their student ID cards. The lab wouldn't have results on the fingerprints for a few hours and anything else would take even longer.

"Excuse me," someone said, interrupting Joseph's thoughts. He turned to see a patrol officer standing in the doorway of the apartment.

"Yeah?" he asked.

"There's a reporter downstairs," the officer explained. "She says she knows you. She won't go away."

Joseph groaned as Hadrian chuckled. Even the man's laugh was slow and stretched.

* * *

Joseph came out of the apartment building to see Sasha Copeland standing behind the police barricade, her bicycle chained to a nearby stop sign. So far, she was the only reporter, though more were probably coming. Joseph remembered Sasha lived around here, but he couldn't recall where at that moment. Her backpack hung on her shoulders and he could see it was only half-zipped. Behind her, he could see her bicycle chained to a stop sign.

"Qaleghqa'mo' jIQuch," Sasha said, smiling.

"Don't I get to have a second morning coffee before you come barging into my life?" Joseph asked. Though they'd bonded over an interested in Star Trek, Sash was definitely the bigger fan. She'd actually learned Klingon.

"I'm a go-getter," Sasha replied.

"You sure it's legal to chain your bike to a stop sign like that? Joseph asked, pointing over her shoulder.

"I didn't see anything suggesting it's illegal."

Joseph sighed.

"What do you want?" he asked. For a moment, he wondered if she believed he didn't know.

"To be first on this story," Sasha replied. "So, who died in there."

"Two girls," Joseph replied. "We're withholding names until we can inform next of kin, but they're probably college students."

"UDC?"

"Looks like it."

"How'd they die?"

"We're investigating that."

Sasha wasn't ready to surrender.

"Got any suspects?" she pressed. "A neighbor? A boyfriend?"

"Nope," Joseph replied in an indifferent tone. "We're considering everything and everyone at this early stage in the investigation."

Sasha sighed.

"Come on, Joe," she urged. "Give me something I can work with."

Now joseph sighed. He glanced around to make sure no one was listening. Neighbors and curious pedestrians were gathering behind the barricades and officers were keeping them back, but the two of them were still away from this growing crowd.

"You didn't hear it from me," Joseph said. "I can't go into too many specifics. The killer posed the victims in a Sexual manner to provoke a reaction. Let's just say it looks pretty horrific up there."

Having taken out her iPad and a stylist, Sasha was writing this down. They both knew Joseph wouldn't speak if she started recording on her phone.

"You think this is a serial killer?" Sasha asked eagerly. "You think he'll strike again?"

"I didn't say that," Joseph defended quickly. "I didn't even say this was a 'he'. We're not ruling anything out. It could still have been personal."

Sasha nodded, her mouth a thin line.

"qatlho'," she said.

Joseph nodded.

"Wish you could be on our team," he remarked.

It wasn't the first time he'd made this comment. They'd known one another since Sasha was an intern at the 2nd District station while studying for her Masters in Journalism and Public Affairs at American University. They understood her deafness, though correctible with her hearing aids, was an automatic disqualifying factor from her wearing a badge.

"Good luck," Joseph said. "Oh, and zip that bag shut."

Stopping to do so, Sasha noticed her right side was silent. In her haste to get out of the apartment and reach the scene, she'd forgotten to change the battery for that hearing aid and it was now dead. She hoped she still had spares in her backpack. Otherwise, the ride to the office could become somewhat precarious.

* * *

"Hey," Matthew Timmons said as Christian entered the library, Lydon leading him as usual.

"How are you?" Christian asked as he slid into his seat, his guide dog settling by his feet.

"Good," Matthew said. "Saw your girlfriend's article. Nice, if a bit sick."

"She didn't commit the murders."

"Still … sick stuff."

During the day, Matthew worked as a Staff Assistant for Congresswoman Amanda Dodson from his home state of Pennsylvania. He was getting a Masters in Criminal Law to move up in the legislative field. He had no intention of ever sharing a zip code with a dead body if he could help it.

"Sasha will probably take that as a compliment," Christian remarked.

Sasha had been on the Washington Post's Local Crime and Public Safety section for two years now. This wasn't the first killing she'd covered, or even her first double homicide, but the prior ones had been things like gang shootings, domestic violence incidents, and murders during robberies. From what Christian could tell, this was different from those pedestrian slayings.

"Lucky me," Matthew said. "You have any theories about this one?"

Christian had written about murder since he was a teenager, keeping a blog on the DC Sniper case as local, state, and federal law enforcement agencies hunted down the two killers. For a while, he also wrote about the unsolved Mid-Atlantic Slayer case until he ran out of theories to share about the killer's motive and identity. He now made a living covering police investigations and criminal trials for various publications throughout the mid-Atlantic region. But, outside of books and the Internet, he had never seen such sadistic behavior.

Sasha's piece on the double homicide was posted on the Washington Post's website within three hours of her hurrying out of the apartment. She had to have sped either to her office or a local coffeeshop with good Wi-Fi to type up the article. Though she could do this on her phone, she carried her laptop in her backpack alongside her iPad.

The article was descriptive, if not specific. It stated two girls were attacked in their apartment on Idaho Avenue and that police were withholding names until their families were notified. Christian supposed the girls weren't D.C. residents before coming here for school. Otherwise, their names would have probably been released already.

The article also stated the victims had been posed for shock value, citing an anonymous source at the scene. Christian didn't want to guess what the killer had done nor who Sasha had convinced to divulge that fact to her.

* * *

Joseph was sure his partner was single-handedly keeping the Washington Post's print edition alive. Hadrian bought a newspaper every morning and evening. If someone managed to convince him to read articles the Post just posted on their website, he still printed them first.

The detectives were at their desks at the 2nd District. The district station was on Idaho Avenue. Though they were many, many doors down from their newest crime scene, they felt a lot closer to where these victims had been murdered than many of the others.

Around them, the squad room bustled as everyone worked their own cases. Washington never had a shortage of crimes needing to be solved. Shoulder-high makeshift walls, acquired at some warehouse sale or something, separated each pair of detectives from all the others. They offered no privacy. Confidential matters were either discussed in hushed voices or the speakers counted on their conversations being masked by the continuous chatter and office hubbub around them.

Joseph and Hadrian's shared cubicle was decorated with opposites split right down the middle. Half displayed family photos, most featuring growing children, while the other presented a love for D.C. United and the UMD Terrapins.

Joseph and Hadrian had more than a dozen open homicides on their desks, none stretching back more than a year. And now, the murders of Rachael Holden and Ellie Stetz would take priority. Two college students, hailing from Michigan and New Jersey, were brutally attacked in their apartment. Neither girl had a criminal record or apparent nefarious connections. The police had found a small amount of pot in the desk drawer in Rachael's bedroom, but even the bag it was in was too small to suggest ties to any kind of drug operation.

Detectives had been sent to the university to canvas alongside the campus police, starting with the girls' professors. Their parents were also in route to D.C., and Joseph planned to meet them personally to ask more questions. Hopefully, all this would lead to friends or even boyfriends, past or present. Maybe a motive would present itself. No one in the department, from the Chief down, wanted these murders to be a random crime. Whether it was or wasn't, they wanted it solved. Innocent dead girls did not make good press. Joseph and Hadrian could argue this was institutional racism, given over half their open cases had victims matching their own skin color, but didn't. A murder was a murder and someone went through a lot of trouble to make these two killings happen. Their adding more racial issues from this case into a volatile climate already blanketing the nation wouldn't help.

"We have to suppose Rachael was the target," Joseph said. "Sure, the killer stabbed them both multiple times and posed them with equal theatrics, but he only raped Rachael."

They would meet with the Medical Examiner to confirm, but no one at the scene had noticed evidence of even attempted penetration on Ellie Stetz's body. The signs of sexual assault on Rachael were hard to miss.

"It is more likely he knew Rachael," Hadrian mused, setting his printout down on his desk. "He stabbed Ellie in the chest and stomach. He'd have seen her face. But he stabbed Rachael in the back. He couldn't see her face when he did it."

"He did rape her first," Joseph said. "She was probably alive for that. And, there were signs of a struggle in the main room. He definitely spent more time with Rachael. I wouldn't be surprised if Ellie turned out to be an incidental victim and he posed her as well to throw us off."

"He might have had no feelings of any kind towards Ellie. Maybe something Rachael did or just something about her set him off. Maybe just a random meeting on the street and he became infatuated with her."

"You mean like John Hinkley?"

Both detectives knew rape wasn't about sex, despite it being called a sex crime. No, rape was about power, the rapist wanting to attain it over the victim. If Rachael Holden was chosen at random or due to some chance meeting she might have never been aware of, that made this killer much more frightening.

"They might have never even met or seen each other before," Hadrian continued. "Maybe he saw something on the Internet. God know what's out there about anyone these days."

Joseph stored the possibility in his mind, having no idea how they would trace this killer if that was the case.

"Maybe he felt remorse after he did it," Hadrian suggested, finishing his thought. "Maybe he felt he had no choice but to kill Rachael then, but he didn't want to look at her when he did kill her."

It was as plausible as anything else right then. They would have to keep working on it.

"Gentlemen," a voice said.

Both detectives looked up to see Captain Gavin King standing in the doorway of their shared cubicle.

"Some light reading?" the captain queried, nodding at the printed Washington Post article on Hadrian's desk. The photo Sasha had taken of the murdered girls' building was quite prominent amongst the text. Considering she wasn't a professional photographer, it was still a good shot.

Joseph and Hadrian knew an answer wasn't expected.

"Watch what you say to the press," Captain King cautioned in a low voice. "Others are already riding the coattails of the Post's story. The frenzy's started."

He wasn't mad, or at least not very mad. If you were called into Captain King's office, you weren't likely to leave it with your badge still in hand. The matter here was serious, but survivable. For one thing, Sasha's byline was in his line of sight and he wasn't commenting on it.

Captain King used to train newly-minted patrol officers. During his service as a lieutenant, he supervised all patrol operations in the 6th District. Despite his widening midsection from too much deskwork, he never lost touch with the streets. He understood how things worked out there, even if he continued to perpetuate the stereotype of cops and doughnuts. He understood what officers and investigators sometimes needed to do or say. Plus, he too knew Sasha from her working at the district.

"This will only get bigger," Captain King said. "Be careful."

Both detectives nodded and he headed back to his office. Seconds later, Joseph's cell phone vibrated.

* * *

Sasha was barely in high school when she saw "All the Presidents Men", after her father dug up a DVD copy of it. Soon after, she saw "The Paper". Much more recently, she and Christian attended a showing of "The Post". By then, her career goals were long-cemented.

The Washington Post, like all newspapers, was a very different place from the settings of those films. Gone were the bustling newsrooms with people running in every conceivable direction while typewriters recorded history for the public's consumption.

Like Sasha, every Post reporter had at least two portable devices on which they could write up a story, some submitting their work while still on sight of their subject matter. Even the ones on local beats like her often spent days, if not weeks, away from the office. On more than one occasion, she'd forgotten which cubicle in the bullpen was hers.

Meanwhile, their editors were in the office more often, supervising the vast geographical spaces outlined by their reporters' whereabouts. E-mails were the most common form of communication, followed by video calls so people could actually recognize one another during future in-person meetings. Of course, Covid-19 helped perpetuate this approach to staff management.

Sasha had met her editors, Nancy Jordan and Eric Williams, about a dozen times since starting on the Post's Local Crime and Public Safety section two years ago. Their reasons for summoning her to the Post's building had varied widely, so she didn't know what to expect when she was summoned the same day as the murders of the two college girls.

"Good job," Nancy said when Sasha was sitting in her office. "The story is getting a dozen new views every minute and we're still waiting on an update about the current number of shares."

She and Eric were both sitting on her side of the desk. Nancy was a Star Wars fan, preferring the original trilogy. Posters, figurines, and a signed photo from Mark Hamill adorned her walls and shelves as though to serve as evidence of this interest.

"Thank you," Sasha said. She was sure her editors had not summoned her just to offer their congratulations. Nancy would consider such an in-person meeting a waste of resources while Eric never had an opinion of any kind about that issue.

"We wanted to talk to you about blowback," the latter editor said. "As I'm sure you know, there's a good chance a killer like this will follow his press."

Eric had been an auxiliary police officer for the New York City Police Department while a student at York College. He always wore bargain-basement suits, similar to the garb of a detective, and kept his hair short. Based on this, he fancied himself an expert on anything crime-related. Problem was, people listened, no matter how dubious or downright outlandish his statements sometimes became.

By contrast, Nancy seemed to prefer more brand-name clothes. She also put a lot of funds into maintaining her dark hair. Even people rarely in the office seemed aware of when she made an appointment with her regular salon. Still, she was as competent in management as her colleagues.

"I haven't received any threats," Sasha tried, not sure how to respond to Eric's suggestions, "and I haven't noticed anyone following me."

"We just want you to be careful," Nancy offered. She was the sweeter of the two. But she was also greener than some reporters on this beat, having covered the financial section prior to her editorial promotion. All that often caused her to believe Eric's notions, despite her competent management skills.

"I will," Sasha said. She certainly didn't think she was a target. She got the story. If not her, someone else would have, and the Post would have still wanted it to be one of their people.

"Stay on it then, I guess," Eric said. "We've gotten a few wacky messages already, but nothing outright alarming yet. We'll let you know if we hear anything."

Sasha just nodded. She did want to know what those wacky messages said, but that was more out of curiosity than anything else. Plus, was Eric expecting something or being outlandish already?

Chapter 3

He was exhausted as he entered the apartment. He couldn't pull these all-nighters and then work all day. For one thing, he wasn't sure how much longer he could afford the volume of coffee he needed to consume in order to make it to quitting time.

But there was an advantage to this routine. The police might figure a killer like him would either not have a day job or wouldn't be at work the day after spending hours in the confined apartment of his Auburn Lovely. He put himself through such grueling hours to avoid suspicion. He'd go to bed early to make up for it. A few good nights of sleep and he'd go out to find another Auburn Lovely. So what if they made up just around five percent of the country's population. He'd seen enough in his life to know he could afford to be patient and pick the right one. He licked his lips.

"Dad!" he called. "Dad, I'm home!"

He received an unintelligible grunt through one of the closed doors on his left. That was as good a reply as he could expect. That was fine. He wanted to just sit and watch TV.

He hung his jacket on one of the wooden red and yellow hooks in the hallway. A previous tenant had erected the gaudy structure and the building's manager never saw fit to take it down despite his and his father's distaste. So, they dealt with its existence by using it.

Heading into the kitchen, he found a beer and some leftover Chinese food in the fridge. He carried his bounty into the small den and plopped himself onto the couch facing the television. The remote was on its side on the far end and he snatched it.

The TV came to life, tuned to a game show. He was absolutely not interested and changed channels. There was no need to surf. He knew what he wanted to see.

There was a chance his Auburn Lovely wouldn't be a hot news item. This was still Washington. There were plenty of killings every day.

But good fortune was on his side. He rose from his seat to shut and lock the den's door. He could already hear the reporter talking about his Auburn Lovely.

"… were murdered in the apartment they shared just off campus," the man was saying. "Both were sophomores at the University of the District of Columbia. Police are continuing to interview friends and neighbors and are asking local residents to come forward with any possible information."

He turned around just as a photo of his Auburn Lovely appeared on the screen. The reporter was talking about her, where she was from, and what she liked to do, but he didn't care. Staring at her pretty face and lovely red mane, he opened his pants. He was never too tired for this.

Muting the television, he began stroking himself. She was so pretty. Staring at her red hair, he realized he ought to have taken something to remember her by. He was already fearing her becoming just a faint memory. Next time.

A series of loud bangs interrupted his self-satisfaction. He jumped in his seat.

"Open up!" his father called through the door.

He gritted his teeth as he zipped up. He rose from his seat and unlocked the den's door. His father could open it himself.

The old man did just that, asking, "What are you doing?"

"Watching TV," he replied. "I've had a long day."

His father strode into the room. Studying the television screen, he nodded as he sat in his leather armchair, set at an angle to the couch and the television.

"Why do parents let their kids go away to school?" he asked, speaking to no one in particular. "You just know something like this will happen."

He nodded as the old man turned his head to look at him.

"Make me a sandwich," his father demanded. "I'm hungry."

Seeing a commercial break had begun, he figured he'd make it back in time with the requested food. It was better than arguing. He always lost.

He turned and walked out of the den as his father grumbled about something.

* * *

With Christian working freelance and Sasha more often being in the field versus the office, both their schedules were flexible. They were therefore able to accept his mother's last-minute invitation for dinner that Thursday evening.

"I wanted to talk to you two about the wedding," Julianna confessed when the casserole was on the table in her small Tenleytown apartment.

"I just got the ring resized," Christian pointed out. "Plus, isn't it the bride who's supposed to immediately go nuts about all these details?"

"BIjatlh'e' ylmev ," Sasha said, slapping his arm. She resumed looking out the window near the table. It offered a nice view of a row of shops and other businesses occupying buildings across the street. It matched Julianna's décor. She'd chosen to hang artwork featuring urban landscapes, explaining she liked how busy and active they looked.

"There's always someone around," she'd added.

The shops visible across the street seemed to always have customers, the volume picking up again in recent weeks.

"I just happen to know about these things," Julianna said as she sat down next to Sasha. She'd long ago chosen to not try and understand her future daughter-in-law's second language or interest in Star Trek.

"What do you have for us, Mom?" Christian asked.

Julianna fancied herself an expert on event-planning in general, despite teaching Computer Science at American University. She had helped her friends plan their weddings and other events and was now doing this for some of their grown children. Christian wasn't sure how much this counted for, but he knew better than to continue voicing that train of thought.

"You're meeting your father this weekend, right?" Julianna asked.

Lydon, who had been in the apartment's main room, strode back into the kitchen. Julianna kept a basket of toys on hand for when her son and his dog visited and he'd selected a green Nyla bone. He settled by Julianna's feet and began chewing on it.

"How worn is that thing?" Christian asked.

"It's still fine," Julianna assured him. "So, your father?"

Even Christian knew her mouth became a thin line whenever his father was discussed, even if she brought up the subject. Christian thought about a phrase his father had taught him. Slovo ne vorobey, meaning a word is not a sparrow.

"Yeah," Christian replied, knowing it was best to confirm it and move on, "we're meeting him for lunch on Saturday."

"Okay," Julianna said, leaning back and pushing some stray strands of her long, red hair behind her ear.

"Mom, you said something about wedding ideas."

Julianna smiled just a bit.

"I had to move the items into my storage unit," she said. "I'm working on specs for a new computer chip."

About a year after Christian moved out, she'd turned his old room into a home office of sorts, working on anything computer-related which came to mind or was requested. Apart from teaching, she also did some consulting for local companies.

"Could you go there and get them for me?" Julianna requested.

"Did you just invite us here to assign this errand?" Christian asked. It wouldn't be the first time.

Julianna didn't reply.

* * *

Rachael Holden never had a serious boyfriend, but Ellie Stets did, at least until two and a half months ago. According to her friend and freshman-year roommate, this boyfriend had tried to flirt with Rachael at the girls' apartment on more than one occasion. It seemed this was a significant factor in the couple's break-up.

Joseph and Hadrian spotted this ex-boyfriend, Kyle Dantana, leaving an office building downtown. A junior at the University of the District of Columbia, he was completing an internship at the law firm of McAvoy & Keller. Careful to not draw the attention of a high-priced lawyer who might feel compelled to provide instant representation, the detectives waited to approach the young man until he was buying some chips and a Coke at the Farragut North Metro station three blocks away.

"What do you want?" Kyle Dantana demanded after introductions were made and badges presented.

"We want to ask you about Ellie Stets and Rachael Holden," Joseph said, keeping a congenial tone. He didn't want to guess how many lawyers' phone numbers were saved in this kid's phone.

The young man's face softened a bit. The three of them stepped over to a nearby ATM so they wouldn't be in the middle of the stations foot traffic.

"I heard what happened," Kyle Dantana said. "I was studying in the school's library until midnight that night."

The detectives wondered how often he watched Law & Order and how close he paid attention to the show. For one thing, the girls were murdered in the early morning, after midnight.

"We're more interested in background," Hadrian said. "You were dating Ellie Stets, right?"

"Sure," Kyle Dantana said. "We dated for a while, but we broke up over the summer."

"Why?" Joseph queried.

"We had our fun and moved on. It wasn't like we were going to get married or anything."

"We heard it was a little more than that," Hadrian said. "We have statements about you being interested in Rachael."

Kyle Dantana sighed.

"Who told you that?" he asked. "Yeah, I hit on her. She was hot and I was interested, so I took a chance."

"We heard Ellie didn't appreciate that and it led to you two breaking up."

"Ellie was looking to get married. I'm trying to play the field and have fun. It'll take you guys about two minutes to find out I hit on a bunch of different girls. That's why Ellie and I split up."

"And you don't resent her for it?" Joseph asked.

"No. Like I said, it wasn't like I was going to marry her or anything. Same with Rachael. I'm looking to have fun."

The detectives exchanged glances.

"How did Rachael feel about your intentions?" Joseph asked.

"She wasn't interested and she then thought I was wrong for Ellie because of me hitting on her," Kyle Dantana said.

"And you never tried to circle back to her after the break-up?"

"No. I'd have liked to, but I never got a chance. So I moved on. Plenty of other babes in this city."

Joseph and Hadrian were starting to think this wasn't going anywhere productive.

"Thanks for your time, Mr. Dantana," Joseph said, handing over one of his business cards. "We'll be in touch if we have more questions."

Kyle Dantana didn't speak as he snatched the card and pocketed it. He turned and walked away.

"Hey," Hadrian called after him.

The young man stopped and looked back over his shoulder.

"Be careful with playing the field," Hadrian advised. "Some of those girls you're looking to have fun with might get the wrong idea. It could get you in trouble."

"What?" Kyle Dantana asked. "Like a Me Too thing?"

"It looks like you've got a promising future. Don't ruin it."

Kyle Dantana frowned, shook his head, and started walking away again.

"What did you think would happen?" Joseph asked, snickering. "That kid would change his ways?"

Hadrian shrugged.

"I've got two girls," he said. "I think about things like that."

Joseph nodded.

"You ready to take him off our list?" Hadrian queried.

"Not quite," Joseph replied. "Come on. We gotta go meet the Medical Examiner."

Hadrian nodded.

"I'm just going to get some water and see if they have those veggie chips," he said, gesturing towards the convenience store Kyle Dantana had exited when they stopped him. "You want anything?"

"No," Joseph replied, chuckling. He was sure his partner would also buy a copy of the Post if this place carried it.

* * *

"Can I help you," the brunette asked as he entered.

"I got a delivery," he said. Hadn't she noticed the logo on his shirt? Why did they issue these things?

"I'll get the manager," the brunette said.

He surveyed the place as he waited. It looked like all the others he visited every day. He'd visited this one many times before, but he could no longer distinguish it from the others. All the cheap furnishings and decorations were the same and the food always matched the ambience.

Thankfully, the manager, a graduate student, if he remembered right, recognized him upon arrival.

"I'll meet you around back as usual," the manager said.

Once the delivery was unloaded, he presented his electronic clipboard and the manager signed it. It was all routine.

"You want something to take along?" the manager offered, returning the clipboard. "I can have someone make you a sandwich or something."

He shook his head. This too was routine.

"I'm good," he said.

He drove back up the alley and stopped at the opening between buildings. Glancing to his left, he did a double-take.

He could see her clearly through the window. She was another Auburn Lovely. He'd found another one so soon. The uniform, flattering on her slim figure, looked even better because it contrasted with her red hair. He couldn't believe she was in the same place he'd just been. How long had she been there? How had he not noticed her?

A siren in the distance snapped him out of his trance. Realizing he needed to move quickly, he took out his phone and snapped a picture. He then pressed down on the accelerator, easing his van onto the street.

He drove a full block and rounded a corner before parking. He jumped out and hurried back.

* * *

David stopped and took Erica's hand in his. He lifted it high above their heads and twirled her on the sidewalk in front of their home. Giggling, Erica let it happen, her long, red hair fanning out around her head.

"You're in a good mood," she remarked.

He'd had several drinks at the engagement party.

"What's there not to be happy about?" David queried, smiling. "I've got a beautiful home, a great gal, and our best friends are now getting married. Most important, we beat them to it."

"Exactly how much have you had to drink?" Erica inquired.

"Just the one, Officer."

Both giggling, they ascended the front steps of their house. Erica kept David from patting his pockets again in the hopes of finding his keys and got her own out of her purse. She'd surely find his in his jacket pocket tomorrow morning.

"Man," David said as they entered. "It's really dark when no one's here."

"Oh, God," Erica said, giggling again as she shut the front door. "You really are wasted."

David froze, seeming to sober up right in front of her.

"Are you okay?" Erica asked.

She heard movement behind her. Before she could turn to check, the cold metal of a gun barrel touched her neck.

"Don't move," a deep voice said. "Don't scream."

Glancing to her right, Erica noticed a figure standing next to her, obscured by shadows.

"What do you want?" David asked. "We don't have any money."

"Shut up," the man said. "Come with me. Move. Now."

He spat out the last two words and the couple quickly realized he was willing to shoot them. There was no point in fighting.

As they walked, they also realized their gun-directed march was heading towards the stairs.

"He goes up first," the man snarled. "Move. Don't try anything."

They obeyed and he directed them down the dark hallway into the master bedroom.

The lights were already on. A chair had been taken from their dining set and placed near the foot of their bed. Several of David's belts had been laid out on the bed, along with a roll of duct tape.

They could see the man now. He seemed to be in his mid to late-twenties like them. He had short, blond hair, a small nose, and large hazel eyes. He seemed to never blink as he stared at them.

Erica couldn't help wondering if he ran like they did. He looked tall and athletic, standing at least half a head over the couple.

The man pointed his gun at David.

"Sit," he hissed, jabbing one finger at the chair.

"You don't have to do this, Man," David protested. "We'll give you all the money we have. It isn't much, but you can take whatever else you want."

He seemed to be on the verge of tears.

The man's eyes narrowed until they looked snake-like.

"Sit or I shoot," he said.

The hand holding the gun was steady. He knew what he was doing.

"Do what he says, David," Erica pleaded.

This got David moving.

Once he was seated, the man nodded and picked up one of the belts. It was brown but not leather. David used it when he wore jeans or similar casual attire.

"Hands behind the chair," the man said, watching David. "Cross your wrists."

He glanced at Erica.

"Tie him," he said, holding out the belt.

Too scared to refuse, Erica took the belt. The thought to run or use this potential weapon never materialized. She just tied David's wrists together behind the chair, hoping she didn't make it too tight. She took the other two belts he handed her, one being from her dresser, and tied her husband's legs to the chair.

"Now gag him," he instructed, holding up a roll of tape. It looked like the roll from their toolbox, normally kept underneath their kitchen sink.

Erica froze.

"You don't have to use that," David said. "We'll be quiet. We promise."

Erica thought about his asthma. It was a warm night, so he'd chosen to forgo a jacket and his inhaler was therefore in her purse.

"Shut up," the man said, tearing off a piece of the thick tape. "Let this happen or it goes over your mouth and nose. I'll make sure the last thing you see is mee screwing her. Then, I'll shoot you in the head just to make sure you're dead."

David didn't speak again, instead taking deep breaths. He didn't move as the man pressed the piece of tape into Erica's hand. Trying not to cry, she turned around and pressed it over David's mouth.

The man set the tape back down and picked up the last belt. It was purple and also belonged to Erica.

"Over there," he said, pointing to David's nightstand next to the bed. He surely couldn't know whose it was. He'd just picked the closer one. Erica didn't dare stop to contemplate this. He followed her as she moved to the indicated spot.

"Very nice, he said, stroking her red hair with the barrel of his gun. He stole occasional glances at her silver watch, a college graduation present from her grandparents.

"Take off your clothes," he said.

Erica gasped as he held the gun up, pointing it at her face to emphasize his command. Tears brimming now, she reached behind her for the zipper on the back of her dress.

The man turned back to look at David, his breaths quickening.

"I'm in charge," he said. "You couldn't stop me if you tried. I always get who I want."

He pivoted back to keep watching Erica undress.

Chapter 4

Joseph and Hadrian arrived in the office of Dr. Everett Mills, somehow making it five minutes early. With the city's annual murder rate ranging between a hundred and fifty to two hundred homicides, the Chief Medical Examiner of Washington DC and his staff always had plenty to do. Still, Dr. Mills personally participated in the autopsies of Ellie Stets and Rachael Holden.

A short, slim man with a receding hairline, the doctor wore a perpetual serious facial expression, even the one time the detectives saw him at his predecessor's retirement party.

"So," Joseph inquired, "how depraved is our killer?"

He and Hadrian could see both girls' files on Dr. Mills's desk.

"Quite depraved," Dr. Mills replied, looking even smaller when seated behind his desk. "Your killer definitely wanted to go for the shock value. I won't be surprised when people write books about this one."

It was an open secret in Washington's law enforcement and medical circles that he had aspirations to be a writer. He'd been working on a novel about a necrophiliac who needs to solve a murder while wanting to find love with a living woman. He'd been working on the project for as long as anyone could remember. Thinking about Sasha's similar ambitions, Joseph figured she'd have better luck.

"We recovered semen from Rachel Holden's vagina," Dr. Mills said, flipping one file open. Despite wanting to be a novelist, he was more often very blunt in his terminology when it came to people's deaths and related traumas.

"Both girls died due to exsanguination," the Medical Examiner continued. "Rachael bled out due to the stab wounds in her back while Ellie bled out through her chest and stomach … we counted twenty-one and nine stab wounds, respectively."

The detectives exchanged glances. This affirmed their theory that Rachael Holden was the killer's target while Ellie Stets was a collateral victim. Joseph remembered the technician at the apartment saying she'd counted eighteen stab wounds on Rachael's back, a number she'd have confirmed at the autopsy. Dr. Mills exceeding that number wasn't welcome news.

"What about the blade he used?" Joseph asked.

"I can't see anything distinguishing about the stab wounds," Dr. Mills said. "We've taken photos and measurements for the lab."

The detectives hoped the department's knife database might yield a viable lead.

"Did the crime scene technicians find some sort of glue at the scene?" Dr. Mills queried. "Stronger than what most people get at Staples for their kids' art projects?"

"We didn't see anything on the reports," Hadrian said, already making a mental note to double-check those reports.

"Your killer definitely used some kind of strong adhesive to keep the girls positioned how he wanted them. Rachael Holden's hands were glued to her inner thighs while Ellie Stetz's hands were glued to her knees. We were able to collect scrapings. Hopefully, the lab can isolate and identify the type of adhesive used."

Joseph and Hadrian could picture how the girls had looked in that apartment. Rachael was laid out with her feet pointed towards the front door, her legs spread, and her hands on the inside of her thighs. Her eyes were open and she was completely naked. Ellie Stets lay face-down on her bed with her backside up and pointed towards the mirror, which enabled anyone entering to get a clear view. Her pants and underwear had been pulled down around her knees while her t-shirt was bunched up around her shoulders. No one had seen the slits from the killer's knife in her shirt until it was cut off and packaged for the crime lab to analyze.

Joseph and Hadrian wondered how the maintenance man who'd found the bodies was doing. He'd come to the apartment because the girls' downstairs neighbor had a leak in their ceiling and he needed to check their ceiling. Finding the door unlocked, he walked right into the first gruesome tableau. Neither investigator had been able to console or get much information from him. He never even made it to the second scene.

Neither detective could think of a reason either girl would keep the type of glue used to position them in the apartment. They'd wait for the lab to identify the brand, but they were already considering the idea the killer had brought the glue.

"We also found an adhesive substance around both girls' mouths and Rachael Holden's wrists," Dr. Mills continued. "It was easier to obtain scrapings at these spots. Look at these."

He pulled some photos out of one file and passed them across the desk. Joseph took them and saw they were images of Rachael's wrists, taken while she lay on the autopsy table. The wide bruises indicated she had been bound, most likely with tape.

"We sent those scrapings to the lab as well," Dr. Mills said. "Like with the adhesive, I hope they can identify a brand."

The detectives again thought back to that apartment. All they'd seen was a small roll of tape in a standard plastic dispenser. Their killer had to have brought the tape used on them as well. He'd been very prepared to cause the maximum amount of carnage and depravity.

* * *

Though she was a quite capable driver, Sasha rarely drove. Her bike and the Metro system usually sufficed for navigating the District of Columbia, even she wanted to get to a fresh crime scene to report the facts.

Still, she owned a blue Mini Cooper, which spent many hours and days in one of the reserved spot in hers and Christian's building's parking garage.

Now, it stood in a Public Storage facility's parking lot in Tenleytown. With Lydon leading Christian, the couple made their way along a row of storage units, each a little bigger than a one-car garage. They found Unit thirty-four and Christian withdrew the keyring his mother gave them.

"What's she got on this keychain, anyway?" he queried. To him, it just felt like a plastic rectangle dangling from the ring.

Sasha grabbed the end of the keychain and studied it.

"It's a picture of Mickey and Minnie Mouse," she reported. "Probably available in any city that's heard of Disney."

Christian nodded and used one key to unlock the padlock on the large door's right side. Trailing his fingers along the riveted panels, he unlocked the left side. He and Sasha reached down and heaved the door upwards. It gave, sliding along its tracks with a low rumble and occasional groan or squeak. Lying on the concrete floor between the couple, Lydon followed its progress with his eyes.

They stared at the stacks of boxes standing among some furnishings covered by plastic tarps. Though there was a lot, there was nevertheless plenty of room to move around.

Stepping over the threshold, Sasha lifted down a box. It wasn't sealed and she opened the flaps. Inside were books, specifically computer textbooks and various manuals for related devices. The box beneath it contained more of the same and she didn't bother with the bottom one in this stack. She also had to stop to sneeze.

"byt' zdorovym," Christian offered.

"Thanks," Sasha said, blowing her nose, "I think."

They surveyed the unit's contents again.

"Does she ever throw anything away?" Sasha asked, moving deeper into the storage unit.

"Not if it interested her at some point," Christian replied, opening another box to find what he assumed were spare computer parts. "I'm sure she's forgotten about some of the stuff in here."

Standing beside him, Lydon began sniffing the floor. Dust moved with every one of the Lab's inhalations and exhalations. He too soon sneezed.

"byt' zdorovym," Christian offered again.

"Where are we supposed to find what she wants?" Sasha asked, looking at the stacks of boxes around her.

Christian wasn't sure. He wondered if his mother even knew where to look. With its paths snaking between boxes and covered furnishings, the storage unit felt like a bad yard sale at IKEA.

Still, with most of them having not been taped shut, it was easy to go through the variously-sized cartons and eliminate their contents as being relevant to the current cause. Sasha soon found herself standing by the back-right corner of the storage unit.

There was one box tucked back there. It seemed to be about the size of the television in their apartment and it looked old and somewhat worn. It too wasn't sealed, but someone had used tape to hold it together.

Doubting its contents were what they wanted, Sasha was nonetheless curious. She supposed it was her reporter's instincts. She lifted the flaps, noticing they were becoming flimsy and susceptible to tearing.

Inside were more textbooks and assorted computer parts. Lifting one book, Sasha saw it had been published back in the late eighties. Putting it back, she saw more books tucked upright along one side. She lifted one out and saw it was a dusty yearbook. Spring Grove Area High School, class of 1988.

A quick search on her phone told Sasha the school was located in York County, Pennsylvania. It took twenty seconds of page-flipping to find Julianna Becker. The eighteen-year-old version of her future mother-in-law looked very pretty. Her auburn hair was adorned by a purple headband. She wore a rose-colored dress and Sasha could see a silver chain around her neck. The photographer had just missed what was on that chain, though one could tell it rested on her sternum. Julianna was a knockout.

Flipping through a few more pages, Sasha saw plenty of signatures from classmates along with several teachers. Julianna had been quite popular.

Sasha pulled out another volume, which was also a yearbook. American University, Class of 1992. Julianna was in there as well, looking just as pretty. Her hair was now styled in a messy bun, some stray red strands framing her face. She was wearing a green blouse and the silver chain was still there. This photographer had aimed a little lower and the top two-thirds of a matching silver locket were now visible. It was a small locket, maybe heart-shaped, and Sasha could tell there was something engraved on it. The yearbook's pages were again adorned with many signatures and phrases expressing warm thoughts and best wishes.

Sasha flipped this yearbook shut and put it back. She then noticed some picture frames also stuffed in this box. There seemed to be about half a dozen. Pulling them out, Sasha saw they were photos of Julianna as a young adult. Most were group shots around Washington, though one seemed to have been taken somewhere in the Caribbean with Julianna wearing a bikini top and long skirt with colorful flip-flops. Sasha was sure she could see glints of light reflecting off her silver locket.

Thinking about the locket, Sasha realized she couldn't recall having ever seen it in person. It seemed to have been important to Julianna. Had she packed it away at some point, like these other trinkets from her past? Was it in one of these boxes?

"I think I found it," Christian announced from another part of the storage unit.

Putting the framed photos back, Sasha turned and rose. Christian was standing a few feet away, holding a box that looked sturdier than the one whose contents she'd been exploring. Lydon stood next to him, wagging his tail.

"What's in there?" she queried.

"Notebooks, photo albums, pamphlets," Christian reported. "I can't think she would keep such an assortment for something computer-related."

"I suppose you never know."

Sasha came over and peered into the box. The pamphlets she could see featured images of wedding scenes.

"Yeah," she said. "This is what we want. MajQa'."

"Thanks, I think," Christian said. "I've seen enough dust. What were you doing, anyway? I heard you rummaging."

"I was looking in some boxes and got caught up in their history. Your mom was always a pretty lady."

Christian nodded.

"She'll want us to clean this box before delivering it to her," he commented. "Plus, I need a shower. Even I can tell I'm covered in dust and God knows what else."

Sasha surveyed his dust-covered physique. She then glanced at herself to see she looked just as bad.

"We both need a shower," she remarked.

She glanced at Lydon, who didn't look too bad. Some dust had clung to his fur. Christian could brush him and he'd be fine.

"Want to save some water?" Christian asked with a grin.

Catching his meaning, Sasha smiled. A shower for two could be fun … and it might save some water.

"Sure," she agreed. "Come on. Let's get out of here."

"Follow," Christian told Lydon and the dog led him to fall into step behind Sasha.

* * *

The water spraying down on him from the shower head for the second time that night, he marveled at his good fortune. His Auburn Lovely had been wonderful. He also marveled at his ingenuity.

He always liked taking two showers. After having his Auburn Lovely and then killing her, the first shower was relaxing. He could refresh before he went to work setting the scene and ensuring the removal of identifying evidence. The second shower was insurance that he wouldn't leave with any blood or other substance on him. And, yes, he thought about his Auburn Lovely both times.

After spotting her during his delivery, he'd driven the truck down a block and parked. He then hurried back on foot and made a casual inquiry about a job opportunity for a non-existent cousin coming to town to go to college. Learning when the shifts began and ended, he made promises to return with said cousin accordingly. The brunette never suspected anything and was likewise sure to forget the encounter soon enough.

True to the prediction, he was not suspected when he casually walked by a little more than twenty-four hours later, wearing a Capitals baseball cap and sunglasses. His Auburn Lovely was getting ready to leave and he kept going. He watched from around a corner and was delighted when she exited and walked in his direction. She never saw him and had no idea how lovely he thought she was. He drank in the sight until she passed him, texting someone as she walked. He began walking a few yards behind her, descending the Metro steps when she led him down there.

He had no clue why she took the train for just one stop. But, she did, and so did he. Another short walk and he watched as she entered her building.

It was another building occupied by a college crowd. He didn't have to wait long for some kid who remained unaware of the world around him to exit.

"Excuse me," he said, having used the time to run to an office supply store. "I've got a delivery for Sonia Baxter."

His quick review of the names on the panel of buzzers and the address written on his package's address label bolstered the lie.

"Sure," the dumb kid said, holding open the front door for him. "The mailroom's in the back. Go straight down that hall."

He thanked the kid and soon found an oblivious equivalent in said mailroom, having disposed of his fake package along the way.

"How you doing?" he said. "Greg Peterson. I just moved in."

Greg Peterson's label on the panel of buzzers looked the least-worn. He figured the building was big enough and its occupants transient enough for his claim to work.

They were and it had.

"Nice to meet you," this second idiot kid said. "I'm Mike."

They shook hands.

"Just between us guys," he'd said, "who's the bombshell I saw down here a little while ago?"

"Who?" Mike asked, opening his mailbox.

"Red hair. Athletic. She looked like she was just coming from work."

Despite counting on the building's occupants not to know their neighbors, he figured his Auburn Lovely would be noticed.

"Only one I know here with red hair is Andrea," Mike told him. "She's on the second floor on the left."

It only took a little more discreet exploration to confirm this was his Auburn Lovely. She did live on the second floor and her small apartment had a balcony the size of a king-sized mattress. That didn't matter. There was a sturdy-looking lattice which ran up from the ground to this balcony and continued on along all the ones directly above it. A six-foot chain-link fence separated this lattice from the alley he stood in. it was easy to traverse and the lattice supported his weight as he climbed it.

As much fun as the research and hunt was, he always preferred having his Auburn Lovely. She heard nothing as he pried her balcony door open with his KA-BAR and entered. It was quick to determine this was a one-bedroom apartment and then to locate said bedroom. She never realized he was there until he slapped the tape across her mouth.

She'd been just as terrified and her eyes pleaded just as much. She was so … lovely. Yes, having her was always better than doing the research.

Once she was bound, gagged, and naked, he let her lie on her bed while he took her. Doing this was admittedly more comfortable than the floor and her muffled moans and squeals sounded just as good. Unfortunately, he again finished long before he wanted to. He had to get better at that. He suspected it was one of the reasons for Susanne's betrayal. His knife made up for it.

Sure enough, he'd gotten another thrill when his Auburn Lovely screamed. He'd taken out his KA-BAR. That muffled scream was the last sound she made before he flipped her face-down on her bed and plunged the blade into her back.

After she was dead and he'd taken his first shower, he spent some time exploring the small dwelling. He had to finish posing his Auburn Lovely before rigor mortis set in, giving him one to two hours at best. That was plenty of time as he had the entire apartment's layout figured out within five minutes. His design was finalized in another ten. With his KA-BAR, it was easy work.

Finishing his second shower, he thought of some final details he wanted to set up before leaving. He turned off the water and reached out for the second towel he'd found in the bedroom closet. He dried himself off and pulled on the set of clean clothes he'd brought in his backpack. His bloody clothes were already in a plastic bag with the first towel he'd used.

Once dressed, he replaced the bloody slipcovers on his sneakers. He walked back into the main room, where his Auburn Lovely sat in an armchair. Knowing it was impossible to avoid all the blood, he was nonetheless careful to step in as little as possible.

He reached his Auburn Lovely and stroked her cheek. She still looked so good. He'd made a mistake last time. He thought his memories would last forever, but that was proving not to be true. He needed something to remember her. Working carefully, he moved his KA-BAR to just behind her left ear. Clutching a clump of her long strands, he sliced them off right near her skin.

He stared at the collection of strands now in his hand. Yes, he'd remember her now. He could relive his time with her over and over again. He could also remember how he left her, as the family-conscious police and media would never show the public that.

Still, he could try and persuade them. He reached for her again, studying the wall behind her. It was just as perfect as everything else. He'd really been meant to visit his Auburn Lovely tonight.

It took less than a minute, even though he had to stretch his arm to reach. He surveyed his work one more time. Much better.

Satisfied, he moved towards the front door. There, he replaced the slipcovers on his sneakers one more time.

Before leaving, he cast one last look at his Auburn Lovely. Yes, he'd chosen well and made the most of what she and this apartment had to give him. He didn't want to leave, but nothing could last forever.

"Good-bye, my Auburn Lovely," he said with a fond smile.

He left her there, naked and seated in the armchair, cradling her own severed breasts in her arms.

Chapter 5

Driving twice in a week's time was a record for Sasha. Nevertheless, she was behind the wheel again, heading down M Street. Christian sat in the Mini Cooper's front passenger seat with Lydon curled up by his feet. He'd always marveled at how deceptively-roomy these cars were.

They were meeting Christian's father at one of his construction sites and driving to a nearby restaurant for lunch. It'd be their first meeting since Christian and Sasha got engaged. According to Christian, his father had expressed his support for the marriage over the phone. Sasha was curious to see that support in person.

"Hu'tegh," Sasha said, tapping her foot on her brake pedal. The cactus mounted on her dashboard, a gift from her niece and nephew, jiggled as the car stopped.

"What?" Christian asked.

"There's traffic," Sasha explained. "A lot more than before."

"It's Saturday. We live in Washington, D.C. There's traffic."

"Not like this. All of the sudden, we're almost at a standstill."

Not only that, but they were also standing two-thirds of the way across an intersection. Sasha was a confident driver, but she still didn't like this position. A chorus of horns surrounded them. A thick fog from that morning was lifting, but it was taking its time and white vapors still decorated the cityscape.

"We've got time," Christian said, unconcerned.

Sasha was more curious than anything else. And, they were still sitting in the intersection.

They moved up a few feet, leaving them three quarters of the way across the intersection. The horns hadn't lessened. How had they ended up in this position?

A few seconds later they moved again, getting out of the intersection.

"Guess they're doing something about it," Christian observed.

Sasha wasn't listening. She could now see flashing red and blue lights through the lingering fog. Had there been an accident? It was possible, given the morning's visibility issues. It would explain the current congestion.

Their progress continued at a steady pace. It seemed the police figured out a way to direct cars around their blockade.

In another few minutes, she could see the police cars as well as a van marked "DC Medical Examiner" in large black letters. There was no sign of a wrecked car. But there were plenty of police officers and other personal entering and exiting the apartment building behind the blockade.

Sasha yanked the Mini Cooper's wheel hard to the left. Thanks to the police cars and related vehicles being in the way, there was no traffic on the far-left lane. Slamming her foot on the brake, she grabbed her backpack from the backseat.

"Wait here," she said. "Don't let anyone make you move the car."

"How would I ..." Christian began, bewildered.

But Sasha had already jumped out of the car, leaving it standing askew in the street as she hurried towards the nearest police officer.

* * *

Joseph stared at Andrea Prady. She'd been in that chair for three hours since the first officers arrived and secured the scene. After the crime scene photographer was finished documenting everything, someone had tried showing mercy and covered her with a clean sheet from the medical examiner's van. The sheet wasn't helping. The only reason she was still here was because everyone was trying to figure out the best way to move her.

Her killer seemed to have glued her to the armchair with her legs spread and her arms wrapped around her torso. A severed breast had been tucked in each crook of her elbows. Her chest, now flat, was covered in her own blood. This was how her friends found her when they came into the apartment to inquire why she hadn't met them downstairs that morning as planned.

Joseph hadn't been on the scene for more than thirty minutes. The first detective had been Erin Jacobs from the 5th District. She arrived when the first responding officers confirmed the presence of a body.

It was Joseph's and Hadrian's good fortune that she kept up with reading the bulletins sent out by detectives across the city. Granted, the information about Rachael Holden's and Ellie Stetz's murders were one of dozens of bulletins about crimes committed just from that night, but the vague details about how the girls were posed after the killings caught Erin's attention. She called Hadrian to report she was possibly at the scene of a similar murder. Seeing how Andrea Prady was left to be found by the first unwitting person to enter her apartment, Joseph and Hadrian were sure this was the same killer. Even though they couldn't see her back, they were sure they'd find fatal stab wounds there once she was freed from the chair.

Hadrian and Erin were on the other side of the room, examining the balcony door. Knowing Andrea's body wouldn't tell him anything else right then, Joseph walked over to join them.

"That's how the killer got in?" he asked.

"Yeah," Erin replied. "The door's definitely been pried open from the outside. It wouldn't have been hard. This is an older building and the door looks cheap."

Joseph stepped out onto the balcony and looked over its metal railing.

"The lattice goes all the way up from the ground along the side here," he reported. "Would have been easy for him to climb up."

"Just like the fire escape at the other apartment," Hadrian mused. "We're probably looking for a younger guy. He'd have to be somewhat athletic."

"The balcony faces north, and there don't seem to be any exterior lights the city would have installed. It might have been pitch-black. No one would have seen him breaking in. What time was she killed?"

"The Medical Examiner's people estimate it was around 2:00 this morning," Erin replied. "Even most of the college crowd would be asleep by then."

Joseph studied Erin as he reentered the apartment. She was African American, like him and Hadrian, but definitely younger. He hadn't heard of her before, but he appreciated her observation skills. Between that and her neat and clean suit, she clearly took pride in her role as a detective.

The three walked back to where Andrea's sheet-covered body sat. they studied the words written on the wall behind her. "Show her". The letters were as reddish-brown as the mattress in the bedroom. The detectives were sure the killer used his victim's blood as ink. The crime scene technicians had examined the writing but found no fingerprints.

"There's a faint impression," a technician said, showing the detectives a close-up image of the spot on the wall. "It's flat, but it's at the natural ending point of the 'R'. I would say he wore rubber gloves."

The detectives were sure those rubber gloves wouldn't be found inside the apartment.

"He left Rachael and Ellie near where he killed them," Joseph recounted to the others, "but he moved Andrea from her bedroom to pose her out here."

The volume of reddish-brown blood on Andrea's bed made it clear where the fatal attack occurred. Her mattress was soaked in it and faint bloody drag marks led from the bed to the armchair.

"Means our guy is strong," Hadrian said. "Definitely athletic. I wouldn't be surprised if he lifts weights or something."

"It also means he wants attention," Joseph added. "We knew he set up the other two bodies to achieve shock value from the first person who entered the apartment and then Ellie's bedroom."

The amount of blood on Andrea's chest and legs, as well as the armchair, made it clear her breasts were severed after she was posed, maybe after her killer applied the glue.

"Guess it wasn't enough," Hadrian said as he studied the killer's message again.

"Those two girls were all over the news," Erin added, "but that was pretty tame compared to what you probably saw at the apartment."

"Definitely," Hadrian confirmed. "I'll bet our guy watched it and wasn't satisfied."

"Show her," Joseph recited. "It's all about him. Andrea, Ellie, and Rachael are basically canvases he wants to display."

"And we definitely have victimology," Joseph said. "Andrea's eighteen and in college, right?"

"A sophomore at Gallaudet University," Erin confirmed. "We're not far from the campus."

"He pays the most attention to his redheaded victims. They're the ones he rapes. Ellie Stets was killed and posed, but just because she was there. Andrea didn't have a roommate, or we'd have another body."

"He likes the redheads," Erin said, staring at the sheet-covered body. "How many more does he have to choose from in this city?"

* * *

"Come on," Sasha complained. "You must know something or you wouldn't be here."

"I'm just watching the barricade," the police officer said, "Dennis" adorning his nameplate. "All I know is that there's a crime scene in there."

"Then it has to be a homicide," Sasha retorted, pointing out the Medical Examiner's van.

"I don't know. Ever hear of an accidental death?"

With a huff, Sasha left him and made her way along the barricade. She spotted a young man by the open back doors of the ominous van.

"Hey!" Sasha called, waving at him.

The young man turned and walked over so only a few feet and the police barricade separated them.

"You're from the Medical Examiner's Office?" Sasha queried.

"I transport the bodies," the young man said, sounding indifferent.

"I'm Sasha Copeland with the Washington Post," she said, presenting the press credentials she kept in her backpack. "Can you tell me who was killed in that building?"

"A girl," the young man said. "I try not to catch their names."

"Is she still up there?" Sasha asked, eyeing the van.

"Yeah. The lead detective said to wait until the other detectives got there."

Sasha raised an eyebrow.

"What other detectives?" she asked, writing on her iPad.

The young man shrugged his shoulders.

"Don't know," he said. "They're up there now. Don't know how we would move the body anyway."

"Why's that?" Sasha asked, looking up.

The young man glanced to his left and right.

"You gonna quote me?" he asked, sounding a little nervous.

"I don't even know your name," Sasha pointed out. "You're just a source from the Medical Examiner's Office."

Unlike the cops, his plastic badge, clipped to his shirt, only displayed his employer's name.

The young man glanced left and right again. He then locked eyes with Sasha and leaned in close.

"The killer left her naked and glued to a chair," he whispered. "She was also cut up a bit."

He looked pale as he stopped talking. He backed away again.

Sasha absorbed this as she made notes. She noticed a cop observing them.

"Thank you," she said, stuffing her iPad back in her bag.

She hurried back along the barricade, seeing another cop standing by her Mini Cooper. He was leaning over a bit, talking to Christian through the open window.

"How did you get the car here?" the officer was asking.

"Sorry, Sasha said, startling him. "It's my car. We'll get out of your way."

She climbed in behind the wheel, made the tightest U-turn she could recall executing, and drove away from the barricade.

"How was your expedition?" Christian queried. "You get a good story?"

"Yeah," Sasha replied, feeling a little queasy.

* * *

Sasha drove to a shopping center two blocks away and parked in front of a Walmart. After getting sodas for herself and Christian, she sat in the car, pecking on her iPad. After twenty-three minutes, she used the Walmart's Wi-Fi to submit the article along with the only snapshot she'd gotten of the police activity outside the apartment building. Finished, she put the iPad back in her backpack and began driving again. They'd need to find an alternate route.

* * *

They arrived at the construction site only ten minutes late. Christian's father, who was walking the perimeter of the nearly-completed office building, waved and came over.

"Dobriy den," Christian said.

"Ochen' khoroshiy," his father, Spartak Fedorov, said with a chuckle. "Very good. I do hope you will one day feel comfortable using the more informal 'Privet'."

Christian and his father were far from the point where their greetings included hugs, let alone informal greetings. Spartak understood it would take time and didn't often comment on it.

They shook hands, followed by Spartak taking Sasha's hand in both of his. She could feel the healed cuts and scratches dotting his palms.

"Pozdravleniya," he offered, eyeing the ring with a broad grin. "Congratulations."

"Thank you," Sasha replied with an apprehensive smile. Though Christian and Julianna had assured her the man was harmless, he was still a foot and a half taller than her and muscular thanks to his work as a construction foreman. His unruly blond hair shone as the sun emerged through the clouds and fog.

"How are things going with the building?" Christian queried, nodding towards the site behind Spartak.

Lydon, bored by now, settled himself by Christian's feet for a nap.

"Very good," his father said in his strong Russian accent. "It's quiet on the weekend, but we are on schedule so far."

Living in a trailer which he towed from site to site with his pickup truck, he simultaneously provided security when work wasn't in progress.

"Let's go eat," he said. "There's a great diner not far from here."

* * *

Sitting in a booth at Duncan's Diner with sandwiches in front of them, Spartak brought up Sasha's article from earlier that week.

"Those poor girls," he lamented. "Wonderful words, but those poor girls. I'm reminded of your mother."

As far as Christian and Sasha knew, he and Julianna hadn't seen or spoken with one another in about twenty-five years.

"She was a beautiful woman," Spartak continued. "I am very sure she still is."

He'd never developed an interest in social media. Christian wasn't sure how his mother would feel if he tried to reach out to her that way.

Sasha remembered the yearbooks and photos she'd found in Julianna's storage unit. Having seen photos of the two murdered girls, she supposed Christian's mother showed the same vibrance at that time in her life … just starting out and seeing the world. And, there was the red hair.

"What happened between the two of you?" Christian inquired. His mother had never given him a straight answer regarding this topic.

"I think you came as a great shock to her," Spartak said. "I was certainly very shocked."

Christian long knew his was not a planned or anticipated conception.

"She was not ready to settle down," Spartak said. "I was prepared to be there for both of you, but she didn't want to do that. So, we fell apart. I am sorry if that sounds as vague as I think it does, but it is the best I can conclude."

He thought for a moment.

"I have considered there was something she didn't want to let happen," he added. "Slovo ne vorobey."

"What does that mean?" Sasha queried. She knew it meant "a word is not a sparrow," but that didn't make much sense either.

"It means that when something is said, it cannot be unsaid," Spartak explained. "It is a Russian proverb. You can catch a sparrow that tries to fly away. You cannot do that with the words that leave your mouth. There is no putting them back."

He took a bite of his sandwich and the next few seconds passed in silence.

"How are your books coming?" he asked.

While making money as professional reporters, both Christian and Sasha aspired to increase their readership by entering the fiction market.

"I've gotten a rough copy out there to a few people," Christian said. "I think Sasha will be the first to get her novel out there for the masses."

"That is the one about the teacher who is taken hostage, right?" Spartak asked.

"Yes," Sasha confirmed. Her novel was actually called "The Teacher".

"Chudesno," Spartak said with pride. "I will read it. I will have to read them all."

* * *

He couldn't believe it. An article about his latest kill was already out there. From what he'd heard while listening on his father's old police scanner, the first officers hadn't arrived until three hours ago. This Washington Post article was amazingly-detailed for being written so shortly after.

Sitting in his den, he checked the byline on his iPhone's screen. Sasha Copeland. He went to his browser's bookmarks and located the Post's article about his other kills. Something about that name looked familiar. He opened the earlier piece.

Yes. Sasha Copeland of the Washington Post's Crime and Public Safety section had written both articles. She was following his work and sharing it with her readers. He had to smile.

Less than a minute of clicking and scrolling on his phone got him a picture. She looked young and petit. She was blonde, which he found disappointing. It would be so wonderful if she could be his Auburn Lovely. But, he reasoned, if he killed her, who would share his work?

He went back to the most recent article. Ms. Copeland was a good reporter. She was being careful not to say he'd killed all three girls, but she pointed out there were similarities which needed to be considered. She wrote about how he posed his victims. He was delighted to see the specific mention about how his Auburn Lovely was "secured" to a chair for effect. Why could she not just say everything he did? Were newspaper editors still such prudes?

He heard the front door open and shut.

"Dad?!" he asked.

"Yeah," his father replied in a gruff voice. He'd gone on one of his usual walks, though his path was always unclear.

"You need anything?" he asked.

"No," his father said and continued on to his room.

He sighed and returned to his phone. Yes, he was becoming a star, but he could still nudge the press along. It wasn't like it hadn't been done before.

Chapter 6

Cassie watched as the man set his gun down on her nightstand, careful to leave its barrel pointed in her direction. She already knew what he wanted. She knew it ever since he ordered her to undress and lie on her bed. Any doubts about his intentions were eviscerated when he used a towel he'd cut into long strips to tie her wrists to her headboard. Now, she just wanted to survive this.

The man opened his pants and climbed onto the bed. Cassie shut her eyes as he moved over her. She could feel him touching her all over, always moving back up to stroke her red hair.

"Open your eyes," the man growled.

Understanding he'd already killed people, Cassie hoped cooperating would leave her alive. Opening her eyes, she looked at him, his face inches above hers. He looked young and his hair was blonde, though it looked like he'd gotten a shaved cut. His small nose sat in the middle of his face. He looked like he walked in the same circles as she did. She'd have never guessed someone like that was capable of doing this. What struck her most of all were his large hazel eyes. They looked calm and relaxed as they stared back at her.

"Good," he said, stroking her long, red hair, having undone her messy bun earlier. "You get it, don't you? I'm in charge."

Cassie didn't dare move as he began to rape her.

"I'm in charge," he said as he moved. "You couldn't stop me if you tried. I always get who I want."

Cassie whimpered. He wrapped his hands around her throat and squeezed. She began gurgling.

"Stay quiet," he grunted.

Everything soon went black … and then came back. Cassie began to regain her senses as he finished inside her. She coughed and spluttered as he got off the bed, zipping up his pants.

He picked up the ring on her nightstand. It was the ring Brian had given her three months ago. The man had pulled it off Cassie's finger before making her lie on the bed.

"Very nice," the man remarked. "Why would a guy who spends a load on this rock then leave it and the gal he gave it to all alone?"

Brian had needed to go on a last-minute business trip to San Francisco that morning. That was why he wasn't here for their usual date night.

Cassie wondered if the man knew about their date night and had anticipated Brian being here. She knew from the news that he'd tied up other men while he raped the women. She didn't dare say anything. The man reached out and patted her bare stomach.

"Stay quiet," he said, pocketing her ring.

He took his gun and left the room. As she heard him rummaging downstairs in the kitchen, Cassie began to cry.

* * *

Christian was surprised to hear someone knocking loudly on the apartment's front door. Their building didn't have a doorman, but people couldn't just walk in. There were buzzers.

"Who's that?" Matthew queried from across the kitchen table. They'd been studying for an upcoming midterm.

"Don't know," Christian replied. With Lydon walking alongside him, he grabbed Sasha's umbrella. Whoever was at the door knocked again, sounding insistent. He unlocked and pulled the door open, only then remembering the chain. He ought to have put that on first.

"Expecting rain?" Hadrian asked with a slight chuckle.

"Relax," Joseph added. "It's Detectives Conway and Hasselle."

"How did you get in the building?" Christian asked.

"Your maintenance man. Where's Sasha?"

Christian decided it'd be best for none of his neighbors to overhear this conversation.

"Come on in," he said, hanging the umbrella back on the coat rack.

The detectives entered the apartment and he shut the door. Matthew sat still at the table, studying the two visitors.

"Where's Sasha?" Joseph repeated.

"Doing her job," Christian replied. "I think she's covering a bank robbery."

"We heard something about that on our radios. You have the day off?"

"We're studying. What do you want?"

He wouldn't bother to introduce Matthew to these detectives.

"We want to talk with Sasha about her last story," Hadrian said.

"She writes a lot of stories," Christian pointed out.

"Here's a hint," Joseph said. "We're not here about any recent works of fiction. She speculated about two crimes being connected."

Christian had suspected why they'd come the moment they'd announced their identities. This suspicion was confirmed when they mentioned the article.

"She didn't speculate anything," he said. "She stated it was the second time in very recent history that people were killed and subsequently posed. Any number of people could have put that together."

Matthew stared, in awe of his friend's willingness to challenge these police officers.

"How did she stumble onto that information?" Joseph asked.

"I don't know," Christian replied. "I wasn't standing next to her."

"Dumb luck, huh?" Hadrian asked.

"Where did she get the information to point out this coincidence?" Joseph asked.

"I don't know," Christian replied. "What, you think the killer helped her put that together?"

They were still standing by the apartment's front door. Bored by the attention not being focused on him, Lydon had stalked away to rejoin Matthew at the kitchen table, curling up at the man's feet.

"No," Hadrian said. "But there are people who are making further leaps than she did after reading her article. They are linking these killings with certainty."

"What?" Christian asked. "They're saying there's a serial killer on the loose?"

"That's what people are saying and thinking," Joseph said.

"Is there?"

From his seat at the table, Matthew had a new reason to grow concerned.

"We're investigating two incidents of murders occurring in separate places on separate dates and times," Hadrian said.

"You two are investigating all these murders?" Christian pressed.

"No comment."

Christian had to smile at this.

"Look," he said. "I honestly have no idea how Sasha got the information she got to suggest a link between these murders and I have no idea when she'll be home. I do know she is responsible enough to not accept the information from some random person. She said her source was on the scene in a professional capacity, so that sounds like a cop or someone similar."

"There's something else," Hadrian said.

"And we're off the record on this," Joseph added.

Christian had to smile again.

"Can we trust him?" Hadrian asked, nodding towards Matthew.

"Yes," Christian replied. "He's cool."

"Thanks, Man," Matthew said, not wanting to be involved in this. he pushed some stray black strands out of his face. He needed a haircut and would dearly love to have the excuse to leave and get one right then.

"Whoever murdered the victim on M Street left a message," Hadrian said. "They want us and, by extension, the media to share what they've done with the general public … every last graphic detail. They want fame for this."

"Why are you telling me that?" Christian asked. "You know Sasha wouldn't desecrate a murder victim like that."

"But someone might want her to, and they probably don't have such scruples. And, they might take more extreme measures to get the attention they crave."

"We're telling you this because we want you and Sasha to be careful," Joseph said. "Her name is on the article and you two don't live in the Witness Protection Program."

"Please let her know to be careful," Hadrian implored.

Christian wasn't quite sure what to say.

"Thanks, I guess," he finally uttered.

"Take care," Hadrian said. He and Joseph then left and Christian returned to the kitchen table.

"This happen often?" Matthew asked, trying not to show how shaken he felt.

* * *

"This is why I became a detective," Hadrian remarked as Joseph, behind the wheel of their unmarked cruiser, rejoined the traffic outside Sasha's apartment building. "Warning reporters to be mindful of stalkers."

Joseph didn't reply. He thought about Andrea Prady. Her murder being high priority, Dr. Everett Mills personally participated in the young woman's autopsy.

Andrea had been stabbed nineteen times in the back, dying due to exsanguination. Semen was found inside her and her body exhibited signs of forcible sex occurring shortly before her death. Residue collected from her wrists and around her mouth suggested she was bound and gagged with tape. She'd definitely been glued to the chair she was found seated in.

"Anyone we need to follow up with?" Hadrian asked.

"No," Joseph replied in a flat tone.

Much like Rachael Holden and Ellie Stets, Andrea had no enemies. There was an ex-boyfriend from her hometown of Annapolis. They'd broken up the summer between high school and college and he'd been in a rehabilitation facility in Pennsylvania for the past twenty-nine days. It seemed he had a drinking problem which might have contributed to their break-up. But, a counselor at the rehab facility was prepared to swear in court that he'd spoken with this ex-boyfriend four hours prior to the murders and five minutes before the facility went into its nightly lockdown. No one entered or exited the facility from the 9:00 lockdown to 6:00 the next morning, when it was lifted. It was an alibi surrounded by brick, metal, alarms, guards, and cameras. With the ex-boyfriend eliminated, there were no other viable suspects in Andrea Prady's murder.

Sure, the lab tests hadn't yet made the connections between the glue and tape residue from Andrea's, Rachael's, and Ellie's bodies. DNA tests wouldn't come back for months. Short of that, anyone with a gold badge was prepared to link the murders. A taskforce was being created and it was expected to be based in the 2nd District, near where the first attack occurred.

Problem was the public was also linking the murders, partly thanks to the suggestions made in Sasha's article. Though the academic year was only half-over, many students in colleges across the city were exploring options to transfer. School administrators were trying to design policies to increase their students' safety, though they were impeded by the fact the people being targeted lived off-campus in buildings the schools had no authority over. Still , suggestions were being made about making sure everything in their homes was locked. Campus police agencies were trying to gain membership on the police taskforce while encouraging their charges to report any suspicious activity occurring anywhere. It was a frenzy Washington hadn't seen in over fifteen years.

"I say we retire after this," Hadrian said. "Catch this prick and go out on a high note."

Joseph had to smile at the idea. He'd been an officer on patrol when John Allen Muhammad and Lee Boyd Malvo went on the spree that paralyzed the DC metro area with fear. He'd responded to the duo's first attack in DC, keeping the crowd back as crime scene technicians and detectives tried to figure out how Pascal Charlot was shot without anyone seeing the shooter. He'd also spent some time on the roadblocks set up to try and ensnare the sniper. He still wondered if he might have let the blue Caprice slip by while on the lookout for the white van.

Yeah, Joseph was ready to retire. It'd be a grim irony if he started and ended on a serial killer case which put DC in a state of panic.

* * *

"Hey!" his boss, David, called.

Seeing the chubby man waving towards him, he stopped loading boxes from the pallet into his van and came over. As he walked, he saw her. Another Auburn Lovely was in the garage, standing next to the man he had to answer to. He shook his head once to focus and not look suspicious. Still, she looked so good. Young, athletic, a nice smile, and that lovely red hair. He couldn't believe it.

"This is Jordan," his boss said. "Jordan, this is Duncan."

He was surprised his boss remembered his name … at least the name he'd provided when he applied. they exchanged half a dozen words in a week's time, if they were lucky, and most of his instructions were instead left on the daily manifests. Then again, how much direction did one require to make these deliveries?

"Jordan's coming on as a driver," David explained. "She wants to make some extra money for college."

His Auburn Lovely gave a small, embarrassed smile.

"I want you to take her along on your run today," David instructed. "Show her how it's done."

He wondered two things. First, could his Auburn Lovely even lift the boxes currently on the pallet by his van? Second, how was he not supposed to pull over and have her right in the van? There was tape in the toolbox behind every driver's seat.

David walked away, indicating his role in this was completed.

"Hi," his Auburn Lovely said, sounding shy. She was so … lovely.

"Hey," he said, struggling to sound indifferent. He thought of Susanne and how close he'd gotten to her. He hoped this wouldn't be the same. If things turned that way, he could kill this one here. That was a fact.

"So," his Auburn Lovely said. "What do you do before you go out?"

He blinked.

"What?" he asked.

"I mean," his Auburn Lovely said. "What do you need to do before you can start making the deliveries? There's gotta be more to it besides loading boxes into the van, right?"

He nodded slowly, resisting the urge to yank out his KA-BAR and start cutting her clothes off right there.

"Come on," he said, motioning for her to follow him. "I just got started."

If nothing else, he'd see how strong she was. It'd be important to keep such a fact in the back of his mind as he decided what to do with her. He also needed to figure out how to explain the brief pitstop he'd intended to make while he was out today. That was too important to postpone.

* * *

Sasha sat in the McDonald's, nibbling at her salad and taking long sips of her milkshake as she worked on the article. The DC Savings and Trust on Pennsylvania Avenue had been robbed. It wasn't the sort of robbery from the movies where someone pumped bullets into the ceiling while shouting demands. No, this perpetrator had walked in, handed a teller a note while displaying the gun in his waistband, and taken all the money she could give him. The whole thing took less than ninety seconds and most bank staff and customers were unaware of what had occurred until the first police officers arrived in the parking lot.

Apart from this thief bringing and showing a gun, this was the much more common M.O. for a bank robbery. According to the FBI agent on the scene, this was the first time he'd seen such a crime committed with a weapon being present. He'd been on the bureau for four years and was assigned to investigate bank robberies nine months ago, investigating at least three cases a month since then. That was good enough to justify his remark about the rarity of a weapon's presence. Sasha identified the agent as "an experienced investigator at the scene" in her article. With his card in her purse, she had a new potential source to stay in touch with.

Finishing the article and submitting it to her editors, she turned to her notes on the person who'd now killed three female college students. She began consolidating her knowledge after the newest victim, whom she learned was Andrea Prady, was discovered and she'd stumbled onto the crime scene.

Sasha could sense the panic. This McDonald's was near American University and every single young woman was accompanied by at least one other person while constantly looking at everyone around her. Groups of three or four were even more common than just pairs and many groups were mixed in gender. The female collegiate body of Washington D.C. was feeling uneasy at best.

Sasha wasn't fearless. She looked around her wherever she was, especially after Christian's text about the detectives' visit. But, she wasn't going to wait and find someone to accompany her everywhere she went.

Plus, she was outside of the killer's preferred victim demographic. It was too much of a coincidence he found two young, Caucasian college students with red hair. Just under five percent of the country's population had red hair, not including dye jobs, and the Washington D.C. population was forty-five percent African American.

Alongside her certainty that this killer was taking the time to find and select his victims, Sasha was also sure he lived or at least worked in Washington. The two crime scenes were just over six miles apart in a city that covered sixty-eight square miles. From what she knew, no locals in either neighborhood reported anyone looking unusual or lost or anything else like that. If the killer was a visitor, he'd stick to a much smaller area in which he'd become comfortable and familiar in. No, Sasha was sure he lived in D.C. and probably had a blue-collar job that let him move around the city without attracting attention.

Considering that last hypothesis, Sasha couldn't help thinking about Christian's father. Spartak was definitely not a suspect. For one thing, he had no criminal record, violent or otherwise. The only overlap he had with her homemade profile was that he moved around the city, living at and overseeing the various construction projects his employers were commissioned to complete.

Sasha considered her profile. She knew it was vague, but it was all she had to go on. The police weren't being very forthcoming, though they now seemed to be admitting there might be a connection between the murders, something easily deduced with the scant information she'd managed to collect.

She'd gotten the e-mail an hour ago. There was to be a press conference held in the media center at the Henry J. Daly Building on Indiana Avenue. The subject of the press conference wasn't mentioned except for it being a public safety matter. That, and it was sent to Sasha, a reporter on the Washington Post's Local Crime and Public Safety section. She was sure she wasn't a recipient due to her prior relationship with the police department.

Sasha couldn't think of anything else occurring in Washington which would warrant her being invited to a press conference at police headquarters. She wondered how much the authorities would share with her and her colleagues. So far, she'd had a leg up on other news outlets, some actually piggy-backing on her articles about the murders. She was sure the police wanted to put all the news media on the same level while keeping themselves ahead of the reporters. She'd have to wait and find out what would be said at the press conference.

Chapter 7

He smiled at his good fortune. Approaching the shopping center on M Street, he spotted a Post Office Box. There seemed to be fewer and few of those around these days. He also spotted a coffeeshop.

"Want something to drink?" he asked, indicating the latter. "I could use a caffeine booster."

They'd been driving for two hours and had three deliveries left to make. Theirs wasn't a market requiring long treks across vast terrains. But, the money was good and the work was easy enough.

"Sure," his Auburn Lovely said in the van's passenger seat, "but I'll buy. It's the least I can do after you took the time to teach me everything."

This was going better than he'd dreamed. Fate was even kind enough to leave a parking spot just twenty feet from the coffeeshop's door and the mailbox nice and empty.

"Wo," his Auburn Lovely remarked as he pressed on the accelerator a little too hard. "You really want that coffee."

"Sorry," he said, relieved when he reached the desired parking space.

"How do you take it?"

"Black with sugar."

"Be right back."

As soon as she was in the coffeeshop, he too exited the van. He moved around the back so his Auburn Lovely couldn't see him through the coffeeshop's large front windows. He dashed forward, willing to risk being spotted as he darted to the mailbox. He shoved his letter through the slot and hurried back.

His Auburn Lovely returned a couple minutes later, carrying his coffee and a water bottle for herself.

"Thanks," he said, his mind still on the letter he'd just mailed. He wished he could see Sasha Copeland's reaction when she opened the envelope.

"I hope I get to come back here," his Auburn Lovely said as they began driving again.

"What do you mean?" he asked, his curiosity actually captured.

"I want to go here to Georgetown."

They were near the campus of Georgetown University.

"I'm taking a couple community college courses," his Auburn Lovely explained. "But this is where I really want to go. Always had this school on my mind."

He nodded, a new thought entering his head. It'd take some work, but the reward would be worth it. Instead of killing her, he could kill in her honor.

* * *

The media center at the Henry J. Daly Building was bustling as a few more reporters trickled in. Every higher-up from the Metropolitan Police Department of the District of Columbia seemed to be in attendance, their suits pressed and their gold badges present and polished. From her space in the second row, Sasha recognized the executive assistant chief of police, both patrol chiefs, and Assistant Chief Clark Blake from the Investigative Services Bureau. A woman stood next to him, the insignia on her uniform suggesting she too was an Assistant Chief for another bureau. And then there was Chief Ehle.

The public face of the department's Office of Communications was Sergeant Emmett Newsome. Sasha only knew him through the e-mail blasts he sent out to the city's reporters, the most recent announcing this press conference. With his neat hair, nice suit, and lack of a firearm on his belt, Sasha was sure he'd only ever served in an administrative role for the department, or at least moved off the streets as soon as he could.

Sergeant Newsome stepped up to the lectern and signaled for quiet. The eager crowd was quick to settle into silence.

"Thank you all for coming on such short notice," the sergeant said. "We know there have been rapid developments, especially in the last forty-eight hours. We called you here today to advise you and the public of the department's actions in response to recent events. Chief Marisa Ehle will now make a statement and take a few questions."

Watching the police chief march towards the lectern, which Sergeant Newsome was hurriedly vacating, Sasha reflected on this woman's ascent to the role of Top Cop in Washington. Her predecessor had resigned in the wake of a bribery scandal and was awaiting trial and the possibility of a ten-year stint in a federal prison. Marisa Ehle had been trying to distance herself from the scandal ever since accepting this appointment. Despite that struggle, she'd earned the respect of the mayor and over half of the City Council. Crime in D.C. dropped three percent during her first six months in charge.

"Good afternoon," Chief Ehle said. "I speak to you and the citizens of Washington during a difficult time. Within a week, three young women were brutally attacked and murdered within the safety of their homes. Circumstantial evidence has led this department to conclude these crimes are connected and are being committed by a single perpetrator with no prior connection to the victims. In other words, Washington, D.C., has a serial killer active on our streets."

If she was expecting reactions of shock and/or horror, they never came. Most of the reporters had speculated on this already. Some, like Sasha, had done so in writing.

"I ask the residents and all those who come to our city every day not to panic," Chief Ehle continued. "Instead, please take caution. Watch your surroundings and report any suspicious activity. Make sure your homes are secure whenever you are out or asleep. Finally, rest assured we are doing everything we can to identify and apprehend this perpetrator."

She paused, glancing to her left.

"Now," she said, "I'd like to introduce the appointed commanding officer for this taskforce, Inspector Harvey Cunningham."

A suited man Sasha didn't recognize stepped forward. Chief Ehle was more graceful as she vacated the lectern for him than Sergeant Newsome had done earlier.

"Thank you, Chief Ehle," Inspector Cunningham said. "I'm honored by your faith and the faith of this city. I have been with this department for twenty-three years and I intend to use all of my experience to lead our men and women towards the person responsible for these brutal slayings."

Sasha had to admit everyone's speeches were well-rehearsed. They sounded professional and somewhat natural.

"I'd like to speak directly to the families of Rachael Holden, Ellie Stets, and Andrea Prady," Inspector Cunningham said. "This entire city offers you our heartfelt condolences. Rest assured we stand with you and we will do everything in our power to find the person responsible for the deaths of your loved ones."

* * *

The parking lot adjacent to the Henry J. Daly Building remained crowded after the press conference concluded. Reporters sat in their cars, hunched over their laptops and tablets, transmitting the police officials' statements to their editors and readers. Not to be outdone, television crews continued filming as on-camera reporters recapped what they'd filmed earlier, using the police headquarters building as a backdrop.

Sasha sat in her Mini Cooper, typing on her wireless keyboard. Her iPad was balanced on her knees while leaning against the steering wheel. She'd put up her windshield shade, depicting the fish from Finding Nemo, to discourage peeking. Her side and rear windows were tinted. She was relatively safe from prying eyes. Nevertheless, she glanced up from her screen every so often to survey her surroundings. Her colleagues were all too busy trying to beat her to the headline to worry about spying on her.

Sasha knew she already had an advantage by being the first to report on the murders. She intended to keep it and knew this required a bold move. And nothing was bolder than to name this killer.

Sasha Finished her article on the press conference by relaying Chief Ehle's warning to the many female college students living throughout Washington, D.C. No curfew had been instated, but they were heeded to avoid going out at night if they didn't have to. They should make sure all doors and windows in their homes were securely locked. And, if possible, they needed to avoid being alone. Finally, they were to carefully monitor their surroundings and immediately report any suspicious activity.

Finished, Sasha surveyed her headline one more time.

POLICE FORM TASKFORCE TO FIND DC COLLEGE KILLER

Sure, she hadn't taken much time to come up with that name, but it sounded catchy. She felt somewhat confident that it'd stick. She clicked "Send".

Turning off her iPad, she pulled the shade off her windshield and started the engine. She'd head home now.

* * *

Due to their luck of having been at both crime scenes, Joseph and Hadrian were assigned to the city's taskforce with little hesitation. Even Captain King seemed somewhat okay with letting them go.

They didn't have to go far. Because the first murders occurred on Idaho Avenue, the taskforce was headquartered in two conference rooms in the 2nd District's station. Inspector Harvey Cunningham was subscribing to the theory that the killer lived in the area and was therefore comfortable committing his first killings there. It seemed the Inspector had taken some profiling courses at the FBI Academy in Quantico.

Though it was made clear he was in charge, Inspector Cunningham was proving to be benevolent. After a short introductory speech to the detectives and officers temporarily assigned under his command, he let Joseph and Hadrian share their findings and theories about the killings, with Detective Erin Jacobs chiming in on Andrea Prady's murder as needed.

After introductions and this share, there was little to go on. DNA evidence, which would likely prove the murders were committed by the same killer, wouldn't be back from the lab for another couple months, and there was no guarantee it would match a known offender. The FBI's Behavioral Analysis Unit in Quantico was working on a profile of the killer, but many suspected the profilers wouldn't come up with anything not already known or suspected.

Still, Inspector Cunningham intended to keep his people busy. Detectives were sent back to the victims' apartment buildings, as well as the campuses of UDC and Gallaudet, to canvas and re-interview neighbors and students. Other personnel were assigned to work with probation departments from D.C., Maryland, and Virginia to investigate paroled felons, particularly sex offenders, who'd targeted redheads.

Of course, the fact the primary victims were redheads didn't escape anyone. Comparisons to the Mid-Atlantic Slayer were being made. Inspector Cunningham was quick to quell any notions that the killings were connected.

"He's been silent for over twenty years," he said in the taskforce's third meeting. "His victimology was completely different. And he would be in his mid-forties today, at best. Everyone here agrees our guy is young and athletic."

His subordinates didn't have much room for counterarguments. Apart from the red hair, the prior victims, adults in their mid to late-twenties, were distinctly different from the college students being hunted now. While it wasn't impossible that the Mid-Atlantic Slayer had changed his victimology, it was highly unlikely he would switch to younger victims who'd be harder to control, especially given he would be older now.

A detective and sergeant, both in their mid-forties, were selected to enter the current victims apartments using the same routes the killer was suspected to have traversed. Though they each made it, the exertion of climbing the fire escape and lattice at the two apartment buildings left the men winded. They needed time to recover, time the killer wouldn't have had being in such close proximity to his victims. Had he not ambushed and subdued them quickly, any of the girls were sure to have heard him in their small apartments.

And, had they gotten a chance to scream due to discovering an intruder, neighbors would have heard this. Though one apartment adjacent to the first crime scene was vacant, no one reported hearing anything alarming. The closest was two young men living beneath Ellie Stets and Rachael Holden. They reported hearing a few thumps on their ceiling, but these sounds were common whenever one of the girls walked through their apartment in great haste. Thus, neither downstairs neighbor followed up on these sounds, instead going back to sleep just as quickly as they'd been woken.

Though not outright dismissed, any suggested connection between the current spree and the Mid-Atlantic Slayer were given low investigative priority.

Also considered unlikely was the idea the killer was a fellow college student. There were less than a dozen transfers between the University of the District of Columbia and Gallaudet University every year. Though both schools had plenty of files on students who'd received disciplinary sanctions, there was no overlap between the schools in this area.

"But there is an overlap somewhere," Inspector Cunningham insisted, making finding a connection between the schools, and in particular the victims, a top priority.

* * *

He smiled as he watched the news. They had a taskforce hunting him and everything. And better yet, that taskforce had no idea who they were chasing. He'd been careful both times, leaving little evidence.

Sure, he could have used a condom every time he had an Auburn Lovely, but he wasn't worried. The police didn't have his DNA to match against what he left inside them. He wanted the world to know what he did to them.

As a commercial played, he surveyed the small room. He was in the armchair this time while his father slept on the couch. They'd switched their usual places without planning such an outcome. The funny thing was the old man wasn't even making full use of the couch, sitting almost exactly in the middle, his head lolled to one side as he snored.

He was relieved the old man was asleep. It was easier to enjoy his fame without the stares, a mixture of suspicion and condemnation. Seeing this expression in his mind's eye, he pushed it away as the commercials ended. He didn't want to miss anything.

Watching the news recapping the taskforce's most recent lack-of-progress report, he considered whether he needed Sasha Copeland anymore. She'd been kind enough to start the media frenzy surrounding his work. Now, plenty of media outlets were making this their own headline without the Washington Post printing it first. He was the Capital's newest sensation. Quite an achievement in a town full of politicians, lobbyists, and hungry people looking to dethrone them. He was a star without having to deal with any of those groups.

He considered whether to kill Sasha. He had no interest in doing her and such a death wouldn't require posing to obtain dramatic flair. He knew where to get a gun. It'd be quick and he'd be gone before anyone could make sense of what he'd done.

But, the idea wasn't growing on him. He supposed he owed a measure of credit for his fame to this lowly reporter. Perhaps they owed each other this. After all, no one knew her name before she became the first to report on his work. If nothing else, this impasse of who owed whom made killing Sasha Copeland less palatable.

Plus, he had a better idea. He'd found another Auburn Lovely. Perhaps, it was time to make his move. He'd found her building just that morning and she'd been so kind to appear in a second floor window as he was walking past, confirming she was the same one he'd seen on the street before.

His Loins tingled as he thought about her. She seemed to not have noticed him studying her, so he was sure he wouldn't encounter anything beyond the usual security measures when he came for her. He could beat anything in the category of "usual".

A noise pulled him out of his reverie. His father was awake, trying to swallow back the drool he'd lost during his nap. This lasted a couple minutes, punctuated by the occasional cough, smack, or splutter.

"What's on?" his father queried.

"The news," he replied, gesturing at the TV screen. The anchor was now talking about a hurricane growing in strength somewhere around the Caribbean.

"They have any scores?" his father asked.

"Not yet," he replied, wondering if his father won or lost on the Capitals tonight. The question only stayed in his mind for a few seconds as he considered if he might need to work more overtime to cover the gap in future bill payments. The downside of all his Auburn Lovelies was they were in college. He'd cleaned out both their purses, as well as the blonde's, and came up with a grand total of sixty-one dollars. Thank God he didn't intend his killings to be financially beneficial.

"I'm getting a drink," he said, not thirsty. "Want anything?"

"Beer," his father replied, his eyes locked on the TV screen in apparent anticipation.

"Sure."

As he walked around the armchair and out of the room, his father turned his head to watch his retreat, his eyes narrowing as the news topic changed to another spike in the mid-Atlantic real estate market.

* * *

Sasha entered the conference room on the seventh floor at One Franklin Square. Her editors, Eric and Nancy were already waiting there, their facial expressions equally grim.

"What's up?" Sasha asked as she pulled out a chair for herself.

"We got another one," Nancy reported. "The Police think it's from the same person."

"He's got quite a set of stones," Eric added, seeming to assume this observation was necessary.

Sasha nodded, remembering the first letter she'd received from the killer of Ellie Stets, Rachael Holden, and now Andrea Prady. The writer, making it clear he wanted to be known as the girls' murderer, congratulated her on being the first to report about his work … "work" was the word he used. He thanked her for getting the piece published and promised more.

"What does this one say?" Sasha asked, thinking about how Andrea Prady fulfilled that prophecy.

Already understanding it was pointless to check if she really wanted to see it, Nancy grabbed a manilla folder and slid it towards Sasha.

"It's not long," she said, "but it's definitely creepy."

Sasha opened the folder to see a single sheet of printer paper, a photocopy of the new message. The original had to be at the crime lab on E Street by now. Lab technicians and police detectives were putting their heads together to think of any test they could subject the message to in the hope of identifying its author.

The letter looked brief. It was handwritten, the writer seeming to take his time to print neatly whenever he put pen to paper. It was probably more to disguise his handwriting than concerns about neatness.

"They're talking about publishing part of it," Eric said. "Maybe someone will recognize the handwriting or the wording, like how they caught the Unabomber."

Sasha nodded, not really listening. Her eyes scanned the page on the table in front of her, trying to analyze the words of a killer herself.

Chapter 8

Dear Sasha Copeland,

I'm flattered you still work hard to pay attention to my work. Your reporting on the latest outcome was as prompt and informative as ever. I'm sure you are likewise pleased with the continuing rise in your readership traffic.

I do wish you would report just how wonderful she was. Words cannot describe that look of terror as I take what I want. It takes my breath away every time.

I assure you this won't be the last time I set out to work. Keep that sharp eye out as it has served you well so far. I will certainly need to see that look of terror again.

I look forward to your next report.

There was no signature. There was no name whatsoever.

Sasha looked up from the letter at Nancy and Eric. The editors stared back at her, seeming to gauge her reaction.

"It came in the mail?" Sasha inquired.

"Yeah, it was mailed a few days ago," Eric replied.

Sasha wondered how soon the killer had sent it after killing Andrea Prady. Maybe he'd mailed it the day after the murder.

"The police are tracing the postmark," Eric continued, "but they think it was probably just put in a mailbox versus someone dropping it off at a post office."

Sasha nodded. There was no way this person would take that risk.

"Has anyone followed you?" Nancy asked. "Have you noticed anyone acting strangely around you?"

Sasha considered for a moment.

"No," she replied.

"Keep an eye out," Nancy said. "The police don't think he'll come after you. They're saying he likes what you've done for his publicity, but still … be careful."

"Of course."

* * *

Sitting on a bench, he watched as Sasha Copeland exited the Washington Post's building. The wait had been far shorter than expected. True, Sasha Copeland wasn't one of those reporters who jetted all around the world and rarely made an appearance at the place that issued her paycheck. She reported on local crimes, including the recent murders of college students.

But, these modern times dictated such a job was mostly remote work. To see her so soon after he'd started this stakeout was extraordinary luck. He wouldn't argue with the results.

He slowly rose from the bench and followed Sasha Copeland as she turned and headed down the block. He noted how careful she was being, walking close to the street as her head darted around. She surveyed her surroundings. Sasha Copeland was not foolish.

Even with his cane, he knew how to avoid looking suspicious, starting with keeping his distance. The sidewalk wasn't crowded at this mid-morning hour. Given how short Sasha Copeland was, not even breaking five feet, it'd be easy to lose her with just a few more pedestrians milling around this commercial area.

Sasha Copeland crossed the street and he allowed the light to go through a cycle before continuing his surveillance. She wasn't walking that fast, so catching up with her wasn't a problem.

Sasha Copeland turned and entered a Panera Bread. As the door closed behind her, he decided to keep going. He had time and he was patient. He'd resume following her another time.

Still, he slowed as he passed the restaurant, glancing through its front windows to see her joining the line by the cashiers.

Turning his head, he saw a cab pulling up to the curb a few yards ahead. A young yuppy emerged, a bag slung over his shoulder.

He quickened his pace, bumping the yuppy as he grabbed the closing cab door.

"Hey," the younger man said, but he ignored the admonishment as he sank onto the cab's backseat.

"Union Station," he said to the startled driver, who was studying him in the rearview mirror.

It took a few seconds, but the driver regained his composure and nodded. A fare was a fare, especially with all the other ride services out there.

* * *

He never showered in his victims' homes. The police had all kinds of methods for retrieving incriminating hairs and fibers from shower drains. No, he brought a change of clothes when he moved in on a selected target. That way, he'd look inconspicuous enough when leaving. He could shower at home, where no crime scene tech would ever have reason to look.

Changed and ready to go, he surveyed the bedroom one more time. He wouldn't dare reenter and get blood on himself, but this view would suffice. Plus, the redheaded woman's hair clips were already in his pocket. Patting the pocket, he remembered her petrified star as he plucked them one-by-one.

The man sat slumped over in the chair, his limps still bound with the shoelaces he'd forced his wife to secure him with. Blood still dripped from the back of his head. Someone would surely call in the paramedics, who'd surely decide there wasn't anything they could do to save him.

The woman, still on the bed with her wrists bound to its headboard with more shoelaces, would likewise be considered a lost cause by the most laymen medical professional. He could see the bullet hole slightly off-center on her forehead. It'd been a good shot, even if he'd done better.

Clutching his bag, he made his way back downstairs to do one final sweep for any remaining cash or valuables he could take with him. He was rifling through the woman's purse, double-checking, when he saw it.

The newspaper was lying next to the phone on the kitchen counter, as though someone had left it there after reviewing its contents with a caller. The Baltimore Sun. He'd heard of it but wasn't familiar with their work. It was folded the way one would find it in a newsstand, but it had been folded over again recently. He could see the crease running down the middle of the pages.

The paper had also been folded over a couple pages, the reader looking for a specific article. The feature facing him was about a Baltimore City Councilman touted to be a leading contender in the next mayoral election. There, for all the world to see, was a large, well-posed portrait of the man and his family.

Anyone who didn't know better would say these were the next Kennedys. The man, seeming to be in his late thirties, a bit older than him, was handsome with a bright, charming smile. His redheaded wife looked stunning. He knew nothing about fashion, but her blouse, jacket and skirt, looked expensive. And she looked beautiful in them. She also looked to be the right age for his taste.

Then, there was the teenager. Skimming the article, he learned she was a fifteen-year-old sister from the wife's side of the family. She was living with the couple while she attended a fancy-sounding private school in Baltimore. Best of all, she too was a redhead.

He'd never thought much about hunting younger girls. The women he'd had were plenty satisfying. Sure, he noticed beautiful girls and young women just as any other red-blooded man, but something about this redheaded teenager required more than an appreciative glance on his part. For one thing, she was as stunningly-beautiful as her older sister, with him supposing their age gap to be around ten or fifteen years. But there was still something more. Why would he want to travel all the way to Baltimore to visit them?

He gasped as it hit him. They looked like the redheaded woman he'd just had.

Grabbing the newspaper, he dashed into the house's den. There, he found what he suspected. Photos on the wall. Family portraits and snapshots. Many featured this redheaded wife and this redheaded teenager. It was more than a coincidental resemblance.

He smiled, imagining the splash this family's deaths would have on the whole country. Two related family's, living so far apart, cut down by the same mysterious killer. Plus, this seemed to be a prominent family in the Baltimore area. Currently in Glen Allen, he hadn't even heard their names as he performed his surveillance for tonight.

Yes, it would be difficult to sort out the logistics required for this venture, but he could already imagine the rewards.

Grinning, he folded the newspaper up along its crease and stuffed it in his bag. No one would miss it. No one would suspect his plan.

* * *

"You think this prick would come after Sasha?" Hadrian asked, looking up at his partner, seated across their desks.

"I doubt it," Joseph mused. "He likes the publicity she's giving him. This guy wants attention. Why would he do anything to jeopardize that?"

Hadrian nodded in agreement. This made perfect sense.

"She's a smart girl," he said. "She'll be careful."

Now, Joseph nodded in agreement.

The technicians at the crime lab were finding precisely nothing on the letter so far. More tests were in progress or due to be run, but it looked like their perp was as careful as ever.

That morning, they'd visited the post office who'd stamped the letter, signifying where it came from. No one there remembered anyone unusual coming to mail something in the past week. This letter definitely hadn't stuck out among the thousands of envelopes they'd processed in that time.

Reviewing their photocopy of the envelope, the Postmaster supposed, like they did, that it was collected from a streetside mailbox.

"No way for us to know who left it there," he said. "Maybe a nearby security camera could help you, but we have no say about that. Best I can do is tell you the letter was mailed last Friday. We collect at five and stamp them the same day."

He pointed out the barely-legible date stamp for the detectives' benefit. They were both just amazed he could read that. But, his supersite wouldn't help them further.

* * *

Sasha swallowed a lump in her throat as she entered the apartment, the day's mail tucked under her arm.

"Hello?!" she called.

"In the bathroom!" Christian called back, his voice faint through the door on the opposite side of their bedroom.

He came out into the main room as Sasha was sinking onto the couch, a glass of wine in her hand.

"Rough day?" he queried, sitting down next to her as Lydon settled by their feet.

Sasha sighed.

"Another letter came," she reported and took a gulp of the wine.

Christian froze.

"From the same guy?" he asked.

"Everyone seems to think so," Sasha replied.

"Are you okay?"

Sasha turned the question over in her mind.

"I guess," she said. "Everyone's worried that this guy might come after me. I guess I've never thought of such a thing happening to me before."

Christian nodded.

"Slovo ne vorobey," he said.

"A word is not a sparrow," Sasha echoed, remembering. She might not have been afraid before. But, now that everyone around her was afraid and had voiced their fears, she couldn't help feeling so as well. The words had gotten out and could not be taken back.

Swallowing another gulp of wine, Sasha studied Christian.

"How do you feel about it?" she asked.

Christian paused, considering her question.

"I'm afraid for you," he said. "I'd keep you locked away in this apartment until they catch that freak, if I could help it. But I know how well you would take that."

In spite of everything, Sasha managed to laugh.

"Nevertheless, are you staying put tonight?" Christian asked.

"Yeah," Sasha replied. "I might try to get some more work done, but I'll do it within these walls."

She drained her glass.

"I gotta go out for a little while," Christian reported. "I'm meeting Matt to prepare for the test next week."

Sasha knew she couldn't make him stay put any more than he could convince her. He'd almost gone insane from the lack of human interaction during the height of the pandemic. Now, he was thrilled to be going out to see people again. Plus, the killer wasn't after him.

"Have fun," she said.

* * *

Tonight was the night. He'd have his Auburn Lovely tonight. But, entering her apartment would be tough. He'd found a way, but it would not be easy.

Standing in his bedroom, he went through his backpack one final time. His KA-BAR, a pair of binoculars, and the tape were there. Everything was set.

He zipped his bag shut, slung it over his shoulder, and exited his bedroom.

"I'm going out for a while!" he called.

His father's grunted reply came from the kitchen, where he seemed to be indulging in some leftover pizza.

Without another word, he left the apartment, his heart racing with excitement.

* * *

"I should get going," Christian mused out loud.

Across their table in the library, Matthew looked up from his notes.

"You sure?" he asked. "It's only been three hours."

For at least the past year, such a short study session was a record for them. But Matthew understood what was going on.

"How's Sasha doing?" he inquired.

Christian studied his friend. He felt he could be honest.

"She's freaking out a little bit," he confessed. "Can't say I'm not going that same way."

"That's rough," Matthew said. "You guys live in a good building though. People can't just walk in and out and your neighbors aren't going to let strangers in."

"I suppose," Christian conceded.

"And if you need to, you guys can stay at my place."

Now Christian laughed, picturing himself, Sasha, Lydon, and Matthew crammed into the latter's studio apartment. Matthew was studying criminal law like him, but he fancied himself a starving artist … without any art.

"I'll keep that in mind," he said, closing his laptop. "I'll see you tomorrow."

"Just remember one thing," Matthew said as Christian and Lydon rose to their feet.

"What's that?"

"Kessler's not gonna let you use this to slide."

Christian laughed again. Matthew's assessment of their strict professor was correct.

"Yeah," he concurred. "On krutoy."

"I suppose you're getting better with the Russian," Matthew remarked, really having no idea.

* * *

Some last-minute surveillance of his intended route never hurt. Last thing he needed was to get caught.

Fate had been kind to him. An apartment on the second floor of the building across the street was vacant and its windows looked directly into his Auburn Lovely's dwelling. Breaking in a couple days earlier required next to no effort and he'd come and gone at his leisure ever since.

He slipped inside and stood by the window frame, where he was almost invisible to the occupants across the street. The sun was setting to his left, casting long shadows onto the street below.

He pulled the binoculars from his backpack and lifted them to his eyes. He stood still, focusing his view.

He soon had a clear line of sight to his Auburn Lovely's apartment, and there she was. She was sitting on her couch, set at an angle to her front windows. Her long, red hair framed her elegant face as the strands came to rest on her shoulders.

She was wearing a sparkling silver top with spaghetti straps. He hoped he might get to the apartment before she changed out of it. He imagined cutting the shiny material off her body while gazing into her terrified eyes.

The outfit didn't quite make sense, mainly because she also wore a skirt. He wondered if she had plans to go out. He hoped she didn't have plans. He'd of course wait for her to return, at which point he'd make his move, but he didn't want to wait if it could be helped. She was possibly the prettiest one he'd had in the past few weeks. He didn't want to wait.

His Auburn Lovely had been sitting stock-still on the couch. But she then moved, turning her head to her left, his right.

He kept watching and couldn't believe what he saw next. He actually gasped.

Chapter 9

He hadn't felt excitement like this in a while … at least not since he began hunting. Even the traffic was working in his favor, or it was at least not impeding his progress.

He reached the Baltimore City limits with enough time for coffee. He found a Duncan Doughnuts and got a large cup … black with sugar.

He kept driving while nursing the cup. This was now his sixth trip up here and he knew where to go. He also knew he was still ahead of schedule.

The shopping center was quiet when he pulled into the parking lot. The spot he wanted, far in a dark corner, hidden from even the setting sun, was available. He pulled in and changed his license plates in under a minute. If anyone looked close enough, his nondescript gray sedan was from the state of Delaware.

He grabbed his bag and hurried past the stores, some of which were closing. He found the gap in the trees behind the buildings and disappeared through it, knowing exactly where to go.

* * *

He'd originally planned to enter his Auburn Lovely's apartment through the same window he'd seen her through the other day, confirming where she lived. But, a last-minute sweep around her building revealed a back door by a dumpster.

He never liked the window. It was a risky entry point, even for him. There was no fire escape or anything else for him to perch on while he worked the window. It also faced the street, where someone could see him, even this late at night.

The door was a stroke of luck. Still, he scolded himself for not finding it sooner. It wasn't exactly a hidden passageway. The thought of having his

Auburn Lovely was consuming him to the point of distraction. He needed to focus.

He moved past the door, which was locked, and further down the alley. Hidden by the shadows of the buildings on either side of him, he waited.

Seconds seemed to stretch into unquantifiable amounts of time. His heart raced as beads of sweat bubbled on his forehead. He checked his phone to see he'd only been waiting three minutes. It felt as though he would have finished already.

The door opened and a young man, a few years younger than him and around the same age as his Auburn Lovely, came out. He knew the building, located just off the campus boundaries of George Mason University, was full of young people, some of whom had to be inattentive enough to suit him.

This one suited him as he left the door ajar. As the young man heaved two bulging plastic bags into the dumpster, he slipped into the building unseen.

He made his way down the dark corridor and into a better-lit hallway. A chipped plastic placard was kind enough to identify the door to the stairwell. He darted through and bounded up the stairs, eager to meet his Auburn Lovely.

* * *

He watched through the bushes as the man and woman, dressed in clothes he couldn't dream of affording, climbed into their shiny black Mercedes and pulled away from their equally-pricy-looking townhouse. It would be very thrilling to kill them. This posh community was sure to have heard all about him. They probably felt they were out of his reach. Tonight would obliterate that belief.

He waited another minute before heading back to the fence boards he'd loosened on a previous trip. He slipped into the small backyard, now protected from prying eyes by the tall privacy fence. Also covered in darkness, he bounded onto the patio. There were two doors, a narrow door with a lock and knob, and a wide sliding glass door. Hoping his speculation was correct, he approached the narrow door and tried the knob, having disabled the lock on another of his previous trips. Yes, the family used the sliding door almost exclusively. They never noticed what he'd done.

He entered the chrome kitchen and moved upstairs. Hearing a shower running, eager anticipation surged through him.

The water stopped as he reached the top of the stairs. He was outside the bathroom door when the girl emerged, clad in a robe. She looked even better than the newspaper photo and his previous, distant observations. Her long, red hair, still wet, clung to her cotton-covered shoulders. He was already imagining how she'd look when she dropped the robe.

She gasped as she turned and saw him. He slapped one hand over her mouth and showed her his revolver. God, those beautiful blue eyes looked even better with this addition of terror.

"Be good and you get to live," he hissed, stroking her damp red hair with his gun.

She stood there, trembling.

"Let's go to your bedroom," he whispered, his lips close to her ear.

* * *

As much as he wanted his Auburn Lovely, he wasn't loving this building. First, he'd had no immediate way of easily gaining access to her apartment. Now that he'd found the back door and was inside, he had to picture the building's front side and guess which door led to the apartment with the window through which he'd seen his Auburn Lovely and through which he'd made an interesting discovery less than hour earlier. Problem was, he couldn't take too long or someone awake this late would stumble onto him.

Walking along the hallways on the second floor, he felt pretty confident in his choice, the third door. Apartment 2K. Withdrawing his KA-BAR, he found prying this door open was as easy as the previous occasions. It was a sickening shade of red, so he didn't mind damaging it as he worked.

He was quickly inside, his eyes adjusting to the dark apartment. Moving past the kitchen and through the main room, he recognized the setup from his surveillance across the street. He targeted the only door, located to the left of the large window. The curtains were now closed. Grinning, he grabbed the knob and turned it.

The bedroom was small and lit only by the dim light pouring in from the main room. Standing in the doorway, he was only able to make out two bodies under the covers of the bed. It was definitely queen or king-sized, taking up over half of the floorspace.

Moving closer, he was able to tell which one was his Auburn Lovely. Neither she nor her brunette companion stirred as he approached the bed. He could hear them breathing.

He'd intended to proceed as he'd done before. Bind his Auburn Lovely, cut off her clothes, and have her. But, the last-minute discovery changed those plans. He now wanted something more elaborate and more fun. He'd read the stories and knew what to do.

He switched on the lamp on the nightstand. Predictably, his Auburn Lovely stirred. He slapped his hand over her mouth. She was definitely awake now, screaming into his palm. Next to her, the brunette stirred and saw him.

"Not a sound," he told both girls, pressing the blade of his KA-BAR against the throat of his Auburn Lovely, "from either of you."

* * *

He couldn't believe this. He'd never been someone's first. It was more exhilarating than he could have imagined and he had to tell himself to calm down or he'd blow it too soon.

Beneath him, the redheaded teenager cried as he moved. She wasn't begging anymore. She wasn't speaking any language he knew. Just blubbers and gasps came out as he took her on her bed, surrounded by posters of bands and movie stars. It wasn't his choice of décor, but it wasn't worth complaining about either. He could just focus on the naked, crying girl beneath him.

"I'm in charge," he said as he thrust. "You couldn't stop me if you tried. I always get who I want."

He soon lost all will and finished with a triumphant grunt. He watched her eyes grow even wider as she realized what was happening, wishing this could have lasted forever.

"Good job," he said as he moved off her and zipped up his pants. He sat on the edge of her bed, catching his breath, as she cried behind him.

The women he'd had before tonight were wonderful. But, he now realized they were a routine. This, a fifteen-year-old girl, was a change he hadn't known he needed. She'd been anything but routine, and every moment was pure wonder. Plus, the night was far from finished.

As though someone could read his mind, he heard a door open and close downstairs, followed by low voices.

Finally.

He picked up his revolver from the nightstand and turned back to the girl.

"Not a sound," he said, aiming the gun at her head.

She didn't move or speak. Satisfied, he left the room.

In the hallway, he could hear the voices more clearly.

"She's probably asleep," the redheaded wife was saying.

"I still say she should have come with us," the man replied. "It's never too early for her to meet people."

"That's not for us to decide,. She's here to go to school."

"Then she should have come anyway, especially with that maniac still out there."

"I know. But she didn't want to. To be honest I didn't want to either …"

The redheaded wife stopped speaking as he appeared behind her husband, his Sig Sauer raised. The man turned and gasped as he saw the same sight.

"Your girl's upstairs," he said. "Try anything, and I'll go and kill her."

* * *

"So girls do it for you?" he asked, moving his knife over his Auburn Lovely like a cook working over a cutting board. Her long t-shirt and panties were soon just shredded pieces of fabric, strewn on the floor next to the bed. His Auburn Lovely replied with a single gasp of fear.

Confident in his control over them, he moved around the bed and cut off the brunette's tank top and boxer shorts. He studied both girls as he worked. Both had long hair and unblemished skin with fading tans, neither of them looking butch. His Auburn Lovely had tan lines while the brunette didn't.

"Good," he said, tossing the last of the tank top against the wall behind him.

"Please," his Auburn Lovely said, tears filling her eyes. "Please don't hurt us."

He smiled, staring at her firm breasts, flat stomach, and sparce pubic hairs. She'd tried to cover herself earlier and the KA-BAR pressing against her throat for a second time made it clear this wasn't an advisable move. The brunette understood this warning without receiving her own hands-on demonstration.

"Be good a little longer and I won't," he said. "Not a sound while I'm gone."

He was out of the bedroom for less than a minute, retrieving a chair from the dining set and setting it in the doorway. He sat on it and opened his pants. Frozen on the bed in full view of him, the girls stared.

"You two start playing with each other," he said with a grin. "Give me a good show."

* * *

"Where's my sister?" the redheaded wife demanded as he marched her and her husband into the master bedroom at gunpoint.

"She's fine," he replied in a growl. "Do what I say and it stays that way."

"Kelly!" the redheaded wife called.

He didn't hesitate, raising his free hand and slapping her across the face. She stumbled but didn't fall and he moved his face close to hers.

"Shut up," he hissed.

She didn't meet his eyes, instead looking past him and a little to her left. He glanced that way and saw her husband. The man just stood there, his hands, not yet bound, at his sides.

"He gets it," he said. "I'm in charge. I suggest you come to understand this."

He spied the necklace. The thin, silver chain shimmered as it ran around her neck and down her front, disappearing behind the seam of her dress. It didn't quite reach her breasts.

"Take off the necklace," he demanded.

The woman whimpered, but she didn't move. The spot where he'd slapped her was turning red.

"Take off the necklace," he repeated in a more threatening tone. He wasn't fond of her defiance.

This time, the redheaded wife obeyed, reaching behind her neck to undo the clasp. He held out his hand as she pulled it out of her dress. She glared as she gave it to him.

He studied the pendent sitting on his palm. He didn't recognize the symbol carved into this piece of silver, but he supposed it was some sort of coat of arms.

"You royalty or something?" he queried as he pocketed the necklace. "Certainly makes things more interesting, especially once we consummate."

He waved his hand towards the bed, where he'd laid out belts, shoelaces, and a couple hair scrunchies, all taken from the girl's bedroom. The woman's look of shock suggested she realized this. Good. He'd hoped for such an effect.

"Bind him," he instructed, pointing out a heavy chair he'd dragged in from a home office down the hallway.

* * *

He moaned as he watched the girls kiss, touch, and try to pleasure each other. They knew better than to deviate from his instructions.

"It's gonna be okay," the brunette told his Auburn Lovely. "Just focus on me. We'll get through this. Just look at me."

She punctuated her statement with loving kisses as they ran their hands over each other.

He kept stroking while taking in the best show of his life. His Auburn Lovely was even crying.

"Stop," he finally said. He was surprised at his own self-control, but he didn't want to finish just yet.

The girls froze, looking at him as he forced his erection back into his pants. That was not comfortable, but it would be just for a little while.

He picked up his bag and dug out a new roll of duct tape. The girls' gazes locked onto this, wondering what he had planned for them.

"Please don't hurt us," his Auburn Lovely pleaded again.

He used his KA-BAR to cut off pieces of tape, sticking each to the nightstand by its edge. When he had enough, he grabbed the first piece and slapped it over his Auburn Lovely's mouth.

"What are you going to do to us?" the brunette asked, trying to sound brave. The whimpers in her words destroyed that effort.

His Auburn Lovely tried to speak through the tape. That went just as well.

"Nothing if you don't defy me," he said, grabbing another piece of tape. He beckoned the brunette over with a wave of his hand.

"Come closer," he said, sweetening his tone.

Shaking, the brunette obeyed and he taped her mouth shut as well. The girls' arms were next, him binding their wrists as he'd done with the others. Then, he bound the brunette's ankles together as well.

With the girls immobilized, he laid them out to his liking. His Auburn Lovely lay on her back, her head resting on her pillow. The brunette lay on her side, facing his Auburn Lovely. She lay a little further down on the bed, her eyes at the same level as his Auburn Lovely's breasts. He'd been kind enough to set a pillow beneath her head as well.

"I wouldn't want you to miss anything," he said.

Both girls protested as he climbed onto the bed. They couldn't be loud enough for anyone to hear.

His breathing quickened as he mounted his Auburn Lovely and unzipped his pants again. Understanding what he was about to do, she began crying again, new tears overlapping with the streaks already framing her face. He thought he could hear the brunette trying to plead with him through her gag. Her bound legs jerked uselessly as she tried to communicate with him. Perhaps she was offering herself so his Auburn Lovely could be spared.

He might have considered such an offer. She was slender with decent knockers and she surely drew men's attention wherever she went. But, she was wrong for him. He wanted his Auburn Lovely. Still, the brunette was appealing enough to cause him to deviate from his prior encounters by not killing her right away. He thought of the stories he read and wondered what having a spectator would do for his performance.

"Watch closely," he encouraged with a smile, looking at the brunette one more time. "Let's see what happens."

He then thrust forward. Both girls cried out through their gags.

* * *

He woke up on the couch in their apartment with a start. Surveying his surroundings, he realized how dark it was. Some shopping show was playing on the television. How late was it? Had Lucas returned yet?

"Lucas?" he called out.

There was no reply.

"Where is he?" he wondered in a lower decibel.

Grabbing his cane, he rose to his feet and hobbled out of the den. Late night walks were not good for his leg. He admitted it was his own fault for falling asleep in front of the TV instead of his own bed. He might have not woken up then.

Lucas's door was slightly ajar. His son had left in a hurry, but maybe he'd returned by now. He entered the small bedroom.

He'd always demanded his son keep his quarters neat. The boy was doing a good job, though he wasn't prepared to pass along such praise out loud. For one thing, one of the pillows on the narrow bed was askew.

He moved closer, hoping his straightening the pillow might send a message. As he grabbed it, he felt his finger brush against something beneath it … something … plastic.

They didn't have a lot of money, but he and Lucas could afford proper bed linens made from cloth. He lifted the pillow.

There, in its apparent hiding place, was a small Ziploc bag. At first, he thought his son was doing drugs. He'd kill him as soon as possible.

He picked up the bag and realized it couldn't be drugs, or anything edible. It was feather-light. Inside was something red. Looking closer, he realized what it had to be and yanked the bag open. He stuck a finger inside, pressing it down deep into the mass. Yes, it was hair … red hair.

Chapter 10

"Bind him," he repeated.

The redheaded wife looked everywhere … towards the bed, the chair, at her husband, , beyond everything towards the bedroom door, and back at him. Tears welled up in her eyes. She knew who he was. She understood he'd killed her sister and her husband down in Glen Allen. She understood what he wanted to do to her.

"Where's Kelly?" she asked, her voice breaking. "Where's my sister?"

He gritted his teeth and tightened his grip on his revolver. Teenagers were supposed to be defiant. But right now, a teenager was being the least defiant person in this house.

"I'll do what you want," the redheaded wife said. "I'll do whatever you want. I just need to see Kelly first."

He considered her words. His victims had tried to bargain before. Many cooperated in the hope of living through the ordeal. He wasn't keen to grant her this wish, but this night wasn't meant to be like the others right from his planning stages. Maybe this was another difference which could serve him well.

He thought another moment before he acted. He pointed his revolver at the man.

"Sit," he snapped.

The man didn't move.

"Sit or no one sees the girl," he threatened.

Now, the man moved forward and sank into the heavy chair. Petrified by fear, he no longer resembled the blond pretty boy from the newspaper.

"Pull it forward," he instructed.

With some effort, the man obeyed, tugging the chair forward.

"Keep going," he directed.

The pattern continued until the man's knees pressed against the footboard of the bed.

"Stay," he threatened. "You move and everyone dies."

He turned back to the redheaded wife, pointing his revolver towards the center of her chest.

"Let's go," he said.

Looking a little relieved, the redheaded wife walked towards the door. He followed, surveying her slender figure and the long, red hair that cascaded down her back. He'd give her only a few minutes with her sister. Then, they'd get back on track.

They walked down the hallway to the redheaded teenager's room. As they got closer, they could hear soft sobs. As they turned to cross the threshold, another sound reached his ears. A distinctive, scraping sound.

He cursed and dashed back the way he'd come.

* * *

His Auburn Lovely was outright bawling as they came together. The brunette was also crying, though her sobs weren't as severe.

"Guess guys do it for you just fine," he said, getting off her and straightening his clothes.

He looked at the brunette. He'd had to threaten her once to keep her eyes open and watch the entire rape. It turned out having her as a spectator did improve this experience. He doubted he'd feel the same if the spectator's gender was different. After all, he had taken care of that in the past so he wouldn't have to find out.

"Stay put," he said. Recalling more from the stories he'd read, he decided to more thoroughly explore the apartment.

Neither girl moved or made a sound as he pushed the chair aside and left the bedroom. He found some beer in the refrigerator and settled onto the couch. He turned on the TV and found ESPN. The news wouldn't have anything to report about him yet, so he'd find satisfaction in watching sports highlights. He leaned back on the couch, nursing his beer as the commentators went on about some Mid-West college football team.

"They could go all the way this year," one of the talking heads offered and the others replied with their own opinions.

He watched until the late-night news came on. The top story was a hurricane, Jordan or Jamie or something like that, which was gathering strength as it passed Cuba at some safe distance.

"We don't suspect the United States will be as lucky," some expert said. "Right now, we believe Jackson will make landfall at the end of next week either in the Carolinas or southeastern Virginia and will continue moving north. The storm will lose strength again as it moves closer to shore, but …"

He turned off the TV and downed the final drops of the beer. He then returned to the bedroom. The girls stared at him as he entered.

"Big storm's coming," he told them. "We should wrap this up."

He retrieved his KA-BAR and moved around the bed to stand behind the brunette. As both girls tried to keep him in their line of sight, he plunged the blade into her back.

* * *

He burst back into the bedroom to find the man standing by the nightstand, pressing buttons on a phone's keypad as he held the receiver to his ear. His finger was over the number 1 key. The chair he'd been sitting in now stood askew by the bed's footboard.

With a roar, he moved forward. In one swift maneuver, he raised the Sig Sauer, settling it inches from the man's head.

"No!" the man cried, seeing it at the last second.

He pulled the trigger. The bang seemed louder than before. Maybe it was because things had gone so wrong.

The man dropped the phone's receiver as he crumpled on the floor, blood spurting out of the gunshot wound in the side of his skull.

He didn't stay put. If the man had tried this, the redheaded wife, who'd been more defiant up to now, wouldn't be waiting for him to return.

Pausing only to yank the phone off the nightstand so its line snapped with an audible pop, he hurried back down the hallway to the redheaded teenager's bedroom. The redheaded wife wasn't standing in the doorway where he'd left her.

She was in the bedroom, crouching by her younger sister's bed. She was trying to undo the knot he'd tied when using the sash from the redheaded teenager's bathrobe to bind her wrists to the bed.

"It's okay, Kelly," the redheaded wife was saying while crying. She had to have heard the gunshot down the hall.

Without a word, he moved up behind her and took aim at the back of her head. The redheaded teenager saw him and tried to say something, but he was quicker.

Another bang echoed through the house. The redheaded wife landed half on the bed, at which point gravity took over and pulled her whole body down onto the floor. Crimson blood sprayed from her headwound across the side of the bed and puddled on the floor. He never liked how blood contrasted with their hair.

The redheaded teenager began to scream, but he lunged forward and grabbed her throat. He squeezed hard, cutting off her cries. It wasn't the first time he'd choked her that night.

Her body no longer aroused him. He would have probably had her again, perhaps after her older sister, but that wouldn't happen anymore.

He kept squeezing her neck. She gasped and spluttered as her eyes rolled upwards. As she began to lose consciousness, he released her and took aim a third time. The bullet struck her above her right eye as she was regaining consciousness.

* * *

His Auburn Lovely was bawling again as the brunette retched, choked, and expired next to her. The latter's blood flowed over the side of the bed. The gag still prevented her from making enough noise to be heard outside the confines of the small bedroom.

"She was becoming a third wheel," he said, moving around the bed to stand by his Auburn Lovely again. He again surveyed her beautiful body. He'd never stayed around this long before, not even when he might have had reason to. And, he'd stayed long enough to serve his needs. But tonight, he wanted to stay longer. She was unlike the others.

His Auburn Lovely shrieked as he climbed back onto the bed. He swung one leg out and kicked the brunette off over the side. He then opened his pants for a third time.

"Just you and me this time," he said.

* * *

He hurried back through the trees. Only when he was behind the shopping center again did he stop. Suspecting neighbors might have heard the struggle and gunshots, he wasn't waiting to find out how long it'd take the police to respond. There was no way to be sure someone hadn't heard something before he'd taken out the phone.

Here, hidden amongst the foliage, he changed out of his blood-spattered clothes. He bunched the incriminating attire into a plastic bag and hefted everything out into the trunk of his sedan.

He didn't bother to change the license plates again. He just got behind the wheel of his car and turned the key in the ignition. He drove out of the parking lot, his adrenaline winding down. At this point, he'd drive towards Delaware if it meant misdirecting some curious party. He just wanted to get out of Baltimore.

Things had not gone the way he wanted. For one thing, he'd only had sex once. Apart from his ex, he didn't know when that last happened. He had really wanted the girl again. He wanted to sample the redheaded wife. After all, she was right in his demographic.

No, as good as his plans had been, things hadn't gone to his liking. And he would need to make his peace with that. they were still dead and the neighborhood would still be shaken. Some goals were accomplished.

He approached a red light. He wouldn't dare commit a traffic violation now. It was best to keep his departure from Charm City as inconspicuous as possible.

As though reading his mind, his concerns in particular, a police car approached the intersection from the opposite direction. It's lights were flashing, but he couldn't hear a siren. No one yet realized how serious the situation was back at the townhouse.

The light changed to enable the police cruiser to proceed unimpeded. He waited until the flashing red lights were shrinking in his rearview mirror before pressing his foot on the accelerator again.

* * *

When he finished with his Auburn Lovely the second time, he knew it was time to go. Without another word, he turned her over and grabbed his KA-BAR. Despite his rush, he still found some satisfaction from stabbing her to death. And, he still took the time to cut off some of her hair for his collection.

He would also stay long enough to shower. It wasn't like he could walk through the city, even this city, covered in blood. Stepping over the dead brunette, he entered the adjacent bathroom, which was about the size of a closet.

He emerged a few minutes later, pulling his shirt back on. He stopped as he again caught sight of the dead brunette. Due to the small space between the bed, the nightstand, and the wall, her head had been unnaturally twisted when she went off the side of the bed. Otherwise, she was lying on her back, making it likely her neck was now broken.

He stared at her. He couldn't help himself. She was just ... worth looking at. Watching her play with his Auburn Lovely had been something his imagination could have never conjured.

He contemplated for a few minutes before deciding she was worth something else as well. He grabbed his KA-BAR and sliced the tape binding her legs together. The space was narrow, but it'd do. He took a moment to arrange her so he'd be more comfortable.

"You don't mind, do you?" he asked and smiled when she didn't respond. She was still pretty warm.

* * *

The next light was also red. Just his luck. Still, he couldn't do anything about it but wait.

He dug into his pocket and withdrew the two necklaces he'd collected. The silver one with the strange pendent belonged to the older woman. The gold necklace with a stone belonged to the girl. The green emerald gleamed in the light from a nearby streetlight as he examined it.

Normally, he cherished these souvenirs as they symbolized successful hunts. Tonight could not be counted as that. But he'd hold on to these items, cherished by the people he'd killed, as he did have the memory of the girl.

The light turned green and he began driving again.

* * *

Christian wasn't sure what woke him. But he was awake. And so was Sasha. She was sitting up in bed, wearing one of the oversized t-shirts she liked to sleep in.

As Christian touched her arm, Sasha jumped. Seeing it was him, she fumbled on her nightstand for her hearing aids. It was a different world when she wasn't wearing them. She could manage fine, but she couldn't communicate well with her fiancée.

"Sorry," she said once they were in her ears. "Did I wake you?"

"I'm not sure," Christian admitted. "Sorry I scared you."

Sasha didn't say anything. It wasn't the first night this scenario occurred. It was just the first under such stressful circumstances.

"What are you doing up?" Christian queried.

"Sleep wasn't working for me," Sasha replied.

Christian could guess why.

"You having nightmares?" he asked.

Sasha sighed.

"Not yet," she admitted. "I just can't help thinking about somebody who can kill, dismember, and pose people who might now be coming for me."

Christian didn't know what to say.

"it's never gotten this real before," Sasha said. "I mean … before this, I reported on fatal robberies and random drug killings. Now, I'm a target just because I got to a scene of a serial killing first."

"That's not your fault," Christian assured her, putting a hand on her arm and moving it up to rest on her shoulder. "You were just ambitious. You wanted to do the best job you could."

"Thanks, I guess," Sasha said, wondering if this was the price she had to pay for being ambitious. And, if one nutcase could do this to her, what would stop another nutcase from following this pattern on the next case she covered?

Christian pulled her closer and wrapped both his arms around her. Sasha was sure the gesture to be in-part protective, but she didn't care. All of it felt good.

"Ya lyublyu tebya," Christian whispered in her ear.

Sasha smiled. It was the only Russian phrase she'd learned and memorized.

"QamuSHa'," she returned, knowing it was the only Klingon phrase he'd learned and memorized.

Smiling as well, Christian held her tighter.

* * *

As always, leaving the apartment was easier than getting in. Like before, he acted casual and strolled out the front door. As before, nobody impeded his path.

He turned left and walked down the sidewalk. The Metro wasn't far away. He couldn't remember which line it was, but that didn't matter. He just wanted to put some distance between himself and the bodies. He'd figure out the best route home after that.

He heard a car come to a stop behind him. He kept walking. Then, he heard a voice.

"Hey!"

He turned. To his horror, he saw a uniformed officer of the D.C Police Department climbing out of his cruiser and walking towards him. Another officer was also getting out, muttering something he was too far away to understand.

"Out late, aren't you?" the first, and younger, officer remarked.

He didn't know why, but he turned and ran.

"Hey!" the officer called out. The sound of his own footfalls followed.

He dashed down the block and across the street, not worrying about if the light was in his favor. There weren't any cars around anyway.

Glancing back, he saw the younger officer was falling behind. His older colleague was far behind both of them.

The younger officer was running and saying something into his radio. He couldn't understand what and he didn't want to find out. The phrase "back-up" had to be exchanged in that conversation.

He turned at the corner of a brownstone and realized too late he'd entered an alley. Worse, at the end of the alley was an eight-foot high fence, beyond which was a fenced-in lot.

He turned again just as the younger officer reached the mouth of the alley.

Trying not to show he needed to catch his breath, the younger officer slowed to a trot as he moved into the alley.

"What's got you so spooked?" he asked with a cocky grin. "Don't you know running from the police makes it clear to us you're guilty of something?"

He wondered why, if this were true, the officer had hailed him to begin with.

"Now," the younger officer continued. "Let's have a dialogue, okay?"

Before he had a chance to respond, the older officer arrived.

"Regis," he managed to bark while taking deep breaths. "What was that about?"

"I …" the younger officer began, turning his head.

"You just ran off like that for no reason. Do you know how many procedures and regulations you ran down in the process? I'll have to write you up at least a dozen times for this, and don't think I …"

A shot rang out. The older officer stumbled and fell forward.

"Jesus!" the younger officer cried, fumbling for his radio as he looked around wildly for the shooter.

Another shot rang out. The younger officer fell back against the building behind him. He collapsed in a slumped-over seated position and didn't move again. His radio fell and shattered next to him.

It all happened in just a few seconds, but it seemed to play out much longer for him. He stood in the alley, frozen as he wondered who decided to save him.

Pools of blood began to spread around both cops' bodies. They were somewhat illuminated by exterior lights from the buildings on either side of the alley.

He looked around, still figuring he'd be next. Then, he gasped as the shooter came down the alley towards him. Before he could grab his KA-BAR, the man spoke.

"Come on."

He couldn't move. He could only gasp again as he realized the man who'd just shot two cops to save him was his own father.

"Come on," the old man insisted again, leaning on his cane. "Someone will be calling that in right now. We're right by the Metro station. Let's go."

He turned and headed back up the alley. Taking a deep breath, he hurried to follow his father.

Chapter 11

The sun was just peeking out over Washington's city skyline when Hadrian stopped the unmarked police cruiser by the barricade. He and Joseph jumped out and badged their way into the scene.

The alley was crowded with police officers, crime scene technicians, and other first responders. Still, the detectives could see the bodies of their fallen brethren. It was clear no efforts were even attempted to save them. Nothing would have helped.

"Officer Keith Regis," an officer told the detectives, pointing towards the young man slumped against the building, his head bloody, "out of the 3rd District. Been with the department two and a half months. That's his training officer, Mike Nichols."

He pointed out the other body, also clad in a navy blue police uniform. The man's cap had fallen off and was lying a few feet away.

"What happened?" Hadrian asked.

"We're not sure," the officer replied. "Radio traffic suggests they were involved in some kind of foot pursuit and the perp somehow got the drop on them here."

This made no sense to either Hadrian or Joseph. How could a suspect the officers chased into this alley then be able to surprise them both and manage to kill them without resistance? There was something else that made less sense.

"Why are we here?" Joseph asked.

The slain officers were from their neighboring district. While it was common for the city to pull resources from wherever possible when a cop was killed, everyone knew Joseph and Hadrian had plenty to do.

"You're at the wrong scene," someone said.

Joseph and Hadrian turned to see a lieutenant approaching them, decked out in in a white shirt, blue blazer with matching slacks, and gold badge.

"Lieutenant Andre Collars," he said. "You two are expected on I Street. That's where this started. Officers canvasing over there found something nasty."

Hadrian and Joseph glanced at one another, trying to make sense of what happened.

"It's not far," Hadrian offered. "Probably easier to go over on foot."

They left the alley and headed down 1st Street.

"You think this is really connected?" Hadrian asked.

"I don't know," Joseph replied. "Our guy's never used a gun. And that's assuming this was our guy."

"It'd be a pretty big leap for him. Killing cops puts a new kind of heat on him."

Joseph nodded as they rounded onto I Street.

"They wouldn't call us in if they didn't suspect a connection to the others," Hadrian pointed out.

"Yeah," Joseph agreed. He shuddered to think what they would find.

They didn't have any trouble identifying the right building. More police were there, walking in and out the front door. They now recognized personnel from the taskforce.

One police cruiser was surrounded by crime scene tape. The detectives could guess who that belonged to. It was parked at an angle, the trunk sticking out onto the street.

"They must have spotted something and got out in a hurry," Hadrian surmised.

They presented their badges to a Sergeant by the front door.

"Upstairs," the Sergeant replied after checking his tablet. "Apartment 2K."

* * *

Bleary-eyed, Sasha and Christian emerged from their bedroom. Having slept through their restless talk, Lydon bounded out, ready for the day.

"I'll put on coffee," Sasha said as Christian grabbed the dog's leash.

"Thanks," Christian said, pulling on his shoes as Lydon circled around him, eager to go out. "Leave plenty for me."

"Sure," Sasha said, figuring she'd shot-gun the first pot herself and put the second on for him. It'd be ready by the time he returned.

As Christian left and the coffeemaker churned, Sasha picked up her phone, which she'd forgotten on the kitchen counter the previous evening. Its usual place was her nightstand. She couldn't recall the last time such an oversight occurred.

More alarming were the volume of text messages and news alerts. Hoping for clarity in the cacophony, Sasha grabbed the TV remote.

She was just in time to catch what had to be a repeat of the breaking news.

"Four people killed in Washington, D.C. this morning," the anchor announced, "and a crime scene stretching over just one mile. Police sources have confirmed the deaths of two George Mason University students and two Metropolitan police officers. Investigators are scouring Foggy Bottom for witnesses and ask anyone who knows anything to come forward. The names of the victims are being withheld pending notifications of their families."

Sasha stared, open-mouthed, as scenes of crime scene tape, canvasing police officers, and multiple vans from the Medical Examiner's office flashed across the screen.

* * *

"Lieutenant Alicia Dye," the woman said, meeting Joseph and Hadrian at the front door of the apartment. She was dressed in a similar attire to her counterpart in the alley and her shield was just as gold.

"You two on the taskforce?" she queried after examining their credentials.

"Yes," Hadrian confirmed. "I thought it was bad enough when we got to the wrong scene."

They could already see the girls. One brunette … one redhead … both naked, their backs bloody. They could see faint bloody drag marks coming from the nearby bedroom. The bed inside said room was also covered with blood. Joseph thought back to Andrea Prady's apartment. He could see the similarities from that scene.

The middle of the main room had been cleared and the girls lay on their sides, their faces buried in each other's crotches. Written on a nearby wall were the words "Had a lot of fun tonight". The detectives were sure the killer's ink was the girls' blood, just like at the previous scene.

"Do we know who they are?" Joseph asked.

"We found their clothes and purses in the bedroom," Lieutenant Dye reported. "The building manager says the tenant renting this apartment is Jennifer Bison. She's the redhead. The brunette's Penelope Grant. They're both students at GWU and hail from Annapolis and Fairfax, respectively."

"I take it Penelope was just visiting?"

The implications of the bodies' positions were hard to miss.

"Best as we can guess," Lieutenant Dye said. "One of the officers interviewed the building manager. He can't be sure, but he thinks he saw her come and go from time to time. The girls weren't causing any problems and the rent came in on time, so he didn't pry."

"Hey, Joe," Hadrian said. He'd stepped over to study the message on the wall.

Joseph didn't miss the nickname. He couldn't recall the last time his partner had used it. Hadrian only did this when he had something serious on his mind.

"What's up?" Joseph Queried, not sure he wanted to know.

"You're thinking the same thing I am, right?" Hadrian asked. "About the girls."

"That they were seeing each other?"

"Yeah. You think our killer knew this?"

Joseph shrugged.

"Maybe," he offered, stepping over to stand next to his partner. He glanced at the girls again. From what he could tell, both looked slender and athletic. Both had long hair. Apart from Penelope Grant's hair color, she was the killer's type.

They had yet to find out how this killer had gotten in. There were obvious pry marks on the front door, but it was still unclear how he'd gained access to the building. They did know he must have studied the dwelling. Maybe he had seen Penelope Grant visiting before last night.

"The scene speaks to how young we think he is," Hadrian said.

"How so?" Lieutenant Dye asked.

Hadrian pointed as he spoke.

"Look at how he posed their bodies. Look at the message. Everything makes it clear these girls were seeing each other, and he liked that."

"Girl-on-girl is hot," Joseph added.

"He used what he found to his full advantage."

"You think he did something different to these girls than his other victims?" Lieutenant Dye asked. "Something we're not seeing yet?"

"Maybe," Joseph said. "He wants attention. He wants to make an impact, even if he uses the most obvious inspiration for how he stages the scene."

"I shudder to think what the autopsies turn up."

"Where are they with getting the girls out of here?" Hadrian asked, casting another look over the bodies.

"Looking for a bigger body bag and stretcher," Lieutenant Dye replied. "They don't want to try separating the girls here. Might contaminate the rest of the scene."

Joseph nodded, having already figured glue was involved when the killer staged this scene. It'd taken almost thirty-six hours to free Andrea Prady from the chair she'd been adhered to. How long would it take to undo this mess?

* * *

Seeing her Mini Cooper was low on gas, Sasha hopped on her bicycle and took it onto the Metro. By the time she reached the police barricades on I Street, the whole area was bustling with television and print/online news media. Chaining her bike to a streetlight, she pushed her way through the crowd until a uniformed police officer stopped her at the barricade.

"That's as far as you go," he said.

Sasha stared at him, unsure of what to say. She looked around at her news colleagues. Many must have also tried to get closer.

Knowing better than to try again, she took half a step back, as that was all the thick crowd allowed her, and pulled out her phone.

* * *

Hearing his phone chime, Joseph stepped away from the others. Moving into a corner of the small apartment, he saw the caller was Sasha. He debated whether to answer, but finally swiped the screen.

"Is it true?" Sasha asked as soon as he pressed the phone to his ear.

Joseph thought about making a smart remark. He decided against it. She sounded distressed.

"Should you be out there?" he asked instead.

"Is it true?" Sasha asked again. "Two girls and two cops, all dead?"

"That's what we know so far."

"Was it him?"

Joseph took a deep breath. The department wasn't commenting on the possible connection between the two sets of killings, let alone a connection to the other murders.

"It looks like the same guy here," he said, figuring there was no point in downplaying that speculation.

He glanced around. No one seemed to be listening.

"You're up there, aren't you?" Sasha guessed.

"Where are you?" Joseph asked.

"Behind your barricades."

Joseph decided a smart remark was warranted now.

"I assure you I did not set up those barricades," he said. "You shouldn't be standing behind them."

There was a pause.

"You think he might be here?" Sasha asked, taking deep breaths.

"I honestly don't know," Joseph said, knowing he had to be very careful now. "This guy changes his playbook to get attention. He might well be seeing how big a crowd he's drawn."

He glanced around again, determining he'd pushed his luck long enough.

"I have to go," he said, "and you should go home. I'll check on you later."

* * *

Hearing Joseph end the call, Sasha pocketed her phone. She studied the crowd around her again. Was the killer here? Did he now need to get his kicks by sticking around at the scene? If that was the case, would he target her here? And, most of all, what had he done to his victims this time?

She recognized a few faces in this gathering of newsmen and women. She'd exchanged greetings with a few while making her way to the barricade earlier. Now, she wondered about the strange faces.

* * *

He sat on the couch in their small den, still absorbing the extraordinary sequence of events from early that morning. His father sat in his usual armchair, waiting, his cane resting between his knees. It had to be the first time in his life that the old man was being so patient.

They hadn't said a word since leaving the alley. The Metro ride home was a silent one. He was thankful no one tried to speak to them. The train had been almost empty to begin with so early in the morning.

He now tried to speak, but it took a few tries just to loosen his jaw.

"H … how did you know?" he asked.

"The hair," his father said. "I then tracked your phone. It wasn't hard."

He surveyed his son.

"So, college girls are your thing," he said. "Can't blame you. They're something to look at. I just always thought they fought to much."

He leaned forward in his chair.

"How did you find out about me?" he asked. Unlike the hair, he didn't keep his souvenirs at home.

"I read the stories," he explained to his elder. "I was hooked. Then, I realized the timeline matched what happened to you. I guess I just let my mind run away with that. Can't argue with the results."

His father nodded slowly.

"I suppose so," he said. "You'd better keep control of that craving for a while. The heat's on you now more than ever. They may still not know who you are, but they'll be as determined as possible to find you."

He nodded, but something nagged at him.

"Why'd you come to that alley?" he asked. "Why did you shoot those cops?"

"They were about to arrest you," his father said in an even tone. "It'd have only been a matter of time before they found out what you did. How long after that would they have found out about me?"

He had to laugh at this.

"That makes no sense," he pointed out. "There's nothing here to prove you did anything. Knowing you, it'd be easy for you to deny any knowledge of anything related to me."

He laughed again.

"You actually care about me," he said.

His father's eyes narrowed and he gripped his cane tighter.

"Believe what you want," he said. "Just know that, if I get snapped up, I'll make sure you pay."

Leaning on his cane, he pulled himself up to his feet.

"I'm going to bed," he announced. "Hide that hair better if you're so intent on keeping it."

He stalked out of the den, grumbling under his breath.

As his father left the room, he looked outside. The sun was still rising. He had a few hours before he had to go to work and the adrenaline of the previous night's events was wearing off quick. He'd get some sleep.

He rose and exited the den as well. Entering his bedroom, he saw his father had left his bag on top of his laptop. He supposed that was to make a point.

He withdrew the hair taken from his Auburn Lovely from his pocket and added it to his collection. He pushed his hand deep into the bag. He felt them all and remembered how good they'd been. He even remembered the brunette.

A yawn overtook him. He sealed the Ziploc bag and tucked it back underneath his pillow. He'd find a better place to hide it once he was more clear-headed … once he'd gotten some sleep.

Chapter 12

He was on the move again. He understood the risk, but the need overtook him. He needed a successful hunt, and he'd taken the proper precautions, even if some shortcuts were required.

* * *

"I'll see you tomorrow," Kristen said, extracting herself from the car. "Or maybe later. What time is it again?"

One of her friends giggled. Kristen wasn't sure who it was as they all had plenty to drink. Then there was the excitement of seeing the strippers. Bachelorette parties were a blast. Kristen knew this as this was her third. The weddings were coming at her in one big wave.

The other girls cheered as the car pulled away from the curb. Kristen waved and broke into a fit of giggles herself as they dissipated into the darkness.

The wedding was next week and her dress had arrived after final alterations the previous afternoon. She'd celebrated her friend's final days of freedom and had already taken a personal day tomorrow to sleep it off.

She was thankful she hadn't worn heels tonight. Flat footwear made the stumbling less hazardous and she reached the front door of her condominium without drawing blood. Things improved further when she got the key into the lock and turned it in the proper direction.

She climbed into her home and fumbled for the light switch. She sobered up in a hurry when someone else turned on the lights and closed her front door.

"Don't scream, Kristen," the man said, showing her his gun. "Do not make a sound."

Despite his warning, Kristen whimpered. She couldn't believe what was happening. It couldn't be real. It couldn't be him.

"What are you doing here?" she asked. She'd never imagined he was capable of this.

He stepped closer and ran the tip of his gun's muzzle along her forehead, pushing aside some stray, red strands.

"I think you know," he said, smiling.

Kristen's legs wobbled. Her heart slammed against the front and back of her ribcage. This wasn't happening.

"You know who I am, right?" he asked. "Who I really am?"

Kristen nodded, whimpering again. He grinned.

"Then you know what I do to those who don't cooperate," he said. "Let's go to your bedroom. Go on."

He beckoned down the nearby hallway. Kristen couldn't believe he knew where her bedroom was. She'd heard he sometimes broke into people's homes as a part of his surveillance before they encountered him.

He had to have done that with her. They saw each other almost every day. How many times had they seen each other while he was preparing for this? Kristen began to cry.

"Sshh," he said with a finger to his lips. "Remember. Cooperation is the key to life here."

Her legs still shaking, Kristen took a step forward. She took another, and then another. It took about two dozen before they were standing at the door to her bedroom.

He nudged her forward and she crossed the threshold. He followed her, turning on another light. She saw her favorite scarf laid out on her bed, near the foot end. He'd prepared everything, just like the news said.

"Take off your clothes," he said, remaining behind her. "Do it slowly. I want to enjoy this."

They saw each other almost every day. She wondered how often he'd undressed her in his mind. She didn't wear provocative clothes when they were at work, but he seemed to have made do.

Knowing she had no choice, Kristen unbuttoned her blouse and let it fall around her feet. Her skirt fell next, and the rest of her clothes followed.

"Step out of those shoes now," he encouraged.

She obeyed.

"Very nice," he said. "Lie on the bed. On your back. Nice and easy."

She'd never imagined this happening to her. She'd never imagined he was this monster. Her imagination, or lack thereof, couldn't help her now as she settled herself on her bed.

He set his gun on her nightstand and grabbed the scarf. He paused for a moment, admiring the golden charms on a chain around her ankle.

"You don't show that off at work," he remarked, caressing the piece of jewelry.

Kristen bit her lip to keep from crying.

"Raise your arm," he said, encircling her wrist with his fingers. "Come on."

Kristen didn't resist as he drew her arm up over her head. He looped the scarf around her wrist twice before making a knot. He then pulled up her other arm and tied it as well. She didn't realize how he'd done it, but she was now tied to the bed. He'd been gentle so far, but she was more terrified than she'd ever been in her life.

"Please don't do this," she pleaded. "I won't tell anyone. I promise."

In truth, she'd leave town the next morning if she survived until then. She could tell the police from anywhere.

He climbed onto the bed and moved over her.

"Please don't do this," Kristen tried again, starting to sound desperate. "Please."

She hoped she could appeal to any sliver of humanity in him. He had to have some decency. He couldn't have put on such a good mask for everyone for all this time.

Hearing his zipper open eviscerated any hope for avoiding what he'd done to so many women before her. Kristen shut her eyes.

"Keep your eyes open," he growled, pushing into her. "Open them, Kristen."

Releasing a choked sob, Kristen opened her eyes and stared up at him.

"I'm in charge," he grunted into her face as he thrust in and out of her. "You couldn't stop me if you tried. I always get who I want."

* * *

"I'm out!" he called.

His father came into the hallway as fast as he could on his cane.

"Where you going?" he demanded.

"Work, Dad," he replied. "I'm already late."

He wouldn't admit it, but his father had a point. The police presence seemed to be heavier all over the city. Colleges were also increasing safety precautions. It was indeed foolish to visit another Auburn Lovely now. Besides, he didn't have any prospects yet.

He did have an errand to run, and he'd run it. His father did not need to know as it would only take a few extra seconds out of his day. But first, he had to get to work.

His father regarded him for a long, cool moment before turning and heading back towards the kitchen. He continued towards the apartment's front door.

* * *

Hearing Lucas leave, he sank back into his chair at the kitchen table just big enough for the two of them. Picking up his fork, he turned his attention back to his half-eaten omelet, which he'd made after sleeping until 11:00.

As he ate, his mind wandered again. He thought about Kristen Donovan. She was the only one whose name he remembered. It was because he knew this information that he didn't consider hunting her at first. The police always looked at the living who were close to the dead first, or at least around them every day. But the debacle in Baltimore caused these plans to require revisions. It was their familiarity first and foremost that he killed her. If anyone could identify him for the police, it was Kristen Donavan. He was also too far gone by the time of that hunt. So many already died at his hand. That was how he intended it every time he hunted. When the rapes no longer paralyzed people with fear, the murders did.

He thought it interesting Lucas now had that same effect, even if his son would never be like him. He was already taking too many risks. It was only a matter of time before risks caused mistakes. And, he knew very well, mistakes led to handcuffs, if not a grave. He'd been lucky enough to teach that lesson rather than learn it, but it still cost him.

He kept eating, unsure if he could even help the kid in the future. Would he even try? Maybe he was insulated enough. He had always been careful.

* * *

Sasha wasn't sure what surprised her more … the fact another letter came or that the Chief Editor and the owner's lawyer were waiting for her alongside Nancy and Eric. Otherwise, the scene looked the same as the last two times. They'd even reserved the same conference room.

"Have a seat," the gray-haired Chief Editor said.

Sasha sat. It took her a minute, but she remembered his name was Ethan Marsh. She hoped he wouldn't realize she'd forgotten her bosses' boss's name. She wouldn't even try with the lawyer as she was certain she had never seen him before.

"Another letter came?" she asked, unable to think of anything else to say.

Nancy slid a sheet of paper over to her. It was another photocopy of another handwritten letter. Sasha began to read.

Dear Sasha Copeland,

I'm sure you've seen my latest work. It was quite a night all around. You and everyone else view it as destructive and devastating … words you throw around to try and describe what you can't put into a category.

I will tell you my Auburn Lovely was wonderful. How can such an experience be destructive and devastating? If she could tell you, she would confess I was the first man she'd ever been with. I swear she never felt anything like it. She felt that pleasure. Maybe I need to show you better.

I will find another and I will cause her such pleasure as well. It's only a matter of time.

Here's hoping you have another good story soon.

Again, no signature. Sasha looked up at everyone.

"I'll say this straight-forward," Ethan Marsh said. "We'd like you to stay home for the time being. Follow up on previous cases and stories. We'll provide you a company phone to conduct interviews if someone doesn't want to use Zoom. It is the safest thing for you."

"We can definitely shuffle the assignments to accommodate that," Nancy offered.

Sasha didn't speak. The idea of her staying home had been floated before, but this was the first time it was outright insisted upon, complete with a plan for her to keep working.

How was she supposed to keep working? The Washington Post's Local Crime and Public Safety section had about a dozen reporters. If the other eleven or so could come and go from the office and their homes as they pleased, they'd have an advantage over her in a matter of days, if not hours. Her career might be stalled for years. She was lucky to have made it this far in spite of the pandemic.

Sasha studied everyone at the table, all of them having power over her right then.

"I need to think about it," she said.

"It would be the best thing for you," Ethan Marsh offered with the owner's lawyer nodding in agreement. "We're only concerned about your safety."

Sasha nodded.

"Thank you," she said, "but I do need to think about it."

She didn't need to say anything else, so she rose and left the room. She darted down the hallway to a bathroom and burst through the door. Grateful it seemed to be empty, she entered a stall and locked the door. Putting the toilet lid down, she sat down on it and cried. She cried for herself and all the people who'd been hurt ... the dead and the living.

* * *

Dr. Everett Mills looked grim as Joseph and Hadrian entered his office. For someone who saw death on a regular basis, he looked troubled. The detectives wondered if he'd ever write about this case.

Dr. Mills had already sent over official copies of the autopsy reports regarding the deaths of Officers Regis and Nichols. As far as killings went, these were unremarkable. Both officers died due to gunshot wounds to the head. The fatal bullets were removed from their skulls and sent to the crime lab for analysis.

Officer Mike Nichols died almost instantly when the bullet severed his spinal cord just below the base of his skull. Officer Regis survived a couple minutes longer, but his killer's bullet entered his brain and ricocheted off his skull several times, causing chips of bone to likewise fly and further damage many areas in his brain. He bled out before the first responders arrived. From a biological standpoint, these deaths did not have nearly the impact the department felt at the loss of two of their own.

"So," Hadrian said as the detectives sat down at the Medical Examiner's desk, "what couldn't you say in writing?"

"Oh, it's all written down," Dr. Mills assured them. "I just haven't seen this before. That's saying something in this city."

"What did he do?" Joseph asked. This had to do with the two girls ... the two newest victims.

"At first," Dr. Mills began, opening a file, "it looks routine, as far as this spree is concerned. Jennifer Bison was stabbed in the back a total of eighteen times. Penelope was stabbed in the back six times. Both were enough to be fatal due to exsanguination."

Remembering which girl had which hair color, the detectives recognized the pattern. Jennifer Bison, the redhead, was again the killer's primary target. They also saw the deviation Dr. Mills was hinting at.

The last time this killer had murdered two victims at once, the blonde, Ellie Stets, was stabbed in the chest. Penelope Grant, another secondary victim, was stabbed in the back, just like all the redheaded girls.

"Jennifer Bison was raped," Dr. Mills continued. "We collected semen for the lab, though I could guess they'll make the connection through DNA someday. Both girls were bound and gagged with tape, which the killer removed after the kills. We collected residue for the lab to probably match, at least in brand. And, yes, they were glued together as you found them. Took us almost a day to separate them. Your killer probably used the same glue."

It all sounded similar to the previous scenes. The only major difference was that Ellie Stets had never been bound. Her killer gagged and stabbed her before she could put up much of a fight and require bindings. Why had he bound Penelope Grant instead of simply killing her? Was it because Jennifer Bison was in the same room? Did he want to gain control of both girls before focusing on one?

"Here is where it starts to get odd," Dr. Mills said.

The detectives considered his words. Was the doctor dismissing the other differences as insignificant? Maybe along the lines of the fact the killer first murdered two people, then murdered one, and then two again?

"We found saliva and vaginal fluids on both bodies," Dr. Mills reported. "These samples were of course collected and sent to the lab."

Joseph and Hadrian didn't find this significant. Friends of the girls confirmed they had been seeing each other since the previous spring. Their neighbors, both in the dorm and apartment buildings, reported them visiting each other often.

"This can't be why you called us in," Hadrian said.

For his part, Joseph was becoming annoyed. They were already taking time off the case tomorrow to attend their slain colleagues' funerals. They needed to investigate, not be told obvious facts which would serve no immediate purpose. They could have read this in the official reports.

Dr. Mills sighed.

"This is why I called you in," he said. "Penelope Grant was bound at her wrists and ankles. As I said, the tape was removed, most likely post-mortem. But this killer always peeled it off, as far as we've been able to tell. That was the case with her wrists ... as consistent as the definition of 'consistent' will allow. What isn't consistent is the very shallow knife wound on the inside of her right ankle. The lack of bleeding suggests this too was post-mortem, though no paramedic with a brain stem would consider this wound serious. It wouldn't even require stitches."

He took a deep breath.

"It looks like Penelope Grant was also raped," he said. "We collected semen from her body too. Let's say it was located deep enough to rule out the possibility of accidental transfer from Jennifer Bison from when either the killer or our people moved them."

Now Joseph and Hadrian were listening. They doubted Penelope Grant had a boyfriend. They'd spoken to too many people for her to be able to have hidden such a secret. So, what made their killer decide to rape her as well? How long was he there for in order to have been able to achieve that?

"We found no signs of bruising, tearing, or similar injuries as we did on Jennifer Bison, or the others," Dr. Mills said, speaking in a slow tone for the first time.

"What does that mean?" Hadrian asked, not sure he wanted to know.

"We think Penelope Grant was raped post-mortem."

Hadrian looked sick. Joseph couldn't make that register.

"Do you mean someone raped her after she was dead?" he asked, not believing this could get worse.

Chapter 13

He was grateful Uber and Lift and all those other companies hadn't rendered the taxicab industry extinct yet. Cash left less of a paper trail than the apps those services required. For this trip, he didn't want a paper trail.

The setup was further improved by this driver not paying much attention to anything, including the morning traffic. He was on the phone, arguing with someone in some foreign language. It made it easier to survey the scenery through the window.

He'd read Sasha Copeland's latest entry in the case. The parents of one of the most recent dead girls had spoken with her, sharing how wonderful their daughter had been. People always shared how wonderful their loved ones were following the loved ones' passing. He'd read articles where such people expressed such sentiments for people fried by the state. The phenomenon wasn't exclusive to death either. People even shared how wonderful he was after he got shot. Society could be so deceptive.

Though this article was insignificant, he wasn't missing Sasha Copeland's involvement in the case. Each of her pieces in the WaPo illuminated more about what was happening, and he worried she might soon expose too much. She was proving to be very intuitive and he needed to learn more about her.

Her bosses at the newspaper were already on alert because of those letters. There was no ruse he could employ to get her personal information, such as an address, from the Post without stirring up way too much suspicion.

So, old-fashioned detective work was his only option. Reviewing all the Washington Post's articles on the case, he knew Sasha Copeland posted the first piece on the killings on Idaho Avenue in the northwestern part of the city, at 9:53 in the morning, before the police released a formal statement. That meant she'd been to the scene or spoke to someone in the department. That meant she had heard about the killings while she was at home, maybe while eating breakfast. He knew many reporters monitored the police and emergency radio frequencies with scanners and there were apps for this now … no more heavy equipment to occupy the trunks of reporters' cars.

Sasha Copeland was the first to get word out about those killings. Therefore, she was first to get close enough to learn something valuable. Therefore, she lived close enough to the scene on Idaho Avenue.

Therefore, here he was, sitting in the back of a cab snaking through the traffic of northwestern Washington, D.C. He'd given the driver an address he'd found on the Internet. If this sweep didn't prove fruitful, a good possibility, he'd find another address and hail another cab. He had enough time and money to work with the vague information available to him. He'd succeeded before using these methods.

He thought the driver was actually shouting at whoever he was on the phone with as the cab pulled up to a red light. He considered saying something to the man as he didn't want to draw unnecessary attention, but another sight caught his eye.

Standing on her bike on the cross street and checking something on her phone was Sasha Copeland, complete with a helmet. Very safety conscious and yet right in his line of fire. Too bad he hadn't brought his revolver. He had just brought temptation.

Without a viable option to kill her, he thought about tossing money onto the cab's front seat like in the movies, hopping out, and following her. His reasoning dictated that would bring on all kinds of unwanted attention, including from Sasha Copeland. Plus, in a battle between her bike and his cane, she'd lose him as soon as the light gave her the right of way. Telling the cab driver to follow her, assuming the guy would understand the request, would also develop unwanted attention.

Studying her and evaluating his options, he noticed something else. Squinting, he realized the safety-conscious Sasha Copeland had gotten her bicycle registered with the city. He could just recognize the long, shiny, rectangular sticker on the crossbar.

Too bad he couldn't read the registration number. He whipped out his phone and activated its camera. With the driver still on his own phone and otherwise oblivious, he lowered his rear window and stuck the phone out. He lined it up and zoomed in. As Sasha Copeland was putting away her own phone, he snapped two photos. His arm was back inside the cab with the window going back up in less than twenty seconds.

A horn behind them alerted the driver that the light had changed. The guy pressed on the accelerator and blew through the intersection.

From the backseat, he turned and watched through the rear window until he couldn't see Sasha Copeland anymore. He pulled up the photos on his phone and scrolled to the most recent one.

The first snapshot was clear enough, which was fortunate. Sasha Copeland was raising her leg to put her foot on her bike's pedal. Her jean-clad thigh obstructed part of the registration sticker in his second shot.

He scrolled back to the first photo and recited the number under his breath. There was a Metro station a few blocks from the coffeeshop he'd told the driver to take him to, so he could disappear from the neighborhood with Sasha Copeland being none the wiser. No further cabs required.

He opened the Contacts list on his phone and made a selection. The driver had finished his angry conversation, but it didn't matter if he overheard now.

Holding the phone to his ear, he listened to the repetitive long tones. Just when he was sure he'd get voice mail, someone answered.

"Hey, Artie," he said in a jovial tone. He did have plenty to be happy about.

"How are you, old man?" Artie asked over the phone.

He never understood that nickname. They were less than two years apart. He'd been smart enough to get out when he did rather than transfer. He also hadn't a crewed three alimonies from women who wouldn't dare to remarry.

"I was thinking when we last had a beer," he said. "Then I realized I couldn't remember when that was."

"I'm sure you've lubricated yourself a few times in-between anyway," Artie said with a chortle.

"How about we hit Vinny's anyway? You free tonight?"

"Sure. I'll catch you there."

Whenever they didn't agree on a time, it would be 7:30. He hung up without another word, thinking how easy things would be … just like before.

* * *

Christian sat on the couch, Lydon resting his head on his knees. He stared at the black television screen. He wished she hadn't, but Sasha insisted on taking a morning bike ride to clear her head. He could understand that, but he wished she hadn't gone out.

"I'll be fine," she'd said. "Besides, all that morning rush hour traffic. There'll be hundreds of witnesses anywhere. He won't try anything."

Her logic made sense … kind of. Now, Christian just hoped she'd come home soon.

They'd had another rough night, though Sasha let him hold her again. In addition to the current stressors, she was thinking about the funerals they'd be going to today. She wasn't just attending as a reporter. She'd worked in a police district as an intern. Dead cops were almost as personal to her as if she wore a badge.

"Any chance you smell her yet?" he asked his guide dog.

Lydon just wagged his tail as he patted his head. It thumped against the carpet again and again.

"I guess it's getting to me, too," Christian admitted. Even if he could see, he wasn't sure how he could protect the woman he loved should anyone try anything.

He heard the key in the front door. He rose as Sasha entered the apartment. Lydon ran over to greet her.

"Hey," Sasha said.

"Hey," Christian returned, moving around the couch and coming towards her. When he was close enough, he threw his arms around her.

Sasha was about to speak when she heard him release a long breath. She understood and stayed quiet, wrapping her arms around his torso as Lydon walked a perimeter around their legs.

* * *

There were all the usual trappings of a police funeral. Crowds of uniformed police officers from across the country stood at attention. Drums and bagpipes played "Amazing Grace". Limos transported the widow, children, and parents. A squadron of helicopters flew overhead, executing a Missing Man formation. It was Sasha's fourth police funeral.

Understanding the publicity surrounding the deaths and wanting to get the formalities over with, the families of Officer Keith Regis and posthumously-promoted Detective Michael Nichols agreed to a joint ceremony, followed by individual, private burials.

Monumental Sports & Entertainment donated the use of the Capital One Arena in the Penn Quarter neighborhood of D.C. for the ceremony. 20,356 people rose as the caskets were carried in.

Seated with the rest of the press, Sasha caught a few glimpses of Joseph and Hadrian. She also saw a few other officers and personnel she knew. It was surreal to see them all in their dress uniforms and standing at attention.

As the mayor spoke, Christian ran his hand down Sasha's arm and clasped her hand in his. She wrapped her fingers around his in return. At their feet, Lydon slept in accordance with his guide dog training. Christian was thankful this wasn't a setting where frequent sitting and standing occurred as the dog was currently using one of his feet as a pillow, successfully anchoring him.

As Merissa Ehle, the Chief of the Metropolitan Police Department of the District of Columbia, stepped forward to speak, Sasha looked at the caskets again. They now stood on risers, each draped by an American flag and adorned with the portraits and caps of the slain police officers.

"These were my men," the Chief was saying. "I feel my own loss as well as the loss felt by this whole department."

Sasha recalled how a source in the 3rd District told her newly-minted Officer Keith Regis was proving to be very impulsive, interrogating people on the street based on the vaguest, sometimes misguided, suspicions. He had a spotty record and the notes from his training officer, Mike Nichols, weren't encouraging. His being African American was sometimes mentioned with people questioning which side he was loyal to in the current national conflict. It was suspected he pursued his killer on similar, perhaps unfounded, assumptions.

Sasha had chosen not to publish these suspicions when reporting about the murdered officers. Though there were whispers throughout Washington about Officer Regis's behavior, no major news outlets seemed to pay it any attention. No one wanted to besmirch a dead cop, especially since there was no clear evidence of wrong-doing linked to his murder. His race was likewise not made a major issue. Many did share the continuing speculation that he'd confronted the wanted serial killer, Sasha's chosen nickname not catching on, eclipsing his questionable but brief law enforcement career.

No, right now, police, citizens, and reporters alike mourned the tragic loss of two police officers who died doing their job.

* * *

He and Artie laughed as they ordered another round. With Artie becoming more and more smashed, he was able to keep water nearby, adding some to his own drinks to lag behind in this race to a blackout.

Artie was probably also motivated to drink after attending the double police funeral earlier that day. It was a bit exhilarating to sit here with him without the man being aware he had his colleagues' killer within choking distance.

"You always could hold your liquor," Artie remarked, in apparent awe of this ability.

A busty waitress brought new drinks to their corner booth, taking the old glasses. He didn't complain about his still being one-third full and being removed nonetheless.

"Man," Artie said when the waitress might have made it out of earshot, "what a rack."

The woman had leaned forward, her plunging neckline revealing her generous cleavage, as she set down his glass. He was sure this was a deliberate ploy to increase her tips. Judging from Artie's reaction, she'd be successful tonight.

"You think I could get her number?" Artie mused to no one in particular.

He laughed because it seemed appropriate.

"You looking to audition her for the role of Wife number four?" he asked.

"She looks like that, I wouldn't mind," Artie said with a shrug and a smile, eyeing the waitress again as she stepped through a door besides the bar.

"I would hope you've learned your lesson," he said. "At least my ex had the good sense to run and never try to squeeze anything out of me."

He paused, feeling a flash of anger surging through him as he talked about her.

"Women," Artie said, taking a gulp of his new drink. "Can't live with them, … I forget the rest."

He drank as well and added some water while Artie closed his eyes, absorbing the taste of the fresh alcohol.

"Speaking of which," he said. "I could use your help."

Artie looked at him, seeming to become more lucid again. He wondered if he'd brought this up too early. Then, his friend's face broke into a wide grin. He relaxed again.

"Bedded the wrong one," Artie said, banging his fist on the table as he broke into a fit of laughter.

"I'm not sure," he said. "We met over at the community center and had drinks a few times."

He had no idea where a community center was nor what event there would have enabled him to meet such a bachelorette.

"Anyway," he continued, having rehearsed this tale, "I take her home one night a few weeks ago and I haven't heard from her since. Thing is, I think she took my father's watch."

Artie's eyes widened as he took two more gulps.

"The Kernel's watch?" he asked in shock.

He nodded, hoping he displayed enough shame.

"Man," Artie said. "That's rough."

He kept nodding, properly averting his eyes.

"I'd just like to get it back," he said. "I'm not looking to press charges. That's more of a mess than I want."

Artie nodded in sympathy.

"She'll say anything," he said. "These days, women get to do that if they don't like having a fling with no strings attached."

He sighed in disgust.

"Yeah," he agreed, wanting to get to his request. "She's a real health nut. She rides her bike everywhere."

"Ah," Artie said. "Only good thing about a woman like that is you want to see her naked."

"I know she got her bike registered with the city. I saw the number a couple times and wrote it down."

He pulled the piece of paper out of his wallet as Artie nodded.

"You always were good with numbers," he recounted, chuckling. "No wonder you were able to get out when you did."

"Yeah," he said, sliding the paper across the table. "Could you check it out when you get a chance?"

Artie looked down at the paper, considering. After almost a minute, he picked it up and jammed it into the inside pocket of his coat. He then drained his glass.

"Sure," he said, smacking his lips. "I'll take care of that for you."

He smiled and took a gulp of his own drink. He hid his distaste as he smiled. Watered-down drinks didn't suit his pallet, but his mission was more important. And, the ploy had succeeded before with Artie never becoming wise to his intentions.

He added more water and finished the drink.

"Another round?" Artie asked, seeming eager to further intoxicate himself.

He shook his head.

"I gotta be able to make it home," he said. This was true as his trek was longer than Artie's and required a greater set of steps to complete.

"Fine," Artie said. "I'll hit the head and we'll settle up."

He shook his head again and waved his hand through the air.

"Tonight's on me," he said.

Artie grinned as though a ploy of his own had succeeded. He didn't care.

"Go take care of business," he insisted.

As Artie extracted himself from their corner booth and stumbled towards the restroom, he went over to the bar and settled their tab, leaving a handsome tip for the brunette waitress. After all, she'd been so kind to use her distracting bosom while supplying enough alcohol to get his friend to agree to this errand, even if she would be none the wiser about her role. While he was sure to not remember their conversation, Artie would find the provided piece of paper in his coat pocket and recall the related request. It had worked so often before and he'd met so many wonderful redheads with this aide. God bless Artie the Drunk for remaining so oblivious all these years, even when he struck close to home.

* * *

"Did you get the prostitute's statement?" Joseph asked.

"Yeah," Hadrian replied, sliding it across the conference table. "I don't see much value in it."

Around them, a dozen or so of their colleagues were likewise exploring new and old information about the ongoing murder spree. More were outside, wearing their soles thin by running down leads and looking for witnesses and informants with information.

Studying the printed transcript, which the seventeen-year-old addict signed and initialed in accordance with a detective's guidance, Joseph had to agree.

"Two or four guys exited the alley after the shooting," he summarized. "One was tall and wearing a UVA jacket."

The hooker had been down the street, looking for a John, when the shooting occurred. According to her statement, she turned towards the sound of gunfire and saw multiple people leaving the alley.

Problem was, a forensic reenactment of the shooting indicated the shooter stood at the opening of the alley, leaving the possibility she would have seen him standing there and turning to leave. Her statement didn't jive with that theory.

"You know this detective?" Joseph asked, indicating the name of the investigator who'd taken her statement in an interview room. Detective Stephen Adin.

"He's good," Hadrian said. "Worked in Narcotics before he moved to Homicide. He knows how to talk to addicts and get something coherent out of them. You'd want him working the murder of a cop."

He seemed to know something about almost everyone in the 3,500-person department.

"This doesn't make sense," Joseph pointed out, indicating the statement.

Hadrian shrugged. This wasn't his friend's fault.

Though other personnel were pursuing outside leads, the taskforce was assigned to investigate any possible connection between the murders of Jennifer Bison and Penelope Grant and the slaying of their brethren. So far, the teenage prostitute seemed to be their only eyewitness and solid lead.

All of a sudden, the door to the conference room opened and Inspector Harvey Cunningham entered, looking grim. He was followed by half a dozen suited personnel, all of whom looked serious. A few people raised their heads at their supervisor's sudden appearance and studied these strangers.

"Everybody stop working!" Inspector Cunningham called out through the large conference room. "Stop working and pack everything up. Download all documents from your laptops and tablets onto flash drives. Everything will be collected by these agents."

He indicated the suited squadron with him, who began moving through the room to commence collecting.

"Make sure you maintain chain of custody of any evidence," he said. "Please speak with me before you go. This taskforce is being disbanded. Thank you all for your efforts and your service."

Chapter 14

Joseph and Hadrian were stunned. Neither could move as a woman in a black suit picked up the prostitute's statement and put it in a manilla folder and then put the manilla folder in a box. They lost track of what then happened to the box.

"What is this?" someone demanded. Others echoed this confusion and outrage.

Inspector Cunningham waved his hand for silence. When the uproar died down, he spoke again.

"I will be speaking with each of you in person to explain further," he said. "New circumstances have necessitated this action. Please, I ask for everyone's cooperation."

This response was met with grumbles as the sergeant, detectives, and officers set to work to help pack up their efforts to solve five, or maybe seven, murders. One by one, boxes were collected by the suited squadron, who said little to nothing as they piled everything onto handcarts and wheeled it out.

Joseph rose from his seat and stepped over to a window. Pushing the blinds aside, he saw two large black vans and a matching sedan parked down on the street, more suited personnel seeming to stand guard by these vehicles.

* * *

Inspector Cunningham surveyed the removal of the taskforce's work product and then remained true to his word. He called Joseph and Hadrian into his temporary office in the 2nd District that afternoon.

Both detectives worked to contain their fury as they sat down and declined their supervisor's offer of water from a cooler someone had dragged in at some point.

"What is this?" Joseph demanded, unable to wait anymore. "What on Earth could warrant shutting down this taskforce after what happened?"

Even the normally-serene Hadrian looked angry.

For his part, Inspector Cunningham regarded the detectives with a calm though troubled gaze.

"I assure you this was a decision that had to be made quickly but couldn't be made lightly," he said. "I found out myself early this morning directly from the Chief. Circumstances have changed and the FBI is in a better position to take the case from here."

"What do the feds know that we don't?" Hadrian asked. He and Joseph had suspected the suited squadron were FBI agents.

"I'm sure you are aware the pressure we've all been under regarding these murders," Inspector Cunningham said. "That extends to our crime lab as well."

Joseph and Hadrian didn't understand this. If the FBI was helping to process evidence, why was the taskforce being disbanded? Law enforcement agencies nationwide, including their own department, sent evidence to Quantico all the time without this drama.

Inspector Cunningham opened a manilla folder on his desk and raised the thin packet of papers inside up to his own face before either detective could read the top page.

"We received some troubling results from the ballistics lab," he said. "The gun used to kill Officer Regis and Nichols has been used to kill before."

"Could be a street gun," Hadrian offered. They'd seen this many times. Maybe their colleagues collided with a drug dealer.

Inspector Cunningham shook his head. He flipped over a couple pages in the packet and turned it, setting it on his desk for the detectives to see.

Joseph and Hadrian leaned forward. It seemed to be a list of names with dates next to each.

Lara Higgins, September 19, 1989

Michael Higgins, September 19, 1989

Katherine Kopell, January 11, 1990

Benjamin Truman Kopell, January 11, 1990

Stephanie Olsen, July 30, 1990

David Anthony Seymour, November 16, 1990

Erica Elaine Seymour, November 16, 1990

Joan Hager-Smith, March 15, 1991

Brian Smith, March 15, 1991

Tyler Sanford, April 22, 1991

Marie Allison Sanford, April 22, 1991

Kelly Porter, April 22, 1991

Kristen Donavan, May 3, 1991

Vincent Andrews, October 30, 1993

Monica David-Andrews, October 30, 1993

Ashley Renee Finley, March 2, 1994

William Conners, March 2, 1994

Seventeen names. It was as random a list as one could come up with, perhaps by throwing darts at pages of a phone book. But Joseph and Hadrian recognized some of the names. Unfortunately, the circumstances were starting to make sense in a way they didn't want them to.

"There's also the attempted murder of Officer Erin Kiefer in Montgomery County back in 1990," Inspector Cunningham said, pushing his glasses back up his sloping nose and showing them another page. "Thankfully, his vest saved him and he lived to die of a heart attack two years ago ... too many ham sandwiches."

The detectives looked up at their superior.

"This is why the FBI is in a better position to move forward with this case," Inspector Cunningham continued. "They're forming a new taskforce in the Washington field office. This case will be enveloped into theirs. You two will be among our personnel assigned to work on that."

With this now being an interstate investigation, such an assignment would normally be a testament to a detective's investigative prowess. But Joseph and Hadrian were still trying to process the fact this cop killer, who might be connected to their current murder spree, could very well be the Mid-Atlantic Slayer.

* * *

In part because of the appointment and mostly to get their minds off the suggested danger, Sasha and Christian met their wedding planner for the first time that Wednesday evening. It was their first serious step since he'd proposed two and a half months earlier.

"Davay sdelayem eto," Christian said, taking a deep breath as they reached the address. Following the instructions on a placard by the front door, both he and Sasha donned masks.

Sasha wasn't sure what to expect, her best reference being Martin Short's eccentricities in "Father of the Bride". But Elliot Wayde looked more like he prepared prenuptial agreements than the ceremonies themselves.

Dressed in a light-gray suit with a black shirt and dark-green tie, Elliot Wayde invited the couple into the expansive office that seemed to take up almost the entire second floor of the brownstone he worked out of.

"First," he began when introductions were finished, along with the usual compliments about Lydon's calm demeanor, and coffee was served, "have you set a date?"

"We want a fall wedding," Sasha replied. "We had November 5th in mind."

Elliot Wayde nodded, typing on his computer.

"Ahead of the holiday rush," he said with apparent approval. "Trust me, it's always a busy season from Thanksgiving through Valentine's Day. And, we're too far into this fall season to even consider anything this year. Plus, the world's still sorting out things with Covid. Then, there's that storm, Jackson. I shudder to think if Washington takes a direct hit."

He punched a few more keys and nodded.

"November 5th, 2022 is available," he said.

According to his website, he never oversaw more than one couple's wedding per day. That way, he and one of his assistants could be on hand for last-minute issues without possible distractions or conflicts.

"Then November 5th it is," Christian declared and Sasha smiled.

Elliot Wayde punched a couple more keys.

"Got it," he said. "Have you given any thought to the venues. You'll need something for the ceremony and the reception, and there's no guarantee they'll be in the same place, especially if you are marrying in a church."

The only thing Sasha and Christian had given serious consideration to was the date, no longer a tentative one. Neither of them were very religious.

"What do you suggest?" Sasha asked.

"That would depend on your budget," Elliot Wayde replied, his hand now palming his computer mouse. "Let me see here. On your questionnaire, you indicated ..."

Despite his joy at planning a wedding with the woman he loved, Christian felt himself becoming nervous about the growing pile of components the wedding planner was already considering.

* * *

Elliot Wayde's office was a pretty easy trip from their apartment. Sasha and Christian sat on the Metro's Red Line, heading north after the meeting.

"What did you think?" Sasha asked, feeling a little giddy.

Christian wasn't sure.

"It's a lot to think about," he admitted.

"HIja'," Sasha agreed.

The date had been by far the easiest thing. They now had to decide between four suggested venues, provide a draft of their guest list, and determine the size of their wedding party, all before their next meeting with Elliot Wayde in three weeks. Crhistian's head was spinning. Why didn't engagement rings come with instruction manuals to warn people about this?

"You sure you don't want to elope?" Christian tried again, half-joking.

Sasha squeezed his hand.

"It'll be fine," she said. "Besides, my mother would kill you and my grandfather would have your corpse court-marshalled."

Her grandfather having once served as the Judge Advocate General for the United States Air Force, Sasha's family were minor celebrities in the D.C. area. Her current growing readership was stirring this fame up again, though her grandfather had long-since retired and relocated to a ranch in Wyoming.

"No military stuff," Christian said, "please."

"No military stuff," Sasha promised. Apart from her grandfather being there, she likewise did not want their wedding to have any sort of military traditions included.

"Next stop," the static-laced P.A. system announced over their heads, "Van Ness-UDC station. Van Ness-UDC is next."

Fast asleep by their feet just a few seconds earlier, Lydon seemed to recognize this name and rose to his feet, taking a moment to stretch despite the train's confined space.

"Poyekhali," Christian said.

Following Lydon's lead, they made their way to the door a few yards ahead of them.

"This is Van Ness-UDC station," the P.A. system announced as the train slowed down to a stop. "Watch your step."

Once Sasha and Christian stepped off, they moved aside and waited for the train to leave before continuing their trek home. It was safer to do it this way with Lydon.

"Your mom's coming by tomorrow night, right?" Sasha asked as the last car left the platform behind.

"Yeah," Christian replied. "Up."

Lydon, who'd sat on his hindquarters after disembarking the train, rose and was then struck by an urge to scratch himself. Christian and Sasha waited as he worked to conquer the stubborn itch. He didn't scratch himself often, but it took up to a full minute when he did.

"He tries to get all the month's scratches in at once," Christian often joked.

"Your mom's coming over tomorrow night?" Sasha asked as they waited.

"Da," Christian confirmed as Lydon finished and stood up straight again. It seemed his mother had found another box of notebooks with wedding ideas in her storage unit. He wondered what prompted her to go explore it herself. He did appreciate the possibility her advice might make wedding-planning easier for him and Sasha.

"Forward," Christian told Lydon.

They began walking, making their way to the staircase at the end of the platform. The walk to their building was three blocks and about five minutes away. They completed the stretch while exchanging few words.

Sasha stopped as they approached their building. She knew enough about police work to recognize an unmarked cruiser. She tried to tell Christian about it, but she felt unable to form words. What had happened now?

They entered the building and Sasha didn't notice anything amiss in the lobby and adjacent mailroom. The staircase looked likewise undisturbed, but they met Detectives Joseph Conway and Hadrian Hasselle by their apartment door.

"What are you doing here?" Sasha asked after updating Christian about their presence.

"Can we talk inside?" Joseph requested.

Wanting answers more than anything, Sasha and Christian led the detectives into the apartment and invited them to sit at their kitchen table. Free from his harness, Lydon gave each man's feet a cursory sniff before crossing the kitchen to his water dish.

"Okay," Sasha said, sitting next to Christian as the dog began drinking in loud slurps and gulps behind them. "VjIjatlh."

The Klingons on Star Trek weren't ones for small talk. She figured such an approach was appropriate here.

The detectives took another moment to survey the couple.

"What we have to tell you isn't public knowledge yet," Joseph said, "but give it time. Do with it what you want."

"It'll be quite the story when it breaks," Hadrian added.

They proceeded to tell Sasha and Christian about the FBI taking over their investigation and forming a new taskforce and about the evidence that led to this development. Sasha and Christian listened, slack-jawed. Despite their mutual love for writing crime, they could not have envisioned this.

"Why are you telling us all this?" Christian asked when they finished.

"A few reasons," Hadrian said. "Obviously, one is the letters Sasha's been getting."

Joseph nodded in agreement.

"We'd also like your help," he added. "Hard as it is to admit, you are one of the foremost authorities on the Mid-Atlantic Slayer."

There was an absolute truth to that statement. Christian kept a blog on the investigation as a teenager, reigniting some interest in the case. Though he'd never authored a book on the serial killer, preferring to write fiction, he'd consulted on two other authors' works on the spree which once paralyzed the region.

"We'd like any notes or anything else you have," Joseph said.

Sasha could see Christian's reluctance.

"Why?" Christian asked.

The detectives exchanged glances.

"We're flying blind here," Hadrian admitted. "Maybe more than before. We want to check every possibility."

"I got most of my information from you guys."

Sasha knew this story. Christian had badgered an Alexandria Police Officer Sawyer, who conducted routine foot patrols in his neighborhood, for weeks. Officer Sawyer finally caved and made some calls, leading a reluctant Detective Holly from a taskforce back then to talk to him. Even from a young age, Christian knew which questions gained the maximum amount of information.

"I need to think about this," Christian said. With this being the biggest break in the case since 2009, he wanted to be prepared for what might come next. Who knew what he could do with this.

The detectives exchanged another glance. They knew they had no grounds to persuade him. After all, they'd admitted they were borderline desperate for a possible lead.

"Could you let us know your decision by the end of the week?" Hadrian asked.

"Sure," Christian agreed.

"And," Joseph added in a firmer tone, "both of you ... be careful. This changes everything and we don't have a handle on who, or what, is out there. Be very, very careful."

* * *

He watched the building from a bench across the street. Once Artie called with Sasha Copeland's address, it was easy to find … just like before. God bless Artie's infamous eversion to reading. The man couldn't name a newspaper if he were being held at gunpoint.

"She sounds familiar," Artie said on the phone after delivering the name and address of the bike registration. "Can't place her though."

He dismissed Artie's speculations and thanked him, wanting the whole matter to be forgotten as soon as possible. He'd waited a few days before going to the building to ensure at least one round of bar-hopping and liquor consumption occurred in his friend's life.

All that was left was how to get into the building, as it seemed anyone without a key needed to be buzzed in by a resident. He was more familiar with penetrating houses and condos, but he wasn't intimidated by this new setting. He'd find a way. If his son could do it, so could he.

He straightened up on the bench as two men emerged from the building. Both were African American, one tall and one stocky. They moved towards what he recognized as an unmarked police cruiser. Detectives.

He didn't bother to speculate why two detectives were in Sasha Copeland's building. The causes were too numerous to quantify. He did wonder if other police personnel loitered around unseen. He would have to conduct more surveillance to be sure before moving to visit Sasha Copeland.

Chapter 15

It took forty-eight hours for the Federal Bureau of Investigation to set up the new taskforce's headquarters in a suite of offices in their Washington field office on 4th Avenue in the northwestern section of the capital. Joseph and Hadrian shared an office with three other detectives, one from the Richmond Police Department and two more from Baltimore City.

"You work the original case?" Joseph asked once he'd acquainted himself with the triple homicide in Charm City.

"No," one of the Baltimore City cops, who'd introduced himself as Daniel Stark, explained. "We got the assignment when your spree got connected to this sicko and our federal friends formed this club."

His partner, Detective Russell Davis, nodded in agreement. Like Hadrian, he was shorter and stocky with reddish-brown hair. Daniel Stark had a Marines haircut framing his thin face. He was the taller of the Baltimore cops, though not as tall as Joseph.

Joseph and Hadrian thought the pair would be all right to work with.

* * *

The man leading the taskforce was Assistant Special Agent in Charge Lloyd Summers. Originally from Annapolis, he made his administrative career in field offices throughout the region as well as Delaware and Pennsylvania. A tall man who could stand to lose ten pounds, he made sure to wear only dark suits. If there were stripes, they were always vertical. He kept his brown hair short and wore elegant frameless glasses.

Everyone met him in an auditorium in another part of the building.

"I thank you all for coming on such short notice," ASAC Summers said, standing in the front of the room. "I know it was indeed short notice and probably caused hailstorms of problems for your departments, but we're hoping that a fast response to these new developments produces positive results."

Getting everyone together for a case that had been cold and inactive for over two decades was an impressive feat. Along with Washington, D.C., investigators from Richmond to Baltimore were appointed to the taskforce in order to clear their own departments' cases. Most were from agencies concentrated in the D.C. Metro area. Representatives from the Maryland and Virginia State Police were also present.

ASAC Summers took a few minutes to recap the Mid-Atlantic Slayer case. Most of the crimes weren't known until 2009, when DNA evidence linked the seventeen murders to forty-one rapes in southern Maryland and northern Virginia and another fifty-seven burglaries. Based on the burglar's modus operandi, authorities estimated he might have committed over a hundred break-ins. During his burglary spree, he masturbated on his victims' beds and stole any loose cash and small valuables. His primary goal seemed to be to acquire women's jewelry, as such items were always taken, regardless of how expensive they looked. None were ever found in pawn shops or similar establishments.

"We believe the burglaries threw off our geographic profile," ASAC Summers admitted. "That may have contributed to his remaining at large."

Acting on the notion that serial offenders started in areas familiar to them, where they felt comfortable, the FBI believed the killer lived in or around Burke, an unincorporated community in Fairfax County, thirty miles south of Washington. That was where his first victims, Lara and Michael Higgins, were murdered. After the discovery of the rapes and fetish burglaries in 2009, the geographic profile now suggested he lived in Prince George's County, where the first quarter of the break-ins were committed. With another nineteen percent having occurred in neighboring Montgomery County, the theory was strengthened.

"Do we know why he stopped?" an investigator from the Maryland State Police asked.

From what they all now knew, the burglaries began approximately fifty years earlier in 1972. The offender evolved to rape in the late seventies and early eighties, committing one assault a month at one point. Lara and

Michael Higgins were killed in 1989, followed by fifteen more victims over the next five years. Some of the rapes overlapped with the murder spree, but neither these victims nor any before them could provide a distinctive description of their attacker. Based on him spending hours with the women he raped, eating their food, exploring their homes, and watching television between assaults, the police surmised he did this in the homes of the people he killed as well. Circumstantial evidence backed up this theory. After raping ten women in Montgomery County, he shifted to targeting couples and making the men watch him during the rapes, though he still sometimes attacked single women.

"We're not sure," ASAC Summers replied. "Of course, all the usual theories have been proposed over the years. Death. Imprisonment. Nothing's ever panned out. And, given what happened in Washington a couple weeks ago, death has become even less likely. Our colleagues in state corrections departments, as well as the Federal Bureau of Prisons, are continuing to investigate recent parolees, but there haven't been any solid leads there either."

The Mid-Atlantic Slayer investigation had remained active long after the final two murders, those of William Conners and Ashley Finley, were committed in 1994. It was the September 11 attacks and the FBI's subsequent shifting of resources to focus on terrorism that put an end to that. Nothing happened until state laboratories, working to clear their backlog, made the discovery of the many more connected cases through CODIS, the national Combined DNA Index System in 2009.

"We have continued to make efforts since that discovery," ASAC Summers said. "More recently, our office has been making use of familial DNA."

A wave of murmurs erupted at this. Many were thinking of how the Golden State Killer, Joseph James DeAngelo, was caught in California.

"We've had to go back six generations," ASAC Summers continued. "We were able to identify fourteen individuals with distant familial connections living in and around this area at the time of the murders. We accomplished this last year and have been working to narrow down that list ever since."

"Gotta be one heck of a family reunion," Daniel Stark remarked and the room erupted in laughter.

Even ASAC Summers smiled, though he soon called for quiet again.

"Let's please focus," he insisted.

The room steadily settled down again.

"Our taskforce will continue running down these leads," he continued. "We are also now the primary investigative body regarding the murders of Washington D.C. Police Officers Michael Nichols and Keith Regis."

He paused. His audience, catching on, also gave the slain officers a moment of silence.

"We are likewise to investigate the current murder spree in which female college students are the victims," ASAC Summers continued after a minute. "I know the FBI's Behavioral Analysis Unit has previously provided Washington detectives with a possible profile of this offender. I will see that you all have this information available to refer to. I would like to invite Metropolitan Police Detectives Joseph Conway and Hadrian Hasselle to speak about their department's prior investigative progress on this case."

He'd earlier met with Joseph and Hadrian alone to let them know this was on his agenda. Reluctant to speak against their new, temporary boss, they agreed to do it and now walked up to the front of the room, their interstate colleagues' eyes on them.

* * *

Sasha and Christian sat at their kitchen table, working on their laptops. Lydon lay on a nearby mat, fast asleep as he wasn't needed for guide work. Sasha and Christian gave up wondering how he slept in the contorted positions he twisted himself into. Today, his head was angled almost ninety degrees while his neck was also turned almost ninety degrees and his body rested against a wall. Somehow, he was breathing deeply, seeming to find comfort while the humans couldn't even find logic.

Wearing earbuds as to not disturb Sasha's progress with his screen reading software, Christian was copying his files about the Mid-Atlantic Slayer onto flash drives. He'd agreed to give the police copies of what he had about the killer. The originals would stay with him.

Sasha was finalizing her article on the new taskforce established to investigate both the Mid-Atlantic Slayer and the DC College Killer. She stared at the second name.

"Ghobe," she said aloud while shaking her head. "I'm still not wild about it."

For one thing, no other media outlets were using it, though no one else had yet come up with a name that did catch on. How had Michelle McNamara made "The Golden State Killer" stick?

"Too bad there's no formula for giving nicknames to serial killers," Sasha remarked.

"That'd probably take the fun out of it," Christian remarked.

Sasha sighed. This wasn't fun.

"What does he use to kill?" Christian queried.

"What do you mean?" Sasha asked.

"How many of these guys have 'caliber' in their name? I'll wager they weren't strangling their victims."

Sasha considered this and then turned her head to double-check that she'd put on the front door's deadbolt and chain.

"He stabs them," she said, turning back to face her fiancée while thinking about the possibility of befalling such a fate. She swallowed.

"Does he use a particular type of knife?" Christian prompted.

Sasha was grateful they were at home. Passersby might find this conversation disturbing.

She opened her Notes file on her One-Drive. She'd managed to talk to a forensics technician at the last scene who'd also been at the first one, the murders of Ellie Stets and Rachael Holden. She'd gotten very lucky as the suspected murder weapon was now a subject of rumors throughout the crime lab and Medical Examiner's Office. It was widely agreed the killer used a KA-BAR, a multi-purpose military knife favored by the U.S. Navy.

"KA-BAR," Sasha muttered under her breath. What to pair that with? The killer stabbed his victims. The KA-BAR Stabber? No, that didn't work. The KA-BAR Slayer? No, she'd be copying too much.

Sasha shut her eyes and pinched the bridge of her nose. She thought about the victims. They were female college students. He preferred redheads, but she wasn't sure what she could do with that. She turned her attention back to the victims' gender. Young women, the apparent demographic for a majority of serial killers. What could she do with that? The College Girl Killer? No.

She thought of the more famous serial killers. Ted Bundy. Richard Ramirez, the Nightstalker. Christopher Wilder. Joel Rifkin, whom the press in New York dubbed "Joel the Ripper" after Jack the Ripper …

Sasha paused. Joel the Ripper. Jack the Ripper. What about … she tried the name out in her head.

The KA-BAR Ripper.

"That works," she said to no one in particular and edited her headline.

OLD AND NEW KILLERS CONNECTED

AUTHORITIES FORM NEW TASKFORCE TO HUNT MIDATLANTIC SLAYER AND KA-BAR RIPPER

Joseph had told her the FBI would be releasing a formal statement that afternoon, announcing the taskforce. Sasha didn't have much time. But she already liked this new name a lot more.

So she reviewed her article one last time and, once satisfied, sent it to Eric and Nancy for final approval and publication. Sure, it might not have been the best idea for her to name the killer herself in the headline with a vague explanation in the article, but someone had to do it.

Finished, she rose to her feet.

"MajQa'," she said, coming around the table and kissing Christian on the cheek. "Thanks."

"Glad to help my gal name a serial killer, I suppose," Christian replied.

* * *

It had been a week since he killed Kristen Donavan, and he was feeling pretty good. All around him, people had been putting up tributes memorializing the young teacher. Before last week, there had been rumors suggesting the unmarried Ms. Donavan was a lesbian. Now, he couldn't walk down a single hallway without running into a student or teacher mourning her.

Their grieving made it easy to build on his supply of pilfered homework papers to save for the police. He made a mental note to get more whiteout.

People didn't mourn Kristen Donavan as much as they feared him. A monster who'd been terrorizing other communities had now violated the safety of their little corner of the world. Their belief they were immune from the depravity was destroyed and they didn't know what to do about it. It was delicious.

Of course, no one realized he was responsible. Why would they? Here he was, walking around with Kristen Donavan's ankle bracelet in his shirt pocket, and they could not fathom he was the one who broke into her house, took complete control, ate her food, watched her TV, and raped her again and again. Yes, the community's fear and lack of awareness were almost as wonderful as the act itself. They just couldn't stop thinking of him.

He was passing a set of large windows that looked out onto the school's front parking lot and the street beyond it. Just then, a beautiful redhead, decked out in running gear, jogged past the property. His glimpse had lasted just a few seconds, but it was enough to know he wanted her. She was athletic, running with ease, and her red hair, secured in a ponytail, looked so enticing. He hoped she was one of those women with a fanatic exercise routine. Maybe he could be prepared when she ran by another day. His heart already pounded, excited as he thought about visiting her. He wondered how close she lived to the school. It'd be another nice shock for the community.

* * *

The buzzer rang and Sasha walked over to answer it.

"Hello?"

"It's Julianna," a distorted voice replied.

"Come on up."

Sasha hit a button and resumed setting the table. When someone knocked on the door a few minutes later, she looked through the peephole before unlocking the deadbolt and opening the door for Julianna.

"Hello," the elder woman said, presenting a large plastic Tupperware with a cardboard box balancing on top of it. "I brought cupcakes for dessert."

Considering she'd announced her intention to do this, it was no surprise. As Sasha took the Tupperware, Julianna shifted her grip to take hold of the box.

"I can't remember why I separated this from everything else," she fussed, setting the box down on a kitchen chair. "It's all about floral arrangements."

Lydon came over and sniffed the box, though it soon became uninteresting as nothing carried an edible scent. He came over to Julianna, who obliged his desire to be scratched behind his ears.

Christian came out of the bedroom and hugged his mother.

"What were you doing that you couldn't come downstairs and help me lug all this stuff up from my Uber?" Julianna chided. "The driver looked at me with all that as though I were nuts."

Tall and lean, she kept fit. Sasha hadn't seen her struggling at the door and she'd somehow managed to knock and ring the buzzer downstairs.

"Sorry, Mom," Christian said. "I fell behind today."

His hair still looked damp from his shower.

"What big writing project are you working on?" Julianna queried. She'd never been fond of her son's chosen profession, thinking freelance writing was an unstable source for a primary income. But, every so often, she exhibited some curiosity.

"It's more research than writing," Christian said, finding Julianna's box on his chair. "What's this?"

"Information about floral arrangements," Julianna explained.

"And you brought actual flowerpots?" Christian asked, heaving the box onto the floor. He and Julianna sat down as Sasha brought over the pot of tomato sauce and meatballs. She set it down next to the pasta she'd set down just when Julianna arrived.

"So what are you researching?" Julianna asked as they began piling food on their plates.

"My own research," Christian replied. "I'm going over my old notes on the Mid-Atlantic Slayer."

Julianna froze, her fork in mid-air with a piece of meatball and a penne hanging off it.

"The police asked him to provide whatever he could for their new taskforce," Sasha added, though her pride evaporated when she saw Julianna looking stunned.

"You know I never liked that," Julianna said, setting her fork down again. "Even when you did that blog. I still cannot believe they gave all that information to a teenager. What were they thinking?"

She sat, stock-still, in her chair.

"It's not like I'm interviewing anyone," Christian said. "With what happened to those cops, the police and FBI think they might finally have a real chance to catch this guy."

Julianna closed her eyes.

"I just don't like it," she said, each word slow as it came out of her mouth. "I thank heaven you didn't turn out like that monster."

"Mom …" Christian began.

"You don't know what it was like. He seemed to be everywhere. Every time someone felt safe, he struck in their neighborhood. Things changed forever when he was around and it took years after he disappeared for any of us to consider feeling safe again."

She'd lived in Alexandria at the time, working for a defense contractor. Christian and Sasha knew Several of the Mid-Atlantic Slayer's rapes and murders took place close to her. She had a right to be upset.

"I just want to help," Christian said. "If something I've got might lead to his front door, I'd rather try than wonder."

Julianna took a few deep breaths and nodded.

"I suppose I can be proud of you for that," she conceded and picked up her fork again.

They all ate in silence for a few minutes.

"So what are your favorite floral arrangements?" Sasha queried, hoping to break the tension.

Chapter 16

"Did my mom seem off to you last night?" Christian queried as the train pulled away from the station.

"She's just scared and worried all at the same time," Sasha pointed out.

"I suppose."

They were heading out to Fairfax County for another lunch with Christian's father. Spartak's current project, the office building in downtown D.C., was just about done and he already had the next one lined up.

"Well, kind of," he'd clarified on the phone. "I have to go backwards first with the demolition. Then, the construction can begin."

Though he wasn't unfamiliar with demolishing old structures to clear land for his projects, that side of the work didn't interest him. He delegated more than anything else.

It seemed a long-decommissioned school, Longbanks Middle School, was being leveled and a new United States Post Office shipping and sorting facility was being built in its place. It had been a minor news headline the previous year when the federal government's interest in the Groveton property broke the stalemate in the Fairfax County Board of Supervisors over what to do with the obsolete school. It was Spartak's first participation in a project born from a federal contract and he therefore chose to forgo his usual brief hiatus between jobs to travel and refresh.

"It is an exciting opportunity," he'd said. "If I complete this, more might come. I would hate to miss this and hope another one comes just because I wanted some vacation time."

He met the couple at an Italian restaurant not far from the new site, which he'd been surveying that morning. The current patronage seemed light as they entered.

"To stay or to go?," the hostess queried. A sign next to her lectern proclaimed, "Please Wear A Mask If You Are Not Vaccinated". The trio was fine.

"Staying," Sasha replied.

The hostess studied the three of them and Lydon for a moment.

"Have a seat," she said, waiving towards the empty tables and booths. "Someone will be right with you."

With Christian preferring booths, they selected the second one beyond the lectern.

"Under," Christian said, directing Lydon beneath the table. He usually had the dog lie in the space between the central table leg and the wall. Sasha slid in next to Christian while Spartak sat across from them.

"They seem to have a lot of paninis here," Sasha observed, picking up one of the menus the hostess set down in front of them. She began reading the items aloud for Christian's benefit.

Spartak quickly settled on a sub and set his menu down again, waiting for the couple to choose. He smiled at the waitress who came over. The brunette seemed to be a college student.

"Good afternoon," she said. "My name is Darla and I'll be taking care of you today. Can I start you off with something to drink?"

"What beers do you have on tap?" Spartak queried.

"We do not serve alcohol."

Spartak's smile faltered.

"Green tea?" he tried.

Darla nodded.

"Wonderful," Spartak said, his smile returning. "I will have that."

"And for you?" Darla inquired, turning towards Christian and Sasha.

"Sprite," Christian ordered.

"Is Sierra Mist okay?"

"Sure," Christian replied. It made no difference to him.

"I'll have Sweet Tea," Sasha added.

"Great," Darla said, jotting everything down. "Would you like another minute to look over the menu?"

Sasha nodded and she stepped away.

"Let me guess," Sasha said, facing Christian. "You're in a quandary."

"You would be too," Christian retorted. "The Calzone Panini or the Antipasta Panini. How does anybody choose?"

Across the table, Spartak chuckled.

The waitress returned with their drinks and everyone ordered, with Christian settling on the Calzone Panini.

"Thank God," Sasha remarked as the waitress left again.

"How's the storm gonna effect you taking down that school?" Christian queried.

"We are investigating this," Spartak replied. "Officially, we start next week. We will go through the building and remove what can easily be removed first. I suspect we will therefore just secure the structure so that neighboring buildings aren't harmed. Of course, we all hope the storm will change course at the last minute. It has happened."

Hurricane Jackson, now a Category 4 storm, was still moving north through the Atlantic, having not deviated from a single meteorologist's prediction so far.

"Where will you go if it does come here?" Sasha asked.

"I have friends out in West Virginia," Spartak replied. "I will probably go there to wait this out."

Since his home was his personal trailer, most often parked on the construction sites he was tasked with overseeing, relocation was an easy matter for him to accomplish. He could drive all the way to California if he so chose. Christian recalled he'd done so maybe twice.

"What about you two?" Spartak asked. "I hope you do not intend to stay in Washington with the storm."

"We'll probably go up north to Philadelphia or something and hunker down in a hotel room," Christian replied.

"As long as you stay safe. Pozhaluysta."

* * *

He'd found another Auburn Lovely. As eager he was to see her, he knew he had to be careful. With the new taskforce looking for him and his father, it wasn't as easy to move around unnoticed anymore.

The colleges were also beefing up their safety policies. With many local landlords cooperating, campus police officers now swept off-campus buildings where students were known to live. Patrols were increased everywhere with the news reporting that the city and schools were paying up to millions in overtime to have a large-enough force on hand at all times. Everyone was urged to not go anywhere alone and to watch for any strange behavior.

In hindsight, he was lucky to snap this photo of his Auburn Lovely. That one couple was eyeing him as he drove away in his van. But, that was three days ago and the police hadn't broken down his door yet. And, best of all, he'd gotten a good picture, so he could hold on to that until he figured out how to have the real thing.

He had to be smart about this. If he thought it through, he could beat all these precautions and advisories and he would have his Auburn Lovely.

He thought back to when he first learned of his father's activities, now dormant minus the one exception. It was the shoebox. He was fourteen when he stumbled onto it, rummaging through his father's jacket for loose change or, if he was lucky, the old man's wallet. But his father was too that. Of course, he himself was persistent.

So, in looking everywhere, he stumbled onto the shoebox, deep in the back corner of his father's closet. Sure, the closet was small, but the box, standing on its side next to a pair of his father's tall black boots, which he hadn't worn in ages, was easy to overlook.

It was curiosity that prompted him to dig further. A thick rubber band held the box shut. Good thing too as it turned out to be bulging and was beginning to fall apart. He hadn't even recognized the shoe brand stamped onto the lid.

Inside, he found cut-out articles from every conceivable newspaper in the area. The Baltimore Sun. The Washington Post. The Richmond Times-Dispatch. There had to be at least a dozen different sources. Every article was about the rapes and killings. The burglaries never merited a wide-spread response from the press.

Like every resident of the region with a pulse, he'd heard of the Mid-Atlantic Slayer, once also known as the Metro Area Rapist. Seeing the articles brought the case into a new perspective for him. With his father out at a card game that afternoon and evening, he devoured the shoebox's contents, learning everything he could and only stopping to order himself a pizza. He ate said pizza in the closet as he continued his research. It would take additional web perusals before he was certain, but he was already developing the theory this infamous killer was his father. The timeline of all the crimes matched his father's history, or what he knew about it.

When he finished reading everything, he put it all back the way it had been and returned the banded box back to its spot. He didn't know then that the articles were a secondary trophy for his father.

"I wouldn't keep the good stuff here," the old man said the night it all came out between them. "They'd nail me in a second if they saw any of that. So, I make do with what the news says and visit my collection when I can."

He now wondered how many of his father's outings were to visit his collection. He couldn't think of where it was hidden, but he understood the sentimental value. It was just like him and his hair.

He wondered about the hair. He was targeting redheads, just like the old man had done. Was it an unconscious impulse because of what his father did? Or, was it a compulsion they shared?

He'd asked his father about the hair, but that was the one thing the old man refused to answer.

"I've got my reasons," he snapped.

He thought of Susanne. She was a redhead and he'd liked that about her. So, maybe it was a fixation they shared even before he decided to kill. The brain was indeed an odd organ.

* * *

Sitting on the couch, Sasha was channel-surfing when she landed on the news.

"Authorities are continuing to question recent parolees, sex offenders in particular, in an attempt to identify the resurfaced Mid-Atlantic Slayer," the anchor was reporting. "Experts caution this is a risky strategy as it might lead to civil suits against local police and the FBI."

"I don't care about risk," Sasha muttered to no one. "Just catch him. Catch them both."

"In a related story, the taskforce released a statement yesterday, confirming the five college students murdered in the last couple months were most likely killed with the same knife. Forensic experts believe the weapon to be a KA-BAR knife, most commonly used by the military. This has earned the killer the dubious title of the KA-BAR Ripper."

Sasha couldn't help smiling.

"Some victims rights groups have criticized this move to name the offender," the anchor continued. "They say this glorifies the killings and fuels dangerous people already looking for attention. We will have more about this topic with forensic psychiatrist Dr. Hannah Lang after the break."

Frowning, Sasha turned the television off as the first commercial began. She was sure she'd be mentioned in the discussion with the forensic psychiatrist, but she didn't want to hear it. This expert would be sure to have something to say about her own state of mind.

But, they had used the name she'd, in a way, proposed. This one would stick. Sasha rose from the couch to get herself something to drink.

* * *

Under other circumstances, the results from the lab might have been something worth celebrating. But, having forensic proof that the fatal stab wounds inflicted on Ellie Stets, Rachael Holden, Andrea Prady, Jennifer Bison, and Penelope Grant were all most likely made by the same knife didn't change much. The taskforce was no closer to identifying who would have such a common knife. And, it had no impact at all on identifying the Mid-Atlantic Slayer.

There had been a debate about releasing the lab results to the public. Many feared the killer would then dispose of the murder weapon, sure to be the best forensic link to his victims once they identified him. Joseph and Hadrian led the opposing group's opinion.

"He needs that knife," they pointed out. "It's as much a part of his killing ritual as anything. Sure, it might have been easy for him to get, but it is worth so much more to him now. He's not going to get rid of it, especially since it's become a part of his identity."

They all knew he meant Sasha Copeland's Washington Post article, in which she christened him the KA-BAR Ripper. The article, and the name, left them likewise divided.

ASAC Lloyd Summers looked troubled when the Washington Post published the article. It had come ahead of his press conference to make a formal announcement about the new taskforce's creation. The article also revealed a possible link between the Mid-Atlantic Slayer and this new killer, something also meant to be shared in the press conference.

Many thought he'd demand the leaker's name. Joseph and Hadrian feared their time on the taskforce, and maybe their careers, was over. But ASAC Summers only demanded no more leaks.

"All information comes from us when we choose to release it," he said.

The ASAC then agreed that there was more of a potential reward than risk in releasing the lab results about the knife wound and scheduled another press conference. This one went to his satisfaction and the matter of a leak seemed to be forgotten.

After the press conference, ASAC Summers authorized the temporary appointment of more civilian staff from the FBI and Washington D.C. Police Department to manage a new hotline to record tips or potential suspects being reported. Along with tracking possible origins of the KA-BAR knife, detectives on the taskforce spent most of their time following up on these tips. It might have been a good use of their time, if such reported tips led anywhere.

* * *

Adjusting the billfold of his Washington Football Team cap, he entered the post office. It was 12:30, and the place was bustling … a perfect time to mail a package unnoticed.

He stepped up to the end of the line., standing behind a woman who was balancing at least half a dozen different-sized packages.

"You need some help there?" he asked.

"Oh, no thank you," the woman replied.

Good. He'd offered. She'd declined. Now, he'd be invisible to her.

The line advanced foot-by-foot. Finally, the woman stepped towards one of the two manned counters, the tower of packages somehow remaining upright as she moved. One had to question the laws of physics while watching that.

Observing the clerk begin processing each of the packages, he noticed the other clerk stepping away. He considered the implication of this as there was no one standing on his side of the counter.

Focusing on the package processing again, he could tell the clerk had been busy and was becoming frustrated. After a solid ten minutes, he passed a receipt through the gap in his plastic barrier.

"Next," he called as the woman headed for the exit.

He stepped forward, setting his thin package on the counter and pushing it through the gap in the plastic barrier.

"Any liquids, perishables, or hazardous materials?" the clerk asked, studying the address on the front of the bubble mailer.

He shook his head, wondering how he'd even get such items into this thin package.

"Looks like it's light enough for standard shipping," the clerk said.

"Great," he said, paying and leaving. That clerk wanted him gone as fast as he wanted to leave, so it all worked out fine. Sure, mailing this was risky, but it was too much to resist. The taskforce wouldn't see it coming. It was time for a few new moves of his own. He wondered if it was also time to visit his collection again. Maybe he ought to move it.

* * *

Christian sat at the kitchen table, frustrated by Writer's Block. It wasn't for work, but his planned debut novel, "2nd Time Around". He'd neglected the piece for far too long, current events only being the latest distraction. But, as Murphy's Law dictated, when he had the time, he did not have the enthusiasm. In that regard, all was right with the world.

Based on past experiences, he knew if he kept pecking at the keys, some juices might start flowing. He also knew current events didn't help in more ways than one. Though Sasha was in their bedroom, taking a nap, he worried as though she'd gone out. Why couldn't they catch this guy? Would this become another Mid-Atlantic Slayer, uncaught for decades?

He actually had something beyond a rough draft of the first part completed, but it was definitely still rough. Not only did it need serious editing, he also had to figure out how to make it just a little longer. Right now, it was too long for a novella, but too short for a novel.

Bol'shoy, Christian thought, I'm Goldilocks, but there's no third length lying around that's just right.

He groaned in frustration. With Matthew in class, he couldn't even call and pick his brain despite the man's distaste for the criminal side of criminal justice.

He switched to browsing the Internet, seeing if there were any new developments on the case, or cases. He quickly determined there wasn't anything he didn't already know.

He supposed the killer was lying low due to the extra safety precautions and scrutiny being given to college campuses and their immediate surroundings. As for the Mid-Atlantic Slayer, he seemed to have disappeared as fast as he'd resurfaced to kill those cops.

Christian wondered why he did that. Why did he announce his continuing existence while making sure all police resources were directed at identifying him, the killer of two of their own? It was such a strange move.

It couldn't be to get attention. His legacy took care of that. There were still new books and documentaries being made about him and some compared the current spree to his one-man crimewave from almost twenty years ago.

Christian figured this guy had to be pushed into doing what he did. Something, or someone, was in danger and those two police officers were the threat. He doubted it had anything to do with race or anything like that. No, the threat was more personal than a social justice issue. He was in danger, perhaps of being discovered. No, the police were still crawling through that neighborhood to this day, looking for clues. They would have found him if he'd left behind something incriminating.

Maybe he wasn't directly in danger, but if those cops found something else, he then would be.

Christian reasoned the assumption that the officers stumbled onto the KA-BAR Ripper, who was fleeing his most recent crime scene, was correct, even if those officers couldn't have known that. The Mid-Atlantic Slayer would only care about the other killer's capture if they knew about each other. But, the profiles suggested they were of different generations.

Christian's eyes widened. What kind of person did just about anything, including killing police officers, for someone else they knew?

"Evrika!" Christian said aloud, realizing only one type of person would do such a thing. A parent.

Christian jumped to his feet. He needed to talk to Sasha.

Chapter 17

Having been engrossed in a new lab report suggesting a foreign fingerprint was found at the last crime scene, Joseph was startled when his phone chimed and vibrated in his pocket. The other four detectives looked up as he pulled it out.

Seeing it was Sasha, Joseph stepped out into the hallway. The small office, not meant for so many occupants, was stifling and he was glad for this excuse to escape, even if for just a few minutes.

"Hello," he said, answering the call.

"Joe," Sasha said. "It's me."

"I don't have anything new for you."

The new lab report wasn't that exciting, at least not until this fingerprint was linked to someone guilty of these murders. But the lab would first go through the elimination prints collected from Jennifer Bison and Penelope Grant along with friends, family, and other known entities who entered the former's apartment in the weeks before the murders.

"I've got something for you this time," Sasha said.

Now Joseph became more attentive. A reporter giving a cop a lead. What was the world coming to?

"What do you have?" he asked, working not to sound so eager.

"Christian and I think these guys are father and son," Sasha reported. "Why else would the Mid-Atlantic Slayer kill two random cops who just happened to corner the KA-BAR Ripper?"

Joseph felt his hopes deflating. The FBI's profilers had already proposed this possibility and the taskforce considered it a viable theory, following up however they could.

"You wouldn't happen to have names to accompany this theory, would you?" he asked, working to sound upbeat.

"No. But that's something, right?"

"Anything's possible. We'll look into it."

Russell Davis then burst out of the shared office. His head whirled left and right before he spotted Joseph. He looked excited and was holding his own cell phone in his hand.

"I gotta go," Joseph said into the phone. "Thanks."

He hung up before Sasha could say anything else.

"What's up?" he asked his Charm City counterpart.

"Up for a ride to Montgomery County?" Russell asked as Hadrian and Daniel Stark emerged from the office. "There's a package we have to check out."

* * *

"What did he say?" Christian queried as Sasha, seated next to him on their couch, set her phone on the coffee table.

"He said they'd look into it," Sasha replied. "I'm not sure how enthusiastic he was about it."

Christian supposed the police might have come to this same conclusion already. They did have more investigative resources than him. Maybe they'd already ruled out this possibility.

"It's a good idea," Sasha said in an encouraging tone. "I'll write about it."

Christian shrugged, not sure what to make of this compliment. He could write about it himself.

Sasha leaned over and kissed him.

"You know you thinking like that does things to me," she said, her tone turning more sultry. "I like smart guys."

She kissed him again. Seeing this as definite affirmation of his investigative prowess, Christian began kissing her back. With all the stress they'd been enduring, it felt good to just be physical with her like this.

They fell back on the couch, only pausing at random intervals to remove one of their own or each other's articles of clothing.

"Ty velikolepna," Christian moaned, running his hands over Sasha's petit frame as she continued exposing herself.

"Try it in English," Sasha said, pushing down his boxers. "I don't want to think now."

* * *

Their destination was Takoma Park in southern Montgomery County. It was more a Washington suburb than a city as its definition suggested and was once home to four women who were detained and raped by the Mid-Atlantic Slayer. They were lucky enough to live through their ordeal. The detectives knew three had since relocated to other parts of the country.

Mixing partners, the team drove in two unmarked cruisers, with Joseph and Russell leading the way.

"How long have you worked homicides up in Baltimore?" Joseph asked as they turned onto 16th Street.

"As long as I can remember," Russell replied.

"You must have been someone's Golden Boy."

"I suppose."

Joseph nodded. He'd worked in homicide for nine years and was ready to retire. The man next to him seemed to hold a special tolerance for the depravity they all encountered just about every day.

"You volunteer for this assignment?" Joseph asked.

"My lieutenant asked if I wanted it," Russell replied. "Figured it'd look good on my record."

Joseph had to admit being on this taskforce would be a shining finish to his career.

"I heard about this guy almost my whole career," Russell continued. "It's still hard to believe I'm now chasing him."

Joseph detected a note of bitterness in his tone.

"You got kids?" he queried.

"A son and a daughter," Russell replied. "My oldest is fourteen now. You?"

"None."

Joseph had never considered having kids.

"You married?" Russell asked, studying his bare hands.

"Nope," Joseph said with some pride. "Lifelong bachelor."

He'd witnessed too many of his colleagues' marriages fall apart thanks to the job. Even a calm guy like Hadrian was on his second wife. He wouldn't put himself through such a mess.

"I suppose I'm one of the lucky ones," Russell remarked.

"How long have you been married?" Joseph asked with a raised eyebrow.

"Met Heidi when I studied abroad. Married her the summer after I got my B.A. So, circa twenty years."

Joseph whistled, admittedly impressed.

"Hope you make it through this," he remarked.

"Jeg også," Russell agreed.

"What?"

Joseph could not comprehend what the man seated next to him just said.

"Sorry," Russell said. "I've known Norwegian since I met Heidi. I sometimes start speaking it without thinking. I was saying 'me, too'."

The handful of taskforce members from outside the Washington Metropolitan Area were staying in a hotel near the FBI field office rather than endure long commutes which wasted too much time. It was another sign the FBI wanted this case wrapped up sooner than later. The Mid-Atlantic Slayer couldn't have more decades of mysterious infamy.

Joseph laughed at the discovery of this lingual talent.

"That ever come in handy on the job?" he queried.

"Not yet," Russell replied, laughing as well."

Joseph indeed hoped his new colleague's marriage would survive this case. He also hoped that, if he didn't retire right away afterwards, he could take a long holiday, perhaps he'd finally learn to ski.

* * *

The Takoma Park Rape Crisis Center had been operational for almost four decades. Unfortunately, it made sense they'd been targeted.

The director herself was waiting in the lobby when the detectives arrived. Francine Powers was short and stout with graying hair, but her frown made it clear she was not to be underestimated. She might have been happy to receive such a quick and large response, but none of the investigators could be sure.

"It's in my office," she said after introductions were made and credentials inspected.

She led the way through a somewhat confusing maze of corridors. The detectives followed, sometimes walking in single file. A few times, they encountered women who darted away as they passed.

"This has caused quite an uproar for everyone," Francine Powers said. "Since the package wasn't addressed to someone in particular, one of our volunteers opened it. She recognized the contents for what they were and alerted our staff. She's speaking with one of the counselors now."

"We'll need to speak with the volunteer as well," Daniel said.

Francine Powers didn't respond to this as they reached her office. They entered, finding it to be a small space for a director.

"I know this is a delicate matter," Hadrian said, "but did the center treat any of the women who were attacked back in the eighties?"

Even now, this center was the only one in the area, nestled at an equidistant point from two suburban neighborhoods. Three of the victims lived within easy driving distance of its address back in the eighties.

Francine Powers's frown deepened.

"Our clients depend on this being a safe space," she chided. "Confidentiality is a key component in maintaining this."

"We understand that," Russell said. "Let's try it this way. If the center did treat any of these women, it would explain why you received the package."

Francine Powers seemed to consider the suggestion, her facial expression not changing.

"Suppose you are right," she said. "I won't say anything beyond that."

The detectives all conceded to this.

"Can we see the package?" Joseph asked.

Francine Powers waved her hand at the desk in the room. The detectives crowded around it.

The bubble mailer had been opened, maybe with a letter opener. They could see the center's address prominent in the middle of the blue envelope. More interested in the upper-left corner, they studied the return address.

Chad Williams

P.O. Box 000456

Philadelphia, MS 39350

It looked just like the addresses from the files. The Mid-Atlantic Slayer usually selected a random city somewhere in the U.S. and made up a name and P.O. Box number. Sometimes, one or both happened to be valid, but they never correlated with one another. Someone would confirm it with the Postal Service, but everyone suspected this would be the same case here.

Lying next to the bubble mailer were several sheets of paper. Donning rubber gloves, Daniel picked them up as the others looked over his shoulder.

They looked like homework assignment sheets, each with the phrase "I'm back to stay. Let them know." scrawled across the top. One was a set of math projects, probably middle-school level. The other two sheets were questions about "Where the Red Fern Grows".

"My kids hated that book," Daniel remarked.

Russell murmured his agreement as he kept skimming the sheets.

All the questions and problems were answered, though the detectives weren't sure if everything was correct. The name had also been removed, or never written in to begin with. The space was blank-white. The sheets looked generic, so they couldn't readily identify what, if any, school assigned the work.

"Well, that's consistent as well," Daniel said.

Throughout his rape and murder spree, the Mid-Atlantic Slayer mailed such homework sheets to various locations, writing a taunting message across each. Recipients included the police, news outlets, counselors assisting victims of sexual assault … sometimes even his surviving victims. But, like everything else about him, the sheets led nowhere.

"I'll go get some large evidence bags," Hadrian volunteered, being the closest to the door. He stepped out of the office.

The team hoped the postmark on the bubble mailer might point to an area from where the package was mailed. Even if this had also not panned out in the past, they still needed to try. It had been over twenty years since the last such mailing was received. They needed to follow up on every possible lead.

They also intended to have the lab examine the sheets. Investigators always suspected identifying information could have been found on such documents, but the Mid-Atlantic Slayer whited such items out and photo-copied the sheets to make anything original undetectable. Maybe the copier's microscopic serial number could be read.

"I doubt he bought his own," Russell reasoned as Hadrian returned, "but if there's a store he frequents, maybe he did it there."

No one could argue with that logic as Daniel packed up the sheets and initialed the envelopes to maintain chain of custody.

* * *

He felt great ... so great. After lying low, he was back inside his Auburn Lovely's apartment. He was back inside his Auburn Lovely.

He hadn't asked his father permission to go out tonight. He wasn't a kid anymore.

After some careful surveillance of his Auburn Lovely's building, a townhouse subdivided into a dozen apartments, he could no longer resist. Her second-floor dwelling faced an overgrown yard surrounded by the loosest definition of a fence he'd ever encountered. And, her small balcony was adjoined by a narrow wooden staircase. Ascending it, he found the lock on the rear door was broken. She was practically inviting him, and who was he to refuse an invitation?

Things only got better from there. After binding his Auburn Lovely and cutting off her clothes, he discovered, upon penetration, she was a virgin. No wonder she'd wailed so much when he positioned her on her couch and opened his pants. He'd never seen anyone cry so much before ... not even Susanne. The cross she wore must have been more than a fashion statement.

"How has no one ridden you?" he asked as he thrust. "God, you are good."

He smiled at the inadvertent religious reference. It had to strike a blow this time.

His excitement led him to again finish too soon. It might be his quickest round ever, but he wouldn't contemplate that possibility.

His Auburn Lovely was trying to say something through the tape over her mouth as he got off her. Her eyes were closed and he wondered if she was praying as tears continued rolling down her flushed cheeks. She was definitely trying to take deep breaths, a task rendered almost impossible thanks to the gag.

The praying unnerved him.

"Stop it," he said.

Avoiding looking up at him, his Auburn Lovely continued praying.

Not wanting to give her the satisfaction, he turned her over on the couch. Like the others, she tried to turn her tear-stained face to see what he was doing. Her eyes widened as she caught a glimpse of his KA-BAR sailing down towards her.

She rived and jerked as he stabbed her again and again. He wondered if she was trying to keep praying in her final moments. But, prayers couldn't help her now.

She soon stopped moving, the air rushing out of her. Blood poured out over her and the couch, dripping onto the floor.

"That's better," he remarked.

Pocketing his KA-BAR, he studied his Auburn Lovely, wondering how to pose her. Her head was turned to the side, her eyes still wide open in shock. He reached over and peeled the tape off her still mouth.

As he removed the tape wrapped around her crossed wrists, he noticed the bookshelf next to her TV. It was half-full and he got an idea.

He pulled his KA-BAR out again and studied the blade, running the tip of his gloved thumb along its edge. Looking at his Auburn Lovely again, he supposed the blade was strong enough.

Leaning over her, he noticed the gold chain for her cross hanging loosely around her neck. He had another idea he could incorporate with the first. This would be his masterpiece.

He set his KA-BAR onto a nearby coffee table. He needed to be gentle as to not damage a vital component of his masterpiece. Pushing her lustrous red hair aside, he found the chain's clasp and released it. Remaining careful, he guided the cross out from underneath her. He took a moment to grope her lifeless breasts, but that was fine. Who was around to judge him for it? They were still firm.

He set the necklace down next to his KA-BAR. Heaving her lifeless body, he flipped his Auburn Lovely face-up on the couch. One of her arms slid off, her hand coming to rest on the woven white and brown rug. Her other hand rested on her stomach, making things easier for him.

He picked up his KA-BAR again. First, he sliced a generous portion of hair from behind his Auburn Lovely's ear for his collection. He paused, studying the room again. Yes, it would take some work, but he could do it. He just wished he could be there when his Auburn Lovely was discovered.

He raised the KA-BAR and moved it down towards his Auburn Lovely's body, ready to work.

Chapter 18

Neither Christian nor Sasha knew what was happening. For the last couple days, they'd found it easier to be more attentive and intimate with one another. They were still keeping up with their work, with Christian making progress on his novel and Sasha submitting her article, suggesting the Mid-Atlantic Slayer and the KA-BAR Ripper might be father and son. According to Nancy and Eric, the feedback was already tremendous in the first twenty-four hours, including a formal statement expressing disapproval of her actions, curtesy of the Metropolitan Police Department and the FBI. And, Sasha's own novel, "The Teacher", was almost ready to hit the printing press.

They lay in bed, thin slivers of sunlight poking through the blinds and slicing over them. Christian tried to remember the last time they'd had sex in the morning, but now, it was time to get up and take care of Lydon.

Sasha followed him, pulling on a bathrobe. They walked into the kitchen. Sasha put on coffee as Christian fed the dog. As Lydon ate, he returned to their bedroom to get dressed to take the dog out.

Filling her first cup, Sasha sat on the couch and turned on the television. As Christian reemerged from their bedroom, she tuned to the news. Her eyes widened as she read the scrolling text.

* * *

He stared at the computer screen. He couldn't remember the last time he felt so horrified. He had to remember he was in a library as he was ready to throw something.

The headline, bold letters that seemed to have been stamped there in front of him for maximum effect, already made things very bad.

D.C. SERIAL KILLERS MIGHT BE FATHER AND SON

Of course, the article was by Sasha Copeland, she having submitted it the previous day. Through some kind of investigation or deduction, she was outlining for her readers the likely relationship between him and his son. She even managed to quote some forensic psychologist in the private sector to back up her assertion.

It was all born from the fact he shot those two cops. Ms. Copeland was speculating he did it to save his son, who was about to be arrested and exposed.

If there were any parental notions behind what he did in that alley, they were on a subconscious level. No, it had been pure self-preservation. Keep his son out of prison … keep himself out of prison. It was about as simple to grasp as two plus two.

Still, Sasha Copeland wasn't grasping it. Problem was, regardless of her flawed reasoning, she was right. And, if she was thinking this, were the police thinking it too? Was that new taskforce closer than he realized?

He cursed under his breath, earning a glare from a passing librarian.

"Sorry," he grumbled in her direction.

He had to think. This required action … a serious response. Except it couldn't look like a reaction. It had to look unlike anything else that was going on. That'd distract the police. He could deliver a red herring and then figure out subsequent steps after that.

Sasha Copeland wasn't the only one who'd done her research. He'd studied her to. According to her Facebook page, she was engaged to a man named Christian Becker. Looking into this man, apparently a successful freelance writer, he stumbled onto a wonderful surprise. Sure, it took a few minutes to recognize the person in the photos thanks to time and ageing, but the connection came. He'd have to figure out how to use it to his advantage.

Bracing himself on his cane, he rose to his feet. Mumbling, he stalked out of the library as it was starting to rain. He'd go after Sasha Copeland soon. But, there was a more pressing matter to deal with tonight.

* * *

"This is getting old," Joseph remarked.

"I think you mean sick," Hadrian offered.

Joseph couldn't disagree.

By now, the taskforce had combined the number of KA-BAR Ripper victims with the number of people killed by the Mid-Atlantic Slayer, including Officers Nichols and Regis. One large bulletin board in their suite of offices displayed all twenty-four photos with names scrawled along the images' bottom edges. Ashley Johnston would join them now.

Half the taskforce was in the UDC junior's small apartment on Connecticut Avenue while the other half canvased throughout the rest of the building and the neighborhood. In Joseph's opinion, the latter half got the better deal.

The young woman's body was laid out on her couch, which was soaked with her blood. One of her hands was glued to her crotch so she looked like she was masturbating. Her other hand was glued to one of her breasts.

The killer had gone further by carving into her thighs, just below her hips. Her right leg bore a cross while the left bore a pentagram, both bloody red.

If that wasn't enough, he'd stabbed her in the chest with a cross from a necklace. The chain hung over the side of her body. The small cross hadn't gone in very deep, but it was deep enough to be able to stand upright between Ashley Johnston's breasts.

"That had to take serious force," one crime scene technician had observed. He and his colleagues were waiting to remove the cross once the body and the scene were fully documented.

To cap off his work, the killer managed to sever Ashley Johnston's head, placing it up in a nearby bookshelf, where it looked down on the rest of her body and the scene. He'd left her eyes wide open and arranged her long, red hair to serve as a nest for her cranium.

A neighbor had noticed Ashley Johnston's door open early that morning and went to investigate. Upon discovering this macabre display, she fainted. Her roommate, hearing the loud thump from across the hall, came running, vomited when she saw the setup, and called 9-1-1. Joseph was ready to puke and pass out himself.

"He's getting bolder," Hadrian offered, looking pale as well.

"How do you mean," a detective from Alexandria queried.

"This had to take time to set up. Probably several hours. He felt confident enough that he'd be left alone all that time to do this."

"Can you even sever a person's head with a KA-BAR?" Joseph asked, addressing a nearby technician from the Medical Examiner's office.

"I suppose it's possible," the tech offered with a shrug. "That's a strong knife. We'll take photos at the autopsy to see if the lab can identify any toolmarks on her spinal cord. It wouldn't have been a clean cut."

In or out of context, that sounded sick.

"How did he get in this time?" Hadrian inquired.

"The back door," another technician offered. "It looks like the lock might have been broken. There aren't any pry marks or anything else to suggest the door was picked or forced. He might have walked right in."

Joseph and Hadrian stepped over to the back door and looked through its window. They could see the balcony and adjoining stairs down to the overgrown yard that gave anyone at least two dozen places to conceal themselves as they approached. The fence beyond didn't look much better. The killer might have been able to stroll right in.

"Her family might have a nice civil case against the landlord," Hadrian suggested.

"Maybe," Joseph muttered, not sure he cared. He wanted this done with. It was getting old.

* * *

He drove through the city, the van's radio tuned to the news. According to his boss, he was finished training his Auburn Lovely and she was on her own now. Good. He could listen to whatever he wanted without raising suspicions.

The news was talking all about the latest murder. It seemed his Auburn Lovely was named Ashley Johnston and she hailed from Chippewa Falls, Wisconsin. He thought about this. A young virgin from a midwestern placed dwarfed by the likes of Washington … it sounded like a cliché.

The news didn't reveal any of the juicy details he'd left behind. Either the police weren't sharing or the radio station thought that too depraved to put on the airwaves. They were all selfish prudes.

He'd have to see what Sasha Copeland wrote about the murder. Her perspective always interested him. And, they were close to where he began killing. It was almost a homecoming for him. It couldn't be considered "full-circle" as he was far from finished.

* * *

Sasha couldn't believe it. Sure, she'd missed crimes before. She was only human. But, she'd missed one of these murders. She'd missed a development in her case.

By now, another Post reporter, Brendan Haynes, had written a basic story on this new murder. It was pedestrian, but he'd gotten it done before she even realized something had happened.

Sasha couldn't recall if she'd ever met Brendan Haynes . She'd started at the Post's Local Crime and Public Safety section in early 2020, just as COVID-19 was developing. She hadn't fully settled into her cubicle when they were all sent home to serve as remote reporters. She was sure she and Brenden were on a Zoom call together at some point, but she couldn't begin to guess what he looked like. And now, he'd beaten her to this scoop, even if she would have handled it better.

She wouldn't blame Christian for this. She'd wanted sex as much as him. She blamed the killer. He put her under house arrest. He caused her stress levels to rise. Now, he'd undermined her efficacy as a journalist. She wanted to catch him just for that.

* * *

Almost as quick as they'd been dispatched to Ashley Johnston's apartment, the taskforce received another development. The unknown print from Jennifer Bison's apartment was linked to a man named Craig Travis. He was a plumber in Arlington, but he'd once been a resident in Virginia's Greensville Correctional Center. His record included a DUI and he was still on parole for two burglary convictions. According to the Virginia Department of Corrections, he was a kitchen trustee who often delivered last meals to Death Row inmates back when the state conducted executions at the prison.

"God only knows what sort of scum he interacted with and what they might have taught him," Daniel Stark commented.

With encouragement from his parole officer, Craig Travis arrived at the FBI's field office and was escorted to an interrogation room. Based on their record in homicide investigations, ASAC Summers chose Joseph and Russell to speak with this suspect.

"You worked in the kitchen while in prison and now you're a plumber," Joseph began when the preliminaries were dealt with and the camera was recording. "How did that happen?"

"You can't call what they did in that kitchen 'cooking'," Craig Travis replied. "My father was a plumber and I used to help him out. Whatever I didn't know, I read about online. My customers have been happy with the outcome so far."

"Self-educated man," Russell remarked. "You're licensed in Virginia?"

"Yeah. My father vouched for me when I got out. It took some time, but the state finally accepted my work from before I got locked up."

"For burglary," Joseph pointed out.

Craig Travis sighed.

"I screwed up," he said. "I was a really dumb kid."

"So you're a changed man?" Russell asked.

"I know it sounds cliché, but yeah. I've been rehabilitated."

Craig Travis took a deep breath.

"Every so often, I grabbed a covered tray and hopped on this golf cart," he described. "A C.O. drove me over to L Building, where they killed those sentenced to die. I walked into this stark room, half of which was a cell. I often never knew the name of whoever was in that cell. There once was a woman in there … Theresa, I think her name was. I set the tray down and took off the cover. They all ordered different things … burgers and fries, pizza, breakfast foods … so many different things. I just walked away after that. I went back later, after the execution was over, to collect the tray. They never said much. Maybe 'hello' or something, but never much. Still, I saw their faces. They were defeated, hours from death, and I never wanted to end up there. That's what it took for me to go straight."

Joseph and Russell exchanged brief glances. They could each tell that the other was wondering how legitimate this story was.

"You're licensed in Washington, D.C., as well?" Russell asked.

"Last year," Craig Travis replied. "I needed more customers. It was another fight, but I won. Even my parole officer vouched for me."

Based on his phone conversation with the haggard-sounding parole officer, Joseph was sure the vouching was based on the fact this felon had no violations on his record and was eighteen months from completing his parole.

"Look," Craig Travis said. "My parole officer said you guys wanted to talk to me about a murder. He said he'd violate me if I didn't cooperate, so I'm here."

Russell picked up a photo of Jennifer Bison.

"You know her?" he asked.

Craig Travis studied the photo for a few seconds.

"She's dead?" he queried.

"Very," Joseph said. "You know her?"

Craig Travis studied the photo again.

"She looks familiar," he said. "Kind of cute. I might have done work for her, but I'd have to check my records. I'd need a name as I don't take snapshots of my clients."

Neither detective was prepared to give him a name.

"She was murdered," Joseph said. "We found your print in her apartment."

"Let me guess," Craig Travis said, his face growing a bit pale. "The bathroom."

The fingerprint had been found on the kitchen counter.

"Not the bathroom," Joseph said. "That would be easily explained."

"I don't just do bathrooms," Craig Travis defended. "Other rooms have pipes and stuff as well. Like I said, I need a name to check my records. Some clients are even nice enough to let me have a drink or something. One old lady once insisted I take a platter of her cookies … chocolate chip and peanut butter. I was ready to refund her after tasting those."

He seemed to be trying to explain the presence of his fingerprint anywhere in the apartment. Joseph and Russell were sure Jennifer hadn't given him cookies, but maybe he'd gotten ideas.

"Where were you on the night of October 4th?" Russell asked.

"Home," Craig Travis replied. "I caught the last of the game."

"Can anyone besides the television vouch for your whereabouts?" Joseph asked.

"I live alone."

Unfortunately, his fingerprint in the kitchen wasn't enough to hold him beyond this interrogation and he hadn't said anything to warrant further investigation. He was a model parolee, so they had nothing to persuade a judge to have him locked up. Best they could do was put him under surveillance until they either got more evidence or a better suspect. ASAC Summers was already working on the arrangements.

"You're free to go," Joseph said, the words tasting bitter as they passed over his tongue.

* * *

It had taken some doing, but he located the redheaded jogger. Without a license plate or something similar to pass to Artie to check in the computers, he had to take a more old-fashioned approach.

Sitting in his cruiser, he waited for her to round the corner on this quiet street. His heart raced in anticipation and it was a struggle to keep his cool. The last thing he wanted to do was draw unwanted attention. He was just out on patrol. Nothing to see here, folks.

The redheaded jogger rounded the corner right on time. His prior glimpses and brief observations told him how punctual she was. This allowed him to time his movements, waiting until she was a few yards past his cruiser. With him tucked away on a side street, she'd probably missed him.

He flipped a switch on his dashboard. His siren emitted a single squawk. Startled, the jogger turned as he pulled out.

"Hey there," he said, exiting the car.

"Hello," the jogger said.

"You new here?" he asked, flashing his badge and putting it away again before she'd be able to read his name.

"I moved here a few weeks ago," she said, looking around and spotting the words stenciled across the side of his cruiser. "Actually, I live over in Alexandria."

He nodded. A few more steps and he'd be able to spit across the county line.

"You're staying safe, right?" he asked. "We can't be too careful."

"I'm fine," she said, sounding annoyed now.

He knew it was time to stop. He'd managed to collect some information he could work with.

"Okay," he said. "Have a good day."

He turned and headed back to his cruiser. Sure, he could have grabbed her and thrown her into the back. He could have arrested her on some bogus charge and taken her to a quiet place to have her.

But there was no fun in that. He wanted to hunt her, to conquer her. He wanted to find her home and be there when she returned one night. Maybe she had a husband or a boyfriend. He hadn't seen a wedding ring, but that didn't always mean anything.

He climbed back into his car. He'd begin the hunt as soon as his shift ended. It was funny to think about how close he actually was to Alexandria ... indeed just about spitting distance.

* * *

He watched the dancers, sipping on his beer. Having checked the club's website, he was waiting for her.

She finally came. A well-endowed redhead wearing a cheerleading uniform with a plunging neckline no school would ever permit.

The music began and the inappropriate neckline was soon a moot issue as the redhead began pulling the uniform off. That was fine with him as she wouldn't be removing her hair, though seeing her breasts wasn't a downside. They'd been under a surgeon's knife, but they looked decent.

The servers in this club didn't take off their clothes, but they did help drum up business for the women who did. He summoned a waitress walking within his general vicinity.

"I'd like a private dance with her," he said, pointing out the almost naked redhead. He hadn't had such success with women in real life, but he could fantasize for a while. Who would suspect any nefarious deeds in relation to him getting a lap dance?

"Sure thing," the waitress replied. "I'll send her over after she finishes her set."

He doubted that would take long. He'd enjoy the redhead for a while. Tomorrow, he'd take care of Sasha Copeland. A man had to have priorities. Plus, he had to wait for his latest package to reach its intended destination. He wished he'd made this discovery earlier, as the shipping would have then been cheaper, but one couldn't have everything. He needed the package to arrive at least on the same day, tomorrow, when he'd visit Sasha Copeland.

The redhead, now clad only in a G-string and heels, finished her routine, gathered her clothes, and left the stage. He could see the waitress getting her attention and smiled in anticipation.

Chapter 19

"With Hurricane Jackson just days away from landfall, Washington Mayor Martin Zayas is urging residents in low-lying areas to evacuate," the news anchor was saying. "No formal order has been given yet, but the mayor's office is continuing to monitor the situation …"

"Come on," Sasha said, exasperated. She didn't need to hear about this. She and Christian already had a plan and would leave in the next couple of days. Right now, she wanted crime reports. What else had she missed.

"I gotta go," Christian said, moving towards the apartment's front door with Lydon, decked out in his guide dog harness, by his side.

"Sure," Sasha said, not turning her attention away from the television. He had an evening class and she might be asleep by the time he got back.

Christian and Lydon left without another word.

As he left, Sasha heard a beeping in her right ear, and then her left. The batteries in her hearing aides were dying. They lasted about two to three days. Her spares were in their bedroom, but she didn't feel like getting them at the moment. So she turned on the television's close captioning.

* * *

Standing across the street, he'd passed the time reliving the lap dance he'd received from the redheaded stripper the night before. True, it made him miss the hunts, but he had to make do. It wasn't like his leg would suddenly get better.

Focusing again, he watched as Christian Becker left the building with his dog. He knew they'd be gone for about four hours. That was plenty of time to get into the building. It was just a matter of finding a beleaguered resident to hoodwink.

* * *

He couldn't believe it. In less than forty-eight hours, he'd found another Auburn Lovely. He quickly snapped a picture and, seeing she and some apparent friends were heading in the direction he had to drive anyway, slowly followed her. Too bad he hadn't chosen to become an Uber driver.

The girls stopped at an intersection. He stopped as well, braking a little too hard. The van emitted an audible squeak as it came to a grinding halt. The driver behind him also braked and then honked before driving around him. There might have also been an obscenity hurled into his vicinity.

Hearing this commotion, a couple of the girls turned, staring straight at him.

"What are you doing?!" one of them, a blonde, asked.

He moved his foot onto the accelerator and pressed down hard. The van squeaked and groaned again as it sped up. They really had to take better care of these things.

He made it through the intersection, seeing the group of girls shrink in his rearview mirror. He'd have to try again another time. He wouldn't give up on his Auburn Lovely.

* * *

"Thanks, Professor Becker," the student said.

Julianna nodded as the young woman backed out of her office. This was the one day of the week where she kept evening office hours. Tonight, she was eager to get them over with.

But, there was a little over an hour to go. With no students waiting outside her door, she dug into the day's mail. A large, blue bubble mailer captured her attention and she pulled it towards her. It was meant for her with American University's address below her name. the postmark indicated it was mailed yesterday by overnight shipping, but she couldn't tell from where. She studied the return address.

Vince Rowel

P.O. Box 000034

Only, TN 37140

Julianna didn't recognize the name or address. A quick search on her phone told her this was a real place. Only was a small unincorporated community in Hickman County, Tennessee. She'd never heard of it and had no clue why someone there would be sending her mail.

Using a letter opener, she slit the envelope open. Inside were several sheets of paper. Pulling them out, she gasped.

It looked like a completed grade-school science assignment, focusing on the human body. There was no name, of a student or a school, but someone besides the person answering the questions had written on it. "I'll pass regards to Sasha" was scrawled across the top of all three pages. She remembered hearing about these sort of sheets a long time ago. The fear of receiving such a packet hadn't entered her mind in years. Now, the fear came crashing back into the forefront.

Julianna trembled. It couldn't be. She had to call … someone, but she couldn't make her hands work to pick up the phone sitting on her desk, right in front of her.

* * *

Sasha stared at her notes, analyzing her revelation and how much weight it held. Ashley Johnston was a waitress at a bar called Kim's, located just off the DCU campus. Christian had once told her it catered to more of an undergraduate crowd and there were plenty of suspicions that people under the age of twenty-one were being served alcohol.

The significant part was that Andrea Prady, the third victim, had held a similar position. She'd been a waitress at a southwestern restaurant called Pparrilla near Gallaudet University. It too was an off-campus hangout for the local student body.

Sasha wasn't sure it was worth mentioning to the police. For one thing, they had to have noticed this already. Also, such servers were often college students, especially when the establishment was near a college campus. With restaurants serving clientele within their walls again, such jobs were becoming available again by the dozens.

A notification popping up on the computer screen interrupted Sasha's train of thought. Someone was at her door. When she and Christian first moved in, they'd installed a wireless transmitter on their front door. It looked and worked like a doorbell. It just didn't make a sound, instead sending a notification to her laptop, phone, and iPad as she was bound to have one near her at any given time. Having not replaced the batteries in her hearing aides yet, this was a prime example of the technology doing its job.

Unfortunately, it also sent a chill up Sasha's spine. Despite the transmitter's existence, people couldn't just walk into the building. They had to be buzzed in.

Another notification popped up on the screen. Whoever was there was trying again.

Sasha rose from her seat. She retrieved a pen and notepad from a kitchen drawer and headed to the door. Looking through the peephole, she could see someone standing in the hallway, holding a large, thin envelope. He wore a Washington Football Team cap and a dark-colored jacket with no logo that she could see.

Sasha wondered what was so important that a delivery man had brought it to her front door. Couldn't whatever was in that envelope be e-mailed? She'd also need to speak with building management. It wasn't the first time a resident let someone in for another resident. But now, the frowned-upon habit was frightening.

Putting on the door's chain, she disengaged the deadbolt and turned the knob.

When she opened the door a few inches, a cane shot through and struck her right in the knee. Sasha's leg buckled as pain surged through her. The pen and notepad fell out of her hand. As she fell over, the cane shot through the gap in the door again, jabbing her in the stomach, hard.

Doubling over, Sasha landed on the floor, groaning. Managing to lift her head, she could kind of see the man through the gap in the door. He looked older and angry, and his cane-wielding arm was coming through, just fitting in the narrow space. She tried to get away, but he was quicker. That was evident when the dark-colored implement came sailing through the air towards her head.

* * *

Leaning against the doorframe, He took deep breaths. Fighting was hard enough, but when one was barred by a chained door and equipped with a bad leg, it was even harder. All things considered, he'd done well.

Recovering, he straightened up again, glad his cane was serving its support role again. He realized he'd been leaning against the button on the door's frame. This confused him until he knocked on the door and got no answer. He recalled reading that Sasha Copeland was deaf. He pushed the button, which allowed him to accomplish what he came to do.

Peering through the gap in the door, he could see Sasha Copeland lying on the floor, a red puddle spreading around her head. She might be dead. Good.

Yes, it would have been easier without the door in the way, but he'd made do. That training never went away. Besides, he never intended to rape Sasha Copeland or anything like that. he just wanted to get her out of the way and keep the police busy with something else for a while. He'd learned that trick when 9/11 took investigators' focus off of him as they instead looked for terrorists all over the world.

It was time to go as his leg ached. Part of him hoped he'd make it home so he could lie down. He'd almost fallen over while using his cane as a weapon, but that didn't happen. Good fortune served him well.

He turned and hobbled down the hallway, holding onto his empty envelope. He'd dispose of it and then take a long nap. He did wonder how a deaf woman and a blind guy could have a relationship. He supposed it no longer mattered.

* * *

Matthew guided Christian down the corridor of Sibley Memorial Hospital, the latter being too distressed to direct Lydon. It was bad enough to arrive home and learn from a neighbor that Sasha had been attacked and was rushed to the hospital, unconscious, but now they couldn't find her in this massive place.

They located the nurse's station in the Emergency Department.

"Can I help you?" a nurse asked, looking at the rain outside the windows beyond the two men.

"M … my … my fiancée," Christian stammered. "She … she's here … some … somewhere."

"Sasha Copeland," Matthew said, taking over. "The paramedics brought her here from 3711 14ᵗʰ Street. She was probably still unconscious."

Christian winced at hearing this.

Turning to her computer, the nurse hit a few keys.

"They're treating her now," she reported. "Are you family?"

"He's the fiancée," Matthew reminded her, gesturing towards Christian.

The nurse nodded.

"I'll need you to wait in the waiting area," she said. "The doctor will come out when they are finished."

She pointed towards a nearby group of chairs. Some side tables between the seats had magazines strewn across them. Matthew wondered who could read in a place like this while a loved one was possibly on the brink of death. The smell of disinfectant made the situation even more sickening.

"Come on," he said, focusing again and taking Christian's arm.

They'd managed to take two steps away from the nurse's station when Detectives Joseph Conway and Hadrian Hasselle burst into the Emergency Department, the whir of an ambulance siren seeming to announce their arrival.

"What happened?" Joseph demanded.

"Sasha was attacked," Christian said, ready to break down. "I don't know what happened. I wasn't there. I wasn't ..."

"We heard about it on our radios when we were heading home," Hadrian explained. "We heard the paramedics were bringing her here and changed course."

"I wasn't there."

Christian's whole body was shaking. Matthew took his arm again and led him to the nearby chairs. The detectives followed.

"We have to ask," Joseph said as Christian sank into the seat. "Where were you tonight?"

Matthew frowned.

"I was in class," Christian said. "I was in class. I wasn't there for her."

"Listen," Hadrian said. "This wasn't your fault. If you'd been there, you might now be here as a patient as well, if not worse."

"Real comforting," Matthew remarked.

The detectives ignored him. This was stuff they had to think about every day, whether someone was close to them or not.

"Listen," Joseph said. "We're going to the scene to see how this happened. Please call us when you know anything. Sasha's as good as one of our own. We'll get whoever did this."

"Got a card?" Matthew queried.

Joseph handed him a business card.

"My cell number's on the back," he said. "Please call us."

As the detectives left, Matthew pocketed the card and sat down next to Christian.

"They're right, you know," he said. "This isn't your fault. I know that doesn't really mean anything right now, but it's true."

Christian began to cry.

* * *

Julianna burst into the Emergency Department of Sibley Memorial Hospital. Looking left and right, and left and right again, she spotted Christian and Matthew seated in the waiting area. She dashed over and hugged her son.

"Oh, thank God," she said. "I called you guys and a police officer answered. I then called your cell phone, but you didn't pick up."

Christian couldn't even contemplate how that had happened. He always had his phone on him and he only turned it off when he was in class.

"The officer told me Sasha was brought here," Julianna continued. "I was so worried you might be ... well ..."

She couldn't figure out how to finish that sentence. She also couldn't figure out how to describe receiving the blue bubble mailer, seeing its contents, and calling him and Sasha over and over again. What she would have said if they'd answered, she didn't know. It didn't matter now.

"Do you know anything about Sasha?" she asked. "How is she?"

"I don't know," Christian replied. "They're still working on her."

Julianna felt tears rolling down her own face. How could this happen? How could it be tied to what happened to her so long ago? Could it be true? How would he have known?

* * *

He groaned as he entered the apartment. It was a struggle, but he'd made it home. Too bad he had to take those detours to get rid of the empty envelope and wipe his cane to remove possible signs of blood. It'd have been easier to just shoot Sasha Copeland, like he'd shot those cops in the alley. But that carried the risk of luring the police right to him.

Despite all that, he made it home. Now, he'd take a leak, take some meds, and crawl into his bed.

Lucas entered the hallway from their kitchen.

"Where were you?" he queried.

"Out," he snapped at his son. He was in no mood for conversation, unless it perhaps had to do with the best way to separate his throbbing leg from the rest of his body. It wasn't like they had a detailed conversation about one another's whereabouts whenever Lucas went out at night.

"You okay?" his son inquired. It wasn't clear whether he was doing so out of concern or curiosity.

"Yeah," he snapped. "Just get out of my way."

He was tempted to beat the kid with his cane. There would be no door in his way this time.

Instead, he gathered his remaining strength and hobbled towards the bathroom, his son no longer impeding him. Maybe he'd just rest on the toilet. After all, Sasha Copeland and her correct deductions weren't a problem anymore. There was no need to rush.

Chapter 20

Joseph and Hadrian surveyed the scene from the hallway. It had all happened by the apartment's front door, which firefighters had broken down so the paramedics could get to Sasha. Thanks to their efforts, there was no need to get closer and disturb potential evidence.

The official investigator on the case was Detective Jason Sisto from the 2nd District's Burglary Division. Since there were no dead bodies, homicide hadn't been called to the scene.

Joseph and Hadrian knew of Jason Sisto by reputation. He was a competent investigator, though there were rumors he was coasting to his retirement. They wanted better for Sasha, so they'd stay close by. So far, no one seemed to mind. In fact, Jason Sisto wanted to talk to them

"You know the resident, right?" he asked.

"She interned at the station a few years ago," Joseph explained. "She's now a crime reporter over at the post."

"Well, it looks personal. The offender obviously never got into the apartment, but they made the effort to attack with the little gap they had to work with. Someone really wanted to hurt her. Any theories?"

Neither Joseph nor Hadrian had any they felt ready to share. Their minds were of course jumping to the subject of Sasha's current articles. They could see her laptop open on the kitchen table inside the apartment.

"You think someone she wrote about did this?" Jason Sisto queried, following their gazes.

"We're not ruling anything out," Hadrian offered. "Seems like a logical conclusion though."

"You know of anything personal going on in her life? Fights with a boyfriend, maybe?"

"She's got a fiancée," Joseph replied. "He's at the hospital. We spoke with him there."

"What's your take on him?"

"No way. He's genuinely broken up about what happened. He's also got a solid alibi."

Jason Sisto nodded.

"I'll still be talking to him," he said.

Joseph and Hadrian understood. They'd be doing the same thing if this were their case. Maybe there was less substance to those rumors than they thought.

* * *

"Copeland," a woman in scrubs said, coming into the waiting area. "Family of Sasha Copeland?"

Christian, Lydon, Matthew, and Julianna rose from their seats.

"I'm her fiancée," Christian said, having managed to collect himself a bit.

"I'm Dr. Zane," the woman said. "Sasha sustained a tear in her left Lateral collateral ligament in her knee. It isn't serious and she'll need to wear a brace and use crutches for a few weeks while it heals. As for her head injuries, she was very lucky. Had her attacker not been impeded, it would have been a lot worse. She sustained two closed, non-penetrating injuries to her skull. There are signs of a concussion and some swelling, but we won't know the full extent of the damage until she wakes up. While there was plenty of blood loss, natural with head wounds, it isn't alarming. Her body is already replenishing what was lost."

"When will she wake up?" Christian asked, wondering if the answer would be ambiguous.

"We are moving her up to the Intensive Care Unit, where our Neurology Department will monitor her around the clock. The swellings already begun to recede, so I expect she could wake up by tomorrow morning or the day after."

Christian tried to calculate how long he'd have to wait, but he couldn't focus.

"Someone will take you up to see her once she's settled," Dr. Zane said. "As I said, she was extremely lucky."

She stepped away.

"I'll go call your cop friends," Matthew volunteered and stepped away as well.

Christian felt ready to cry again. Sure, the doctor had said Sasha would most likely be okay, but she shouldn't be in this place to begin with.

Julianna put a hand on his shoulder, trying to think of something to say. No wisdom came, in part thanks to what she did not feel ready to disclose.

* * *

"Dad!" Lucas called from their den.

Clutching the bag of chips he'd just pulled out of the cabinet, he went to see what the kid needed.

"What?" he snapped as he entered the den.

His son pointed at the TV, which was showing a car commercial.

"You want me to buy a Crisler?" he asked.

"No," Lucas said, angry. "The news was just on. They said someone attacked a Washington Post reporter named Sasha Copeland in her apartment. What did you do?"

He stared at his son, seeing no reason to get upset.

"She was getting too close," he replied. "You wanna go to prison because some brainy blonde figures out who you are?"

"She didn't know anything," Lucas snapped.

"That just shows you don't know anything. Did you even read her last article?"

"Sure I did."

That he could believe. Lucas wouldn't miss a possible opportunity to admire his own fame.

"Then you know exactly what she figured out," he said.

"So?" Lucas asked, incredulous. "People put out stuff like that all the time now. How many podcasts out there have different theories about you?"

He sighed, wondering how his kin could be such an idiot.

"It doesn't matter if it's a theory, intellectual guesswork, or a psychic vision," he said, exasperated. "Even if it's dumb luck. The point is she was right. Someone only has to be right so many times before the police break down your door with a warrant. And she wasn't just right about you. She was right about you and me. I am not going to prison over that."

He glared at Lucas.

"It's done," he pointed out, gripping the bag of chips even harder. "You gonna report me?"

He turned and left the den. He'd eat the chips in his room.

* * *

Like Joseph and Hadrian, the taskforce felt certain enough that the attack on Sasha Copeland had to do with the articles she'd written on The Mid-Atlantic Slayer and the KA-BAR Ripper. They also took a moment the following morning to celebrate the fact she was expected to survive and recover.

Unfortunately, their day did not improve otherwise. Craig Travis was cleared as a suspect. Unbeknownst to the felonious plumber, a bank diagonally across the street from his apartment building had a camera aimed towards the frontside of his residence. Obtaining the footage, the taskforce saw him arrive home in his plumber's van, enter the building, and not leave again until the next morning, well after Jennifer Bison and Penelope Grant were murdered. While the apartment had a back door, one still had to circle around the structure and emerge on the sidewalk in the front, where they'd also be caught on camera. Craig Travis was nowhere to be seen between his arrival and departure the next morning. He wasn't their killer.

"A rehabilitated man," Daniel Stark snarked. "Who knew."

As for other leads, their best source was the hotline. With the killing of Ashley Johnston, the call volume increased again. People reported their neighbors, ex or current lovers, strange homeless people, and supermarket check-out clerks who leered too much. At least three psychics had called to offer their services and some people suggested that, based on the most recent victim's surname, this was all linked to the JFK assassination.

"We oughtta require people to get full-time, in-office jobs," Daniel suggested. "No way they'd then have time to come up with this stuff."

Joseph couldn't disagree. He feared that, in the volume of useless tips, legitimate information might be overlooked. He'd hate for the KA-BAR Ripper to remain unidentified and gain a legacy equivalent to that of the Mid-Atlantic Slayer.

* * *

It was his day off and he did not want to spend it with his father. So, he returned to Lisa's Pasta Hut, where he'd seen his Auburn Lovely the other day. Given how close the restaurant was to the college campus, she was sure to be a regular. He'd overheard enough students complaining about their school's food over the years.

No one recognized him as he entered, and he was fine with that. He secured a table in the corner for himself and ordered a Mountain Dew and the Ravioli with meat sauce and garlic bread on the side. Taking as much time as he dared, he ate while his eyes swept back and forth across the dining area.

He was pretty sure she wasn't an employee. Sure, it could have been her day off when he saw her, but why would she then come to her workplace with her friends? Off-campus eateries were a dime a dozen around all the colleges in D.C.

He saw someone with long, red hair tied into a ponytail enter the restaurant, but it turned out to be a man. He could not understand what sort of fashion statement the guy was trying to make, but it wasn't working.

With his garlic bread gone and him being down to his last couple of ravioli, he felt relief wash over him when his Auburn Lovely entered the restaurant. She was again accompanied by other girls with less-appealing hair colors. He couldn't recall if these were the same friends who'd been with his Auburn Lovely the other day. Still, he'd be careful. These girls seemed to be heeding the city's advice to not go out alone.

They were getting food to go this time and seemed to have ordered in advance. They were already receiving Styrofoam cartons in plastic bags while one presented her credit card to a cashier.

As the group turned to leave, he put forty dollars beneath the handle of his fork and donned a UDC cap. He rose and followed them out onto the sidewalk. He stopped to retie his shoe, watching them move towards the intersection. The light was red, so he waited.

When the light turned green, he started walking again. They were crossing the street, about a hundred yards ahead of him. He'd just make it across the street as well before the light would change again. There were enough people around to obscure him, should any of the girls look back. Last thing he needed was for one of them to notice him again.

The walk took them all to the end of the next block, where the girls turned left and crossed the street again. He again waited until just before the light changed before he kept following.

Halfway down the next block, the girls turned and entered a building. Seeing the front door had an almost full-length window in it, he picked up the pace. The panel of buttons next to the door told him he couldn't just walk in, but that didn't matter.

Though the glass was fogged, he could still make out the group of girls. His Auburn Lovely was turning left while pulling out a key and sliding it into a lock of a door just down the hall from the front door. He had her.

He jogged to the end of the block so he could grin with glee without drawing suspicion from any of the building's residents. When he was calm again, he walked back.

There was a driveway next to the building, leading to a rear lot he supposed was reserved for the building's residents. Seeing no guard or gate to obstruct him, he walked down this driveway, glancing in through the windows he passed.

He saw them in the third window and ducked down as these windows weren't fogged. They were settling down in the den, their purchased food laid out on the coffee table.

Knowing his presence would look suspicious to anyone coming up or down the driveway, he rose again and hurried away. He knew everything he needed to know and he'd come back tomorrow night with his supplies. He just hoped these girls weren't planning to all sleep over as a part of sticking together for safety.

These concerns were soon replaced by the possibilities of how he could pose his Auburn Lovely this time. So many possibilities. He had to admire his own imagination.

* * *

While Matthew stayed in the ICU's waiting area with Lydon, Julianna led Christian into Sasha's room. The D.C. Police had stationed an officer at the door and they both had to present photo identification before entering.

Part of Sasha's head had been shaved and bandaged. Tubes in her nose provided oxygen and an IV line provided nutrients and medications. An EKG next to the bed emitted a consistent rhythm of beeps.

"It sounds like she's doing okay," Julianna offered as she placed one of Christian's hands on the armrest of a chair by the bed. Another doctor had earlier given them a second positive prognosis. It was consistent with what Dr. Zane had told them.

Christian didn't say anything as he sat down. He stared in Sasha's direction, seeming to keep a vigil over her. Julianna knew this couldn't last. The nurse had only given them fifteen minutes.

She wished there was something she could do or say to help or comfort. But this situation wasn't in a mother's manual, if such a manual even existed. Her mind went back to the bubble mailer and the sheets it contained. They were all hidden in the bottom drawer of her desk in the office and would be destroyed soon enough.

She was not ready to share their existence, having never anticipated having to tell anyone anything before tonight.

* * *

With his cruiser sticking out in Alexandria, a sight that would lead to uncomfortable questions, he used his personal car instead. He put on a D.C. license plate as a precaution.

He knew the redheaded jogger had to live nearby, so just across the county line. Why else would she regularly jog in the area? He just had to drive around, not look suspicious, and watch everyone.

He located a residential neighborhood and drove around through it from 5:00 onwards. He hadn't been able to get the day off, or he'd just look for her around the time she went jogging. It was an odd hour, suggesting she kept odd hours. He wondered where she worked.

* * *

"Spasibo, Christian," Spartak said into his phone. "I am here if you need me. Please let me know if anything happens."

After receiving an update about Sasha, he pocketed his phone and stepped out of his trailer. He needed some air.

He'd known about Christian's existence back when Julianna was pregnant. But neither of them were ready to settle down for different reasons. So Spartak moved on and roamed from construction site to construction site until Christian contacted him a couple years ago. He then stayed in the D.C. area while getting to know his son.

Given their upcoming nuptials, Sasha had become like a daughter to him. Now, she'd been attacked and was in serious condition in the hospital. Spartak was not prepared to be put in this position, but he couldn't do anything about it.

It was cold, but he didn't care. He stared up at the stars, hoping for a suggestion about what he could do now. No answers came.

He turned his gaze towards the school building, which his crew had worked on stripping throughout the day. Even less wisdom emerged from that sight.

He thought it was ironic. He was within jogging distance of Julianna's old home in Alexandria, back when she worked for that defense contractor. She and Christian lived there a little while longer before she moved them into the city. He'd never been sure why she chose to do that. He saw no point in asking now.

Running a hand through his blond hair, he studied the school building. A couple more days and it would be ready for the actual demolition, though that might have to wait until Hurricane Jackson passed through the area. He wondered what he might be able to salvage before then. He sometimes found discarded but decent decorations or furnishings he could keep or resell.

It began to rain and Spartak hurried back to his trailer. Hurricane Jackson was still out on the ocean, but the havoc was already being reeked on the residents of the D.C. Metro area.

* * *

Matthew drove Christian home and accompanied him into the apartment. A new door had been installed and an envelope with new keys lay on the kitchen table. Sasha's laptop was also still there and still open.

"What's on the screen?" Christian queried.

"It's black," Matthew replied. He tapped the trackpad and the log-in screen appeared.

"You wouldn't happen to know her password, would you?" he asked.

"No," Christian replied. He sighed as he sat down at the table.

"You want me to stick around?" Matthew asked, getting himself a soda from the fridge.

Christian didn't know. A police officer had been stationed in the building's lobby in case the assailant tried to return.

"I think I'll be okay," Christian said.

Matthew sat on the couch next to him, not sure about this statement. He opened the can and took a large gulp.

Chapter 21

Joseph sat at his desk, studying photos Jason Sisto had sent him of Sasha's head injuries. They weren't easy to look at … almost as eerie as when he stood in the alley where Officers Keith Regis and Mike Nichols were killed.

He could tell where she'd been struck, the hospital shaving part of her hair off to treat the wounds. She'd definitely been hit twice. Looking closer, he thought the bruises looked long and thin.

Joseph considered the possibilities. The injuries looked too narrow to have been made by a baseball bat. A golf club, maybe? He'd helped canvas the building for possible witnesses. No one reported seeing anyone with a golf club or golf bag. Neighbors did report seeing a delivery guy, a plumber, and another man with an envelope and a cane.

Joseph's eyes widened.

"A cane," he said under his breath.

"What?" Hadrian asked from the next desk over. The others in the office looked up as well.

Joseph slid the photos over for his partner to see.

"What do you think made those wounds?" he asked.

Hadrian picked up one of the snapshots and examined it.

"A golf club," he suggested. "Maybe a narrow pipe?"

Joseph thought back to Craig Travis, the now-exonerated plumber.

"What about a cane?" he suggested.

Hadrian looked at the photo again. He then nodded.

"It's possible," he agreed.

"Well," Joseph said. "Who are we looking for who might now be walking with a cane?"

Hadrian's eyes widened in understanding. Sasha's attacker might very well be the Mid-Atlantic Slayer.

"He's getting worried," Hadrian said.

Joseph nodded with satisfaction. Despite what happened, he enjoyed it when a perp got worried. When they got worried, they made mistakes.

* * *

Sasha woke up early in the morning, about thirty-six hours after arriving at the hospital. By then, she'd been moved to a private room outside the ICU. In the meantime, Christian had gotten somewhere between four and six hours of sleep at home. Matthew promptly drove him to the hospital.

Sasha had been moved out of the ICU to a private room. Another police officer was guarding this door and photo IDs were again required to gain access.

Sasha smiled as the two men entered with Lydon.

"Hey you," she said in a weak voice. If she could manage it, she'd probably have spoken louder.

Christian released a long breath he hadn't realized he'd been holding.

"Hey," he said, moving towards the sound of her voice.

His leg bumped a chair, which seemed to be standing in a similar spot as its counterpart in the ICU room. He reached the bed and hugged her.

"Oh," Sasha said. "My IV. Be careful."

Christian backed away and bumped into the chair again.

"Maybe you should sit down," Matthew suggested from the door.

"Sorry," Christian said.

Sasha paused, reading his lips.

"It's okay," she said. The hug had been welcome.

Christian situated himself and sank into the chair. Lydon settled down at his feet while Matthew disappeared from the doorway.

"Brought you something," he said. He pulled a plastic bag out of his coat pocket and set it on the nightstand. Picking it up, Sasha saw that inside were her hearing aids, along with a pack of spare batteries. Moving as quickly as she could, she replaced the small batteries and slid the hearing aids into her ears. As sound came back to her, she glanced at the notepad on nightstand, which she'd been given to communicate with hospital staff and investigators.

"How did you get them back?" she asked, remembering she'd been wearing the hearing aids the last time she could recall.

"One of the paramedics noticed them when they were putting you on the stretcher," Christian explained. "He collected them in the ambulance and left them with a nurse. She dug a pack of batteries out from somewhere and gave them to me when we were here the other night."

Despite her joy at hearing his voice again, Sasha frowned as the context of the scenario was referenced.

"Are you okay?" Christian asked, now unable to think of anything else to say. What did people say in these situations?

"I'm okay," Sasha said. "Let me tell you … Percocet is good stuff."

"Have the police been here?" Christian asked.

Sasha's smile faltered.

"Yeah," she said. "A detective, Sirus or something, asked me some questions. I wasn't able to give him much. All I could remember is that the guy looked older. He had a cane."

She stared past Christian and out the window. A generic office building was all she had to look at. Of all the structures in D.C., she lamented.

"What floor am I on?" she asked. She wasn't sure why she needed to know.

"The third, I think," Christian told her, not remembering which button Matthew had pressed in the elevator. "What did the doctor say?"

"She was also here," Sasha said. "She thinks I can go home tomorrow or the day after. The swelling's going down."

She touched the bandaged part of her head, her hand trembling.

"I never thought this would happen to me," she said, shifting her gaze to the opposite wall. "He didn't get into the apartment, right?"

Christian shook his head.

"The fire department had to break down the door because the chain was on," he described. "The landlord already had it replaced and is working on getting reimbursed by the city."

"Fast work," Sasha remarked. She thought about how lucky she was to not have been raped. Likewise, her laptop was probably still in the apartment. Given she was sure who had attacked her, she needed to find a way to fight back.

* * *

Making use of the light provided by a nearby streetlight, he made his way back up the driveway. He found the window again. Someone had drawn the curtains shut, so he couldn't see inside this time. Still, he was sure he had the right one.

He pulled out his KA-BAR and set to work. This building was newer, so it took some time. The window opened horizontally, so he had a better idea then just trying to pry it open. He wedged the tip of his KA-BAR between the two plastic frames encasing the glass panels. He moved it up until he felt the obstruction. He jiggled his knife and felt the latch loosen. He pushed upwards again and felt it lift to his will.

He pulled the KA-BAR out and tried the window. It slid aside. He stepped through. The curtains rustled as he entered the apartment, but this didn't seem to cause a stir inside the dwelling.

Keeping the curtains in place to obscure anyone's view from the outside while he worked, he closed the window. He made his way into the den he'd seen earlier and froze.

On the couch lay a large form under a blanket. Stepping closer, he saw it was a man … a large man. He had no idea who this was and would need to deal with him before anything else. But first, he'd look around some more. He needed to know where he'd later find his Auburn Lovely.

He spotted a kitchenette, which was empty, and a hallway beyond it. There were two doors. He tried the first door and discovered a bedroom. The curtains on this room's window were ajar and the moonlight shone onto his Auburn Lovely, fast asleep in the bed in the middle of the room. His heart raced as he anticipated having her, but he made himself focus. He needed to take care of the unexpected factor first.

The other door led into a small bathroom, which was empty. He returned to the den, withdrawing his KA-BAR. He moved towards the couch and the sleeping man.

His leg struck the coffee table and he heard something fall and break. So did the man on the couch. He stirred and groaned.

"Laura?" he asked.

He lunged forward, his knife raised. The man became coherent enough in time to raise his arm. He bellowed as the blade sank into his tricept. Raising his other arm, the man managed to grab him while rising from the couch.

He heard glass crunching as they continued struggling. He also heard the man wince as he likely stepped on the shards without wearing shoes.

He pulled his arm back and thrust forward again. The man had no training as a fighter and he managed to stab him in the abdomen. As his quarry stumbled backwards, he caught sight of his Auburn Lovely coming down the hallway to investigate the noise.

"Ali!" she cried, seeing what was happening.

The man, Ali, turned and spotted her.

"Run!" he cried as he moved forward and stabbed him again. The man wasn't a good fighter, but he was bigger. He had to take advantage of any distraction he could get.

With their struggle blocking her path to the front door, his Auburn Lovely ran back towards her bedroom. Knowing he had to get to her quickly, he thrust two more times. The man weakened and fell, blood continuing to pour from his wounds.

He stabbed his opponent in the chest two more times to be sure he was vanquished. He then hurried to his Auburn Lovely.

She was scrambling to hide beneath her bed when he entered. Her slim frame made it possible for her to just fit beneath the low frame. He reached forward and grabbed her leg. He heard her gasp as he pulled.

He dragged her out and flipped her onto her back. Leaning in close, he pressed his bloody blade against her neck.

"Peek-a-boo," he said with a lecherous grin.

Could her eyes get any wider? She looked so scared. He could hear her hastened breaths.

"Not a word now," he said, setting his backpack down next to her. Pulling out his tape, he had her wrists bound behind her back in less than fifteen seconds.

After gagging her, he peered beneath the bed. She had to have been calling 9-1-1, but he couldn't see a phone down there.

She was a college student living off-campus, perhaps alone most of the time. She had to have a phone.

He inspected the nightstand and realized the lamp, charging station, and a book were in disarray. Checking the narrow gap between the nightstand and her bed, he found the phone. No wonder she hadn't managed to call for help.

"Lookey here," he said, holding up the phone for her to see. Spotting a small fish tank on her dresser, he stepped over and dropped the precious device in the water. The two goldfish scattered at this intrusion on their habitat.

"Now we're all alone," he said, coming back to his Auburn Lovely and placing his hand on her breast. Squeezing her, he realized she wasn't wearing a bra beneath her t-shirt. Good.

"Let's continue," he said, sliding his KA-BAR beneath her shirt.

She whimpered and whined as he cut, baring all she had. Her fear was intoxicating and he felt his breaths quicken in anticipation of the next step.

Then, he stopped, hovering over his naked Auburn Lovely. Noticing something odd, he took a closer look. Beneath her firm breasts and flat stomach, he saw a faint, blonde patch of fuzz.

Blonde? It couldn't be. Moving up, he leaned in close and examined her hairline. Her anxious breathing filled his ears as he spotted them. Blonde roots.

His Auburn Lovely wasn't what she portrayed herself as. She was a liar … a fake … a charlatan. He couldn't believe it.

His mind went back to Susanne and how she'd played with his emotions. Now, this girl was lying to him as well.

Seeing the enraged expression on his face, the girl … the blonde … gasp. She had the gall to be scared?

With a roar, his fist sailed through the air and connected with her collarbone. Tears now streaming down her face, she cried out through the gag as he gave her the beating she so richly deserved.

* * *

With lights and sirens doing their best to clear the late-night traffic, Joseph and Hadrian hurried to the scene. Giving up on Michigan Avenue, they left their car by the curb and ran the last two blocks.

The street in front of the apartment building was blocked off. Joseph counted at least a dozen police cruisers, plus vans and ambulances. Headlights illuminated the dark neighborhood, making it feel almost like daytime. Officers were already moving to neighboring buildings to begin canvasing. The nearby Catholic University of America had locked down its campus, though most of the student body were sure to still be asleep.

Joseph and Hadrian spotted Assistant Special Agent in Charge Lloyd Summers talking to a man in a white shirt , blue pants, and police-issued jacket. This had to be a captain or lieutenant from the local district.

The ASAC's suit looked rumpled, like he too had been called out of bed for this and put on yesterday's attire again. He seemed alert though and gave Joseph and Hadrian a single nod of acknowledgement as they dashed into the building.

Russell Davis and Daniel Stark were standing in the hallway just off the lobby, steering clear of the crime scene technicians who were documenting the long, dark stains on the carpeted floor. Joseph and Hadrian didn't need to guess which apartment was everyone's focus point. They could see the reddish-brown blood on the open, white door.

"What do we have?" Joseph asked.

"We're working on figuring that out," Russell said. "Nobody's sure this was our guy. We might have all gotten out of bed for nothing. Uflaks."

Joseph realized the man had slipped into spouting out some Norwegian again.

"What happened?" he asked, focusing.

"A bartender was on her way home after closing time," Daniel described. "She was walking down the street when she saw a man burst out of the front door of this building. I mean, he flew out of this place like he'd just set the timer on a bomb to go off in the next ten seconds. Anyway, he passes under a streetlight and she sees he is covered in blood. I mean, head to toe. Naturally, she freaks. He keeps running and she calls 9-1-1. Of course, it was easy for the first responding officers to follow his trail back to this apartment. Let's say we know where the blood came from."

"Did anyone find him?" Hadrian asked. He wondered if this case might be finished. Maybe he was hoping that was what happened.

"No," Russell said. "He was gone by the time the first officers arrived and the bartender never got a good look at him beyond 'a white guy covered in blood'."

"But you have doubts that it's our guy?" Joseph queried.

"Let's have a look," Russell suggested, nodding towards the apartment.

The four detectives entered and saw the man lying on his side by the couch, dressed in a green t-shirt and boxers. Blood covered his chest, waist, and legs.

"Ali Qazi," Russell said. "Originally from King George, Virginia. A junior at the Catholic University of America. Looks like he put up quite a fight before he died."

Seeing the couch and coffee table in disarray and a shattered beer bottle on the floor, Joseph could agree.

"Why don't you think this is our guy?" he asked. The KA-BAR Ripper had killed other occupants in his primary victims' homes before. It was only a matter of time before he'd encounter a woman with a live-in boyfriend.

"That's in the bedroom," Russell said.

He and Daniel led Joseph and Hadrian down a short hallway to a bedroom. Inside, they could see a young woman lying on the floor, or what was left of her. She seemed to still be bound and gagged with duct tape, but her body was a bloody mess. There was more blood all over the floor and crimson sprays arced across the walls.

Two technicians from the Medical Examiner's Office were in the room with her.

"ID in the purse on the dresser says she's Laura Fields," Daniel reported. "A sophomore at CUA. The building manager says she's the resident of this apartment, having moved in at the beginning of the semester."

"What happened?" Hadrian asked.

"Someone beat her until they couldn't beat her anymore," one of the technicians responded, looking up from the body. "I haven't finished counting how many broken ribs she has. Worst part is she might have still been alive for a few minutes after he was done. Those would have been nothing but pain and agony with no relief to come."

"Was she stabbed?" Joseph asked, wondering how they'd even be able to tell in this mess.

The technician shook his head.

"She was hacked," he described. "It's the sloppiest butchering job I've ever seen, but it took serious rage to do it."

Joseph could see the blatant inconsistencies with their previous scenes. But he wasn't ready to rule this victim out. For one thing, they still needed to know if Laura Fields had been raped. There was no way anyone would find evidence of that here.

"Let's say this was our guy," he proposed. "What about her could have set him off that he beats and then hacks her to death?

No one had an answer.

"He selects these girls at random, most likely based on the color of their hair," Hadrian reminded everyone.

The problem was they still didn't know how the killer found his redheaded victims to begin with. It was there best shot at identifying him. But there lay the possibility he traveled through Washington at random and simply chose his victims as he happened to encounter them.

"Did he shower before he left?" Joseph asked, hoping to find more consistencies with the previous scenes apart from the victim's hair color. He glanced down the hall at the open door to a small bathroom, the sink and half the toilet falling into his line of sight.

"No," Daniel replied. "The shower's dry. And, the bartender saw him fleeing this place covered in blood, remember? That'd be the least effective shower in history. No, it looks like no one used this bathroom apart from the victims. I saw hair of hers in the bristles of a brush, so …"

His eyes widened and he walked into the nearby bathroom. He opened the mirrored cabinet and rummaged for a few seconds. The others watched with curiosity.

"Ah-ha," Daniel soon said in triumph.

He came back into the hallway, holding something.

"Here's his trigger," he said. "Maybe it is our guy after all."

Everyone stared at the bottle of red hair dye he was holding out for them to see.

Chapter 22

"So our guy's a purist," Hadrian mused. "He saw Laura Fields color was a dye job and his rage boiled over, so he went off on her."

He shuddered, remembering the carnage in Laura Fields's bedroom. He also considered the possibility that the female collegiate population of Washington now faced a danger on two fronts. Laura Fields couldn't have been the only one who dyed her hair red, even if some girls were probably now trying to undo this choice in hairstyle. Thank God his daughters weren't into that.

The detectives were standing outside the apartment building, consulting amongst themselves as well as with ASAC Summers and Luke Abrams, the captain of the night watch for the 4th District.

"I've called in helicopters and dog teams," Captain Abrams said. "I'm hoping this prick is still in the area."

The detectives were sure the neighborhood was about to get an early and abrupt awakening, at least those residents who weren't already up and standing behind the barricades set up at each end of the block.

A uniformed officer came running over, holding his radio.

"9-1-1 call just came in from a McDonald's three blocks from here," she reported. "Witnesses reported being held up by a man wearing bloody clothes."

It had to be their guy.

"Do we know if the perp's still there?" Daniel asked.

"They're saying he fled," the officer replied.

"Still," Captain Abrams said, "no one goes in without vests. We've seen what this guy can do with a knife and we have no idea if he has any other weapons."

* * *

After some hasty, impromptu organization, a squadron of six uniformed and armored officers entered the McDonald's and cleared it. When the place was secure, the detectives entered.

The witnesses consisted of two employees, four late-night customers, and an apparent security guard who was pressing a dripping bag of ice against the side of his head.

"What happened?" Joseph asked.

A young man stepped forward. The tag pinned to his gray t-shirt made his role clear.

Adam Evers

Manager

"This guy came in, covered in blood," the young man described, his voice and body shaking. "Before anyone could stop him, he locked himself in the bathroom."

"You call 9-1-1?" Daniel asked.

"Not right away," Adam Evers admitted. "We needed help quicker than that. We called the Wawa down the street. The guard on duty there agreed to come and check this out."

He gestured at the man with the ice pack. Joseph decided not to point out what a stupid idea this was … at least not yet.

"He got here just as the guy came out of the bathroom," Adam Evers recounted. "The guy was holding some sort of knife."

The security guard rose from the table he'd been sitting at and came over, still pressing the melting ice against the side of his head. The detectives noticed the holster on his belt was empty. His nametag read "Officer Chris White". There was no security company name and the logo on his shoulder patch didn't look familiar.

"I tried to disarm the subject," the guard said, picking up the story. "We struggled and he managed to disarm me and get my gun. I thought we were all goners, but he just told us to count back from a hundred. He then left."

"We all did as he said," Adam Evers added. "Then we called the police."

A police officer, still wearing a bulletproof vest, came over.

"We've got bloody clothes in the garbage bin inside the bathroom," he reported. "There's also some blood on the floor."

"Secure that room," Hadrian instructed. "We'll get the crime scene techs down here to get samples for the dogs and to bag everything as evidence."

The units at the nearby apartment building could afford to spare a few techs for this. It was by far the best lead they had.

"Not sure how much the dogs will help," Officer Chris White said. "The guy managed to hail a cab. Not sure how far he might have gotten."

"Any chance anyone caught the name on the cab?" Russell asked.

There was no response. Joseph glanced up, noticing a camera on the ceiling in one corner of the dining area. Could their luck be that good?

"You got those outside as well?" he asked, pointing at the camera.

"Yeah," Adam Evers replied. "Two, I think. But we don't have any footage here. It all gets sent to the owner's home computer."

Joseph's heart rate increased. This was the first time where getting an image of the suspect seemed like a plausible possibility. He wondered what the killer of eight, or maybe more, would look like.

"Call him," he insisted, reasoning they needed to look at the camera's footage first.

* * *

Lying in his bed, he heard Lucas coming home. Things must not have gone well as his son didn't so much enter as storm into their apartment.

The boy went straight to his room, slamming this door as well. He could hear him muttering and cursing through their shared wall. He considered what the neighbors might think and wondered if the police might be summoned. How would he explain this? Thanks to Sasha Copeland's article, he couldn't claim ignorance of his son's activities anymore.

Lucas seemed to settle down after a few minutes, or at least he didn't hear him anymore. He waited a while longer, but he didn't hear any sirens. Sure, if the police suspected anything, they might not announce their arrival, but they would have come charging into the apartment by now.

Relaxing a little, he rested his head back on his pillow and closed his eyes. Maybe it was time to cut his ties and truly disappear once and for all.

* * *

He was at an intersection when he saw her. Across the street, in a medium forest-green Jeep SUV, was the redheaded jogger. He was staring right at her through their windshields. Wearing formal attire instead of her running clothes, she didn't seem to notice or even recognize him.

The light turned green and she drove forward, crossing the street right towards him. He didn't dare make a U-turn to follow her. Instead, he drove straight, watching the back of her SUV in his rearview mirror.

He saw her turn right at the next intersection and disappear. He made an immediate U-turn and headed back the way he'd come. He made the same right turn she did and saw her. Parked on the fourth driveway down was the green Jeep. As he passed it, he saw her getting out. He kept going, again watching her via his rearview mirror. She was walking down her short driveway and checking her mailbox.

He pumped his fist, hitting the roof of his sedan. Regardless of the pain, he was happy. He'd found her. He'd do more surveillance and then he'd visit her.

* * *

As she sat on the edge of her hospital bed, Christian helped Sasha put on the sneakers he'd brought from home. Being granted permission to enter, Matthew came in and scooped up the overnight bag his friend used to supply his fiancée with proper clothes and toiletries for her departure.

"Good thing you grabbed the poncho," he remarked, looking out the window. "It's really coming down out there."

Hurricane Jackson was expected to make landfall in northeastern Virginia within the next forty-eight hours and the wind and rain were intensifying in apparent preparation for this.

"You guys were going to a hotel, right?" Matthew queried.

"Yeah," Christian replied. Their apartment probably wasn't in danger of serious damage or flooding, but they could afford to play it safe, especially after what happened.

Matthew shook his head.

"You guys can just come stay with me and my parents in Philly," he insisted. "I'll have to run back and forth to the Congresswoman's office, but there's plenty of room. Your mom can come too."

Sasha and Christian glanced at one another.

"We'll think about it," Sasha said. "Thanks."

"Please don't think too long," Matthew said. "I'm just about packed and ready to go."

* * *

There was no going back to sleep for anyone on the taskforce. After helping officers canvas the neighboring apartments and businesses at the scene of the murders and the hold-up at the McDonald's, they returned to their headquarters at the FBI's field office. ASAC Summers ordered out for extra coffee and breakfast sandwiches as they began evaluating these new developments.

Most of the victims' friends and family were still asleep, so they didn't have much background yet. A second sweep of the apartment indicated that Ali Qazi was not a regular overnight guest of Laura Fields. The obvious signs, like a second toothbrush in the bathroom and spare clothes stored in a drawer in the bedroom, were absent. It also looked like he'd been sleeping on her couch.

"Lover's spat?" Daniel suggested. "Early in the relationship?"

They needed more information.

Joseph was reviewing Ali Qazi's social media presence, which he seemed to use to exhibit his artwork, when Russell stuck his head in the office door.

"There are some girls downstairs," he reported. "They want to talk to us about Laura Fields. An agent is bringing them up and Daniel's securing an interview room."

Joseph drained the rest of his … he wasn't sure how many cups of coffee he'd drunk since dragging himself out of bed. Chucking the empty cup into a wastepaper basket, he rose and followed Russell out of the office.

* * *

It was three girls, one blonde and two raven-haired. They all looked like college students.

Once they were crowded into the interview room, Joseph and Hadrian took charge.

"You knew Laura Fields?" Hadrian asked.

"She was our friend," one of the raven-haired girls, Courtney, replied. "We all hung out together all the time."

"Was Laura having any issues with anyone?" Joseph asked.

"Just her English professor," the blonde, Traylor, said. "He gave her an unfair grade on her paper. She was fighting to get it changed, but he was being really stubborn about it."

Joseph and Hadrian doubted Laura Fields was murdered over a bad grade.

"Did Laura have a boyfriend?" Hadrian asked.

"No," Traylor replied. "Guys tried to ask her out a lot, but she didn't really date."

"What was her relationship to Ali Qazi?" Joseph inquired.

"They were both from King George," Courtney described. "Ali was a year ahead of her. He looked out for her when she came to CUA. They were friends."

"Why was he sleeping on her couch?"

"To protect her. We've all seen what was going on. We all thought Laura could become a target. She couldn't get the dye out right away, so Ali agreed to sleep on her couch to keep her safe. He was a big guy, so we all thought she'd be safe."

"We should have all stayed with her," the second raven-haired girl, Melissa, added. "We should have stayed with her, or she should have stayed with one of us. She'd still be alive then."

"You don't know that," Hadrian pointed out. He'd seen how determined this killer was.

"Can you think of anything else?" Joseph tried, seeing they were getting nowhere. "Anyone exhibiting strange behavior or paying any unusual attention to Laura? Anything like that?"

The blonde's eyes widened, as did those of one of the raven-haired girls.

"The van," Traylor said.

"What van?" Joseph asked, his interest peaked.

"We were all at Lisa's Pasta Hut the other day," Courtney recounted. "We were leaving and we realized this van was following us. I yelled at him and he sped away."

Joseph and Hadrian looked at one another. They wondered if either Russell or Daniel were having heart palpitations in the adjacent observation room.

"Can you describe the driver?" Joseph asked.

"I didn't see him well," Courtney said. "He was white and I think he had a shaved head. He was wearing a black, brown, or dark-blue jacket and white shirt."

It wasn't much of a description, but Joseph wanted to play on a hunch.

"Excuse me," he said and left the interview room.

He returned a couple minutes later, carrying a manilla folder. He set it on the table in front of the girls and pulled out a photo.

"Is this him?" he asked, showing them a still shot from the McDonald's security cameras. Those cameras hadn't gotten a good look at the cab, but the interior camera got a few clear views of the killer. This image was of the non-bloody variety.

All three girls studied the image. A young man with short, blond hair and brown eyes stared back at them. Those eyes were wide open and his teeth gritted. It was the least-intimidating image available to them and every member of the taskforce now had copies available for an occasion just like this.

"He might be," Courtney said, looking up from the image. "I'm not sure. His van's windshield wasn't very clean and he took off so fast when I confronted him."

Joseph nodded in understanding. It was still the best news he'd gotten this week.

"What about the van?" Hadrian asked. "Could you describe his van?"

"It was blue, but not real dark-blue," Melissa said. "It didn't have any windows in the back, so I guess it's used for deliveries or something."

Joseph and Hadrian felt their own heart palpitations. If the killer chose his victims due to random encounters, tracking him through an employer's vehicle could be by far the best break they'd get.

"Did it say anything?" Hadrian asked. "Did the van have any type of logo on it?"

The girls were all silent, seeming to try and remember.

"I think it had a crossed fork and knife on the side," Traylor said. "It might have had writing as well."

Courtney shut her eyes.

"It said …" she tried. "It said … Rivers Dishes and Cutlery."

* * *

Having decided to take steps to leave the Washington area once and for all, he took the Metro and a cab to his destination.

"You sure you want to come here?" the driver asked, surveying the address he'd provided.

"Yeah," he said. "I'm just feeling a little nostalgic."

"You shouldn't take long. They're tearing this place down. Plus, the hurricane's just about here. I'm bailing as soon as my shift is over."

He nodded. He intended to disappear among the evacuees.

"You gonna be long?" the driver asked.

"No," he said. He just needed to pick up something.

"Ten bucks and I'll wait five minutes," the driver said.

He considered the offer and decided it'd be fine. Groveton was a quiet place. He wasn't sure when or where he'd get another cab.

"Five minutes," he said, handing over a ten-dollar bill.

He entered the building and took the route he knew well. The guidance office had been cleaned out, but he saw his old desk. How kind of them to leave it there. He'd never thought much of them either.

The tall filing cabinet in the corner was also still where he remembered it. One of its drawers was ajar and empty. As a younger man, he'd moved it aside as needed. Now, he reached out with one hand and pulled it over, letting gravity take care of the rest. It fell with a thunderous crash, but he wasn't concerned. Besides him and the cab driver, who else was around to hear it?

He checked the time. He had three minutes left. Stepping forward, he stopped when he heard something.

"Hello?!" someone was calling. "Is anyone in here."

Whoever it was, they were coming closer. They'd stumble onto him soon enough as he couldn't get away quick enough with his cane. If they saw him carrying something, he'd have things he couldn't explain away.

He cast a longing look at the corner once blocked by the filing cabinet.

"Hello?!" the voice called again. The speaker seemed to have an accent.

He turned to leave. Exiting the guidance office, he saw a tall and beefy man coming down the hallway, holding a crowbar in one hand.

"Hey!" the man called in the accent. "What are you doing here?! Stop!"

He whirled around and hurried down the hallway, his cane tapping on the linoleum floor with every step. He turned left and exited the way he'd come. Hearing the man catching up, he moved as fast as he could.

"You okay?" the driver asked as he collapsed onto the cab's backseat.

"Yeah," he said, catching his breath. "I'd like to get back to the station."

The driver shrugged and drove away from the school building as he straightened himself upright in the back. Glancing out the window, he saw the tall and beefy man coming out of the door he'd fled through.

* * *

Cursing under his breath, Spartak watched the car pull away and disappear. He thought it might have been a cab of some kind, but he couldn't be sure. He pulled his phone out of his pocket and dialed.

"I need help," he said when someone answered.

Chapter 23

"We deal in quantity, not quality," the manager, David Ferris, explained as though this fact was a source of pride. He was leading Joseph and Hadrian through the garage/warehouse of Rivers Dishes and Cutlery as he spoke. The location was in southeastern D.C., near the Fairfax County line.

"We're headquartered up in New York, east of Albany," David Ferris continued. "This location made sense thanks to the volume of business we get here. You've got eateries by the dozen around every college in this city. They all need plates, glasses, silverware, etc. These are cheap places for poor college kids, so they don't want to put out too much dough. Enter us. Plenty of plastic plates and everything else to go around. And, since things always break in those hectic places, we're constantly restocking. And, since the pandemic, we've gotten into take-out cartons."

Joseph and Hadrian didn't care about the company's business model. They realized the KA-BAR Ripper must have been finding his victims while making deliveries for Rivers Dishes and Cutlery. Two of the women he killed were waitresses at restaurants who had accounts with this supplier. If they did some digging, they'd find the others were regular patrons at such establishments. Who would have ever thought of the guy delivering new dishes and cutlery in any context, let alone as the perpetrator of a series of brutal rapes and murders?

"So, who did you say you were looking for?" David Ferris asked. He seemed to have forgotten why they'd come.

"Do you recognize this man?" Hadrian asked, showing him the photo of their suspect. It was the same image Laura Fields's friends had been shown that morning.

David Ferris studied the picture.

"I think that's Duncan Ericson," he said. "He's one of our drivers."

"He give you problems on the job?" Joseph asked.

David Ferris considered the question.

"He's middle-of-the-road," he said. "Most of my people are. No one sticks out one way or the other. Like I said, we deal in quantity, not quality."

He thought for a moment.

"He did seem a bit agitated when he came in this morning," he recalled. "I didn't think much of it because he got to work right away. We're buried in orders right now."

Joseph realized the suspect would be agitated considering what happened the night before.

"What'd you say he did?" David Ferris asked, studying his tablet.

They hadn't, and they'd cropped the gun he'd been holding out of the photo before showing it to anyone.

"We need to speak with him," Hadrian said. "Is he working today?"

"He's out making deliveries," David Ferris replied. "All the restaurants are stocking up in anticipation of needing to feed people after the storm."

The detectives wouldn't wait for him to return.

"Can you call him?" Hadrian asked.

"Sure," David Ferris said. "Who can't you call nowadays?"

"Call him," Joseph insisted. "Let him know he forgot some inventory."

* * *

He'd calmed down from the night before. It couldn't be helped now and he didn't want to draw suspicion onto himself. He'd find another Auburn Lovely, though they were beginning to evacuate the city thanks to Hurricane Jackson's immanent arrival. That's why he was making these deliveries. All the restaurants were anticipating having an influx of customers and orders while people waited for their power to be restored. They all needed dishes, cutlery, and take-out cartons.

He supposed he could use this opportunity to move on to somewhere else. He had no special connection to Washington, D.C. He certainly had no love for his father. It'd be easy to pack up and leave.

His phone, in a holder clamped to the van's air-conditioning vent, rang. He swiped the screen to answer it.

"Yeah," he said.

"Duncan," his boss said. "Where are you?"

"On M Street," he replied. "What's up?"

"I need you to come back. There's … You forgot some boxes you need for your run. We have to get everything out as soon as possible and then get this place ready to weather the storm. How soon until you can get back? We need to get this stuff out right away."

He thought for a moment, considering the question and glancing at his manifest. He had three stops left.

"Twenty to twenty-five minutes if I head back now," he replied.

"Great," his boss said. "I appreciate that. Carl will have everything waiting for you by the door."

"Sure."

The call disconnected.

He was not going back to the warehouse. His boss never appreciated him for anything. And, if something was forgotten, he made the drivers continue and then go back out at the end of their runs, all the while complaining how they were bleeding the company.

It was a trap. Somehow, the police knew who he was and they were waiting for him. They were probably also tracing the van. He had to ditch it.

He made a sharp left turn and pulled up the Contacts in his phone. He selected whom he wanted, wondering why she'd given him her number at all.

"Hey," he said when she answered. "Where are you?"

* * *

He wasn't surprised to find the apartment was empty. Lucas was probably at work, clueless as usual. That was fine. A good-bye between them wasn't necessary.

He went into his bedroom and yanked his duffel bag out from under his bed. It was the same bag he'd been issued in the Navy. Old Faithful.

Clearing out his closet and dresser, he tossed the clothes into the bag. Beneath his socks was his old service revolver, a Sig Sauer six-shot revolver, in its holster. He hadn't fired it in years, but he'd maintained it. He clipped the holster to his belt. He dug his second revolver, more recently-fired, out from beneath his mattress and strapped its holster to his left calve.

The two firearms were almost identical. Their primary difference were their significance in his life. One had one body on it. The other had all the others.

He surveyed the small room. In mere minutes, he'd packed everything in his life which ever mattered. He'd have liked to take his treasures, but that wouldn't be so. He couldn't try to go back anymore. That guard, or whoever he was, would be on alert for future intrusions. He had to have called the police. Even if they didn't have time to investigate right now, they'd be on alert.

He zipped his bag shut and was about to pick it up when he got an idea. He went next door to Lucas's room. It looked decent as usual. The boy's laptop was on his small desk, where he always kept it. He grabbed one of the pillows from the bed and leaned his cane against the frame. Putting as much weight as he could on his good leg, he drew his service revolver. Pressing the pillow over the barrel, he fired twice, hearing two soft pops.

Both bullets struck the laptop and continued on into the desk beneath it. Satisfied, he threw the pillow back onto the bed and grabbed his cane. Steadying himself, he holstered his service revolver and left the room.

It'd be a nice red herring for the police. Nothing on that laptop would tell them anything they wouldn't already know. But, his efforts to destroy the device would lead them to think there was something worth looking for. They'd waste their time while he left their jurisdiction behind forever. With the pillow having muffled the gunshots, none of his neighbors would have reason to call 9-1-1 and bring investigators to the apartment earlier than necessary. As for Lucas, he could get a new laptop if he managed to not get himself arrested. All he really used it for was to search for porn featuring redheads.

He returned to his room and heaved his bag over his shoulder. He hobbled back to the front door of the apartment, not looking back.

* * *

Since they'd been packing their things into Matthew's SUV, the trio, plus Lydon, used Sasha's Mini Cooper to drive down to Groveton. Spartak was waiting for them in the parking lot of the condemned school building. It had begun to rain again and he directed them around the building to where his trailer was parked, walking the route back himself. It was tricky helping Sasha maneuver on the slippery terrain, but Christian and Matthew held her arms as she walked on her crutches.

Christian had been inside his father's home on two prior brief occasions. The trailer seemed to be of average size, with a bedroom and airplane-worthy bathroom on one side and an eating/sitting area on the other. A television was mounted on the wall with a couch situated for comfortable viewing. The entrance was in the middle with a counter, stove, sink, refrigerator, a few cabinets, and a microwave across from this entrance. It was anyone's home compressed in order to be able to move on wheels.

"What was so important?" Christian asked once they were all inside and Matthew and Spartak were given proper introductions.

"A few hours ago, there was a man here," Spartak recounted. "I was out back, cleaning up, when I heard a big crash inside the building. I went to see and found a man there. He was hurrying away, but he could not go very fast. He was far enough ahead of me and managed to get to a car and drive away. So, I called the police."

"Are you giving us a news scoop?" Christian asked, incredulous, as Sasha maneuvered on her new crutches so she could sit at the trailer's kitchen table.

"Not entirely. Some men, police officers, came. They looked around and found nothing wrong. I showed them where I saw the man. They said it was probably a prank and left. I was not so sure. The man did not look young, you see. So, I checked where I saw him come out of. It was some offices. I saw the filing cabinet had been knocked over. That is what must have made the loud crashing noise I heard from outside. I went to look closer and I saw the wall. It was strange. It was bent in one corner."

Christian and Sasha couldn't decide if his English was failing him. Matthew didn't know what to think.

"I touched it and discovered it was cardboard," Spartak continued. "Who would make a wall out of cardboard? I pulled it off ... a whole piece of cardboard made to look like the wall and stuck to the real thing with tape. It was hiding something. Someone made a hiding space there. I found this in the hiding space."

He stepped over to a cabinet over the kitchen sink. He lifted out a metal box with a latch.

"I brought it in here in case the man returned to try and get it," he explained.

Christian, Sasha, and Matthew watched as he set it down on the table. Even Lydon looked up from the spot he'd picked to lie down on. The box was a dull gray and measured about eighteen by twelve inches. Two silver latches kept it closed.

"I already looked inside," Spartak said, flipping open the latches. "I do not understand."

The box squeaked as he lifted the hinged lid. They all peered into it and saw jewelry ... various, mismatched jewelry. There were also some hair clips, scrunchies, and one pair of glasses. Christian's eyes widened as Sasha and Matthew began describing the contents.

"Dad," he said, "you said it was an older man, right?"

"Yes," Spartak confirmed. "It looked like he could not walk very well. He had a cane. I could hear it tapping as I went to talk to him."

Sasha was beginning to realize what her fiancée was thinking.

"It can't be," she said, even while staring down at the evidence on the table.

"What?" Matthew asked.

"The Mid-Atlantic Slayer took jewelry or similar items from his female victims," Christian explained. "He did it even when he was only committing rapes. The police always suspected he was keeping this stuff as trophies. It looks like we found his treasure chest."

Matthew backed away, his face pale, until he bumped into Spartak's refrigerator. Spartak also looked a little sick.

"I will call the police again," he said, stepping away.

Sasha pulled out her own phone as well. She was selecting a contact when she froze.

In one corner of the metal box, something silver caught her eye. It wasn't the only silver item in the box, but the small, heart-shaped portion she could see grabbed her attention. She grabbed it with her fingertips and lifted it. It was a chain … with a locket hanging on it. It was a heart-shaped locket.

No one was paying attention to what Sasha was doing. Turning the locket carefully, she gasped when she saw the letters "JB" engraved on the heart. Pictures from the past flashed through her mind … images long stored away in boxes.

"You okay?" Christian asked.

"Yeah," Sasha replied, setting the necklace down again. "Just overwhelmed."

She had no idea how to tell him what she'd just realized. Instead, she picked up her phone again.

* * *

"Det er det," Russell declared, spotting the blue Rivers Dishes and Cutlery van parked in the AMC parking lot. He grabbed his radio.

"Hey, Joseph," he said. "Low-jack paid off. I'm looking at the van."

"You see the driver anywhere?" Joseph asked over the radio.

Parking his unmarked cruiser a few spots away, Russell studied the van. The driver's seat seemed to be empty.

"I don't see anyone," he reported. "We'll approach and let you know what we find."

He and Daniel exited the cruiser and met up with the dozen cops who'd been in the area and responded when he announced his discovery.

"Let's be careful," Russell advised. "This guy may prefer knives, but that doesn't mean he doesn't know how to use a gun."

"His old man might also be hiding out around here," someone pointed out."

Russell grimaced, remembering the circumstances which led to the taskforce's formation.

"Be careful," he repeated.

They spread out and, moving between parked cars, approached the van on all sides. Everyone had their weapons drawn and all reported seeing no one in the front of the van.

Getting closer, Russell noticed the driver's door was ajar.

"Driver's door is open," he reported on his radio.

With Daniel behind him, he approached and nudged the door open.

"Police!" he shouted, springing up with his pistol pointed into the van's cab.

Around him, other officers charged forward, yanking open the passenger side door as well as the rear doors.

The doors turned out to all be unlocked. The van was empty and only a few boxes remained in the back. The key was still in the ignition, all other keys which might have hung on the same ring nowhere to be seen.

"Joseph," Russell said into his radio, "this guy's gone."

"We'll send reinforcements to get a search started in the area," Joseph replied. "Stay safe."

"Copy," Russell said, knowing what else he ought to do. He looked at Daniel.

"Let's see if our borrowed cruiser has any fingerprint-collecting tools," he said.

* * *

After receiving the update from Russell Davis, Joseph and Hadrian confronted David Ferris in his cluttered office adjacent to the garage/warehouse. So far, the manager had proved helpful. But now, their suspect, Duncan Ericson, was missing.

"You tip him off in any way?" Joseph pressed.

"No!" David Ferris defended, sinking into the seat behind his desk. "I swear. I told him to come back for forgotten inventory, just like you told me to do."

"Do you know where he might go?" Hadrian asked. "Someone he might go to for help?"

The address Duncan Ericson provided didn't exist and the bank account where he had his paychecks deposited was linked to a Post Office box under another name. The KA-BAR Ripper was still a ghost.

"I don't know," David Ferris said. "We never made any small talk."

"What about someone else here?" Hadrian queried. "Was there a co-worker he was friendly with?"

David Ferris thought about this.

"Not really," he said after almost a minute. "Maybe the girl he trained."

"What girl?" Joseph asked.

"A new girl who started here a few weeks ago. People come and go here and our drivers just train each other. It's not like they have a hard job."

Joseph felt himself becoming impatient.

"Who's the girl?" he pressed. "What's her name?"

David Ferris checked something on his tablet, his hands sweating.

"Jordan," he said. "Jordan Hunt."

"Where is she?" Hadrian asked.

"She's out driving as well. Like I said, we're slammed with last-minute orders."

"We need to find her," Joseph insisted. "Track the van like you did before. Also call …"

His phone began ringing in his pocket. Yanking it out, he saw it was Sasha. He moved to decline the call, but he answered it instead.

"What?" he snapped, kicking himself for the mistake.

Listening, he nearly dislocated his eyes from their sockets.

"You have what where?" he asked, stunned.

* * *

The receptionist didn't recognize the young man who'd just entered, so she called him over the radio. As he made his way to the front doors, he thought about the redheaded jogger. He was just about ready to visit her.

He was getting more and more excited, having caught his usual glimpse of her through the window a few minutes ago.

He was still grinning when he reached the lobby.

"What's up?" he asked, figuring the issue was a disgruntled parent. The rising rate of divorces brought such people around from time to time.

It was only then that he realized the young punk standing there had drawn a gun from a jacket pocket.

"Drop it!" he shouted as the secretary dove beneath her desk. His training kicking in, he reached for his holster on his belt.

He couldn't believe this was happening. True, he'd been posted here to prevent such an occurrence, but how often did these things happen? If he died, the world would forget about him in no time.

He was drawing his service revolver when the young punk pulled the trigger. The loud bang filled the lobby.

The bullet ripped through his leg and it buckled. He hit the ground hard but managed to keep a grip on his service revolver. Pain shooting through every cell in his body, he still found enough energy to focus. He needed to live and visit the redheaded jogger. He'd been so close.

As his shooter advanced on him to finish the job, he raised his service revolver and fired. Blacking out, he wasn't sure how often he pulled the trigger. He just knew he needed to live.

* * *

He waved as he saw his Auburn Lovely approaching. She pulled the van to the curb and he climbed in. He noticed she was chewing gum again. He'd take care of that first.

"What happened?" she asked. "Where's your van?"

"I had to ditch it," he said. There was no harm in being honest.

She stared at him.

"Ditch it?" she inquired as though she hadn't heard right. "Why would you …"

He pulled out the gun he'd taken from that security guard at the McDonald's. Raising it, he aimed it at her face. He'd save his KA-BAR for later.

His Auburn Lovely gasped as her mind registered this new dynamic between them.

"No more questions," he snarled. "Just drive. Go where I tell you."

"What are you doing?" his Auburn Lovely asked, shocked.

"Just drive. Don't think I won't pull the trigger."

She kept driving, doing as she was told. He pulled the gun away from her head, keeping it in his lap where she could still see it but people outside the van would remain oblivious.

"Why are you doing this?" his Auburn Lovely asked, sounding desperate.

"Make a left here," he directed, pointing through the windshield.

She did as instructed.

"You're smart," he said. "You know why I'm doing this. You've figured out who I am. You know what is going to happen."

His Auburn Lovely began to cry. He smiled. In spite of everything going wrong in his life right then, he was thrilled to be enjoying this moment.

"How you cooperate determines what happens to you," he said, tightening his grip on the gun.

Chapter 24

The average time it took to drive out to the former Longbanks Middle School in Groveton was thirty minutes. With their lights and sirens, and sometimes making use of sidewalks and highway shoulders, Joseph and Hadrian made it in twelve. It wasn't enough time for them to process everything they'd learned. Were all their big breaks coming in a single day?

Christian, Sasha, Lydon, Matthew, and Spartak met the detectives outside of Spartak's trailer. Two cruisers from the Fairfax County Police Department were also waiting at Joseph's request. The rain had let up a little, but it was still coming down.

"Where is it?" Joseph asked.

"Inside," Sasha said, nodding towards the trailer behind her.

"You all touched it?" Hadrian asked.

"I didn't," Matthew quickly replied.

"We'll take elimination prints anyway," Hadrian said with an amused smile.

Spartak and Christian led the detectives into the trailer. The box sat on the table where they'd just left it.

Joseph moved towards the open box. Peering inside, , he froze. This was real. With the Mid-Atlantic Slayer case files having been brought out of storage, he could recognize some of the jewelry and similar keepsakes right away.

"Where did you find it?" he asked.

Spartak again recounted hearing the filing cabinet's crash, encountering the intruder, and finding the hiding place. It turned out one of the responding Fairfax County Police cruisers had been there earlier when he'd called 9-1-1.

"We'll need to see that hiding place," Hadrian said.

Spartak nodded.

"Where are you staying during the storm?" Hadrian asked as Joseph went back outside to consult with their Fairfax County counterparts. They had to see about getting some crime scene technicians to the former school. It was slated to be demolished, if the storm didn't do the job first.

"I will drive west until the storm passes," Spartak replied.

"You'll come back?" Hadrian asked.

Spartak nodded again.

"Of course," he said. "My work is here. My son is here. I will return."

* * *

Unable to stand anymore, Sasha went to sit in her Mini Cooper. It was just a few minutes before someone was knocking on her window. Startled, she looked up to see Joseph standing there, his raincoat being whipped around by the rain-laced wind. She lowered the window, raising her arm to guard against the onslaught of the downpour.

"You okay?" Joseph asked, his voice raised to be heard over the wind.

"Yeah," Sasha said, hoping their conversation would be carried away and people standing a few yards away didn't hear. She eyed Christian, who, with Lydon by his side, was standing by the school building's back doors with Matthew, Spartak, and one of the Fairfax cops, somewhat shielded from the rain.

"Yeah," she said.

"It's overwhelming, isn't it?" Joseph guessed.

You have no idea, Sasha thought. He couldn't guess what she'd seen and deduced.

"Yeah," she said again.

"This is a game-changer," Joseph said. "We might finally get this guy, and you guys made it happen."

His hood was up, so it was hard to tell, but Sasha thought he might be smiling. He didn't have any devastating conclusions interfering in his head.

"When are you heading out?" Joseph asked.

"As soon as we get home and finish loading up," Sasha replied. Her being on crutches hampered the process as she was unavailable for heavy lifting, but Spartak's call downright detoured their plans.

"Good," Joseph said. "It's gonna get nasty here. You're better off staying out of that."

Sasha agreed one hundred percent. Problem was she had to find out something first.

They both noticed a van arriving in the parking lot. Joseph waved and hollered. Sasha wondered if the crime scene techs would hear him over the increasing wind. Despite her efforts to deflect the rain, she and the inside of her car were drenched.

"You'll need to come back out," Joseph said, turning back to look down at her. "They need to take your prints. They'll probably want to set up inside the building where it's dry."

Sasha studied the wet pavement around her, considering how stable her crutches would be on it.

"I'll help keep you upright," Joseph promised, noting her concerned expression.

* * *

Rain poured down Russell's face. But he moved towards this second blue Rivers Dishes and Cutlery delivery van, parked in a far corner of a Costco parking lot. It'd been as easy for the taskforce to track as the first one. They hoped they'd find better results.

They again had the van surrounded, though this parking lot was emptier. This Costco was already shuttered in anticipation of the storm. Russell, with Daniel on his left, could see the dark forms of other officers approaching.

"Police," someone said. They might have been shouting, but the wind carried away most of their verbosity.

Russell and Daniel were five feet from the van when they noticed its rear doors were ajar, being kept from just blowing open by several long pieces of gray duct tape. The wind was certainly trying, buffeting the doors and making the tape pieces look like they were straining to fulfill their responsibility.

Gripping his pistol in one hand, Daniel pulled his pocketknife out of his pants pocket. Flipping out the blade, he raised his arm and sliced through the four thick pieces of tape at once. His movements were almost ninja-like.

The doors flew open, Russell jumping back to avoid being hit.

"Herregud!" he cried.

Up front, some officers got the cab doors open and seemed to find no one there.

Russell and Daniel did find something. Lying among the boxes, covered in blood, was a body.

"Christ!" Daniel cried and jumped into the van.

She was a redhead. She was naked and bleeding badly. Daniel could see shredded remains of her clothes lying among the boxes, some pieces now being blown out.

Daniel couldn't believe it. Their killer, the subject of a manhunt throughout the city, if not the region, actually stopped to attack another woman. He grabbed her arm, hoping he might find a pulse. The KA-BAR Ripper wouldn't have had the time he'd had with his other victims. Maybe he wasn't able to attack with the same level of deadly depravity.

As he touched her arm, the woman turned her head. She opened her mouth and blew a bloody bubble.

"Oh man!" Daniel cried. He whirled around to see Russell standing by the open van doors.

"She's alive!" he shouted to be heard. "Get an ambulance here, now!"

As Russell grabbed his radio, he turned back to the young woman, leaning close to her face.

"Help's on the way," he said. "Hang on."

Staring at her face, he could see she was crying. Beyond her head, he spied a piece of plastic. He reached over and grabbed it before the wind could.

It was a nametag from Rivers Dishes and Cutlery. The young woman was Jordan Hunt, the employee David Ferris identified as a trainee of the man he knew as Duncan Ericson.

He whipped off his jacket and covered her with it, using one hand and a knee to keep the wind from blowing it away. He grabbed her hand again and leaned close.

"Hang on, Jordan," he said. "Come on. Squeeze my hand."

Nothing happened. Jordan Hunt just stared.

"You can do it," Daniel encouraged. "Come on. Just squeeze my hand. Stay with me."

Over the roar of the wind, he heard a faint siren.

"Help's almost here, Jordan!" he called. "Stay with me."

Jordan kept staring as she squeezed his hand.

* * *

Turning and waving his arms to flag down the approaching paramedics, Russell felt his phone vibrating in his pocket.

* * *

Matthew drove Sasha's Mini Cooper back to its spot in hers and Christian's building's parking garage. His Dodge Charger stood in their other reserved spot, Christian never having any use for the space. Now, the SUV was weighed down with everyone's bags and supplies, accounting for the possibility of not being able to return for up to three weeks. Climbing out of the Mini Cooper, Lydon eyed the one and a half giant bags of dog food, visible through one of the SUV's side windows.

"Listen," Sasha said as they surveyed the SUV, "I gotta go take care of something. I should be back in about an hour."

"Are you nuts?" Christian asked. "Even I can tell how bad the rain is getting."

For his part, Matthew was looking back to the garage entrance, where some of said rain was getting in.

Balancing her crutches under her arms, Sasha pulled out her phone and ordered an Uber. She looked up at her fiancée, wishing she could just explain her mission. But she needed to be sure first, and the mission was needed to accomplish that. It was a Catch-22 if she ever encountered one.

"I'll be fine," she said. "I'll be back as soon as I can."

Getting a notification on her phone that an Uber driver accepted her trip and was seven minutes away, she turned and headed towards the garage entrance.

* * *

"Lucas James Stoller," Russell announced, recapping the call and report he'd received from the crime lab regarding the fingerprints he'd collected from the suspect's abandoned van outside the movie theater. "The lab says it's a ten-point match."

With the exception of Daniel, they were back at their headquarters, drying off. Some of the taskforce members were preparing the office for the storm while others continued following up leads. Two FBI agents were ensuring that all information about the case was on the field office's remote back-up drives. The Maryland state troopers were outside, helping the maintenance crew cover all windows with boards while the state police from Virginia helped arrange sandbags. Daniel had accompanied Jordan Hunt in the ambulance to the hospital.

Russell held up a photo of their suspect. It wasn't a mug shot. Joseph guessed he'd gotten it from the DMV, maybe under the "Duncan Ericson" alias. The man looked to be in his late-twenties with short, dark-blond hair and brown eyes. The photo didn't suggest the monstrous acts this ordinary-looking young man had committed.

"Does he have a criminal record?" Hadrian asked.

"Not criminal," Russell replied. "He's in the Armed Forces database."

They all knew the Armed Forces Fingerprint database was linked to the FBI's national Integrated Automated Fingerprint Identification System.

"He was military?" Joseph asked.

"U.S. Marines," Russell said. "Served one tour before receiving a general discharge. We're waiting on more information from the Pentagon."

"Let them know what he's suspected of doing. That might speed things up."

"Do we know anything about his parents?" ASAC Summers queried, joining the group.

"Born to Marilyn Pataki and Christopher Stoller," Russell replied. "We're getting more information on them as well."

They were all thinking the same thing. Was Christopher Stoller the Mid-Atlantic Slayer? Who and where was Marilyn Pataki?

"We'll see if his prints are on file," Joseph promised before ASAC Summers could open his mouth. The metal box of jewelry and other keepsakes taken from the victims was already at the lab.

"I'll update my boss, your Chief, and the mayor," ASAC Summers said. "They'll be thrilled to hear we're looking for two killers in the middle of this storm."

He left the office suite.

"Christopher Stoller has an address in D.C.," Hadrian said, reading something on his computer screen. "We should have enough for a warrant."

"And enough reason to go in with the SWAT team," Joseph added, rising from his seat.

* * *

Lucas Stoller ducked under an awning which was sure to not survive the storm. It wasn't shielding him from the rain now.

The police had to know everything about him by now. They had to have found his father's apartment. In less than an hour, he was homeless and wanted, not to mention outside as a hurricane could be seen from the Virginia and Maryland shorelines.

At least he'd gotten his Auburn Lovely, even if he now knew never to have one in the back of a delivery van again. Even while he was on top, it was a less-than-comfortable experience. The only salvation came from his Auburn Lovely's discomfort and distress. It still felt good to plunge the knife into her afterwards.

He'd get out of Washington. If he was lucky, his building would be leveled by the storm. If he was really lucky, it would take his father with it. He'd find another city and he'd find another Auburn Lovely. He wasn't finished.

But first, he had to find shelter from the storm. Knowing the awning for what seemed to be a florist's shop wouldn't do, he hurried forward.

* * *

Hearing the urgent knocking on her front door, Julianna abandoned her almost-packed suitcase on her bed to answer it. She was surprised to encounter an out-of-breath Sasha standing there.

"Are you all right?" she asked.

"Stairs ... with ... crutches ... are ... interesting," Sasha replied, taking deep breaths. Julianna lived on the third floor of a building that didn't have an elevator.

"Come in," Julianna said. She guided Sasha into her kitchen and into a chair, leaning the crutches against the wall behind her.

"Is everything okay?" she pressed. "I thought you guys left already. What are you doing here?"

She'd declined Christian's relayed offer from Matthew to accompany the group to Philadelphia. She was staying with a friend in Cumberland, an area in western Maryland expected to only endure the very outskirts of Hurricane Jackson. With her friend needing to stay at the prison where she worked to help ensure the security system didn't fail, she'd have the condominium to herself. With everything that happened over the past few weeks, she needed to be alone so she could think.

"What are you doing here?" she tried again, sitting down as well.

Sasha caught her breath and looked at Julianna.

"I found your necklace," she said.

"What necklace?" Julianna asked, confused.

"The silver one with the heart-shaped locket. I saw it in all your yearbook photos, but not in more recent photos. It had your initials carved into it."

Julianna's face became pale with realization. Sasha thought she could see the woman's heart stop beating for a few seconds.

"He took it, didn't he?" she asked.

Julianna didn't speak. It was possible she couldn't speak. All Sasha could hear was the wind and rain pounding against the boards over her kitchen window.

"Ho ... How did you find it?" Julianna asked.

"We found his collection," Sasha explained and launched into the story about Spartak's encounter with the intruder on the site of the old school in Groveton and the subsequent discovery.

"The police will probably know who he is very soon," she said. She'd read about how serial killers cherished their trophies. The Mid-Atlantic Slayer would want to feel his trinkets and wouldn't wear gloves to impede this. Considering his efforts to conceal his treasure, he'd have never anticipated the possibility of someone else finding it, let alone making the connection to his killings.

"He raped you, didn't he?" Sasha asked. She wasn't sure how to ask in a more sensitive manner and she didn't have a lot of time.

Julianna's eyes began to moisten.

"It's not that simple," she said.

"Okay," Sasha conceded. "But is the fact he raped you a part of this?"

Julianna was silent again.

Sasha didn't know what to say. Sure, she was attacked by the same perpetrator, but it was still different. For one thing, she wasn't raped ... not even close. Nevertheless, she tried to find a way to connect with her future mother-in-law.

Julianna released a long breath.

"Yes," she said, her whole face seeming to quiver. "He raped me, and I found out I was pregnant soon after."

Chapter 25

He'd parked his car behind the main building of a gas station about a mile away. Even the clerk would forget about it there. Jumping the fences in order to remain unseen from the streets was becoming tougher thanks to his leg, but he intended to persevere. He wanted to visit the redheaded jogger and no punk with a gun would get in his way. The physical therapist said he was back to normal. This was the ultimate field test of that theory.

He'd already outlived thirteen people and terrorized so many communities. Then came the eighteen-month wait he had to endure thanks to the punk. Tonight, he was back. He could already taste the fear sure to ignite when the redheaded jogger's body was discovered tomorrow.

He reached her condominium. He hadn't been able to prepare a door ahead of time without raising her suspicions, but the lock on her back door was easy enough to overcome. Inside, he took the now-familiar route to the redheaded jogger's bedroom. She always worked late on Tuesday nights and was due home in about an hour. He'd be ready when she arrived, exhausted thanks to working on some big project for the government … those details didn't matter.

The important thing was she was still here. He'd feared she would have moved during the time he was in physical therapy and couldn't surveil her. But, he'd gotten the license plate number of her Jeep and he hadn't needed to use it earlier. Now, Artie was able to confirm she still drove the Jeep and still lived at the same address. It only took a couple trips to refamiliarize himself with her home and he was ready to make his move tonight. Now, all the redheaded jogger needed to do was come home.

* * *

Julianna blinked as the car zipped past her in the opposite lane, its headlights cutting through the dark, suburban night. The long hours were getting to her, but they were almost done. She'd take a long vacation when the final specs were approved. Maybe she and Spartak could take a trip to somewhere in the Caribbean together. She'd had a blast the last time she'd gone, and she could definitely afford it.

Relief swept over her when she reached the intersection with her street. Four more houses and she'd be pulling into her own driveway. It was a lot safer there than nodding off while driving.

She turned right into her driveway and jammed her foot on the brakes. Glad to be home, she didn't care she'd parked her car crooked. She grabbed her purse and got out.

Her legs felt like lead as she struggled up her walkway. Fumbling with her keys, she got the right one into the lock of her front door. Everything around her was dark and still. That's how late it was.

Her house was just as dark and quiet. She'd been meaning to install a timer on her lights to make it look like she was home earlier than what reality dictated.

She shut the front door and felt the cold, metal muzzle of the gun on the back of her neck. She froze as a hand snaked forward and flipped the deadbolt.

"No company tonight?" a voice asked, his lips by her ear. "That's fine. We're all the company we'll need."

Julianna felt her legs go weak. Her whole body swayed.

"Don't try that," he insisted. "Let's go to your bedroom first."

Julianna realized exactly who had gotten into her home. Despite his insistence, she couldn't move. She couldn't believe he'd come back and chosen her.

A hand crept up her back and gripped her neck.

"Let's go," he said, squeezing to emphasize this wasn't a suggestion.

Julianna found herself walking. He led her to her bedroom. It was clear he knew where it was. This wasn't his first time in her home.

They stopped by her bed, where he'd laid out some of her stockings.

"Turn around," he snarled.

She did. He was standing right there. Tall, athletic, blond-haired, and armed. He looked familiar, but Julianna couldn't place his face. Had they met before? He also seemed to be surveying her. It got worse when he grinned.

"Take off your clothes," he said.

Julianna froze again. She'd read about what he did. This instruction came as no surprise. Still, hearing it was shocking. She did not undress for strangers.

He took a step forward so their faces were meager inches apart. He glared down at her.

"Take off your clothes," he repeated. "Now."

He was staring at her necklace, his eyes trailing the silver chain up one side of her neck and back down the other.

Again understanding she had no choice, Julianna reached to her side and pulled down the zipper. Her dress soon hit the floor, something she'd only allowed a few men to be present for in the past.

He licked his lips as she removed her underwear. Surveying her naked body, he gave a nod of apparent approval.

His eyes fell on her necklace again. He stared at her silver locket, now visible as it rested on her sternum. Julianna turned her head to not see this. Her father gave her the necklace before he left for Grenada. Having this psycho seem to admire it was sickening.

"Get on the bed," the man instructed, grabbing the stockings he'd laid out. "On your back."

Her body didn't hesitate to cooperate this time. If she survived this, she'd burn the bed.

When she was lying down, he pulled her arms up towards the headboard. He used the stockings to secure her wrists. To Julianna's shock, he then reached down and straightened out her necklace so her locket was lying on her chest again.

"Don't," she tried.

"Don't what?" he asked. It wasn't clear if he was confused or mocking her.

Setting his gun on her nightstand, he climbed onto the bed and moved over her. Julianna shut her eyes as he put his hands on her.

"Open your eyes," he growled as he molested her.

Drawing in choked breaths, Julianna opened her eyes. Staring up at the man, she thought he might be in a trance as he touched her. His hazel eyes never moved while his hands went everywhere.

"Oh yes," he was muttering under his breath. "Yeah. It's been too long.

Julianna gasped as he forced her legs open and unzipped his pants.

"Sshh," he said, positioning himself.

A sob escaped her throat. She didn't want this.

"Please don't do this," she pleaded as softly as she could.

He pushed into her and began to thrust. Julianna began to cry.

"Quiet," he growled in her face.

He wrapped his hands around her neck and squeezed. Julianna gagged as her lungs soon ached from the depravation of oxygen. She wriggled and rived as her vision grew spotty and then black.

* * *

Oh, yes. Eighteen months and he hadn't lost his touch. The redheaded jogger gasped for air as he choked her. He leaned in close to watch her eyes roll towards the back of her head while her body struggled for life under his weight.

He released her at just the right moment. She gasped for air, taking large gulps of it, as he kept thrusting inside her.

"I'm in charge," he said. "You couldn't stop me if you tried. I always get who I want."

He soon finished with a series of grunts. Oh, yes. It was good to be back at it.

The redheaded jogger lay trembling on the bed as he rose and zipped up his pants. He smiled down at her as he picked up his revolver.

"Rest," he said. "I don't want to hear a sound out of you. Got it?"

She whimpered and nodded, her eyes wet. Still smiling, he left her alone in her bedroom, hitting the light switch as he exited.

* * *

She was alive. He'd ambushed her. He'd raped her. He'd choked her. But she was still alive.

Julianna gave silent thanks for that. She then wondered what would happen next.

She could hear him. He was on the other side of her condo, rummaging through the fridge and kitchen cabinets. After a couple minutes, everything was silent again. Then, her TV came on. He was flipping through the channels before he settled on what sounded like a home-shopping show.

Her whole body ached and she could still feel him in her. Julianna wondered if he still planned to kill her. She knew he stayed a while, but for how long?

She looked at her nightstand, but her alarm clock had been turned so she couldn't see its face. She had no sense of time. How long had the rape lasted? How long had it been since he left the room? When would he leave altogether?

The clock in her head was soon playing tricks on her. She was no longer sure if seconds or hours passed. The only recognizable sound she heard from the rest of the house was the flush of her toilet. How long did that last?

Then, there was a long stretch of silence. Had he left? Her heart raced. He'd warned her to stay quiet. He'd choked her to emphasize his point. Could she risk trying to free herself.

She carefully moved her wrists, testing how secure her bindings were. Her mattress squeaked as she moved.

A light came on and he appeared in the middle of her room. His face looking ghoulish, he moved close to her. What Julianna saw in his expression of glee would haunt her nightmares forever.

"You're making noise," he said, the shadows on his face moving as he spoke.

He pinched her chin between his thumb and forefinger.

"Should I kill you right now?" he asked.

Some shred of logic in Julianna's head told her not to respond. She tried to block out the sight of his face, still very close to her.

"Good," he said in a long, low tone. The light then turned off and he disappeared.

* * *

He chuckled as he moved back into the den of this condo. Her shock at his sudden appearance was intoxicating. He indeed still had it.

He moved back up the hallway and stood outside her bedroom, drinking in the sounds of her shuddering breaths. He wished he could see her naked body quiver, but she'd then see him and the majesty would be ruined.

His leg began to ache. He returned to the den again and sat on the couch. He conceded he'd put his body through a lot tonight. He needed to leave soon to conserve some energy in order to make it back to his car unseen. But, he wanted her one more time, and he still had to kill her.

* * *

Julianna gasped as the bedroom light came on again. He was standing in her doorway.

There were no theatrics this time. He stepped forward and got onto the bed again.

"No," Julianna said. Not again.

He didn't speak as he again unzipped his pants and positioned himself. He stared at her face as he pushed himself inside her a second time.

* * *

His leg ached, but he blocked this out as he had her a second time. The redheaded jogger was worth it.

She gasped, whined, and spluttered beneath him. He wouldn't try choking her again. Plus, he liked these sounds.

She suddenly cried out. He was ready to snap her neck right then when he realized she'd had an orgasm. He missed that too.

He finished and stayed over her, catching his breath. He stared down at her necklace again. It was again askew and he reached down to straighten it. He wasn't sure what possessed him to keep doing this. He'd been with women who wore necklaces before. He'd taken plenty of them. But tonight, he kept feeling compelled to straighten this one out. If nothing else, the redheaded jogger didn't like it, and that was delicious.

He stayed there, one finger still on the necklace.

* * *

Julianna lay still as he straightened her necklace again. She wouldn't dare try to object to him doing this again despite her disdain.

He kept staring at it. Then, his hand moved up and around her neck. Horrified, Julianna realized he found the clasp.

"No!" she cried. "Please don't."

He pulled his hand back and slapped her across the face.

"Shut up," he snapped.

Stunned by the blow, Julianna couldn't move as he reached behind her neck again. He undid the clasp and pulled the necklace off her. He smiled as he saw how upset this made her.

"No!" Julianna cried again.

Her father gave her that necklace before he left for Grenada. It was her strongest tie to him. He couldn't take it.

But he was. He closed his fist around it and left the room.

* * *

He sat on the couch in the den again. His leg was throbbing. He admired the necklace in his hand. It would be a good addition to his collection as the redheaded jogger obviously cherished it.

He could hear her sobbing back in her bedroom. Losing the necklace must be worse than anything else he'd done. Maybe letting her live would make it worse.

The throbbing in his leg lessened again, but he knew it was time to go. Yes, he would let the redheaded jogger live without this precious necklace. He'd let others live before and he was still free. At this point, there was nothing more he wanted to do here. He'd go home and sleep.

* * *

Julianna's sobs finally subsided. She strained to hear anything. She wanted to see him again and get her necklace back.

But there was nothing. She couldn't hear a sound. Was he taunting her again? Would he pull another terrifying routine with his face?

She decided to try freeing herself again. She pulled and tugged at the stocking-made bindings. She could hear her bed squeaking.

He didn't come back. She kept yanking and tugging. She finally heard fabric tearing. He still didn't come.

The stockings kept tearing until her arms fell free. Julianna jumped to her feet, ready to fight in case he was waiting for this. She'd fight for her life and her necklace.

He didn't appear. She was standing in the middle of her bedroom, naked with the remains of the stockings hanging from her wrists.

She burst out into the hallway. It was dark and empty. Becoming oblivious to her nudity, she dashed down to the den. There was nobody there either. The kitchen was likewise empty, though she didn't stay there. There wasn't anything to prevent a neighbor from seeing her through the window, even if it was unlikely that someone besides her was awake now.

He was gone, and so was her necklace. Tears streaming down her face, she walked back to her bathroom. She turned on the water and stepped beneath the shower. She didn't want to think about what to do next. She just wanted to erase the experience from her memory and her body.

* * *

"I never called the police," Julianna confessed to Sasha, who was downright stunned to hear all this. "I've never told anyone until now."

"Why not?" Sasha asked.

They were still sitting in Julianna's kitchen. The rain was still coming down outside as the roaring wind sent it off in every conceivable direction.

"I didn't see it making a difference," Julianna said. "By then, he'd done so much and hurt so many people. The police were nowhere near catching him. I didn't want to go through an exam and repeat what happened over and over again for nothing. I got myself tested for STDs and everything was negative, so that was a relief and another reason to just put it behind me. It was so overwhelming, I didn't even think about the possibility of becoming pregnant until ..."

Her voice trailed off. Sasha didn't want to know, but she had to.

"Christian?" she asked.

Julianna nodded, wiping some tears away.

"Who's his father?" Sasha asked. She didn't want to know, but she had to.

Julianna wiped her eyes again.

"I'm not sure," she admitted. "I was dating Spartak at the time, and we ... you know."

Her sex life alone was an uncomfortable topic to discuss with her future daughter-in-law. Talking about this was almost impossible.

"I don't know for sure," Julianna admitted. "Christian looks like Spartak, but he also looks like ... I don't know if I'm imagining it and I never dared to do a paternity test. I just tried to be his mother. He didn't do anything wrong."

Sasha needed to go.

"Christian and Matthew are waiting for me," she said. "I should go."

She pulled out her phone to request an Uber. Julianna reached out and placed her hand over the screen.

"You'll never get anything now," she insisted, looking determined. "I'll drop you off. You'll need help getting back downstairs anyway."

Chapter 26

Amidst the roaring wind and pounding rain came the sound of a crashing door.

"Police!" the SWAT team members shouted as they executed their entrance into the apartment.

It took less than a minute for the four-man team to go through the apartment's five small rooms and its central hallway.

"Clear."

"Clear."

"Bathroom's clear."

"Clear."

"I gotta get this door!"

"Clear."

"Okay. It's clear."

The apartment was empty and secure.

"Come on up," the team leader said into his radio headset.

* * *

Joseph and Hadrian made their way to the fifth floor of the apartment on 4th Street. Their search was bolstered by the crime lab's recent match of fingerprints on the discovered jewelry which matched Christopher Stoller. They'd identified the Mid-Atlantic Slayer, though the match raised the question why his prints were in the system without an accompanying criminal record.

The detectives entered the apartment. Walking from room to room, they encountered cheap furnishings and sparsely-filled or empty drawers and closets. The residents of this apartment were gone.

"You think they're running together?" Hadrian asked.

"I don't know," Joseph replied. He was prepared to expect anything in this case at this point.

"We ambushed Lucas Stoller," he mused. "He wouldn't have had time to pack, but his father had a chance."

None of the former's co-workers had noticed him loading any personal luggage into the delivery van when he started his last shift. There was also no evidence Lucas Stoller owned a car. The young man was running with nowhere to go and little to carry.

In one of the bedrooms, they found a laptop which someone had shot.

"Let's get this to the lab," Joseph said. "Someone took the time to destroy this. There might be something worth finding."

Hadrian nodded in agreement, noticing a pillow on the bed. Looking closer, he saw the two bullet holes, just centimeters apart and surrounded by dark-gray gunpowder residue.

With an officer keeping this room secure until the crime scene technicians arrived, the detectives moved into the other bedroom. Joseph stepped up to the closet, noticing a jacket which had been left behind. "Eleanor Roosevelt High School" was stenciled across the back of the blue jacket in bold white letters. Dust coating the jacket suggested it hadn't been worn in quite some time. The fact it was still here also spoke to its sentimental value.

"Where's that school?" Joseph wondered out loud as his phone rang. He pulled it out of his pocket.

"Hello?" he asked.

"I'll start with the very bad news," Russell said. "Daniel just called from the hospital. Jordan Hunt died on the operating table."

Joseph cursed under his breath. Couldn't someone encounter Lucas Stoller and live?

Hadrian came over. Joseph slid a single finger across his throat and his partner nodded once, closing his eyes.

"The rest isn't much better," Russell said. "I got some background on Christopher Stoller. You're not going to believe this. He was a cop."

Joseph almost dropped the phone.

"He was a cop?" he asked, not believing it.

Hadrian's eyes widened in shock.

"Yeah," Russell replied over the phone. "Fairfax County Police. He was a School Resource Officer for most of that time, assigned to the now-decommissioned Longbanks Middle School in Groveton."

"That's where we were," Joseph realized. It was where Sasha and the others found the metal box now being examined at the FBI's crime lab in Quantico.

"The information Fairfax Police sent over is pretty bland," Russell said. "Only thing that stands out is a fatal shooting."

"That's really got to stand out," Joseph said, putting Russell on speakerphone so Hadrian could hear.

"Ja, it does. He stopped a school shooting in September 1992. It seems a former student who'd failed in life since came back to get revenge on some teachers. SRO Stoller confronted him in the school lobby. The kid got off one shot, which hit Stoller in the leg. Stoller than drilled him. He died before the paramedics could find their keys."

Joseph remembered a long gap between the Mid-Atlantic Slayer killings in 1991 and late 1993.

"How bad was Stoller wounded?" he asked.

"The bullet lodged in his femur," Russell reported with the sound of rustling papers in the background. "He went through a couple surgeries until the doctors decided it was safer to just leave it there. He went through months of rehab to properly walk again and return to work in 1993."

"And killing," Hadrian added.

"It didn't last. He took a disability retirement in 1994."

"When the rapes and killings stopped altogether," Joseph said, eyeing the abandoned jacket in the closet again. "Can you check if there were any schools in the area called 'Eleanor Roosevelt High School'?"

He could hear Russell typing over the phone. As he waited, he noticed a pair of boots still in the back corner of the closet. They looked like they were meant for working or hiking … he couldn't be sure.

He then noticed something else. Needing to hold the phone, he gestured to Hadrian, pointing out the box, which was standing on its side between the boots and the wall. His partner knelt and, wearing rubber gloves, pulled it out.

"Looks like it's falling apart," Hadrian remarked.

"What?" Russell asked over the phone.

"This box we just found in the closet," Joseph explained as Hadrian removed a rubber band holding the thing closed.

Inside, they found newspaper clippings. Flipping through the variously-sized pieces of paper, they realized it was all articles about the Mid-Atlantic Slayer's spree, going back to the few reports on his initial burglaries.

"Someone was collecting these," Hadrian said. "Judging from the dates on these articles, I'd say they're Daddy's. Something to hold on to alongside what we found at the school."

"He must have ran in a real hurry to leave these behind," Joseph remarked.

Russell coughed over the phone.

"Looks like it's still active," he reported. "Eleanor Roosevelt High School in Greenbelt. That's in Prince George's County, just north of D.C."

"How does it connect to the Stollers?" Hadrian asked.

"I can't tell. The school isn't kind enough to list staff or alumni who've taken on serial killing on their website."

They knew Lucas Stoller was born in Alexandria in 1993. Problem was Christopher had already divorced his first wife, Francis Stoller, who was found dead in an apartment in Minneapolis ten years later. A new boyfriend of hers was serving a thirty-year prison sentence for her murder until he was killed in a prison fight in 2000. His choice of weapon, an aluminum baseball bat, was nowhere close to the Mid-Atlantic Slayer's M.O. it was still unclear where Lucas came from and who and where Marylyn Pataki was.

"The divorce was finalized in June of 1989," Russel reported. "That's three months before the first murders."

"It's a trigger if I've ever seen one," Hadrian remarked. "Don't suppose you found a photo of the ex."

"No such luck. But I know what you're thinking. I'll bet she's a redhead."

"Probably wasn't a stable marriage," Joseph pointed out. "He was already raping women by then."

There was a pause.

"Oh, boy," Russel then said. He muttered something else, but Joseph and Hadrian couldn't be sure if he was speaking English or Norwegian.

"What now?" Joseph asked.

"I just got an e-mail from the Navy JAG's office. They must have seen our request for more information about Lucas Stoller's time as a Marine."

Joseph and Hadrian stared at one another. It would make sense if NCIS sent them this kind of information, but why would the JAG's office be doing so? What more could Lucas Stoller have done?

"Yeah, it's not good," Russell said. "Seems our boy Lucas wasn't a clean-cut Marine. He was a suspect in a 2019 rape and murder in … oh, man. How do you pronounce this? … Böblingen, Germany. That's just off the Panzer Kaserne Military Installation. Lucas Stoller was stationed there for most of his tour."

"What happened?" Joseph asked.

"A local woman, Susanne Kraus, was attacked in her home just off the grounds of the installation. She was raped and stabbed. Her boyfriend, U.S. Army Sergeant Patrick Fuller, wasn't so lucky. He died at the scene … seven stab wounds and clear signs of a struggle. His wife didn't take that well."

"Oh man," Hadrian remarked, unable to withhold a chuckle. He'd worked a few homicides which unearthed adultery.

"The Kriminalpolizei from Germany's federal police were in charge of the case," Russell continued. "Due to the proximity of the scene to the military installation and the fact one of the victims was U.S. Army, they involved CID almost from the beginning. NCIS was called in later."

"How did Lucas Stoller become a suspect?" Joseph asked, wondering what else they'd uncover about this killer.

"Looks like he dated the female victim for a while. She worked in the Base Exchange. They broke up a few weeks before the murder and … wonderful … she filed complaints that he was harassing her. No formal charges were brought though."

"What about the attack?" Joseph asked. "Were charges ever filed in that?"

"Doesn't look like it."

Joseph's heart sank. The nine murders in their jurisdiction might have been preventable.

"Seems the victim was too terrified to identify who attacked her," Russell elaborated. "She thanked God she was alive and got out of town right after that. He didn't use a condom, so they got semen, but the DNA was inconclusive. Seems there was some screw-up at the lab. So Lucas Stoller walked on this before they ever got the cuffs on him. The Marines transferred him stateside to their Air Station in Yuma, Arizona, and he got a general discharge earlier this year."

"Where he then moved back east?" Hadrian asked.

"Looks like it. That's the same time Christopher Stoller relocated to the D.C. apartment where you two are hanging out now."

Hadrian paused to think.

"Doesn't the military have a DNA database?" he queried.

"That's strictly for identifying bodies," Russell clarified. "No exceptions."

Joseph was sure he didn't need to hear more.

"Thanks, Russell," he said. "Let us know if you hear anything else."

"Will do," Russel replied. "Daniel's on his way back from the hospital and I doubt he'll be in a good mood."

The call ended there. Joseph and Hadrian studied each other.

"You think Lucas Stoller knew what his father did?" Joseph wondered aloud.

"I wouldn't be surprised," Hadrian replied. "There was definitely some inspiration from one spree to the other. Bet we'll find both their prints on these articles."

"Prints and inspiration won't help us catch them now."

* * *

Her windshield wipers doing their best to grant her any visibility, Julianna pulled her electric Nissan Leaf to the curb in front of Sasha and Christian's apartment building. Good thing she'd already charged it in preparation for the storm.

Inside the car, Sasha and Julianna looked at one another. Julianna put her hand on Sasha's shoulder.

"Please don't tell Christian," she pleaded. "He's my son. That's all that ever mattered to me."

Sasha couldn't comprehend the idea of keeping such a big secret from the man she was about to marry. Then again, she couldn't imagine how she'd tell him either. She studied Julianna's distressed face.

"I'll let you get going," she said. They both needed time to process this before any further moves were even contemplated.

The Nissan was small and it was a tight fit, but she managed to get the door open and maneuver herself out and onto her crutches. Julianna watched as she climbed the two steps and made it through the building's front door. She then drove away, heading north.

* * *

Sasha had been out in the rain for maybe thirty seconds when she trekked from Julianna's car to the front door. But, those thirty seconds were enough to again soak her. Water still dripped from her hair and clothes as she entered the apartment. This didn't stop Lydon from bounding forward to greet her.

"Where have you been?" Christian demanded.

She'd seen his missed calls and text messages. She'd chosen to ignore them.

"I had to find out something," she said, not looking at him. "Sorry."

"What?" Christian asked. "For what? A story? Sasha, there's a killer storm baring down on all of us. It might be called a 'Superstorm' now, but that's no better than a hurricane in my book. Matthew's waiting down in the garage. We gotta go."

Sasha nodded.

"I'll just change," she said. There had to be something decent and dry left in her closet.

"I'll help you," Christian said. "It'll take you forever with your bum leg."

"No," Sasha said, stopping and raising a hand. "I got this. Just give me five minutes. I promise."

* * *

Washington, D.C., Mayor Martin Zayas prided himself on staying healthy and consequently dodging most of the medical maladies which plagued so many people these days. Now, he was pretty sure he was experiencing at least one aneurism.

His office, as well as the offices of the D.C. City Council, in the John A. Wilson Building had been evacuated. They were now operating out of a building on the Washington Navy Yard. Currently, he was seated across a table, serving as his temporary desk, from D.C. Metropolitan Police Chief Marisa Ehle. The room they sat in had gray walls and one, boarded-up window with florescent lighting illuminating their grim situation. FBI Director John Brooks was joining them via Webex on the mayor's laptop.

"Call it off," the mayor was demanding, not for the first time in the past hour.

"Sir," Chief Ehle protested, "they've just identified these killers."

"Does anyone know where they are?" Mayor Zayas inquired.

Neither Chief Ehle nor Director Brooks said anything. Everyone knew there were no viable leads as to the whereabouts of Christopher and Lucas Stoller.

"We need to worry about everyone in this city," Mayor Zayas insisted.

Many D.C. residents had evacuated, but many had not. He'd have to go on TV and the radio soon to announce that it was now too dangerous to send police or rescue personnel out to help anyone in danger. People would have to stay sheltered until help could come several hours later.

Growing up, he'd watched many community leaders make such statements when facing these monster storms and always hoped he'd never have to say those words.

But he had to say them now. He'd gone to the roof of the building earlier and saw the worst of Superstorm Jackson, still a few miles from shore, with a pair of fancy binoculars the Navy had on hand. He wouldn't ask anyone to face that.

"The police need to work on helping residents for as long as they can," the mayor said. "They can't go looking for these guys when they don't even know where to look."

"And what if one or both of these killers gets into someone's home?" Chief Ehle asked. "What if that home is occupied? We could have a hostage situation and don't even know it. Or worse, they could assault and torture their captives and disappear when the storm lets up."

The scenarios sounded crazy, but Mayor Zayas knew he couldn't rule them out based on that notion. He looked at FBI Director Brooks, the man's face plastered on the laptop screen between them.

"Do your profilers have any idea about what these men might do?" he queried.

On the screen, Director Brooks shook his head.

"These men have both been smart and careful," he explained. "That's why they are still out there, though a large amount of luck also played a role. This storm basically upends the chessboard for both of them. They might find a way to ride it out or they might use it as an opportunity to disappear. Chief Ehle's scenarios aren't out of the question, but the best the BAU has given to any of that happening is fifty-fifty."

Mayor Zayas sighed. He'd never seen the use of these profilers. If he could, he'd have shut that whole unit down. What made it worse was this was all being perpetuated in the media, leaving the public with misguided beliefs about the capabilities of law enforcement.

"What do you suggest?" he asked the FBI man.

"As a father of a daughter, I say call in the military and turn D.C. upside-down," Director Brooks admitted. "As a professional lawman, I can't see a plausible way for things to be resolved safely right now."

Despite realizing she was outnumbered one to two, Chief Ehle kept a calm composure. It wasn't like the Mayor and the FBI Director weren't right.

"I'm not indifferent," Mayor Zayas said, trying a new tactic. "Believe me. I grew up here in Washington. I know what the Mid-Atlantic Slayer did. He terrorized entire communities and hurt a lot of people. If I knew where he was, I'd order the SWAT team in myself."

Those were cops who could get things done.

"But no one knows where these men are," he continued. "I cannot ask our police force to put themselves in harm's way for a possibility of maybe finding something or someone. Not now."

He sighed.

"Tell everyone to help whoever they can for the next two hours," he instructed, making it clear these orders were final. "Then, they are to ensure their own safety."

* * *

Ten minutes after arriving at the apartment, Sasha hobbled through the garage to Matthew's SUV. Her leg and arms ached. She looked forward to being able to rest during the long drive to Philadelphia.

"What took you guys?" Matthew complained.

From his spot on the backseat's footwell, Lydon looked up. With his plush, green-and-blue bed somewhat folded around him so it'd fit, he looked like a multi-colored hot dog.

"Sorry," Sasha replied as Christian helped her climb into the front passenger seat.

Once seated, Sasha checked her pocket to make absolutely sure she'd taken her phone. She saw her backpack, where she'd already stored her laptop and iPad, resting by her feet. Christian understood the priorities.

The only appropriate thing left in her closet had been American University sweatpants with a hooded sweatshirt which at least matched in color but was one size too big. Matthew didn't comment as he glanced at the baggy attire.

Christian took Sasha's crutches and stored them in the back and then climbed in behind her.

"All set?" Matthew asked. "Any other errands/suicide missions?"

Sasha didn't respond as he backed out of the parking space and maneuvered towards the garage exit. She leaned her head against the seat's headrest, still contemplating everything she'd deduced, confirmed, and learned in the past few hours. She wondered if it was too early to retire from Journalism. Had Woodward and Bernstein discovered this much so fast? How had they coped?

Slovo ne vorobey, she thought miserably. A word is not a sparrow.

Here, nothing said could be taken back. The proverb was truer than ever.

Chapter 27

Christopher Stoller stood inside the bus stop, the glass and metal panels somewhat shielding him from the wind and rain. How much longer would they hold up against this vicious onslaught? His cane hanging on a rail, he braced himself against one of these panels as he used a pair of binoculars with night vision capabilities to watch the building down the street.

He couldn't remember why he'd purchased these at an Army Surplus Store maybe ten years ago. It wasn't like he could surveil potential redheads anymore. But he'd been picking up a few things there and they were on sale. Now, they came in handy.

His leg ached and he knew he'd have to leave soon, but he could afford to stay a little while longer.

Staring through the binoculars, he thought back to that punk. He still wondered what part of the idiot's brain told him walking in through the school's front doors and shooting specific teachers, most of whom hadn't seen him in almost a decade, as a form of revenge would be a plausible plan? Even before Columbine, schools were taking precautions against this sort of thing. That's why he'd spent so much of his police career stuck in that middle school as a School Resource Officer.

Then, that posting cost him everything. The doctors decided leaving the bullet in his femur was the safer option. He lost so much time with the redheads because he needed to learn to walk right again. It took over a year of physical therapy for him to feel confident enough to proceed. He then had to start over with his surveillance to be sure nothing had changed in the interim. Too much time was lost.

He remembered his night with the redheaded jogger. His leg ached so much a few hours into that. He'd actually conceded and fled without killing her. He had completed more physical therapy and visited two more redheads after that, both with husbands. He'd stuck around to kill everyone both times, but the ache didn't go away. After the second time, he decided to retire from his profession and his passion. Since then, he'd regretted killing the punk in the school lobby. He should have made him suffer first.

The community rallied around him after that shooting and this attention had satiated him for a while. Parents thanked him for saving their offspring. Teachers thanked him for stepping between them, their pupils, and the danger that walked into their school. He received all kinds of perks, from complimentary meals to prime seats at local sporting events. Women even flirted with him. He enjoyed the attention the redheaded women gave him. But it didn't last, so he tried what worked before until his leg no longer allowed him to kill.

Unfortunately, that community support also produced Lucas as well. He'd met the boy's mother at a bar. A cocktail waitress at some dive he couldn't remember, she'd recognized him from the news. They talked and she went home with him ... a standard one-night-stand. She then turned up in his life again two months later to report her pregnancy. Lucas was born and the paternity test proved the lineage.

The redhead eventually left the boy with him, wanting to return to college and study abroad. The closest she came to the latter was getting shipped to a nuthouse for ... he forgot the reason ... some kind of paranoia maybe. That was the last he'd heard about her. He'd made the best of the situation, raising Lucas while pursuing his passion until his leg couldn't take it anymore.

His memories were interrupted when he saw an SUV emerging from the building's garage. He doubted it would mean anything to him as he didn't recognize it, but he focused in on it nonetheless. It wasn't like he had anything better to do.

Surprised, he saw Sasha Copeland sitting in the front seat, next to a man he didn't recognize. The man's identity didn't matter. He'd defied the odds and waited. He could still get revenge for her articles ruining his life.

The SUV turned and drove towards him. Christopher Stoller pulled out his Sig Sauer and took aim.

* * *

"What was that?" Christian asked from the backseat.

They all heard the metallic clunk up and to the left of Matthew's side.

"Sounded like something hit us," Matthew replied, leaning forward to try and see anything through his windshield.

"What's that?" Sasha asked, leaning forward and pointing.

They could barely see anything through the swirling rain. It looked like someone was standing at the bus stop. Sasha and Matthew could just make out a dark silhouette.

"Jesus!" Matthew cried as something hit the rearview mirror on Sasha's side of the SUV.

He pressed on the accelerator. The SUV surged forward. Their hearts all raced as Christian also realized someone was shooting at them.

They heard glass shattering, followed by a metallic thunk.

"I think he hit my taillight," Matthew said, daring to look back for a second.

* * *

Christopher Stoller watched the SUV pass him and disappear into the sheets of rain. He pulled the trigger one more time before giving in. He was sure he'd hit something with at least one of his shots … maybe, he'd hit someone. It would be the best he'd get.

He pocketed his service revolver and grabbed his cane. It was time to get out of here. Tucking his raincoat around himself, he walked away from the bus stop and in the opposite direction the SUV had fled. Good riddance, Washington, D.C.

* * *

Matthew drove for a solid minute before stepping on the brakes. The SUV fishtailed and swerved to the left. They came to a complete stop standing sideways on the street.

"How did we not hit anything?" Matthew wondered aloud, breathing heavily. He must have raced down three blocks to be sure they were out of the line of fire.

Her hands shaking, Sasha pulled out her phone and selected a contact. 9-1-1 couldn't help them now.

"Hello?" Joseph asked after two rings.

"Joe," Sasha said in an urgent tone. "It's Sasha."

"Sasha?" Joseph asked, bewildered. "Where on Earth are you?"

"We were leaving and someone started shooting at us. I think we lost them."

"Well, keep going."

Joseph didn't hesitate with his response. Sasha was stunned.

"You heard me, right?" she asked. "I said someone's shooting at us."

"We can't get out there now," Joseph explained, speaking quickly. "The Mayor and the Chief will shut us down altogether very soon and we're focusing on being ready for that and helping people get away while we still can. I'll check out your neighborhood when this is over. Just get out of town and stay out until you hear from me."

Sasha couldn't argue with that advice.

"Stay safe," she urged, surveying the black-and-gray scenery outside the SUV.

Matthew didn't need to be told anything. He was already straightening out the SUV and resumed driving at a safer speed. He turned on the radio, tuning to the news.

"With the local rivers almost reaching capacity," the anchor was saying, "officials continue to be concerned about flooding in Washington's low-lying areas. Residents are urged to evacuate or proceed to the nearest emergency shelter. We have a list here, which we will read now ..."

* * *

Christopher Stoller didn't know how long he'd been walking. Every step was a struggle as he sought shelter or a way out of D.C. He'd abandoned his duffel bag a while back, having no attachment to anything in it. He didn't need the dead weight.

The busses and Metro had been shut down and he saw no cabs driving by, often not even seeing streets. According to his phone's Uber app, there were no available drivers anywhere near him. He was on his own.

His leg was killing him, but it wasn't like he could stop to rest. He'd already dodged two airborne tree branches ... at least he assumed they were branches, glimpsing each at the last second and ducking. He tried any door he could find, all being locked. If anyone could hear him knocking, they ignored it. He hadn't found a door in a while.

He could hear rushing water, but he'd lost all orientation in this wind and rain. It was so loud. He was stepping into one large puddle after another. For all he knew, he was walking around the inside of a giant toilet bowl. It certainly smelled right.

* * *

While Officer Heath Jesperson drove, Officer Carol Reed did her best to survey the river to their right. They were supposed to drive up and down Route 295 and monitor the Anacostia River to make sure no one was stupid enough to go out there in this storm. They looked forward to being called off this suicidal assignment.

"At this point, we're more likely to wind up in that river," Officer Reed remarked. Her partner nodded in agreement.

Their headlights barely cut through the blackness all around them. They were running their lights and siren, but they doubted anyone could see or hear them in this mess.

Suddenly, their headlights became useful, illuminating the feet, legs, and cane of someone walking along the highway.

"Christ!" Officer Jesperson cried, stepping on the brakes.

* * *

He stopped, hearing something that sounded like … a siren. He turned and could just make out a car about ten feet back, its red and blue lights flashing through the darkness. The officers inside seemed to be getting out.

One of them seemed to be shouting something, but he couldn't hear. He moved towards the car, sliding his hand into his pocket. Sure, these officers would take him somewhere safe and dry. Then, possibly as soon as they got him into their cruiser, they'd recognize him under any source of light. That safe, dry place would become a jail cell.

Christopher Stoller had another, better plan. He'd wait for these cops to get closer. Then, he'd kill them. In the dark, they could look right at him and never see it coming. Then, he could take their car. He'd use the GPS to drive through the rain and get out of town. By the time anyone could look for the cops or their car, he'd have ditched it far outside Washington, near another mode of transportation that could take him far away.

Christopher Stoller gripped his Sig Sauer. At least one of them was moving forward, still shouting something unintelligible. He slowly drew his service revolver, bracing himself on his cane.

* * *

"Come here!" Officer Reed shouted to be heard. "Come towards my voice!"

The figure didn't move. They probably couldn't hear her. She took another careful step forward. Her feet were sliding on the soaked asphalt.

She thought she saw the figure move. Then, she saw a flash and something flew by her right ear.

"Shooter!" she shouted, wondering if her partner could hear her. She drew her weapon and pulled the trigger, taking aim at another muzzle flash from the same spot. She could just barely hear her own pistol being fired.

* * *

Christopher Stoller didn't realize they were returning fire until two bullets slammed into his chest and abdomen. He stumbled backwards, losing his cane and service revolver. His vision grew bleary, but he thought he saw the cops moving. He raised his arm.

Another slug struck his shoulder and he hit something hard behind him. As his upper body kept falling over, his hand brushed metal.

Christopher Stoller realized it was a guardrail, and he was falling over it. His body, rendered useless by the cops' gunfire, flailed as he landed hard on the grass and mud in the other side. Rolling to his left, he concluded he was on an incline and couldn't stop himself. He hit several hard stones as he kept rolling.

Then, he hit the water with an inaudible splash. He wriggled and flailed, trying to resurface. Nothing worked as he felt the current drag him away. His lungs filled with water, and his vision went black.

* * *

Officer Reed was sure they'd hit the figure, having seen Officer Jesperson's muzzle flashes to her right as she fired. She couldn't see their assailant anymore. She carefully moved forward again. She couldn't see anyone ahead of her now.

Her foot hit something and she reached down. It was a long stick … a cane. She gripped it tight and used it to feel around for signs of a body. She could hear her partner shouting, but she couldn't understand what he was saying.

The cane's tip hit something else. Daring to holster her weapon, Officer Reed reached down again and felt something metal. Feeling further, she realized it was a gun, and the muzzle was warm.

She grabbed the gun and retreated towards the flashing red and blue lights on the patrol cruiser's roof. She found a door and pulled it open.

She didn't realize until she slid in that she was in the back, where the doors couldn't be opened from the inside. She looked up front to see Officer Jesperson back behind the wheel, speaking into the radio. Through the small holes in the plastic barrier separating them, she could hear what he was saying.

"We think he went into the river," he was saying. "I'm sure I saw him go over the guardrail."

Officer Reed tapped the plastic barrier. Getting his attention, she held up the gun, a revolver, and cane for him to see.

"We've got a weapon," Officer Jesperson reported. "No sign of the shooter."

"Come on back and file the report," the dispatcher said. "We can't send anyone out to you now."

"Copy. We're on our way back."

Officer Jesperson set down the radio and shifted into Drive.

"Can you let me out?" Officer Reed requested from the back. "I feel like a perp back here."

Officer Jesperson shook his head.

"Neither of us is going out there again while we're standing here," he insisted. "I'll let you out when we're back at the station."

He drove forward, wanting to get away from this spot as fast as he could while remaining alive.

* * *

Matthew's parents were as hospitable as advertised, even converting a downstairs office into a guestroom for the crutch-baring Sasha. She now lay on the couch/bed, finally alone.

She knew from overhearing a phone conversation between Christian and his mother that Julianna had made it safely to Cumberland, where, like Philadelphia, the weather was far less harsh. Spartak had texted his son, reporting he was likewise safe at a campground near Huntington, West Virginia. The weather was also better at his location.

Christian was kind enough not to mention their run-in with a gun-wielding figure to either of his parents. Per Matthew's request, Mr. and Mrs. Timmons were likewise left in the dark about this part of the group's journey/evacuation.

"They'd never let me out of the house again," Matthew had pointed out as they drove down his old street towards the house.

Christian and Sasha were happy to comply. For his part, Matthew pulled his SUV up next to the house so his parents couldn't readily notice any damage. He confirmed one of his taillights was definitely broken.

"God only knows how I'll explain this at the Bodyshop," Matthew remarked before they'd gone inside.

They'd sat in the Timmons' den earlier, watching news coverage of the storm. Their drive had improved once they made into Maryland and could almost be considered pleasant by the time they crossed the border into Pennsylvania. It was raining in Philadelphia as well, but this rain looked normal, not like someone could die before it passed. Watching the television, they could hardly see Washington anymore.

"Glad we didn't stay," Christian remarked at one point.

After a dinner of homemade meatball subs and fries, Sasha said she was tired and retreated to her temporary room. Since the couch could in no way accommodate two people, Christian would be staying in the Timmons' upstairs guestroom.

She checked in with a few friends from the D.C. area, all of whom had evacuated or were in an area not in danger of flooding or major storm damage. Based on people's replies, she concluded her adventure had been the most harrowing. She supposed it couldn't have been a contest, or at least not a close one.

With no nefarious characters knowing where they were and everything as settled as it could be, Sasha's thoughts returned to Julianna's revelation. She could have never dreamed this up, not even for a book.

In her first year at American University, a friend of hers was raped at an off-campus party. Sasha had no idea it happened until a few weeks later, when Fay was starting to make her peace with what happened. She wondered if Julianna had made her peace with what happened at some point before she revealed all to her future daughter-in-law. Had she ever been able to make any peace with it given her son's father might be her rapist and a monster?

Sasha considered the possibility Christian could be the son of the Mid-Atlantic Slayer. She'd never seen anything to suggest he held dark, violent impulses. Still, if it were true, could she look at him the same way again? Could she still marry him? What if word of this possible kinship got out?

She also wondered if there were more offspring out there, apart from the KA-BAR Ripper. In addition to seventeen murders, the Mid-Atlantic Slayer raped almost fifty more women … maybe more than fifty if others like Julianna didn't report the assault. What were the odds only one child was conceived in those statistics, even factoring in the contraceptive medications rape victims received at the hospital?

These thoughts were becoming as complicated as anything else in this case. Sasha turned over to face the couch, the green-and-gray cushion centimeters from her face, staring back at her. Thank God it couldn't make things more complicated.

Chapter 28

Joseph burst into the department's 5th District's station. All around him, personnel were trying to set the place right again. Outside, the rain was letting up.

Superstorm Jackson made landfall around 11:00 the previous night. It moved right over Washington about ninety minutes later, leaving approximately seven inches of rainwater. Flood damage wasn't as severe as predicted and many people were returning to their homes as the morning sun broke through the clouds.

Joseph, having stayed at the 2nd District through the night, didn't care about this at the moment. He was interested in what happened to two D.C. Metropolitan Police Officers on Route 295 along the Anacostia River.

He spotted their captain and hurried through the bustling squad room. The taskforce was likewise checking the state of their homes and office and ASAC Summers assigned him to follow up on this report.

"You're the detective I'm waiting for?" the captain, Caspen Turner, asked.

"That's me," Joseph confirmed and introduced himself, presenting his credentials. "What happened?"

At the captain's insistence, they entered the man's office. Joseph noticed one of the windowpanes was broken, a plastic bag taped over that section. Part of the carpet still looked wet and he smelled something off.

"We won't stay in here long," Captain Turner said, shutting the door and sitting behind his desk. "Internal Affairs and the crime scene technicians are just headed out to Route 295 now to see if they find anything. I'm inclined to doubt it. I've heard the officers' accounts and it's about as straight-forward as things can get under these circumstances."

"What did they say happened?" Joseph asked, sitting down as well.

"Seems they were patrolling on 295 along the river when they encountered someone crazy enough to be walking around out there. They tried to hail them to take them to a shelter. When they got out of their cruiser, the subject opened fire on them. Thankfully, they weren't harmed. The officers returned fire and are sure they hit the subject, who disappeared. The theory is the subject fell over the guardrail and went into the river. They're insisting it all happened in a matter of seconds."

Joseph sighed. With last night's wind and rain, not to mention the strewn debris left behind, neither Internal Affairs nor the crime lab technicians would find anything. Whoever fell into the Anacostia River was likewise unlikely to resurface, especially if they'd been shot.

"And you think it was Christopher Stoller?" he asked. He wouldn't use the nickname "Mid-Atlantic Slayer" anymore. The monster had a face and a real name.

"It's suspected," Captain Turner replied. "The Coast Guard, Navy, and our own Marine Unit will conduct a search for a body."

"But why do you think it's him?"

Captain Turner reached down behind his desk and soon reemerged with a long object wrapped in paper, a Chain of Custody card attached to it. Joseph could tell it was a cane. His heart raced. Could this be over?

"Exhibit A, counselor," Captain Turner remarked. He set the package down again and pulled another smaller package out of a desk drawer. It was likewise wrapped in paper with a Chain of Custody card attached.

The captain donned a pair of rubber gloves and carefully opened the package.

"Don't worry," he said. "It's not loaded anymore."

Lying there was a Sig Sauer six-shot revolver. It looked old but well-cared for, even if it was recently exposed to some harsh elements.

Joseph's mind raced. He could feel himself sweating, remembering the case files. Christopher Stoller used a Sig Sauer six-shot revolver to kill his seventeen victims. D.C. Police Officers Keith Regis and Mike Nichols were killed with that same Sig Sauer six-shot revolver. Sig Sauer stopped making these particular models in the mid-1990s.

"I'm waiting for the crime lab to pick up this stuff," Captain Turner reported, rewrapping the revolver and adding his name to the Chain of Custody card. "It had three bullets left in it when Officer Reed brought it in. I've already e-mailed the serial number to a friend at ATF. I expect to hear back later today. I don't think they got hit as hard down there."

Joseph could only nod. It now seemed realistic that Christopher Stoller, a man who terrorized the region for almost forty years, was gone. Still, he knew it wasn't over yet.

But, one monster might be gone for good. Sitting in this captain's office, Joseph could feel weights being lifted from his shoulders.

* * *

Using her crutches, Sasha walked around the Timmons' backyard, Lydon and the couple's two Golden Retrievers keeping an eye on her. She was grateful for the six-foot wooden fence which surrounded the property. No one in the neighborhood could see her shaved and bandaged head. No one inside the house had commented on it, which she was also grateful for.

The sun was shining today, a far cry from the horrific meteorological circumstances they'd left behind less than twenty-four hours earlier. They had yet to hear any news from Washington except that the rainfall was lessening and a search had been launched for someone who seemed to have fallen into the Anacostia River.

"He's a goner," Matthew had remarked upon seeing the bulletin.

His mother was quick to chide him for expressing such a crass opinion. Sasha silently agreed with Matthew. It'd be difficult to survive that under any circumstances.

She'd texted Joseph for a status update, but the detective had yet to reply. She hoped he'd survived the storm. The news said seven people were killed in the Mid-Atlantic region. Two names had been mentioned, neither of them him. Sasha couldn't help wondering.

She studied the swing set. It seemed Matthew's older sister and her husband had a two-year-old who loved to come out here to play when he visited his grandparents. Sasha once dreamed of having her own family with children and her own home with a swing set in the backyard. Would that happen anymore?

"Come on," she told herself. Julianna had lived with this secret and this possibility for almost twenty-seven years. She wasn't able to make it through twenty-seven hours. Sure, this man had attacked her, but he'd raped Julianna.

She started walking again. One of the Timmons' Golden Retrievers then found a burst of adrenalin somewhere. He darted forward, passing her, towards a squirrel who was already three-quarters back up a tree. The dog reached the tree and jumped up, pressing his large paws against the trunk and barking. If the squirrel looked back, Sasha couldn't tell.

Sasha's phone chimed and vibrated in her pocket. She stopped and pulled it out. She'd received a text message from Julianna. She wished she hadn't.

I will tell him. He deserves to know.

Sasha grimaced. On one hand, the burden of keeping this secret would be lifted from her. On the other hand, she feared what might happen next.

Sure Julianna wasn't expecting a reply, she deleted this message and slid her phone back into her pocket. She turned back to the house. Through the rear windows, she could see Christian, Matthew, and Mr. Timmons playing some sort of card game. Mr. Timmons was touching the corners of his cards in apparent curiosity and fascination. Sasha was sure he was investigating the braille symbols printed there for Christian's benefit. She hardly noticed things like that anymore.

She then saw Christian reaching down. He pulled his own phone out of his pocket and held it up to his ear. Sasha stood frozen in the yard, wondering, or fearing, who was calling and why.

* * *

Sure that Christopher Stoller was gone, the taskforce took a few minutes to celebrate with somebody procuring pastries from a nearby coffeeshop. The Mid-Atlantic Slayer was gone. Even Hadrian, whose living room was currently occupied by a fallen tree, was able to make it.

"Hey!" ASAC Summers admonished, entering the suite of offices. "Hey!"

Everyone settled into prompt silence as their temporary boss moved towards a bulletin board on the wall. The two Stollers' photos had been hung up there the day before and someone had drawn a large, black X across Christopher Stoller's face.

"He's still out there," ASAC Summers said, pointing at the adjacent photo of Lucas James Stoller. It was an image from the McDonald's security camera, the same one the taskforce had been showing witnesses.

"Find him," ASAC Summers demanded in a firm tone, "or show me proof he's gone like his old man."

* * *

Sasha jumped when someone knocked on the door of her makeshift guestroom.

"Come in," she said. The door was unlocked. She was sitting on the couch. There was nothing compromising to see and she hoped her face didn't betray her current thoughts and feelings.

Christian opened the door and entered, Lydon following him.

"Hey," he said. "Matthew wants to see about returning to D.C. tomorrow."

"Lu'," Sasha replied. Joseph had texted her back earlier that day, confirming he was okay. He'd also advised it was "probably safe to return," though he refused to elaborate.

Christian came over to the couch and sat down.

"You okay?" he asked. "You've been very quiet."

Sasha studied him. He didn't look like life as he knew it had been upended. And, she knew he trusted Joseph's assessment of their safety back home, even if the cop had been vague.

"A lot's happened," she said, hoping he wouldn't push. "You know."

Christian nodded.

"We're on the other side, aren't we?" he said. "We're relatively intact. Vse v poryadke."

Sasha supposed he was right. She just wondered when Julianna planned to come clean.

"Come on," Christian said. "You should get out. Matthew wants us to try genuine Philly Cheesesteaks. He says there's a place not far from here."

Matthew too seemed to have made his peace with what happened. He'd spent most of the day at a garage, getting his broken taillight and mirror repaired.

"I'm just glad to get away without a ticket," he'd said when he returned a little while ago. "If they found any bullets, they didn't say anything. Regardless, let's make that the last adventure with guns, all right?"

Sasha considered the suggestion of food. She was getting hungry. And, she'd remembered to pack a Washington Post baseball cap. It would hide her injuries and horrific hairdo for the most part.

"I'll be right there," she said. She supposed she could just be happy for the moment. Her world didn't have the potential to come crashing down until at least when she returned to Washington. She could enjoy sandwiches and company in Philadelphia.

* * *

The sun rose, presenting Washington, D.C., with another beautiful day. The floodwaters were reseeding, the cleanup and repairs were progressing well, and evacuees continued returning to their homes. All in all, the city fared better than experts had predicted.

Apart from the nice weather, Lucas Stoller didn't care about any of this. Having managed to find an abandoned townhouse, he hid there during the storm, avoiding the worst of the falling debris as the fierce wind took down part of the decrepit structure. He'd managed to get some sleep when things settled down, but he now wanted a real bed. He also wanted aspirin as his head was still pounding.

He wasn't quite sure where he was. He supposed he was still in D.C., though he found it hard to believe there was an area of the city he hadn't driven through when making deliveries.

The gun and his KA-BAR rested in his jacket pockets. He had some money, which he hoped to use to get some distance between himself and the Capital. He was fine with the inevitable prospect of robbing people for more funds, but he wanted to do it somewhere where he'd draw less attention.

He knew his old life was over. The police had to be in his apartment by now. He had no idea what had become of his father, nor did he care to find out. It was a million to none for reasons to get out of town and reinvent himself. Soon, Lucas Stoller wouldn't exist anymore.

He also wanted a change of clothes. Between walking outside during the early stages of a hurricane and spending over twenty-four hours in a condemned building, he looked and smelled filthy. The only upside was no one wanted to come near him. They didn't even want to look at him. Given his face had to be plastered all over the news by now, Lucas Stoller was fine with their aversion. He wasn't in any hurry to find a razor and take care of his blond stubble.

His head was killing him. Wasn't there a pharmacy open somewhere? He'd gladly splurge a sizable chunk of his meager funds on painkillers.

Heck, he'd endure another night in some building which aspired to be a slum if he had a bottle of pills with him.

Where was he? How long had he been walking? Where did the sun rise? If he could figure that last one out, he'd have a better sense of where he could go. Yes, that made sense.

He crossed the street and stopped. He blinked, not believing what he saw. There, maybe two hundred yards ahead of him, walking away from a bus stop, was an Auburn Lovely. Dressed in a suit or something like that and carrying a large bag over one shoulder, she was talking with two brunette girls.

Lucas Stoller felt a new need overtake him as the group headed his way. He needed her. He had the gun. He could use it to take her somewhere. Once they were alone, he could have her. Then, he could still plunge his KA-BAR into her back. Yes, the mere thought of doing this already made his headache recede.

The group of girls sped up as they walked mere inches past him. One of the brunettes threw a look of disgust his way.

Lucas Stoller didn't care. Yes, he smelled, but the brunette's opinion didn't matter to him. She didn't matter.

He turned around and followed them, waiting for the perfect time. His hand slid into his pocket and gripped the gun. It felt strange. He hadn't fired a gun often in his life, but that didn't matter. He wanted to scare people with it, and he could still shoot if he needed to. His Auburn Lovely would be terrified when she felt its muzzle touch her smooth, soft skin.

His heart raced in eager anticipation. He felt a stir in his pants. Lucas Stoller knew he deserved this. After everything he'd endured, he deserved to have her the way he wanted. He thought of Susanne and this strengthened his resolve. He wouldn't bother to surveil her. He didn't need to know where she lived and with whom she lived. He would just have her.

"Did you get a whiff of that guy back there?" one of the girls asked. "Oh my God."

Her friends, including his Auburn Lovely, said something he couldn't understand. Lucas Stoller didn't care what they said.

"You'd smell him coming anywhere," the first girl continued.

Lucas Stoller had to smile at this. He was about to destroy her theory. None of these girls had even looked back and noticed him in pursuit.

As they all kept walking, he stared at his Auburn Lovely. He wondered about the things he could do with her. How could he pose her? No one would expect it. It would be glorious. She would be glorious.

The group crossed another street and he hurried to catch the light. Stepping onto the curb on the other side, he noticed something about his Auburn Lovely. Her shoelace was becoming loose. She wore elegant, black leather boots with thin laces. He looked forward to pulling them off her feet soon enough.

They were approaching a building. Lucas Stoller studied it. He knew it from somewhere. Glancing down to make sure he didn't lose his Auburn Lovely, he looked back up at the domed roof. The sun shone of it, making it look even brighter. It looked so familiar. Where were they? His head was aching again.

"Hey," someone said.

Lucas Stoller snapped back to attention and realized one of the brunettes was talking to his Auburn Lovely. He sped up to hear.

"Your shoe's untied," she was saying.

His Auburn Lovely stopped and looked down to see her laces swing back and forth with her steps. One got caught beneath her shoe as she stopped walking.

"Go," she said to her friends. "I'll catch up."

Setting her bag down, she crouched and fumbled with the troublesome laces. Her friends hurried forward to the steps and began to ascend.

Knowing he'd never get a better chance, Lucas Stoller moved forward, ready to draw the gun.

* * *

Jodi Brooks stopped to push some stray red strands out of her face and tucked the ID card hanging around her neck beneath one arm so she could get this done. She knew she was already running late. It was one little thing after another today, starting with almost poking her own eye out when putting her contacts in that morning. She needed to get up earlier. That, and someone needed to fix the hot water in her apartment. Her whole body still felt chilled.

She was retying her shoe when she heard footfalls approaching from behind her on the concrete path. It was early and things weren't bustling yet, but there were people around, mainly security and groundskeepers. Why did these footfalls bother her?

She thought of the homeless man she and her friends had passed earlier by the bus stop. He looked creepy and his dirty visage came to mind. Jodi shook her head and focused on her shoe. She was being ridiculous. Not only did she need to get up earlier, she needed to sleep. Her father's constant warnings about all the world's dangers didn't help either.

"You're a pretty girl," he'd always said. "People will notice that. Be careful."

Jodi shook the words out of her head. She couldn't wait for this semester to be done. Maybe she could visit her cousins in Aspen. She needed a break. She was finally focusing enough to correctly tie her shoe, but that had taken way too long.

Finished, she began to rise, her ID swinging back out in front of her. Standing almost straight and adjusting her bag's strap on her shoulder, Jodi froze. Out of the corner of her eye, she noticed a shadow approaching from behind her. Then, she heard a voice. She smelled something … something bad.

Chapter 29

"Hey," a voice said.

Daring to take his eyes off his Auburn Lovely, Lucas Stoller glanced right to see a police officer approaching. With a few yards to go, he quickened his pace, his gun ready to be revealed.

"Hey!" the officer said loudly. "Stop!"

He reached out to grab his arm.

Lucas Stoller raised his arm and swung back, striking the officer in the face. His opponent stumbled backwards but didn't fall. He managed to right himself and reached out again.

* * *

Hearing a scuffle, Jodi Brooks turned to see a Capital Police officer struggle to grab ... the homeless man from earlier. She couldn't believe this. Had he followed them? What was he going to do?

Jodi couldn't move. She could see other uniformed officers and black-suited Secret Service agents hurrying towards the altercation. The first officer had managed to grab the homeless man now and they were struggling. It seemed to be an even match, with the homeless man managing to keep the officer from reaching for his holstered gun on his belt.

Someone grabbed Jodi's shoulder and she jumped. She turned to see another Capital Police officer standing beside her.

"Get inside," the woman barked, pointing towards the steps and the doors beyond. "Now!"

Jodi's legs managed to cooperate. She grabbed her bag and hurried up the steps, willing herself not to stumble. At the top, she glanced back to see more officers and agents struggling with the homeless man, who had now pulled out a knife.

Not wanting to see blood, Jodi grabbed the door and yanked it open. Shrieking alarms filled her ears as she rushed into the building.

Another officer was standing there. He grabbed the ID card hanging around her neck and studied it for a second.

"Go in there," he said, pointing to a nearby door. "Stay in there until someone comes and gets you."

Jodi could hear him speaking into his radio as she hurried to obey.

The room she'd been sent to was small and bland. A single desk with no occupant stood in the middle, two metal filing cabinets and a bookshelf half-full of random books standing behind it. There were no windows and a single florescent light in the center of the ceiling gave the room an eerie glow. Still, the homeless man wasn't here, so that was an improvement.

Jodi shut the door behind her. The noise of the shrieking alarm lessened. Dropping her bag, she sank down onto the floor. Breathing heavily, she started to cry.

* * *

It took about thirty seconds and six personnel to subdue and secure the strange, disheveled man who'd wandered onto the grounds of the United States Capital. That was enough time to both cause panic and get most Representatives and Senators locked down in secure locations within the building.

When Lieutenant Ivan Erdai arrived at the scene of the melee, one of his officers was patting down the subject, now lying face-down on the pavement with his wrists cuffed behind his back. The lieutenant was told a loaded Colt 1911 pistol was found in the suspect's jacket, along with the knife he'd used to try to fight back against the officers.

"Log them," Lieutenant Erdai instructed. "Cuff his legs before you get him up."

Until he knew everything about this disheveled man and why he'd come onto the grounds of the U.S. Capital, he would not take any chances.

"Greene's getting shackles," an officer reported, still out of breath.

Lieutenant Erdai couldn't believe this. He hadn't learned about the President's plan to speak at the Capital until this morning, before he'd even finished his first cup of coffee. He'd hoped that the last-minute scheduling would prevent the lunatics from trying anything and he'd have a quiet shift, relatively speaking. It'd been a nice dream.

Another officer arrived with the shackles and the subject's legs were secured. He wasn't resisting anymore. Still, no chances would be taken.

"Okay," Lieutenant Erdai said. "Get him up."

An officer and a Secret Service agent grabbed the subject beneath his underarms and hauled him to his feet. There was no ceremony in their process. Once upright, they held him both as a matter of security and to steady him so he wouldn't faceplant back onto the ground.

Lieutenant Erdai stood still as the subject's eyes met his own. Was it possible he was actually seeing this? They needed to confirm it quick. The news media were probably already on their way.

The subject frowned at the lieutenant, seeming to size him up.

" You'll wish you had killed me," the disheveled subject said.

* * *

Driving across the Delaware Memorial Bridge, Matthew, Christian, and Sasha all paid closer attention to the radio when the breaking news was announced.

"We are getting reports an arrest was made at the United States Capital this morning," the news anchor was saying. "Capital Police Officers and

Secret Service agents, preparing for an emergency address by President Biden later this morning in the wake of Superstorm Jackson's devastating impact on the Mid-Atlantic region, struggled with and subdued an armed suspect who'd wandered onto the grounds."

Sasha again silently lamented missing a good story.

"Details remain sketchy," the anchor continued, "but eyewitnesses are reporting the suspect, now in custody, resembles wanted fugitive Lucas James Stoller, identified earlier this week as the prime suspect in the recent KA-BAR Ripper spree of murders. Both the Capital Police and Washington Metropolitan Police officials offer no comment on these speculations …"

Now Sasha really wanted to be back in Washington. Fumbling around, she found her phone. Using the hands-free mode on his own phone, Matthew was already calling a friend in Congresswoman Dodson's office.

* * *

By this point in the case, Joseph could admit he'd dreamed about being the one to put the cuffs on the Mid-Atlantic Slayer and the KA-BAR Ripper. Now, that was likely to remain a dream.

Nevertheless, he didn't hesitate to head to George Washington University Hospital with most of the taskforce and the D.C. Metro Police's SWAT team. No one was taking any chances this time.

Though he could have faced a long federal prison stretch for his actions at the Capital, the federal government decided to forgo pressing charges and would instead transfer custody to D.C. authorities. Nine consecutive life sentences without parole sounded a lot better than twenty years with time off if he managed to behave himself.

While his fingerprints were taken at the Capital Police station on D Street, Lucas Stoller complained of a severe headache. Officers guarding him reported seeing blue and black bruises around his head, though

Stoller refused to answer anyone's questions about these. Consulting with FBI ASAC Lloyd Summers, the lieutenant in charge of securing the suspect had him brought to the hospital for tests … after the fingerprint match confirmed who he had in custody.

Meanwhile, the crime lab, having not sustained too much damage from the storm, reported some interesting developments. Striations found on bullets fired from the revolver found on Route 295 were inconsistent with the bullets used to kill the Mid-Atlantic Slayer's seventeen victims as well as Officer Keith Regis and Detective Mike Nichols. The gun found on that highway, while having surely been used to fire on Officers Jesperson and Reed, was not the murder weapon. The lab double-checked to make sure, but there was no possibility of an error, even though the discovered gun was also a Sig Sauer six-shot revolver.

The Bureau of Alcohol, Tobacco, Firearms and Explosives had better news. The revolver, though at least thirty years old, was well-maintained. Its serial number was easy to read with the naked eye. A quick check with Virginia authorities revealed the Sig Sauer was issued to Christopher Stoller by the Fairfax County Police department after he graduated from the academy. Further digging revealed Stoller bought an identical Sig Sauer six-shot revolver from a private vender in Maryland in 1988, using his parents address in Prince Georges County. Murder might have not been the initial motive for this purchase, but everyone felt sure it was the weapon used by the Mid-Atlantic Slayer. They were also sure this gun was now lost in the Anacostia River alongside Christopher Stoller.

The D.C. lab did theorize the injuries Sasha sustained were consistent with having been made by the cane found with the gun out on that highway. Joseph supposed they'd never know for sure. Both the FBI and ATF intended to run further tests on all the evidence, but these results were satisfying enough. Plus, Joseph and the other detectives could put Lucas James Stoller away for the rest of his life.

It seemed the hospital didn't advertise who was being treated within their walls. Nor did the administration forewarn the staff and patients of the arrival of over a dozen detectives and agents and six armed SWAT officers. People scrambled to get out of the way as the group traversed the corridors. Knowing the attention their presence created, they intended to leave as soon as possible … at least before the press arrived.

Lucas Stoller had been moved to a private room on the second floor. Three Capital Police Officers stood inside the room, armed with batons, tazors, and mace while wearing body armor, helmets, and face shields. Five additional personnel were stationed in the hallway and the adjacent rooms on either side had been cleared. Doctors and nurses making rounds in this corridor made it a point to come and go as quickly as they could.

When the taskforce arrived outside Lucas Stoller's room, the SWAT team entered first to take over security of the prisoner. Meanwhile, Joseph, Russell, Hadrian, and Daniel spoke with a Dr. Kimberly Monroe, the physician placed in charge of their suspect's care.

"He has a mild concussion," the doctor reported. "Nur logical tests show no long-term impact on cognitive function and we treated his headache with Tylenol. He should be observed for the next twenty-four to forty-eight hours."

Joseph nodded. This wouldn't be a problem for the infirmary staff at the District of Columbia Jail. Lucas Stoller could continue his recovery in a single cell.

One of the Capital Police officers handed Hadrian a milk crate full of small plastic bags, each baring its own Chain of Custody card.

"We've escorted the weapons he was carrying directly to your lab," the officer added as Hadrian took the crate.

The SWAT Team captain reemerged in the hallway to announce everything was ready.

"Let's do it," Joseph said as Daniel escorted Dr. Monroe away.

Another SWAT officer emerged from the room, followed by Lucas James Stoller. The killer was cuffed and shackled for his trip. Two more SWAT officers escorted him while the rest of the team brought up the rear.

Joseph and Hadrian studied the man they'd spent weeks looking for, encountering nine dead college students in the process. He glowered back at them, his mouth a straight, thin line beneath a pair of brown eyes and pointed nose. The detectives could see the bruises on his shaved head.

"Rough night?" Hadrian asked.

Lucas Stoller bared his gritted teeth. The SWAT officers on either side of him tightened their grips.

"Doesn't matter," Joseph said. "Lucas James Stoller. You're under arrest for murder."

He wouldn't give this killer the satisfaction of listing the names of the people he'd slaughtered.

"You have the right to remain silent," he continued. "Anything you say can and may be used against you in a court of law …"

He might not have put the cuffs on this perp himself, but this still felt pretty good.

* * *

The mission to pick up Lucas Stoller and transport him to the D.C. Central Jail was kept on a need-to-know basis. Chief Ehle planned to hold a press conference to announce the arrest in a couple hours at the Henry J. Daly Building. The e-mail from Sergeant Emmett Newsome in the department's Office of Communications was sent out that morning. Still, about half a dozen reporters made it to the hospital to document the killer's escorted exit.

Propped on her crutches on the sidewalk across from a seldom-used door, Sasha watched as the KA-BAR Ripper, now deprived of his signature weapon, came out. Next to her, Kassim Nazir snapped photo after photo. Though newspapers no longer hired full-time photographers as much as they used to, the

Washington Post still had a few on staff. Nancy and Eric made sure Kassim was available to meet Sasha at the hospital in time to document this. they understood the value such photos would have after she'd confirmed the man arrested at the U.S. Capital was indeed Lucas Stoller, the KA-BAR Ripper.

Sasha studied the killer as he made the short outdoor trek from the door to a police cruiser, one of four in a convoy waiting by the curb. He looked so … ordinary. She'd been to court a few times to conduct follow-up pieces and it always struck her how the people accused of horrific crimes no longer fit the majesty of their deeds then, especially now that they were cuffed and surrounded by officers intending to prevent further harm. Lucas Stoller now looked more like the homeless man people at the Capital initially believed him to be.

She spotted Joseph and Hadrian emerge from the building behind the cuffed man, along other detectives. Hadrian was carrying a milk crate full of small plastic bags.

As they walked to an unmarked cruiser parked at the end of the convoy, both men looked over and briefly met her eyes. Sasha held their gazes for a few seconds before looking down at her iPad, studying her three-line headline.

KA-BAR RIPPER IN POLICE CUSTODY

MID-ATLANTIC SLAYER LIKELY DROWNED

THE VICTIMS ARE REMEMBERED

Sasha did the math. Twenty-eight people died at the hands of these two men. Hundreds more, including herself and Julianna, were attacked and terrorized or just impacted by their actions. "The Victims Are Remembered" was the least she could say.

Thinking about Julianna, Sasha wondered how many, like Christian, were out there, unaware of their connection to the violent crime spree. As far as anyone knew, Julianna's rape never happened. Other attacks might likewise have never been documented or connected to Christopher Stoller. She again wondered if there were any more offspring's than the two she knew about.

* * *

They sat in the SUV in the hospital parking lot, around the corner and out of sight of the action. Matthew was fine with that. He'd had enough of being involved with serial killers. He was ready to go back to his passion of serving politicians.

"No comment," he warned Christian, who was seated in the SUV's passenger seat.

"I wasn't going to say anything," Christian said, though he couldn't withhold a chuckle.

They'd indulged Sasha's insistence to come here so she could document the arrest. They were sure it wouldn't take long and began to wonder what was keeping her.

"It's not like they're putting on a parade for this guy," Matthew remarked.

Christian checked his phone again, the voice-over feature telling him it was 11:04. They still needed to get home to drop off their things. Then, he had to have lunch with his mother. It sounded important to her that they did this.

* * *

With Lucas Stoller in custody, the taskforce packed up their makeshift headquarters. While the search for Christopher Stoller continued, their work was done. The case was solved. No further investigation required. It was now just a matter of securing all the evidence for the prosecutor's use in future legal proceedings.

The bulletin board was empty again, as it had been when the taskforce first moved in. The victims' photos were in their respective file boxes with other materials and evidence from their individual cases. The photos of Christopher Stoller, which bore the large, bold X, and the one of Lucas James Stoller, now with "CAPTURED" scrawled across the top, were also packed away. With one dead and the other in custody, no one wanted to look at those faces anymore.

"It's been fun," Daniel said, stacking another box of documents onto a handcart.

"Yeah," Hadrian said. "Let's do it again, but without all the dead bodies."

Daniel chuckled.

"Baltimore's not that far away," Russell pointed out, clearing his temporary desk nearby. "You guys come up some time, we'll show you where the best beer and crab cakes can be found. Hvordan det?"

At his own temporary desk, Joseph smiled. That sounded like a good idea.

Chapter 30

Sasha hadn't been home for ten minutes when Nancy and Eric asked her to come to the office at One Franklin Square. It turned out they wanted to congratulate her on the story. Her leg aching, Sasha wished they'd done so over the phone or Zoom. Someone had also left a fresh-looking bouquet of flowers on the desk she rarely sat at. Eric found a vase and promised to have the maintenance staff water them regularly.

"Thank you," Sasha said, eager to get home and sleep in her own bed. She didn't care how early it was. She was sure she'd stay asleep until well into the next morning, no matter when said slumber began.

Christian had come and gone even faster than she had. Sasha silently wished him luck as he headed out with Lydon to meet his mother for lunch. When she returned two hours later, he was packing a suitcase in their bedroom. Seeing his angry face and shaking body, Sasha understood what had happened.

"She told you," she concluded.

"Yeah," Christian replied in a tone as Shakey as his body.

He glanced her way for just a second. His eyes looked beet-red.

"I'm sorry," Sasha offered. She wasn't sure what to say.

"She also told me she told you a few days ago," Christian said, grabbing some t-shirts from his dresser and throwing them into his suitcase. "It seems you figured it out and confronted her."

"She begged me not to tell," Sasha replied and stopped. She wasn't sure it was fair to blame Julianna.

Lydon came over to the bed on which Christian's suitcase lay open. Seeing one of his Nyla Bones lying there, he reached out and snatched it.

"Hey!" Christian snapped, hearing the bone being dragged across the linens.

Both Sasha and Lydon flinched. Christian reached out and found the dog, yanking the bone out of his mouth. Sasha had never seen him so upset. Deprived of his toy, Lydon stalked out of the room.

"How long have you known?" Christian asked, throwing the toy into the suitcase.

"I didn't know until she told me," Sasha explained. "I recognized her necklace in the box. I'd seen it in her yearbooks and other old photos of her."

"I was there with you. You couldn't have said something to me then?"

Sasha supposed he was right. She'd taken advantage of his lack of sight to keep this information to herself. But she'd had her reasons.

"I needed to be sure," she defended. "I didn't want to tell you something and be wrong."

"You were pretty sure, right?" Christian asked, adding more clothes to the suitcase.

"I don't know … maybe."

"Sure enough to hurry off to talk to my mother right as a storm was coming at all of us."

"I needed to know. I wanted to tell you then, but …"

Sasha didn't know how to finish that sentence. She could imagine how Christian reacted when his mother told him everything.

"Where are you going?" she asked.

"I don't know," Christian replied. "Somewhere far from here."

He made a decent enough living as a freelance writer to be able to afford living on his own. But Sasha didn't want him to go. How could she make him stay?

"When will you be back?" she asked. What could she say to make him stay? Best she could come up with was fish for information about his plans so she could employ any useful snippets to talk him out of this.

"Doesn't matter," Christian said, thrusting out his hand. "I want the ring back."

Sasha's heart fell out of her chest. He wasn't just leaving. He was ending their engagement. She looked down at her left hand. He'd given her that ring just three months ago. They'd been so happy then.

"Christian …" she said, looking back up at him. "Please. Let's talk about this. I understand you're upset. But you're not thinking clearly. Please, let's talk. I don't want you to go."

Christian just stood there, his hand held out towards her. Sasha looked past him and around their bedroom. They'd bought the bed, nightstands, and dressers together when they decided to live here the previous year, before she knew of his plans to propose. She couldn't give this up. She couldn't lose him.

But she couldn't figure out what to do or say to get him to stay either. The news he'd received was too devastating and his distress and anger too overwhelming.

Reluctantly, Sasha raised her hands, hoping her crutches would again support her. Tears flowing down her own face, she pulled the ring off her finger and placed it in the center of his palm. She didn't let go of it.

"Please," she tried again. "I'm sorry. I'll help you with whatever you need. Please don't do this."

But his face looked resolute. Taking large gulps of air, Sasha released her grip on the ring.

Feeling her hand leaving his, Christian closed his fingers around the ring. He thrust it into his pants pocket. Without another word, he closed his suitcase and wheeled it out of the bedroom. Sasha turned to follow him.

In the main room, Christian used a bungee cord to strap Lydon's bed to the suitcase's handle.

"Lydon," he said.

The dog, seeming to understand what was happening, came over very slowly.

"Come here," Christian demanded.

Lydon didn't pick up the pace.

"He's coming," Sasha said, though she wasn't sure her words were heard.

When Lydon reached him, Christian put him in his harness and clipped his leash to his collar. He then pulled his backpack onto his shoulders, grabbed the suitcase again, and headed out the front door.

As the door swung shut behind him, Sasha saw he'd left his key to the apartment on the coffee table. She collapsed onto a nearby couch and sobbed.

* * *

A grand jury didn't take long to indict Lucas James Stoller. There were thirty-three charges, including multiple counts of murder, sexual abuse, and burglary, most with varying degrees.

Seventy-two hours after his arrest at the hospital, Lucas Stoller appeared in the Superior Court of the District of Columbia to be arraigned on the charges. He pled not guilty and bail was denied without argument from any of the attorneys. Given the notoriety of the case, these proceedings were downright unremarkable by comparison.

Nevertheless, Sasha came to court to see this. It definitely kept her busy, which she needed. Also, given her involvement in the case from the beginning, she needed some closure. She couldn't wait for the trial, which might be years away. She was one of about fifty reporters in court that day, though she was sure everyone else's motives were different.

Lucas Stoller never spoke during the hearing, remaining cuffed and shackled at the defense table. One of his court-appointed public defenders entered his not guilty plea for the record.

Sasha knew the killer likewise refused to speak with detectives after he was released from the D.C. Jail's infirmary. He seemed to be letting the press's coverage of the case sell his notoriety for him. There was plenty of evidence pointing towards him and he seemed to recognize the wisdom behind not giving authorities a confession.

Through a friend on the WaPo's International Section, Sasha learned about an attack just off a military base in Germany. Some quick research of her own revealed Lucas Stoller was indeed stationed there during the time of the murder of U.S. Army Sergeant Patrick Fuller. With the DNA from that case compromised thanks to a lab error, charges were likely never to be filed. Sasha had never managed to reach Patrick Fuller's family for comment and the woman Stoller had raped in that same incident was likewise unavailable for comment.

Other women were coming forward, claiming to have noticed one Stoller or the other stalking them or describing an interaction they once had with either man. At least two said they were raped by Christopher Stoller back in the 1980s but never revealed this before now. One woman from Columbus, Ohio, told anyone who'd listen she was Marylyn Pataki, the mother of Lucas James Stoller. Though her credibility was still being verified, some magazines and talk shows were already granting her interviews. One fact bolstering her claim was that she was a redhead.

The proceedings for the D.C. crime spree were concluded in less than ten minutes.

"Take the prisoner back into custody," the judge ordered, banging her gavel. "We'll take a ten-minute recess before hearing the next case."

Sasha couldn't miss the fact this woman had graying red hair. She recalled rumors that notorious serial killer Ted Bundy's executioner in Florida had visible long lashes beneath their hood. With the death penalty not being an option here, this might be the closest Lucas Stoller would ever come to encountering such a karmic irony.

Lucas Stoller remained stone-faced as two court officers led him away through a side door to the holding cells. He was being given special transportation and confinement arrangements wherever he went in order to segregate him from other prisoners. Some might be eager to challenge this notorious killer to bolster their own reputations. Sasha supposed those measures would need to exist, in one way or another, for the rest of his life. She hoped it'd be a long life.

She left the courtroom and made her way out of the building. The prosecutor was already on the front steps, giving an impromptu press conference about the arraignment and next steps in the process. Sasha noticed the large crowd, recognizing a few parents she'd spoken to for her articles on the murders standing near the front of this gathering.

She also saw signs being waived. Some were about Women's Rights. Others were about Victims' Rights. Some protested the fact Washington, D.C. did not have capital punishment. A city council member spoke on a talk show the day before, lamenting this same issue and promising to draft the proper legislation to rectify this.

"Lucas Stoller is the reason why this jurisdiction needs to bring back the ultimate punishment," he said into the camera, his teeth shining to compliment his neat hair. "We must have something to protect our citizens from the worst of the worst criminals."

Sasha didn't need to comment on any of this. She'd already submitted her article about the arraignment. She wasn't sure if she'd report on anything else having to do with this case.

Baring her weight on her crutches and her good leg, she crossed the street to the parking lot, where her Mini Cooper was waiting. At her last exam, her doctor said her knee had healed well enough for her to drive again, provided she didn't overdo it.

"Keep doing what you're doing and you'll be off those crutches within a week," the doctor had added.

Sasha did not disclose her plans to the doctor. So what if she'd be on the crutches a little longer than that. She refused to wait.

"Sasha!" someone called.

Sasha stopped and turned to see Julianna hurrying across the lot towards her. She wondered if her former future mother-in-law had been in court. She also considered if such a title actually worked.

"How are you doing?" Julianna asked.

They'd talked twice since Christian broke off the engagement. Neither had heard from him since he'd walked out of the apartment. He'd blocked both their numbers on his phone.

"He'll turn up," Julianna insisted. "He just needs time to process all this."

Sasha wondered whom she was trying to convince.

"Are you ever curious?" she asked. "Do you ever just want to know for sure who his father is?"

She was sure that, if placed in that situation, she would want to know. In this case, the father could very well be a man who'd brutally murdered seventeen people.

"What would I gain?" Julianna asked. "He's my son. That's all that ever mattered."

Sasha nodded. She supposed she needed to accept that.

Julianna studied Sasha and her Mini Cooper, packed with all her things.

"You're really doing this?" she asked.

Sasha nodded. She needed to process this as well. She'd already managed to find someone to sub-let her apartment and her furniture was now locked in a storage unit, much like Julianna's own past.

"Where will you go?" Julianna asked.

"I don't really know," Sasha admitted. "I might go see my brothers. Then …"

She really didn't know where she wanted to go. She looked west, picturing the possibilities the country held. Nancy and Eric had already approved her idea to report on crimes throughout the United States, a sort-of travel log.

Julianna wiped her eyes.

"I guess you know what you're doing," she said. "Take care of yourself."

She stepped forward and hugged Sasha.

"I'll be okay," Sasha promised, daring to release one of her crutches to wrap an arm around the woman's shoulders.

Julianna turned and walked away, off to locate her own car and head home.

Sasha turned again and maneuvered herself behind the wheel of the Mini Cooper. She then managed to settle her crutches between the driver's and passenger seat without hitting the shifter.

Pulling on her seatbelt, she glanced at Julianna and the courthouse beyond her one last time.

"TlhIngan Hol: meQtaHbogh qachDaq Suv qoH neH," she muttered. It seemed like a more appropriate proverb at this point. Plus, having lived through "Slovo ne vorobey", she was sick of that saying.

There was no upside to fighting now. She wasn't prepared to give up on having a life with Christian. She'd fight for them again someday ... after she'd figured out some things.

Sasha started the engine, pulled out of the parking space, and drove through the lot towards the street. Stopping at the curb, she turned on her radio. Looking ahead again, she was confronted with her first decision in this new endeavor ... left or right?

"In local news," a news anchor was saying on the radio, "the Coast Guard has suspended the search for the body of Christopher Stoller. The FBI has named Stoller as the likely perpetrator of the Mid-Atlantic Slayer killings from the late 1980s and early 1990s. Experts surmise that, with his presumed injuries, the suspected serial killer likely drowned after a confrontation with police officers which caused him to fall into the Anacostia River during Superstorm Jackson ..."

The End!